DragonLance® Saga

The Second Generation

DragonLance® Saga

The Second Generation

Margaret Weis and Tracy Hickman

Poetry by Michael Williams
Illustrations by Ned Dameron

TSR Inc.

**To everyone
who wanted more**

**DRAGONLANCE® Saga: The Second Generation
©1994 TSR, Inc.
All Rights Reserved.**

First Printing: February 1994
Printed in the United States of America
Library of Congress Catalog Card Number: 93-61435

Cover art by Larry Elmore.

Interior art by Ned Dameron.

9 8 7 6 5 4 3 2 1

ISBN: 1-56076-822-3

TSR, Inc.
P.O. Box 756
Lake Geneva, WI 53147
United States of America

TSR Ltd.
120 Church End, Cherry Hinton
Cambridge CB1 3LB
United Kingdom

Contents

Prologue

It is always the map of believing,
the white landscape
and the shrouded farms.
It is always the land of remembrance,
of sunlight fractured
in old, immovable ice,

And always the heart,
cloistered and southerly,
misgives the ice, the drifting
for something perplexed and eternal.

It will end like this,
the heart will tell you,
it will end with mammoth and glacier,
with ten thousand years
of effacing night,
and someday the scientists
rifling lakes and moraines,
will find us in evidence,
our relics the outside of history,
but your story, whole and hollowed, will end
at the vanishing edge of your hand.
So says the heart
in its intricate cell,
charting with mirrors
the unchartable land
of remembrance and rivers and ice.

This time it was different:
the town had surrendered
to the hooded snow,
the houses and taverns
were awash in the fragmented light,
and the lake was marbled
with unstable ice,
as I walked through drifts
through lulling spirits,
content with the slate of the sky
and the prospect of calendared spring.
It will end like this,
the winter proclaimed,
sooner or later

in dark, inaccessible ice,
and you are the next one
to hear this story,
winter and winter
occluding the heart,
and there in Wisconsin,
mired by the snow
and by vanishing faith,
it did not seem bad
that the winter was taking
all light away,
that the darkness seemed welcome
and the last, effacing snow.

He stood in the midst
of frozen automobiles,
cars lined like cenotaphs.
In a bundle of coats
and wool hats and mufflers
he rummaged the trunk
for God knows what,
and I knew his name
by the misted spectacles,
the caved, ridiculous
hat he was wearing,

And whether the courage
was spring in its memory,
was sunlight in promise
or whiskeyed shade,
or something aligned
beyond snow and searching,
it was with me that moment
as I spoke to him there;
in my days I am thankful
it stood me that moment
as I spoke to the bundled
weaver of accidents,
the everyday wizard
in search of impossible spring.

Tracy, I told him, *poetry lies*
in the seams of the story,

in old recollections and prospect
of what might always and never be
(And those were the words
I did not say, but poetry lies
in the prospect of what should have been:
you must believe that I said these words
past denial, past history),
and there in the winter
the first song began,
the moons twined and beckoned
on the borders of Krynn,
the country of snow
resolved to the grasslands
more brilliant and plausible.
And the first song continued
through prospects of summer,
where the promise returns
from the vanished seed,
where the staff returns
from forgetful deserts,
and even the northern lands
cry out to the spirit,
this is the map
of believing fulfilled;
this is the map of belief.

Where's my hat? You took it! I saw you.
Don't tell me it's on my head! I know better! I . . .
Oh, there it is. Decided to bring it back, did you?
No, I don't believe you. Not for a minute. You've
    always had your eye on my hat, Hickman. I—
What? You want me to write what?
Now? This minute?
Can't do it. Don't have the time.
Trying to recall the words to a spell.
Fire sale. Fire engine. Great balls of fire. . . .
That's close. . . .
Oh, very well. I'll write your blasted foreword.
    But just this once, mind you.
Here goes.

Foreword

A long time ago, a couple of doorknobs named Margaret Weis and Tracy Hickman decided to leave their homes on Krynn and go out adventuring. I'm afraid there's some kender blood in those two. They just couldn't resist traipsing off to visit other new and exciting worlds.

But Weis and Hickman are like kender and bad pennies—they keep turning up. And so here they are again, all set to tell us about the wonderful things that are happening in Krynn.

Some of these stories we've heard before, but they have a couple of new ones, too, all about the children of that small band of adventurers who are now known as the Heroes of the Lance.

Many years have passed since the war. The Heroes' children are growing up, going off on adventures of their own, heading out into a world that, I'm sorry to say, still has plenty of danger and trouble left to go around.

Now, as you read these stories, you will notice that sometimes Weis and Hickman contradict certain other stories you may have heard. Some of you might find yourselves more than a little perplexed over their accounts of the Heroes' past lives—accounts that differ from other accounts.

There is a perfectly simple explanation.

Following the War of the Lance, Tanis and Caramon and Raistlin and all the rest of the Companions stopped being ordinary people and became Legends. We liked hearing about the Heroes' adventures so much, we didn't want the stories to end. We wanted to hear more. To fill the demand, bards and legend-spinners came from all over Krynn to tell the wondrous tales.

Some of these knew the Heroes well. Others simply repeated stories they'd heard told by a dwarf who had it from a kender who borrowed it from a knight who had an aunt who knew the Heroes . . .

You get the picture.

Some of these stories are absolutely, positively true. Others are probably almost absolutely, positively true, but not quite. Still others are what we refer to in polite society as "kender tales"—stories that aren't true, but sure are a hoot to hear!

And so you ask: Fizban, Great and Powerful Wizard, which stories are which?

And I, Fizban, Great and Powerful Wizard, answer: As long as you enjoyed the stories, you doorknob, what does it matter?

Well, well. Glad we got that settled.

Now, go pack your pouches. Pocket your hankies. Grab your hoopak. We have a lot of adventuring to do. Come along! Forget your cares! Travel with Weis and Hickman through Krynn once again, if only for a little while. They won't be here long, but they do plan to come back.

(Maybe next time, they'll return my hat!)

What was my name again?

Oh, yes.

I remain, yours sincerely,

Fizban the Fabulous

1

At the edge of the world
the juggler wanders,
sightless and pathless,
trusting the venerable
breadth of his juggler's hands.
He wanders the edge
of a long-ago story,
juggling moons,
parading the fixed
anonymous stars in his passage.
Something like instinct
and something like agate
hard and transparent
in the depths of his reflexes
channels the objects
to life in the air:
stilettos and bottles,
wooden pins and ornaments
the seen and the unseen—all reassemble
translated to light and dexterity.

It is this version of light we steer by:
constellations of memory
and a chemistry born
in the blood's alembic,
where motive and metaphor
and the impulse of night
are annealed by the morning
into our countenance,
into the whorls
of our surfacing fingers.

Something in each of us
yearns for this balance,
for the vanished chemistries
that temper the steel.
The best of all jugglery
lies in the truces
that shape our intention
out of knives, out of filament
out of half-empty bottles
and mirrors and chemistries,
and from the forgotten
ore of the night.

Kitiara's Son

Chapter One

The Strange Request Of a Blue Dragon Rider

It was autumn on Ansalon, autumn in Solace. The leaves of the vallen-wood trees were the most beautiful they'd ever been, so Caramon said—the reds blazing brighter than fire, the golds sparkling more brilliantly than the newly minted coins that were coming out of Palanthas. Tika, Caramon's wife, agreed with him. Never had such colors been seen before in Solace.

And when he stepped out of the inn, went to haul in another barrel of brown ale, Tika shook her head and laughed.

"Caramon says the same thing every year. The leaves are more colorful, more beautiful than the year before. It never fails."

The customers laughed with her, and a few teased the big man, when he came back into the inn, carrying the heavy barrel of brown ale on his back.

"The leaves seem a tad brown this year," commented one sadly.

"Drying up," said another.

"Aye, they're falling too early, before they'll have a chance to completely turn," another remarked.

Caramon looked amazed. He swore stoutly that this wasn't so and even dragged the disbelievers out onto the porch and shoved their faces in a leafy branch to prove his point.

The customers—longtime residents of Solace—admitted he was right. The leaves had never before looked so lovely. At which Caramon, as grati-fied as if he'd painted the leaves personally, escorted the customers back inside and treated them to free ale. This, too, happened every year.

The Inn of the Last Home was especially busy this autumn. Caramon would have liked to ascribe the increase in trade to the leaves; there were many who made the pilgrimage to Solace, in these days of relative peace, to see the wondrous vallenwood trees, which grew here and nowhere else on Krynn (despite various claims to the contrary, made by certain jealous towns, whose names will not be mentioned).

But even Caramon was forced to agree with the practical-minded Tika. The upcoming Wizards' Conclave was having more to do with the increased number of guests than the leaves—beautiful as they were.

A Wizards' Conclave was held infrequently on Krynn, occurring only when the top-ranking magic-users in each of the three orders—White, Red, and Black— deemed it necessary that all those of all levels of magic, from the newest apprentice to the most skilled sorcerer, gather to discuss arcane affairs.

Mages from all over Ansalon traveled to the Tower of Wayreth to attend the conclave. Also invited were certain individuals of those known as the Graystone Gem races, whose people did not use magic, but who were involved in the crafting of various magical items and artifacts. Several members of the dwarven race were honored guests. A group of gnomes arrived, encumbered with blueprints, hoping to persuade the wizards to admit them. Numerous kender appeared, of course, but they were gently, albeit firmly, turned away at the borders.

The Inn of the Last Home was the last comfortable inn before a traveler reached the magical Forest of Wayreth, where stood one of the Towers of High Sorcery, ancient headquarters of magic on the continent. Many mages and their guests stopped at the inn on their way to the tower.

"They've come to admire the color of the leaves," Caramon pointed out to his wife. "Most of these mages could have simply magicked themselves to the tower without bothering to stop anywhere in between."

Tika could only laugh and shrug and agree with her husband that, yes, it must be the leaves, and so Caramon went about inordinately pleased with himself for the rest of the day.

Neither made mention of the fact that each mage who came to stay in the inn brought with him or her a small token of esteem and remembrance for Caramon's twin brother, Raistlin. A mage of great power, and far greater ambition, Raistlin had turned to evil and very nearly destroyed the world. But he had redeemed himself at the end by the sacrifice of his own life, over twenty years ago. One small room in the inn was deemed Raistlin's Room and was now filled with various tokens (some of them magical) left to commemorate the wizard's life. (No kender were ever permitted anywhere near this room!)

The Wizards' Conclave was only three days away, and this night, for the first time in a week, the inn was empty. The mages had all traveled on, for the Wayreth Forest is a tricky place—you do not find the forest, it finds you. All mages, even the highest of their rank, knew that they might spend at least a day wandering about, waiting for the forest to appear.

And so the mages were gone, and none of the regulars had yet come back. The townsfolk, both of Solace and neighboring communities, who stopped by the inn nightly for either the ale or Tika's spiced potatoes or both, stayed away when the mages came. Magic-users were tolerated on Ansalon, (unlike the old days, when they'd been persecuted), but they were not trusted, not even the white-robed mages, who were dedicated to good.

The first year the conclave had been held—several years after the War of the Lance—Caramon had opened his inn to mages (many inns refuse to serve them). There had been trouble. The regular customers had complained loudly and bitterly, and one had even been drunk enough to attempt to bully and torment a young red-robed wizard.

That was one of the few times anyone in Solace could remember seeing Caramon angry, and it was still talked of to this day, though not in Caramon's presence. The drunk was carried out of the inn feetfirst, after his friends had removed his head from a fork in a tree branch grown into the inn.

After that, whenever a conclave occurred, the regulars took their business to other taverns, and Caramon served the mages. When the conclave ended, the regulars returned, and life went on as normal.

"But tonight," said Caramon, pausing in his work to look admiringly at his wife, "we get to go to bed early."

They had been married some twenty-two years, and Caramon was still firmly convinced that he had married the most beautiful woman in Krynn. They had five children, three boys: Tanin, twenty years old, at the time of this story; Sturm, who was nineteen; sixteen-year-old Palin; and two small girls, Laura and Dezra, ages five and four. The two older boys longed to be knights and were always off in search of adventure, which is where they were this night. The youngest boy, Palin, was studying magic. ("It's a passing fancy," Caramon said. "The boy'll soon outgrow it.") As for the little girls . . . well, theirs is another story.

"It'll be nice," Caramon repeated, "to get to bed early for a change."

Sweeping the floor vigorously, Tika pursed her mouth, so that she wouldn't give herself away by laughing, and replied, with a sigh, "Yes, the gods be praised. I'm so tired, I'll probably fall asleep before my head hits the pillow."

Caramon looked anxious. He dropped the cloth he was using to dry the freshly washed mugs and sidled around the bar. "You're not that tired, are you, my dear? Palin's at school, and the two older boys are away visiting Goldmoon and Riverwind, and the girls are in bed, and it's just the two of us, and I thought we might . . . well . . . have a little time to . . . uh . . . talk."

Tika turned away so that he wouldn't see her grin. "Yes, yes, I am tired," she said, heaving another weary sigh. "I had all those beds to make up, plus the new cook to supervise, and the accounts to settle . . ."

Caramon's shoulders slumped. "Well, that's all right," he mumbled. "Why don't you just go on to bed, and I'll finish—"

Tika threw down her broom. Laughing, she flung her arms around her husband—as far as they would go. Caramon's girth had increased markedly over the years.

"You big doorknob," she said fondly. "I was only teasing. Of course, we'll go to bed and 'talk,' but you just remember that 'talking' was what got us the boys and the girls in the first place! Come on." She tugged playfully at his apron. "Douse the lights and bolt the door. We'll leave the rest of the work until morning."

Caramon, grinning, slammed shut the door. He was just about to slide the heavy wooden bar across it when there came a faint knock from outside.

"Oh, blast!" Tika frowned. "Who could that be at this time of night?"

Hastily, she blew out the candle in her hand. "Pretend we didn't hear it. Maybe they'll go away."

"I don't know," the soft-hearted Caramon began. "It's going to frost tonight—"

"Oh, Caramon!" Tika said, exasperated. "There are other inns—"

The knocking was repeated, louder this time, and a voice called, "Innkeep? I'm sorry it's late, but I am alone and in desperate need."

"It's a woman," said Caramon, and Tika knew she'd lost.

Her husband might—just might—be persuaded to allow a man to go in search of another inn on a cold night, but a woman, especially one traveling alone—never.

It didn't hurt to argue a bit anyway. "And what's a lone female doing wandering about at this time of night? Up to no good, I'll wager."

"Oh, now, Tika," began Caramon, in the wheedling tone she knew so well, "you can't say that. Maybe she's going to visit a sick relative and darkness caught her on the road or—"

Tika lit the candle. "Go ahead. Open up."

"I'm coming," the big man roared. Heading for the door, he paused, glanced back at his wife. "You should toss a log onto the kitchen fire. She might be hungry."

"Then she can eat cold meat and cheese," Tika snapped, slamming the candle down on the table.

Tika had red hair and, though its color had grayed and softened with age, her temper had not. Caramon dropped the subject of hot food.

"She's probably real tired," he said, hoping to pacify his wife. "Likely she'll go straight to her room."

"Humpf!" Tika snorted. "Are you going to open the door or let her freeze out there?" Arms akimbo, she glared at her husband.

Caramon, flushing and ducking his head, hastened to open the door.

A woman stood framed in the doorway. She was not what either had expected, however, and even the soft-hearted Caramon, at the sight of her, appeared to have second thoughts about letting her in.

She was heavily cloaked and booted and wore the helm and leather gloves indicative of a dragon rider. That in itself was not unusual; many dragon riders passed through Solace these days. But the helm and cloak and gloves were a deep blue, trimmed in black. The light caught a glint of blue scales, glistening on her leather breeches and black boots.

A blue dragon rider.

Such a person had not been seen in Solace since the days of the war, for good reason. Had she been discovered in daylight, she would have been stoned. Or, at the very least, arrested and made prisoner. Even these days, twenty-five years after the end of the war, the people of Solace remembered clearly the blue dragons that had burned and leveled their town, killed many of their kin. And there were veterans who'd fought in the War of the Lance—Caramon and Tika among them—who recalled with hatred the blue dragons and their riders, servants of the Queen of Darkness.

The eyes in the shadow of the blue helm met Caramon's steadily. "Do you have a room for the night, Innkeep? I have ridden far, and I am very tired."

The voice that came from behind the mask sounded wistful, weary . . . and nervous. The woman kept to the shadows that had gathered around the door. Awaiting Caramon's answer, she glanced over her shoulder twice, looking not at the ground, but at the skies.

Caramon turned to his wife. Tika was a shrewd judge of character—an easy skill to acquire, if you like people, which Tika did. She gave a quick, abrupt nod.

Caramon backed up and motioned for the dragon rider to enter. She took one final look over her shoulder, then hastily slid inside, keeping out of the direct light. Caramon himself took a look out the door before he shut it.

The sky was brightly lit; the red and the silver moons were up and close together, though not as close as they'd be in a few days' time. The black moon was out there, too, somewhere, the moon only those who worshipped the Dark Queen could see. These celestial bodies held sway over three forces: good, evil, and the balance between.

Caramon slammed the door shut and dropped the heavy bar across it. The woman flinched at the sound of the bar thudding into place. She'd been trying to unlatch the clasp of the pin that held her cloak together—a large brooch wrought of mother-of-pearl that gave off a faint and eerie glow in the dimness of the candlelit inn. Her hands shook, and she dropped the brooch to the floor. Caramon bent and started to pick it up. The woman moved quickly to forestall him, attempted to hide it.

Caramon stopped her, frowning. "An odd adornment," he said, forcing open the woman's hand for Tika to view the pin. He found, now that he studied it, that he was loath to touch it.

Tika peered at the brooch. Her lips tightened. Perhaps she was thinking her infallible judge of character had failed her at last. "A black lily."

A black, waxen flower with four pointed petals and a blood-red center, the black lily is reputed by elven legend to spring up from the graves of those who have met their deaths by violence. The black lily is said to grow from the heart of the murdered victim and, if plucked, the broken stem will bleed.

The dragon rider snatched her hand away, slid the brooch back into the black fur that trimmed her cloak.

"Where've you left your dragon?" Caramon asked grimly.

"Hidden in a valley near here. You needn't worry, Innkeep. She's under my control and completely loyal to me. She won't harm anyone." The woman withdrew the blue leather helm she wore to protect her face during flight. "I give you my word."

Once the helm was removed, the frightening, formidable dragon rider disappeared. In its place stood a woman of perhaps middle age; it was hard to tell how old she was by looking. Her face was lined, but with sorrow more than years. Her braided hair was gray, prematurely gray, it seemed. Her eyes were not the cruel, hard, merciless eyes of those who serve

Takhisis, but were gentle and sad and . . . frightened.

"And we believe you, my lady," said Tika, with a defiant glance at the silent Caramon—a glance that, to be honest, the big man didn't deserve.

Caramon was always slow to react, not because he was thick-witted (as even his best friends had once thought, in his youth), but because he always considered each new or unusual occurrence from every conceivable angle. Such rumination gave him the appearance of slowness, and frequently drove the quick-thinking among his comrades (including his wife) to distraction. But Caramon refused to be hurried and often came up with some astonishingly insightful conclusions in consequence.

"You're shivering, my lady," Tika added, while her husband stood flat-footed, staring at nothing. Tika left him be. She knew the signs of her husband's mind at work. She drew the woman close to the fire pit. "Sit here. I'll stir up the blaze. Would you like some hot food? It will take me only a minute to whip up the kitchen fire—"

"No, thank you. Don't bother about the fire. It's not the cold that makes me shiver." The woman said the last in a low voice. She fell more than sat on a bench.

Tika dropped the poker she was using to stoke the fire. "What is wrong, my lady? You've escaped some dreadful prison, haven't you? And you're being pursued."

The woman lifted her head and looked at Tika in wonder, then the woman smiled wanly. "You are near the mark. Does so much show in my face?" She put a trembling hand to her lined and faded cheek.

"Husband." Tika stood up briskly. "Where's your sword?"

"Huh?" Jolted from his thoughts, Caramon jerked his head up. "What? Sword?"

"We'll wake the sheriff. Turn out the town militia. Don't worry, my lady." Tika was busily untying her apron. "They won't take you back—"

"Wait! No!" The woman appeared more frightened of all this activity on her behalf than she was of whatever danger threatened her.

"Stop a minute, Tika," Caramon said, resting his hand on his wife's shoulder. And when Caramon spoke in that tone, his headstrong wife always listened. "Calm down."

He turned to the dragon rider, who had jumped to her feet in alarm. "Don't worry, my lady. We won't tell anyone you're here until you want us to."

Breathing a sigh of relief, the woman sank back down onto the bench.

"But, darling—" Tika began.

"She came here on purpose, my dear," Caramon interrupted. "She didn't stop at the inn just for a room. She came on purpose to find someone living in Solace. And I don't think she escaped some evil place. I think she left." His voice grew grim. "And I think that when she leaves here, she's going back—of her own free will."

The woman shuddered. Her shoulders hunched, her head bowed. "You are right. I have come to find someone in Solace. You, an innkeeper, you would know where I could locate this man. I must talk to him tonight. I dare not stay long. Time . . ." Her fingers, in their blue gloves, twisted together. "Time is running out."

Caramon reached for his cloak, which hung on a peg behind the bar. "Who is it? Tell me his name, and I'll run to fetch him. I know everyone living in Solace . . ."

"Wait a moment." The prudent Tika stopped him. "What do you want with this man?"

"I can tell you his name, but I cannot tell you why I want to see him, more for his sake than my own."

Caramon frowned. "Will this bring whatever danger you're in down on him as well?"

"I can't say!" The woman avoided looking at him. "Perhaps. I'm sorry for it, but . . ."

Slowly, Caramon shook his head. "I can't wake a man in the middle of the night and take him to what may be his doom—"

The woman lifted anguished eyes. "I could have lied to you. I could have told you that all will be well, but I don't know that. I know only that I bear a terrible secret and I must share it with the one other person alive who has the right to know it!" She reached out, caught hold of Caramon's hand. "A life is at stake. No, sir, more than a life! A soul!"

"It's not up to us to judge, sweetheart," said Tika. "This man, whoever he is, must decide for himself."

"Very well. I'll go fetch him." Caramon flung his cloak around his shoulders. "What's the name?"

"Majere," said the woman. "Caramon Majere."

"Caramon!" repeated Caramon, astounded.

The woman mistook his astonishment for reluctance. "I know I'm asking the impossible. Caramon Majere—a Hero of the Lance, one of the most renowned warriors of Ansalon. What could he have to do with the likes of me? But, if he won't come, tell him . . ." She paused, considering what she might say. "Tell him I've come about his sister."

"His sister!" Caramon fell back against the wall. The thud shook the inn.

"Paladine help us!" Tika clasped her hands together tightly. "Not . . . Kitiara?"

Chapter Two

Kitiara's Son

Caramon took off his cloak. He intended to hang it on the peg, but missed. The cloak slid to the floor. He didn't bother to pick it up. The woman watched all this with growing suspicion.

"Why aren't you going to fetch this man?"

9

"Because you've already found him. I am Caramon Majere."

The woman was startled, then obviously dubious.

"You can ask anyone," Caramon said simply, waving a hand to indicate the inn and beyond. "What would I gain by lying?" He flushed, patted his broad belly, and shrugged. "I know I may not look much like a hero . . ."

The woman smiled suddenly. The smile made her seem younger. "I was expecting a great lord. I'm glad you're not. This will be . . . easier."

She studied him intently. "Now that I look at you, I might have recognized you. She described you to me—`a big man, more brawn than brains, always thinking of where his next meal is coming from.' Forgive me, sir. Those were Kitiara's words, not mine."

Caramon's expression darkened. "I suppose you know, my lady, that my sister is dead. My half-sister, I should say. And you know that Kitiara was a Dragon Highlord, in league with the Queen of Darkness. And why would she tell you anything about me? She may have been fond of me, once, I suppose, but she forgot about that in a hurry."

"I know what Kitiara was, better than most," the woman said, with a sigh. "She lived with me, you see, for several months. It was before the war. About five years before. Will you hear my story from the beginning? I have traveled many hundreds of miles to find you, at great peril."

"Maybe we should wait until morning—"

She shook her head. "No, I dare not. It is safer for me to travel before dawn. Will you hear my story? If you choose not to believe me . . ." She shrugged. "Then I will leave you in peace."

"I'll make some tarbean tea," said Tika. She left for the kitchen, first laying her hand on her husband's massive shoulder, silently enjoining him to listen.

Caramon sat down heavily. "Very well. What is your name, my lady? If you don't mind my asking."

"Sara Dunstan. I am—or was—a resident of Solamnia. And it is there, in a small village not too distant from Palanthas, where my tale begins.

"I was about twenty years old then. I lived alone, in a cottage that had belonged to my parents. They had both died of the plague, some years before. I caught it, but I was one of the lucky ones who survived. I earned my trade as a weaver; having learned the craft from my mother. I was a spinster. Oh, I'd had chances to marry, when I was young, but I turned them down. Too picky, the townsfolk said, but the truth was, I never found anyone I loved, and I couldn't settle for less.

"I wasn't particularly happy. Few were in those hard times before the war. We didn't know what lay ahead of us, or we would have counted ourselves blessed."

She accepted a glass of hot tea. Tika took her place beside her husband and handed him a mug of tea. He accepted it, put it down, and promptly forgot about it. His face was grim.

"Go on, my lady."

"You shouldn't call me a lady. I'm not. I never was. As I said, I was a weaver. I was working at my loom in my home, one day, when there came a banging on my door. I looked outside. I thought at first it was a man standing on my stoop, but I suddenly realized it was a young woman, dressed in leather armor. She wore a sword, like a man, and her hair was manlike, black, and cut short."

Tika glanced at Caramon to see his reaction. The description fit Kitiara exactly. But Caramon's face was expressionless.

"She started to ask me for something—water, I think—but before she could say anything, she passed out at my feet.

"I carried her into my house. She was very ill. I could tell that much. I ran to the old woman, a druidess, who was the village healer. That was in the days before the clerics of Mishakal had returned to us, but the druidess was skilled in her own way and saved many lives. Perhaps that's why we never fell for any of those false clerics and their tricks.

"By the time the druidess came back, the woman—Kitiara, she said her name was—had recovered consciousness. She was trying to get out of bed, but was too weak. The old woman examined her, told her to lie back down and stay down.

"Kitiara refused. 'It's only a fever,' she said. 'Give me something for it, and I'll be on my way.'

" 'It's not a fever, as you well know,' the druidess told her. 'You're with child, and if you don't lie down and rest, you're going to lose the baby.' "

Caramon's face went white, all the blood draining from it in a rush. Tika, pale herself, was forced to put down her mug of tea, for fear she might spill it. She reached out and took hold of Caramon's hand. His grip on hers was thankful, crushing.

" 'I want to lose the brat!' Kitiara began to curse, savagely. I'd never heard a woman talk like that, say such foul things." Sara shuddered. "It was dreadful to listen to, but it didn't bother the old druidess.

" 'Aye, you'll lose the baby, but you'll lose yourself at the same time. You'll die if you don't take care.'

"Kitiara muttered something about not believing a toothless old fool, but I could tell that she was scared—perhaps because she was so weak and sick. The druidess wanted to have Kitiara carried to her house, but I said no, I would take care of her. Perhaps you think this was strange, but I was lonely and . . . there was something I admired about your sister."

Caramon shook his head, his face dark.

Sara smiled, shrugged. "She was strong and independent. She was what I would have been if I'd had courage enough. And so she stayed with me. She was very ill. She did have the fever; the kind you get from swamps. And fretting about the baby. She obviously didn't want it, and her anger over being with child didn't help her any.

"I nursed her through the fever. She was sick for almost a month or more. At last she grew better, and she didn't lose the baby. But the fever left her very weak—you know how it is. She could barely lift her head from the pillow." Sara sighed. "The first thing she asked, when she was well, was for the druidess to give her something to end her pregnancy.

"The old woman told Kitiara that, by then, it was too late. She would kill herself. Kitiara didn't like that, but she was too weak to argue, too weak to do much of anything. But from that day, she began to count the days until the baby's birth. That day 'I'll be rid of the little bastard,' she'd say, 'and I can move on.' "

Caramon made a gulping noise, coughed, and looked stern. Tika squeezed his hand.

"The time of the birthing came," Sara continued. "Kitiara had recovered her strength by then, and it was well she did, for the birth was a long and difficult one. After two days of hard labor, the baby was finally born—a boy. He was strong and healthy. Unfortunately, Kitiara wasn't. The druidess (who didn't like her) told Kitiara bluntly that she was probably going to die and that she should tell someone who the baby's father was, so that he could come and claim his offspring.

"That night, when she was near death, Kitiara told me the name of the baby's father and all the circumstances surrounding the child's conception. But, because of those circumstances, and who the father was, she forced me to vow not to tell him.

"She was vehement about that. She made me swear an oath—a terrible oath—on the memory of my own mother. 'Take the boy to my brothers. Their names are Caramon and Raistlin Majere. They will bring my son up to be a great warrior. Caramon, especially. He's a good fighter. I know, I taught him.'

"I promised her. I would have promised her anything. I felt so sorry for her. She was so low-spirited and feeble, I was certain she was going to die. 'Is there something I can take to your brothers that will convince them the child is yours? Otherwise, why would they believe me?' I asked her. 'Some piece of jewelry they would recognize?' "

" 'I have no jewelry. All I have is my sword. Take my sword to Caramon. He will know it. And tell him . . . tell him . . .' Kitiara glanced weakly around the room. Her gaze went to the baby, who was screaming lustily in a cradle by the fire.

" 'My little brother used to cry like that,' she whispered. 'He was always sickly, Raistlin was. And when he'd cry, Caramon would try to tease him out of it. He'd make shadow figures, like this.' She held up her hand—poor thing, it was all she could do to lift it—and she formed her fingers into the shape of a rabbit's head. Like this.

" 'And Caramon would say, 'Look, Raist. Bunnies.' "

Caramon gave a great groan and lowered his face into his hands. Tika put her arm around him and said something to him softly.

"I'm sorry," Sara said, concerned. "I forgot how terrible this must be for you. I didn't mean to upset you. I only meant to prove—"

"It's all right, my lady." Caramon lifted his head. His face was haggard and drawn, but he was composed. "The memories are hard sometimes, especially coming . . . like this. But I believe you now, Sara Dunstan. I'm sorry I didn't before. Only Kit or . . . or Raist . . . would have known that story."

"There is no need to apologize." Sara took a swallow of the tea and wrapped her chill hands around the mug to warm them. "Of course, Kitiara did not die. The old druidess couldn't believe it. She said Kitiara must have made a pact with Takhisis. I often thought about that, later on, when I heard Kitiara was responsible for the deaths of so many. Did she promise the Dark Queen souls in exchange for her own? Was that why Takhisis let her go?"

"What a dreadful fancy!" Tika shivered.

"Not a fancy," said Sara, subdued. "I've seen it done."

She was silent for long moments. Caramon and Tika stared at her in horror. They saw her now as they had seen her when she first entered—wearing the helm of evil, wearing the death lily as an ornament.

"The baby lived, you said," Caramon stated abruptly, frowning. "I presume Kit left him behind."

"Yes." Sara resumed her tale. "Kitiara was soon strong enough to travel. But while she was recovering, she had taken a liking to the baby. He was a fine boy, alert and well formed. 'I can't keep him,' she said to me. 'Momentous things are about to happen. Armies are forming in the north. I mean to earn my fortune with my sword. Find him a good home. I'll send money for his upbringing and, when he is old enough to go to war with me, I'll come back for him.' "

" 'What about your brothers?' I ventured to suggest.

"She turned on me in a rage. 'Forget I ever said I had kin! Forget all I told you. Especially forget what I said about the father!'

"I agreed. And then I asked her if I could keep the child." Sara stared at the fire, her face flushed. "I was so lonely, you see. And I'd always wanted a baby of my own. It seemed to me that the gods—if there were gods—had answered my prayers.

"Kitiara was pleased with the idea. She had come to trust me, and I think she even liked me a little—as much as she could ever like any other woman. She promised to send me money, whenever she had any. I said I didn't care about that. I could support myself and a child. And I promised her I would write her letters, telling her about the boy. She kissed the child, when she left, and then put him into my arms.

"What will you name him?' I asked.

" 'Call him Steel,' she said. And she laughed when she said it—a kind of joke, considering the baby's surname."

"That would be 'Half-Elven,' " Caramon muttered aside to Tika. "I don't see much joke in that, except on poor Tanis. All these years." He gave a gloomy shake of his head. "Never knowing."

"Hush!" Tika whispered. "You can't say that for sure."

"What?" Sara overheard. "What are saying?"

"Sorry, but I don't get the joke," said Caramon. "About the baby's name. 'Half-Elven,' you see."

"Half-Elven?" Sara was perplexed.

Blushing, extremely embarrassed, Caramon coughed and said, "Look, we all knew about Tanis and Kit, so you don't have to hide it anymore—"

"Ah, you think the baby's father was Tanis Half-Elven," said Sara, suddenly understanding. "No, you're wrong."

"Are you sure?" Caramon was puzzled. "Of course, there could have been someone else—"

"Any man in trousers," Tika muttered beneath her breath.

"But you said this baby was born four years before the war. Kit and Tanis were lovers. And that must have been just after she left Solace with—" Caramon's breath caught in his throat. He stared at Sara. "That's not possible!" he growled. "Kit was lying. I don't believe it."

"What do you mean?" Tika demanded. "I don't understand! Who are you talking about?"

"Don't you remember back then—"

"Caramon, I was a little girl when you and Raistlin and the others left Solace. And no one of you ever talked about what happened during those five years."

"It's true we never spoke of those journeys," said Caramon slowly, formulating his thoughts. "We went in search of the true gods, that was our goal. But, looking back on it, I realize now that we really went in search of ourselves. How can a man or woman describe that journey? And so, we've kept silent, kept the stories in our hearts, and let the legend-spinners, who are only after a steel piece, make up whatever fool tales they choose."

He gazed long and sternly at Sara, who stared down at the mug of tea, grown cold in her hands.

"I admit I have no proof. That is," she amended, "I have proof, but nothing I can produce at this moment."

She raised her head defiantly. "You believed me up until now."

"I don't know what to believe anymore," Caramon said heavily. He rose to his feet and walked over to stand by the fire.

"Would somebody tell me what's going on? What's the baby's name?" Tika demanded, exasperated.

"Steel," Sara answered. "Steel Brightblade."

Chapter Three

White Rose, Black Lily

"May all the gods preserve us!" Tika gasped. "But that would mean . . . What a strange lineage! Blessed Paladine!" She stood up, staring, horrified, at Caramon. "She killed him! Kitiara killed the father of her own child!"

"I don't believe it," Caramon said thickly. Hands shoved in the pockets of his trousers, he kicked moodily at a log that threatened to roll out of the grate, sending a shower of sparks up the chimney. "Sturm Brightblade was a knight—in his soul, if not by the rules of the order. He would never—" Caramon paused, his face flushed. "Well, he wouldn't."

"He was also a man. A young man," Sara said gently.

"You didn't know him!" Caramon rounded on her angrily.

"But I came to, later. Will you hear the rest of my story?"

Tika laid her hand on her husband's broad shoulder. " 'Closing your ears won't shut truth's mouth,' " she said, repeating an elven proverb.

"No, but it silences gossip's wagging tongue," Caramon muttered. "Tell me this: Is that baby still alive?"

"Yes, your nephew lives," Sara answered steadily, her expression sad and troubled. "He is twenty-four years old. It is on his behalf that I've come."

Caramon heaved a great sigh that came from the ache in his heart. "Go on, then."

"As you said, Kitiara and the young knight left Solace, headed northward. They sought news of their fathers, who had both been Knights of Solamnia, and so it seemed logical that they should journey together. Although, from what I gather, they were an ill-matched pair.

"Things went wrong between them, right from the beginning. The very nature of their searches was different. Sturm's quest was a holy one. He went looking for a father who had been a paragon of knighthood. Kit's quest wasn't. She knew, or at least suspected, that her father had been cast out of the knighthood in disgrace. She may have even been in contact with him. Certainly something was drawing her to the Dark Queen's armies, forming in secret in the north.

"Kit thought that young Brightblade, with his serious-minded dedication and religious fervor, was amusing at first. But that didn't last long. She was soon bored by him. And then, he began to seriously annoy her. He refused to stay in taverns, claiming they were places of wickedness. He spent every night saying his ritual prayers. By day, he lectured her sternly on her sins. She might have tolerated this, but then the young knight made a terrible mistake. He sought to take charge, to take command.

"Kitiara could not permit this. You knew her. She had to be in control of any situation." Sara smiled sadly. "Those few months she spent in my house, we did things her way. We ate what she wanted to eat. We talked when she wanted to talk.

" 'Sturm was infuriating,' Kit told me, and her dark eyes flashed when she spoke of him, months later. 'I was the elder, the more experienced warrior. I helped train him! And he had the nerve to begin to order me around!'

"Another person would have simply said, 'Look, my friend, we're not getting along. This isn't working out. Let us each go our own separate ways.' But not Kitiara. She wanted to break Sturm, teach him a lesson, teach him who was stronger. At first, she said, she considered goading him into a duel, beating him in a contest at arms. But then she decided that wasn't humiliating enough. She devised a suitable vengeance. She would prove to the young knight that his armor of self-righteousness would buckle at the first blow. She would seduce him."

Caramon's jaw was set, his face rigid. He shifted his great bulk uncomfortably from one foot to the other. Much as he wanted to doubt, it was obvious—knowing the two as he did—that he could see the truth of what had happened much too clearly.

"Brightblade's seduction became a game for Kit, added spice to what had become a dull, uneventful trip. You know how charming your sister could be when she wanted. She stopped quarreling with Sturm. She pretended to take seriously all he said and did. She admired him, praised him. Sturm was honorable, idealistic, perhaps a little pompous—he was young, after all—and he began to think he had tamed this wild woman, led her to the paths of goodness. And, I've no doubt, he was falling a little bit in love with her. It was then she began to tempt him.

"The poor young knight must have struggled long with his passions. He had taken vows of chastity until marriage, but he was human, with a young man's hot blood. At that age, the body sometimes seems to act with a will of its own, drags the reluctant spirit along with it. Kitiara was experienced in such matters. The unworldly young knight was not. I doubt if he knew what was happening to him until it was too late, his desire more than he could bear."

Sara lowered her voice. "One evening, he was chanting his prayers. This was the moment Kitiara had chosen. Her vengeance would be complete, if she could seduce him from his god.

"She did so."

Sara fell silent. All three were silent. Caramon stared bleakly into the dying fire. Tika twisted her apron in her hands.

"The next morning," Sara continued, "realization came to the young knight. To him, what they'd done had been sinful. He intended to do what he could to make reparation. He asked her to marry him. Kitiara laughed. She ridiculed him, his vows, his faith. She told him it had all been a game. She didn't love him. In fact, she despised him.

"She achieved her goal. She saw him crushed, shamed, as she had hoped. She taunted him, tormented him. And then she left him.

"She told me how he looked," Sara said. " 'Like I'd driven a spear through his heart. The next time he's as white as that, they'll bury him!' "

"Damn Kit," Caramon swore softly. He beat his fist into the brick fireplace wall. "Damn her."

"Hush, Caramon!" Tika said swiftly. "She is dead. Who knows what dread retribution she now faces?"

"I wonder if her suffering is enough," Sara said quietly. "I was young and idealistic myself. I could only imagine how the poor man must have felt. I tried to say as much to Kitiara, but she grew angry. 'He deserved it,' she claimed. And, after all, he'd had his revenge on her. That was how she viewed her pregnancy—his revenge. And that was why she made me promise not to tell anyone that he was the father."

Caramon stirred. "Then why are you telling me? What does it matter now? If it's true, it's best forgotten. Sturm Brightblade was a good man. He lived and died for his ideals and those of the knighthood. My own son's named after him. I won't have that name dishonored." His face darkened. "What is it you're after? Money? We don't have much, but—"

Sara rose to her feet. Her face was livid; she looked as if he'd struck her. "I don't want your money! If that was what I was after, I could have come to you years ago! I came to seek your help, because I heard you were a good man. I obviously heard wrong."

She started toward the door.

"Caramon, you lummox!" Tika ran after Sara and caught hold of her, just as she was putting on her cloak. "Please, forgive him, my lady. He didn't mean it. He's hurt and upset, that's all. This is a shock to both of us. You . . . you've lived with this knowledge for years, but this has hit us right between the eyes. Come back, sit down."

Tika drew Sara back to the bench.

Caramon's face was red and hot as the embers. "I'm sorry, Sara Dunstan. Tika's right. I feel like an ox that's been felled by an axe. I don't know what I'm saying. How can we help you?"

"You must hear the rest of my story," said Sara. But she staggered as she tried to sit down and would have fallen but for Tika's hold on her. "Forgive me. I'm so tired."

"Shouldn't you rest first?" Tika suggested. "Surely there would be time in the morning . . ."

"No!" Sara sat up straight. "Time is what we lack. And this weariness is not of the body, but of the spirit.

"Kitiara's son was six weeks old when she left him. Neither he nor I ever saw her again. I can't say I was sorry. I loved the baby as much as if he were my own. Maybe more, for, as I said, he seemed to have been given to me as a gift from the gods to heal my loneliness. Kitiara kept her promise. She sent money to me and gifts to Steel. I could keep track of Kitiara's rise in fortune over the years, because the sums of money increased and the gifts were more costly. The presents were all warlike in nature: small swords and shields, a small knife with a silver hilt carved with a dragon for his birthday. Steel adored them. As she had foreseen, he was a born warrior.

"When he was four, the war broke out. The money and gifts stopped coming. Kitiara had more important matters on her mind. I heard stories of the Dark Lady. I heard how she had risen in favor with Highlord Ariakas, the general of the armies of evil. I remembered what she'd said to me—how, when the boy was old enough to ride to battle, she would return for him. I looked at Steel. He was only four, but he was stronger and taller, more intelligent, than most children his age.

"If I ever missed him, I was sure to find him in the tavern, listening with open mouth and eager eyes to the stories of battle. The soldiers were mercenaries—a bad lot. They made fun of the Knights of Solamnia, called them weak men who hid inside their armor. I didn't like what Steel was learning. Our town was small and unprotected except for this rabble, and I feared that they were in league with the Dark Queen's forces. And so I left.

"My son"—Sara cast Caramon a fierce look, daring him to defy her—"and I moved to Palanthas. I thought we would be safe there, and I wanted the boy to grow up among the Knights of Solamnia, to learn the truth about honor and the Oath and the Measure. I thought this might . . . might . . ."

Sara paused and drew a shivering breath before she continued. "I hoped it might counteract the darkness I saw in him."

"In a child?" Tika was disbelieving.

"Even as a child. Perhaps you think it's because I knew the disparity of the two strains of blood that ran in him, but I swear to you, by the gods of good, whose names I can no longer say in innocence, that I could literally see the battle being fought for his soul. Every good quality in him was tainted with evil; every evil quality gilded with good. I saw this then! I see it more now."

She lowered her head. Two tears slid down her pale cheeks. Tika put an arm around her. Caramon left his place by the fire and stood protectively near her as she continued her tale.

"It was in Palanthas that I first heard about Sturm Brightblade. I heard the other knights talk about him—not in particularly approving tones. He was said to associate with outlandish folk—an elf maid, a kender, and a dwarf. And he was defying authority. But the ordinary people of the city liked and trusted Sturm, when they didn't like or trust many of the other knights. I talked about Sturm with Steel, took every opportunity to make Steel aware of his father's nobility and honor . . . "

"Did Steel know the truth?" Caramon interrupted.

Sara shook her head. "How could I tell him? It would have confused him. It's odd, but he never asked me who his parents were. I never made any secret of the fact that I wasn't his real mother. Too many in my small town knew the truth. But I lived—I still live—in dread of the question: who are my real father and mother?"

"You mean"—Caramon looked astonished—"he doesn't know? To this day?"

"He knows now who his mother is. They took care to tell him that much. But he has never once asked his father's name. Perhaps he doesn't think I know."

"Or perhaps he doesn't want to find out," Tika suggested.

"I still think he should have known," Caramon argued.

"Do you?" Sara cast him a bitter glance. "Think of this. Remember the battle for the High Clerist's Tower. As you know, the knights won. The Dragon Highlord, Kitiara, was defeated, but at what a terrible cost. As you said, she killed Sturm Brightblade, killed him as he stood alone on the battlements.

"I was horrified when I heard this news. Can you imagine what I felt? To look at Steel and know that his mother had slain the man who was his father. How could I explain such things to a boy when I didn't understand them myself?"

Caramon sighed. "I don't know," he said moodily. "I don't know."

Sara went on. "We were living in Palanthas when the war ended. And then I was truly frightened, terrified that Kitiara might start searching for her son. Maybe she did. At any rate, she didn't find us. Some time later, I heard she had taken up with the dark elf mage, Dalamar—apprentice to her brother, Raistlin, who was now Master of the Tower of High Sorcery in Palanthas."

Caramon's face softened, grew grave and wistful, as always, when Raistlin was mentioned.

"Forgive me, Caramon," Sara said softly, "but when I heard the stories about your brother Raistlin, all I could think of was—here is more dark blood, running in my child's veins. And it seemed to me that Steel drifted deeper into the shadows every day. He wasn't like other boys his age. All boys play at war, but, for Steel, war wasn't a game. Soon the other children refused to play with him. He hurt them, you see."

Tika's eyes widened. "Hurt them?"

"He didn't mean to," Sara said quickly. "He was always sorry afterward. He takes no pleasure in inflicting pain, thank the gods. But, as I said, the games weren't games to him. He fought with a fierce ardor that shone in his eyes. Imaginary enemies were very real to him. And so the other children shunned him. He was lonely, I know, but he was proud, and he would never admit it.

"And then came the war over Palanthas, when Lord Soth and Kitiara attacked the city. Many people lost their lives. Our home was destroyed in the fires that raged through the city, but I wept with thankfulness when I heard that Kitiara was dead. At last, I thought, Steel is safe. I prayed that the dark cloud would be lifted from him, that he would begin to grow toward the light. My hopes were dashed.

"One night, when Steel was twelve, I was awakened by a knocking at the door. I looked out the window and saw three figures, cloaked in black, riding horseback. All my fears returned to me. They frightened me so much, in fact, that I woke Steel and told him we must flee, escape by the back door. He refused to go. I think . . . I think some dark voice called to him. He told me to run, if I wanted. He would not. He wasn't afraid.

"The men battered down the door. Their leader was . . . Do you recall, I spoke of Ariakas?"

"Highlord of the Red Dragonarmy. He died in the temple, during the final assault. What has he got to do with this?"

"Some say he was Kit's lover," Tika inserted.

Sara shrugged. "She wouldn't have been the first, and likely not the last. But, according to what I've heard, Zeboim, daughter of Takhisis, was enamored of Ariakas, became his lover, and bore him a son, named Ariakan. Ariakan fought in the ranks, under his father's command, during the War of the Lance. He is a skilled warrior who fought courageously in battle. When he was captured, more dead than alive, by the Knights of Solamnia, they were so impressed with his courage that, although he was their prisoner, they treated him with every respect.

"Ariakan was their prisoner for many years, until they finally released him, mistakenly thinking that—in these times of peace—the man could do no harm. Ariakan had learned much during his enforced stay with the knights. He came to admire them, even as he despised them for what he considered their weaknesses.

"Shortly after his release, Ariakan was visited by Takhisis, in the form of the Dark Warrior. She commanded him to start an order of knights dedicated to her, as the Solamnic Knights are dedicated to Paladine. 'Those who are boys now will grow up in my service,' she told him. 'You will raise them to worship me. I will own them, body and soul. When they are men, they will be prepared to give their lives in my cause.'

"Almost immediately, Ariakan began to 'recruit' boys for this unholy army."

Sara's voice sank. "Ariakan was the man at the door."

"Blessed Paladine!" Tika murmured, stricken.

"He had found out about Kit's son." Sara shook her head. "I'm not sure how. Ariakan claimed that Kit had told his father about the boy. I don't believe that. I think . . . I think it was the wizard Dalamar, evil Master of the Tower of High Sorcery in Palanthas, who led Ariakan to us—"

"But Dalamar would have told me," Caramon protested. "He and I are . . . well—"

Sara stared at him, her eyes wide.

"Not friends," Caramon said, thinking the matter through, "but we have a mutual respect for each other. And the boy is my nephew, after all. Yes, Dalamar would have told me—"

"Not likely!" Tika sniffed. "When all's said and done—he's a black-robed mage. Dalamar serves the Dark Queen and himself, not necessarily in that order. If he saw that Steel might prove valuable . . ." She shrugged.

"Perhaps Dalamar was only following orders," Sara whispered, glancing fearfully out the window, into the night. "Takhisis wants Steel. I believe that with all my heart. She has done everything in her power to take him . . . and she is close to succeeding!"

"What do you mean?" Caramon demanded.

"It is the reason I am here. That night, Ariakan made Steel an offer. Ariakan would make Steel a dark paladin." Sara reached for her cloak, held up the brooch of the black lily in a trembling hand. "A Knight of Takhisis."

Caramon was aghast. "Such an evil order doesn't exist."

"It does," Sara said in a low voice, "though few know it. But they will. They will." She sat silently shivering and, at length, drew her cloak back around her.

"Go on," Caramon said grimly. "I think I see where this is heading."

"Kitiara's son was among the first Ariakan sought. I must admit he is shrewd, is Ariakan. He knew exactly how to handle Steel. Ariakan spoke to the boy man-to-man. He told him he would teach him to be a mighty warrior, a leader of legions. He promised Steel glory, riches, power. Steel was entranced. He agreed, that night, to go with Ariakan.

"Nothing I said or did, no tears I shed, moved Steel. I won only one concession—that I could come with him. Ariakan agreed to this only because he figured I could be useful to him. He would need someone to cook for the boys, mend their clothes, clean up after them. That . . . and he took a fancy to me," Sara finished softly.

"Yes," she added, partly ashamed, partly defiant, "I became his mistress. I was his mistress many years, until I grew too old to please him anymore."

Caramon's face darkened.

"I understand," said Tika, patting the woman's hand. "You sacrificed yourself for your son. To be near him."

"That was the only reason! I swear to you!" Sara cried passionately. "I hate them and what they stand for! I hate Ariakan. You don't know what I have endured! Many times, I wanted to kill myself. Death would have been far easier. But I couldn't leave Steel. There is good in him, still, though they've done all they could to trample out the spark. He loves me and respects me, for one thing. Ariakan would have rid himself of me long ago, but for Steel. My son has protected me and defended me—to his own detriment, though he never speaks of it. He has watched others rise to knighthood ahead of him. Ariakan has held Steel back, all because of me.

"Steel is loyal. He is honorable, like his father. Both to a fault, perhaps, for as he is loyal to me, so he is loyal to them. His life is bound up in this evil knighthood. And, at last, he has been offered the chance to become one of them. In three nights' time, Steel Brightblade will swear the oath, make his vows, and give his soul to the Queen of Darkness. This is why I have come to you, why I have risked my life, for if Ariakan discovers what I've done, he will kill me. Not even my son will be able to stop him."

"Faith, my lady," said Caramon, troubled. "What do you want me to do? Give you refuge? That is easily handled—"

"No," said Sara. Timidly, she touched Caramon's hand. "I want you to stop my son—your nephew—from taking the vows. He is the soul of honor, though that soul is dark. You must convince him that he's making a terrible mistake."

Caramon stared at her in astonishment. "If you—his mother, a woman he loves—haven't been able to change him, all these years, what can I do? An uncle he never knew, a stranger. He won't listen to me."

"Not to you," Sara agreed, "but he might listen to his father."

"His father's dead, my lady."

"I've heard that the body of Sturm Brightblade is enshrined in the High Clerist's Tower. I've heard it said that the body possesses miraculous holy powers. Surely, the father would reach out to help his son!"

"Well . . . maybe." Caramon appeared dubious. "I've seen some strange things in my life, but I still don't understand. What is it you want me to do?"

"I want you to take Steel to the High Clerist's Tower."

Caramon's jaw sagged. "Just like that! And what if he doesn't want to go?"

"Oh, he won't," Sara said confidently. "You're going to have to use force. Probably take him at sword point. And that won't be easy. He's strong and a skilled warrior, but you can do it. You're a Hero of the Lance."

Perplexed, baffled, Caramon gazed at the woman in uncomfortable silence.

"You must do it," Sara pleaded, clasping her hands in supplication. Tears slid unheeded down her cheeks; weariness and fear and sorrow finally overcame her. "Or Sturm's son will be lost!"

21

Chapter Four

Caramon Tries to Remember Where He Put His Armor

"Well," said Tika, jumping briskly to her feet, "if you two are going to leave before dawn, you'd better get started."

"What?" Caramon stared at his wife. "You can't be serious."

"I most certainly am."

"But—"

"The boy's your nephew," Tika informed him, hands on her hips.

"Yes, but—"

"And Sturm was your friend."

"I know that, but—"

"It's your duty. And that's that," Tika concluded. "Now, where did we pack away your armor?" She eyed him critically. "The breastplate won't fit, but the chain mail might—"

"You expect me to go riding a blue dragon into a . . . a—" Caramon looked at Sara.

"Fortress," she told him. "On an island, far to the north, in the Sirrion Sea."

"An island fortress. A secret stronghold filled with legions of dark paladins dedicated to the service of the Dark Queen! And once in this fortress, I'm supposed to snatch up a trained knight in the prime of his life and haul him off to pay a visit to the High Clerist's Tower. And if I even get there alive, which I doubt I'll do, then you expect the Solamnic Knights to just let us stroll in? Me and a knight of evil?"

Caramon was forced to shout this last. Tika had walked out on him, into the kitchen.

"If one side doesn't kill me," he bellowed, "the other will!"

"Hush, dear, you'll wake the children." Tika returned, carrying a bag, redolent with the odor of roasted meat, and a waterskin. "You'll be hungry by morning. I'll just go fetch you a fresh shirt. You'll have to see to the armor. I remember—it's in the big chest under the bed. And don't worry, dear," she said, stopping to give him a hurried kiss. "I'm sure Sara has devised a way to get you inside the fortress. As for the High Clerist's Tower, Tanis will come up with a plan."

"Tanis!" Caramon regarded her blankly.

"Well, of course, you're going to pick up Tanis on the way. You can't go alone. You're not in the best of shape. Besides . . ." She glanced at Sara, who had donned her cloak and was standing impatiently by the door. Tika took hold of her husband's ear and pulled his head down to her level. "Kitiara may have lied," she whispered. "Tanis may be the real father. He should see the boy.

"Then, too," she added aloud, as Caramon rubbed his ear, "Tanis is the only one who can get you into the High Clerist's Tower. The knights will *have* to let him inside. They wouldn't dare offend him or Laurana."

Tika turned to Sara with an explanation. "Laurana is Tanis's wife. She was one of the leaders of the Knights of Solamnia during the War of the Lance. She is highly revered among them. Now she and Tanis are both serving as liaisons between the knights and the elven nations. Her brother, Porthios, is the Speaker of the elven nations. To offend either Tanis or Laurana would be tantamount to offending the elves, and the knights would never do such a thing. Would they, Caramon?"

"I s'pose." Caramon looked dizzy. Events were happening too fast.

Tika knew this was the case, knew how to handle her husband. She had to keep things moving fast. If once he stopped and got to thinking about it, he'd never budge. As it was, she could already see him mulling it over.

"Maybe we should wait until the boys come back from the plains," he hedged.

"No time, dear," Tika said, having anticipated this. "You know that they always spend a month with Riverwind and Goldmoon, going out hunting and learning woodcraft and that sort of thing. Besides, once they set eyes on Goldmoon's beautiful daughters, our boys will be even less anxious to leave. Now, off with you." She pushed Caramon, blinking and scratching his head, toward the door that led back to their private chambers. "Do you remember how to reach Tanis's castle?"

"Yes, I remember!" Caramon snapped quickly.

Too quickly. And therefore Tika knew he didn't remember; he was having to think about it, which was good, because that meant he'd be occupied with trying to figure out how to reach Tanis's dwelling for the length of time it would take him to get ready. Which meant he'd be well on his way before it occurred to him to consider anything else.

Like the danger.

Once he was out of sight, Tika's briskness evaporated. Her shoulders sagged.

Sara, keeping watch out the window, turned at the sudden silence. Seeing the bleak and unhappy look on Tika's face, Sara walked over to stand beside her.

"Thank you for what you've done. I know this can't be easy for you to let him go. I won't say there isn't any danger. That would be lying. But you're right. I have thought of a way to sneak him inside the fortress. And taking Tanis Half-Elven with us is an excellent idea."

"I should be used to it," said Tika, clutching the meat sack in her hands. "I sent my two boys off yesterday. They're younger than your son. They want to be knights. I smile when I tell them good-bye. I call after them that I'll see them in a week or a month or whatever. And I don't let myself think that I may not, that I may never see them again. But the knowledge is there, in my heart."

"I understand," said Sara, "I've done it myself. But at least you know your boys are riding in the sunlight. They are not shrouded by darkness . . ." She put her hand to her mouth and choked back a sob.

Tika put her arm around her.

"What if I'm too late?" Sara cried in a low voice. "I should have come sooner, but . . . I never believed he would really go through with it. I always hoped he would give it up!"

"It will be all right," Tika soothed her. "It will all be all right."

Caramon came out of the bedroom. He was draped in chain mail, which fit well over his shoulders, but didn't quite do its job covering his middle. The big man wore an aggrieved expression.

"You know, Tika," he said, solemnly, staring down at the clanking mail with a frown. "I don't remember this stuff being this heavy."

Chapter Five

Tanis Half-Elven Has an Unpleasant Surprise

Caramon did finally recall how to reach Tanis's castle, located in Solanthus, but he knew the directions only by traveling overland, not by dragon back. Sara, however, was familiar with the entire continent of Ansalon—a familiarity Caramon found disquieting.

"Ariakan has excellent maps," she said, in some confusion.

Caramon wondered just why the Knights of Takhisis had excellent maps of the continent. Unfortunately, the reason wasn't difficult to guess.

The journey took hardly any time at all. Far too little time, for Caramon, who sat hunched on the back of the dragon saddle, cold and hungry (he'd long since eaten the meat), all the sleep startled out of him. He was trying to think of how he was going to explain this strange tale to his friend Tanis.

And what if Tanis is the father? Caramon mulled the matter over. Am I doing him a favor by springing a son on him? What will Laurana say? She never had any use for Kit, that's for damn sure. And what about Tanis's own son? How will this make him feel?

The more he thought about it, the sorrier Caramon was he'd decided to come. At length, he ordered Sara to turn back, to return him to his inn, but she either couldn't hear him—for the rush of the wind in their ears—or was pointedly ignoring him. He might jump out of the saddle, but—from this height—that was out of the question.

It did occur to Caramon that he was armed and that he might overpower Sara. But, after giving this some serious thought, he realized that even if he did manage to overpower Sara, he would never be able to control her blue dragon, which was giving him suspicious looks as it was. And by the time Caramon had reached this conclusion, they had landed on a hilltop overlooking Tanis's castle.

Caramon dismounted from the dragon. It was not yet dawn, but sunrise wasn't far off. Sara calmed the dragon, left it orders to stay put—or so Caramon assumed, since he couldn't understand what she was saying—then she began walking toward the palatial dwelling. Realizing Caramon wasn't following, she turned to him.

"What's wrong?" she asked anxiously.

"I'm not sure," Caramon said, considering.

Sara looked frightened, as if she might start to cry again.

Caramon sighed. "Yes," he said gloomily. "I'm coming."

"Caramon Majere! Of all the lame-brained— Excuse us a moment, will you, mistress?" Tanis said politely to Sara.

Grabbing hold of Caramon's arm, the half-elf dragged the big man to the far side of the large, firelit room.

"This could be a trap," Tanis whispered. "Did you ever consider that?"

"Yes," Caramon said.

"And?" Tanis demanded.

"I don't think it is," Caramon responded, after a moment's thought.

Tanis sighed. "You obviously haven't—"

"I mean," Caramon continued, "why would these dark paladins set a trap for me, a middle-aged innkeeper? That doesn't make much sense, does it?"

"No, but—" Tanis looked embarrassed. "Maybe the trap wasn't meant for you . . ."

"I know," Caramon said, nodding wisely. "You're far more important. But it was Tika who suggested I talk to you, not Sara. And," he added gravely, after another moment's profound thought, "I don't believe Tika's setting a trap for you, Tanis."

"Well, of course, she isn't," Tanis snapped. "It's just . . . All right, so maybe it's not a trap. Maybe I . . . I don't want . . ." He shook his head and started over. "I remember that terrible day Kitiara died. She had tried to kill Dalamar, remember? He stopped her. . . ."

Tanis paused and swallowed. "She died in my arms. And then the death knight came to claim her. I could hear her voice, pleading with me to save her from that dread fate. 'Even now, in death, she's reaching out to you . . .' Dalamar told me then. She's still doing it, Caramon."

"No, she's not, Tanis. This is her son . . ."

"If you believe that woman, Sara."

Caramon was troubled. "Don't you?"

"I don't know what to believe. But, you're right. We have to find out the truth, and do what we can to help this young man, no matter whose son he is. Besides, it will give me a chance to see what Ariakan is up to. We've heard reports of these dark paladins before now, but we had no way of knowing if they were true or merely rumors. It appears"—he glanced grimly at Sara, a chilling figure in her blue helm and black-trimmed cloak—"that they are true.

"But now," Tanis added with a wry smile and a shake of his head, "I have to face the truly difficult task. I have to go tell this to my wife."

Tanis spent an hour alone with Laurana. Caramon, pacing the entry hall of the half-elf's mansion, could well imagine the nature of the conversation. Tanis's elven wife, Laurana, knew all about the relationship between Kitiara and her husband. Laurana had been understanding, especially since the affair was over and finished long ago. But what about now—when there was the possibility of a child? A very good possibility, as far as Caramon was concerned. He simply could not bring himself to believe the father was really Sturm.

"Yet, why would Kit lie?" he asked himself.

The answer was beyond Caramon. But then he'd never been able to explain why his older half-sister had done half the things she'd done.

Tanis came out of the room, his arm around his wife. Laurana was smiling, and Caramon breathed easier. She even paused to say a few whispered words to Sara, who sat, slumped, weary and exhausted, in a corner near the fireplace. Caramon noted then how young Laurana looked, in comparison to her husband—the tragedy of elven-human relationships. Though Tanis had elven blood in his veins, the human blood was growing gray, as the saying went. When the two had wed, over twenty years ago, they had looked to be of equal age. Now they could have been father and daughter.

"But they knew this when they married," Caramon said to himself. "They're making the most out of the time they have together. And that's what counts."

Tanis was ready to travel almost immediately. As official ambassador and liaison between the Solamnic Knights and the elven nations, he spent much of his time on the road, as did his wife. He had donned a suit of leather armor—favored by elves—and a green cloak. Seeing him thus, Caramon was reminded poignantly of their old adventuring days.

Perhaps Laurana was thinking the same, for she ruffled the beard that only a half-human elf could grow, and made some teasing comment in Elvish that caused Tanis to smile. He bid his wife farewell. She kissed him gently, and he held her fondly.

Then he bid farewell to his son—a frail and weak youth, doted on by both parents, who watched him with anxious, loving eyes. The young man was elven through and through, with no trace of his father visible. His complexion was the sickly white of one who rarely steps outside.

Not surprising that Tanis and Laurana keep him locked in a cage like a baby bird, Caramon thought, considering the number of times they've nearly lost him. If he was all elf, he'd be content to spend his time with his nose in a book. But he's human, too. Look at those eyes, Tanis. Look at him when he watches you ride off to adventure, to see wondrous sights he's only read about.

"Someday, Tanis," Caramon said softly, "you're going to come home and find the cage empty."

They trudged up the hill, to where the blue dragon was dozing, its wings folded at its sides.

"What are you muttering about?" Tanis asked Caramon grumpily.

The half-elf was regarding the blue dragon with a grim face, keeping a close watch on it. The dragon was apparently not pleased at the smell of elf.

It woke up instantly, its nostrils flared. Tossing its head in disgust, the beast snaked out its head and showed its fangs.

Sara Dunstan was a skilled dragon rider, however. With a sharp word of reprimand, she brought her mount swiftly, if sulkily, under control. Caramon climbed into the saddle first, then reached down from his rear seat in the two-person dragon saddle to haul up his friend with an easy swing of a massive arm.

"I was thinking to myself that your boy looks well," Caramon lied.

Tanis squirmed to get into a halfway comfortable position, practically an impossibility. He would be forced to cling to the back of Caramon's seat—either that or sit in the big man's lap.

"Thanks," said Tanis, brightening, his proud gaze going to his son, who stood on the lawn, gazing at them with wide, almond-shaped eyes. "We think he's getting better. If we just knew what was wrong with him! . . . Not even Revered Daughter Crysania can tell us."

"Maybe he just needs to spend some time in the fresh air. You should let him come visit us," Caramon suggested. "My boys would take him out riding, hunting . . ."

"We'll see," Tanis said politely, in a not-on-your-life tone. "Any signs of pursuit, mistress?"

Caramon scanned the skies. It had been near dawn when they'd arrived. The morning was well advanced now, the late autumn sun burning off night's chill. There was no sign of any other dragons that he could see.

"With luck, they haven't missed me," Sara said, though she looked worried. "I'm a dragon trainer now. I am often gone, exercising the mounts. I foresaw the need for this."

She spoke a word to the dragon. The blue leapt into the air, propelled by its powerful hind legs, strong wings beating to lift it. They circled the castle once, in order for the dragon to get its bearings, then they soared northward.

"We will arrive at the fortress after dark," Sara told them. "I regret the loss of this day, but, it can't be helped, and what time we've lost we will hopefully make up. Will there be trouble with the Solamnic Knights?" she asked Tanis anxiously.

"There will always be trouble with the Solamnic Knights," Tanis growled. He was in an ill humor, for which Caramon really couldn't blame him. After all, the half-elf might well be journeying to meet a son he never knew he had. "But with Paladine's help, we'll get through it."

The blue dragon glared round at them ferociously. Sara spoke sharply, and the beast sullenly turned its head.

"I wouldn't mention that god's name again," she suggested quietly.

None of them could think of anything to say after that. Talking was difficult anyway; they were forced to shout over the rush of air created by the dragon's powerful wings. And so they traveled in silence, flying far beyond Ansalon, far beyond known civilized lands, flying into darkness.

Two days left.

Two days to save a soul.

Chapter Six

The Fortress of Storm's Keep

"My god!" said Tanis grimly, taking care not to mention which god he was calling on to witness his astonishment. "It's huge!"

"What's the fortress called?" Caramon asked Sara.

"Storm's Keep," she answered. Her words were blown back to him by the violent wind, and it seemed to Caramon that it was the wind that spoke. "Ariakan named it. He said that when those gates open, a storm will be unleashed on Ansalon that will destroy everything in its path."

The fortress was located far north of Ansalon's mainland. Vast and forbidding, Storm's Keep was built on a large island of jagged rock. The glistening black walls of the stronghold were continually bathed by the spray from the crashing waves of the Sirrion Sea. Watch fires burned on the tall, tooth-edged towers. The light served to guide the flight of dragons, whose wings were black silhouettes against the stars as the beasts wheeled and turned in the night sky.

"What's all the commotion?" Caramon asked nervously. "This isn't on your account is it?"

Sara reassured him. "It's just the soldiers, practicing night attacks. Ariakan says that was a mistake the Dragon Highlords made during the last war—fighting in daylight. The knights and their mounts are being trained to fight in the dark, use the darkness to their advantage."

"Not a ship could get near this place," Tanis muttered, eyeing the white foam of the breakers smashing against the steep rock shoreline.

"The seas are far too rough to sail. Not even the minotaurs will venture this far north—one reason Ariakan chose this island. It is accessible only by dragon and by magic."

"At least no one should notice us in all the activity," said Caramon.

"Yes," Sara agreed. "This is what I was thinking."

No one did notice them, or at least pay much attention to them. A gigantic red dragon shrieked at them in irritation, when the smaller blue dived between the red and the tower under "assault." The two dragons exchanged curses and snarls in their own language; the soldier atop the red added his own insults, which Sara answered in kind. She held her course, her destination in sight, cutting swiftly through the mock battle.

Caramon, subdued and appalled, stared around in horror, awed by the strength in numbers and the daring skill of the black-armored paladins, who were easily routing the towers' "defenders." And the dragons were not even using their most powerful weapon—their breath, which could spew acid, belch fire, cast lightning. Tanis's face was stern and grim, noting and attempting to impress on his mind every detail.

Sara ordered the dragon to land in a cleared area far from the main part of the fortress. This section of the compound was relatively quiet, in sharp contrast to the commotion going on at the battle site.

"These are the stables," she said in a low voice to Caramon and Tanis, as they dismounted. "Keep quiet and let me do the talking."

Both men nodded, then hunched their shoulders deep into blue cloaks trimmed with black, which they wore over their own armor. Sara had brought one with her, thinking she would only have to disguise Caramon. She gave Tanis her own cloak, first taking care to remove the black lily brooch.

"You mustn't touch it," she warned him. "It has been blessed by the dark clerics. It might do you harm."

"You touch it," he said to her.

"I am used to it," she returned softly.

The blue dragon settled down in the vast, open yard, an enormous landing site located outside the fortress's walls. Beyond, a long row of stalls echoed with the frustrated, eager whinnies of horses. Excited by the sounds of battle, they wanted their turn.

"The knights are taught to ride and fight on horseback, as well as dragon back," Sara told them.

"Ariakan thinks of everything, doesn't he? Where do you keep the dragons?" Tanis asked. "Surely not here."

"No, the island isn't large enough. The dragons have homelands of their own. No one is quite certain where. They come when summoned."

"Hsst!" Caramon tugged on Sara's sleeve. "Company."

A hobgoblin was running over to stare at them.

"Who's that?" the goblin demanded suspiciously, holding up a torch that sputtered in the rain. "No blues out tonight! What the— Ariakan's woman!"

Sara took off her helm and shook out her hair. "*Lord* Ariakan to you, worm. And I am no one's woman, except my own. You do remember my name, don't you, Glob? Or has it slipped your pea-brained mind?"

The goblin sneered. "What you doing out this night, S-s-s-ara?" He hissed the name mockingly. "And who be these two?" Little piggy eyes had caught sight of Caramon and Tanis, though the men took care to stand well out of the torchlight.

"If I were you, I wouldn't ask too many questions, Glob," Sara replied coolly. "Lord Ariakan doesn't like underlings who meddle in his affairs. See to it my dragon has whatever she wants. You two." She didn't look behind her, but motioned to Caramon and Tanis. "Come with me."

The two walked past the goblin, who appeared somewhat daunted at the mention of Ariakan's affairs, and stepped back. But the goblin squinted intently as the two, shrouded in their cloaks, passed him. And at that moment, as ill luck—or the Dark Queen—would have it, a gust of wind swept round the stable yard and whipped back Tanis's long, graying hair to reveal a shapely, pointed ear.

The goblin sucked in a shrill breath. Leaping over to Tanis, he caught hold of his arm and thrust the lighted torch in his face, so close that he nearly caught the man's beard on fire.

"Elf!" the goblin shrieked, adding a curse.

Caramon had his hand on his sword, but Sara threw herself in between the big man and the goblin.

"Glob, you fool! Now you've done it! Ariakan will have *your* ears for this!"

Snatching the torch from the goblin's hand, Sara hurled it into the mud. The flame sputtered and went out.

"What you mean?" demanded Glob. "What I do? He be a damn elf! A spy!"

"Of course, he's a spy," Sara snarled. "You've just unmasked one of my lord's double agents! You may have jeopardized the entire mission! If Ariakan hears of this, he'll have your tongue cut out!"

"Me no talk," Glob returned sullenly. "Lord-man know that."

"You'd talk fast enough if some white-robed mage got hold of you," Sara predicted grimly.

Caramon had released his sword, but he stood large and threatening. Tanis flipped his cloak over his face and glowered balefully at the goblin.

The goblin's face twisted in a scowl. He stared at Tanis with hatred. "I don't care what you say. I go report this."

"It's your tongue," said Sara, shrugging. "Remember what happened to Blosh. And if you don't, go ask him. But don't hold your breath, waiting for him to answer."

The goblin flinched. The aforementioned tongue flicked nervously over its rotting yellow teeth. Then, with another glare at Tanis, the goblin ran off.

"This way," said Sara.

Caramon and Tanis trudged after her. Both cast oblique glances at the goblin and saw the creature accost a tall man in black armor. The goblin, talking in a shrill voice, pointed at them. They all caught one word: elf.

"Keep walking," Sara said. "Pretend you don't notice."

"I should have wrung the creature's neck," Caramon muttered, hand on his sword hilt.

"Nowhere to hide the body," Sara said in cool, practical tones. "Someone would have found the wretch and there would have been the Abyss to pay. Discipline is strict here."

"Ariakan's whore . . ." The goblin's voice carried clearly.

Sara's lips tightened, but she managed a smile. "I don't think we have much to worry about. Ah, there, see?"

"Speak of Mistress Sara with respect, toad!"

The knight struck the goblin across the face, sent the creature sprawling backward into the stable muck. Then the knight strode on about more pressing matters.

Sara continued walking.

"This business about us being spies. That was fast thinking," said Tanis, at her shoulder. Caramon, glancing around watchfully, brought up the rear.

"Not really." Sara shrugged. "I had already planned out my story, in case we were seen. Ariakan has been bringing his agents here, mostly to impress them, I think. A goblin made the mistake of blabbing that he recognized one. Ariakan had the creature's tongue cut out. That gave me the idea."

"Will the dragon say anything?"

"I've told the dragon the same story. Flare is loyal to me, anyway. Blues are. They're not like reds."

"That knight seemed to respect you . . . " Tanis began.

"Unusual—for a whore." Sara finished his sentence for him.

"That wasn't what I meant."

"No, but it's what you were thinking." Sara walked on in bitter silence, her eyes blinking against the rain and spray that lashed her face.

"I'm sorry, Sara," Tanis said, resting his hand on her arm. "Truly."

She sighed. "No, I'm the one to apologize. You spoke only the truth." Lifting her head proudly, she turned to face him. "I am what I am. I'm not ashamed. I would do it again. What would you sacrifice for your own son— your wealth? Your honor? Your very life?"

Clouds scudded across the night sky and, suddenly, for one instant, Solinari, the silver moon, was free of them. Its bright light shone down on Storm's Keep, and for a strange instant, Tanis saw the future illuminated for him, as if Sara's words had opened a door of a moonlit room. He had only a swift glimpse of danger and peril, swirling about his frail son like the driving rain, and then clouds blew back across Solinari, hiding it from sight, blotting out its silver light. The door shut, leaving Tanis disturbed and frightened.

"Ariakan didn't mistreat me," Sara was saying somewhat defensively, mistaking the half-elf's shaken silence for the silence of disapproval. "It was always understood between us that he would use me for his pleasure, nothing more. He will not take a wife, not now. He is over forty, married to war.

" 'All true knights should have only one true love,' he says. 'And that true love is battle.' He considers himself a father to the young paladins. He teaches them discipline and respect for their fellow knights, respect for their enemies. He teaches them honor and self-sacrifice. Such things, he deems, are the secrets of the Solamnic Knights' victory.

" 'The knights did not defeat us,' Ariakan tells the young men. 'We defeated ourselves, by selfishly pursuing our own petty ambitions and conquests instead of banding together to serve our great queen.' "

" 'Evil turns upon itself,' " quoted Tanis, trying to banish the terror that haunted him, the afterimage of the startling vision of his son.

"Once it did," said Sara, "but no more. These knights have been raised together from childhood. They are a close-knit family. Every young paladin here would willingly sacrifice his life to save his brother . . . or to further the Dark Queen's ambitions."

Tanis shook his head. "I find that hard to believe, Sara. It is the nature of evil to be selfish, to look out for oneself to the detriment of others. If this were not so . . . " He faltered, fell silent.

31

"Yes," Sara urged him to continue. "What if it were not so?"

"If evil men were to act out of what they perceive to be noble cause and purpose, if they were willing to sacrifice themselves for such causes . . ." Tanis looked grave. "Then, yes, I think the world might well be in trouble."

He drew his cloak more closely about him. The chill, damp air made him shiver. "But that just isn't the way things work, thank the gods."

"Reserve your judgment and your thanks," Sara said in a soft, trembling voice. "You haven't yet met Sturm's son."

Chapter Seven

Why Have You Never Asked?

Sara's house was a two-room dwelling, one of a number huddled against the outside walls of the fortress, as if the house itself was frightened of the crashing waves beating on the rocks and sought the protection of stolid walls. Tanis could hear the boom of the waves, crashing with monotonous regularity less than a mile away from where they stood. Salt spray blew against their cheeks, left brine on their lips.

"Hurry," Sara said, unlocking the door. "Steel will be off duty soon."

She hustled them inside. The house was small, but snugly built, warm and dry. Furnishings were sparse. An iron pot hung in a large stone fireplace. A table and two chairs stood near the fire. Behind a curtain, in another room, was a bed and a large wooden chest.

"Steel lives in the barracks with the other knights," Sara said, bustling about, hastily throwing meat and a few vegetables into the pot, while Caramon stirred up the fire. "But he is permitted to eat his meals with me."

Tanis, lost in his own gloomy reflections, still haunted by that vision of his son, said nothing.

Sara poured water in the pot. Caramon had a roaring blaze going beneath it.

"You two hide back there, behind the curtain," Sara instructed, pushing them toward the bedroom. "I don't need to warn you to keep quiet. Fortunately, the wind and the waves generally make enough noise that it's sometimes hard to hear ourselves talk."

"What's your plan?" Tanis asked.

In answer, Sara removed a small vial from her pocket, held it up for him to see. "Sleeping potion," she whispered.

Tanis nodded in understanding. He was about to say something more, but Sara shook her head warningly and drew the curtains shut with a snap. The two men, left in semidarkness, backed up against a wall and stood opposite each other. In case the young man happened to thrust the curtain aside, all he would see at first glance was an empty room.

Caramon discovered a tear in the fabric, which permitted him to see what was going on. Tanis found his own peephole. Both looked and listened in wary, tense silence.

Sara stood near the pot. She held the vial—unstoppered—in her hand. But she didn't pour it.

Her face was pale. She bit her lip. Her hand shook.

Tanis cast a look of alarm at Caramon.

She's not going to go through with it! the half-elf's eyes conveyed warningly.

Caramon's hand closed over his sword hilt. The two braced themselves, though neither had any very clear idea what they would do if she didn't.

Suddenly, with a mutter that might have been a prayer, Sara poured the contents of the vial into the stew pot.

A thundering knock sounded on the door. She poured the vial into the heart of the blaze and wiped her hand hastily across her eyes.

"Come in," she called.

Grabbing a broom, she began to sweep up water and mud that had been tracked across the floor.

The door opened. A young man entered. Caramon nearly fell through the curtain in an attempt to see. Tanis waved at the big man, urged him back, but the half-elf himself had his eye plastered to the hole.

The young man had his back to them. Taking off his wet cloak, he unbuckled his sword belt from around his waist. He leaned the sword, sheathed in its black scabbard—decorated with an axe, a skull, and the black lily—against the wall. He took off his breastplate, then removed his helm with a quick, impatient gesture that made Tanis's heart constrict with painful memories. He'd seen Kitiara remove her helm with that very gesture.

Leaning over Sara, the young man kissed her cheek and placed a hand on her shoulder. "How are you, Mother? You don't look well. Have you been ill?"

Sara had trouble answering. She shook her head. "No, just busy. I'll tell you later. You're wet to the bone, Steel. Go warm yourself. You'll catch your death."

Steel untied a leather thong and shook out a quantity of dark hair. Both the hidden watchers recognized those dark curls. Kitiara had worn her hair short; her son wore it long, tumbling over his broad shoulders. As he stepped over to the fire and held his hands out to the blaze, the flames lit his face. . . .

His face . . .

Caramon gave a great, wheezing gasp.

"What was that noise?" Steel glanced around sharply.

Caramon clapped his hand over his mouth and moved away from the curtain. Tanis, hardly daring to breathe, held perfectly still.

"It's the wind, rattling that broken window," Sara responded.

"I fixed it the last time I was here," Steel said, frowning. He took a step toward the curtain.

"Well, the latch is loose again," Sara said. "Come, eat your dinner before it gets cold. You can't do anything to mend the latch while this storm lasts."

Steel cast a last glance at the curtained room, then turned and walked back to the fireplace. Shifting his position slightly, Tanis could continue to see what was happening.

Steel took a bowl and ladled out broth and meat. A puzzled look crossed his face. He sniffed at the bowl.

Tanis shook his head and gestured toward the living room, warning Caramon to make himself ready. The two of them, catching the younger man off guard, might stand a chance.

Lifting a spoon, Steel tasted the broth, grimaced, and tossed the bowl's contents back into the pot.

Sara, stricken, stared at him. "What—what's the matter?"

" 'Eat it before it gets cold,' " Steel repeated. He was fondly teasing, mimicking her voice. "Mother, I'd have to set that stew out in the storm for it to get much colder. It's not cooked yet!"

"I . . . I'm sorry, dear."

Sara was limp with relief, and so was Tanis. But he was worried about her. She was trembling, her face ashen. Steel couldn't help but notice.

"What is it, Mother?" he asked, once again serious. "What's wrong? I heard you were out this night. What were you doing?"

"I . . . I was ferrying a couple of spies . . . from the continent—"

"The continent!" Steel's dark brows came together in a frown. "Spies! This is not safe, Mother. You take too great a risk. I'll speak to Lord Ariakan—"

"It's all right, Steel," Sara said, regaining her composure. "He didn't send me. I took the task upon myself. It was either that or let some stranger ride Flare. I couldn't permit that. You know how temperamental she can be."

Turning her back on the young man, Sara picked up the poker and stirred the fire.

Steel watched her, his countenance dark and thoughtful. "I find this talk of ferrying spies odd, Mother. I didn't think you were that committed to our cause."

Sara paused in her work. "It's not the cause, Steel," she said in a low voice, her eyes on the flames. "You know that well. I do this for you."

Steel's lip curled. His expression was suddenly hard and cold. Tanis, watching, knew that look. So did Caramon. The big man tensed to jump.

"You ferry spies for me, Mother?" Steel's tone was mocking, suspicious.

Flinging the poker down on the stones, Sara stood up and faced her son. "Someday, Steel, you will ride to war. Whether I approve or not, I will do my part to keep you safe." She clasped her hands. "Oh, my son! Reconsider! Do not take these vows! Do not give up your soul—"

The young man was exasperated. "We've gone over this before, Mother—"

Sara flung herself at him, caught hold of him. "You don't mean it, Steel! I know you don't! You can't give your soul to Her Dark Majesty. . . ."

"I don't know what you mean, Mother." Steel returned. He wrenched himself loose from his mother's grip.

"Yes, you do. You have doubts." Her voice dropped low, and she glanced somewhat nervously out the window into the rain-lashed dawn. "I know you do. That's why you've waited this long to take the vows. Don't let

Ariakan pressure you—"

"The decision is mine, Mother!" Steel's voice had a knife's edge. "War is coming, as you say. Do you think I want to go into battle on foot, leading a party of hobgoblins, while men with half my ability fight on dragons, attain honor and glory? I will take the vows, and I will serve the Dark Queen to the best of my ability. As for my soul, it is my own. And it will stay that way. It belongs to no man, to no goddess."

"Not yet," Sara said.

Steel did not respond. Thrusting her aside, he stalked across the room, stood staring into the stew pot.

"Is that edible yet? I'm starving."

"Yes," said Sara, with a sigh, "it is hot. Sit down."

At her sorrowful tone, he looked around, grudgingly remorseful. "You sit down, Mother. You look exhausted."

Respectful, attentive, he led Sara to a chair and held it for her. Sara sank into the chair, then gazed at him with wistful eyes. The young man obviously found her silent pleading disturbing. He turned from her abruptly. Ladling out two bowls of soup, he placed one in front of each of them.

Sara stared at hers.

Steel began to eat his with a healthy appetite. Tanis let out a relieved breath and heard Caramon do the same. How long would it take the potion to act?

"You're not eating," Steel observed.

Sara was watching him. Her hands, beneath the table, were curled into fists in her lap. "Steel," she said, in a strange voice, "why have you never asked me about your father?"

The young man shrugged. "Perhaps because I doubted that you would be able to give me an answer."

"Your mother told me who he was."

Steel grinned—a crooked grin that brought back such vivid, painful memories, Tanis was forced to shut his eyes.

"Kitiara told you what she thought you wanted to hear, Mother. It's all right. Ariakan has told me all about Kitiara. He told me about my father, as well," Steel added offhandedly.

"He did?" Sara was astonished. The hands in her lap ceased to move.

"Well, not his name." Steel ate more stew. "But everything else about him."

Damn, this is a slow-acting potion! Tanis thought.

"Ariakan said my father was a valiant warrior," Steel continued, "a noble man who died courageously, gave his life for the cause he believed in. But Ariakan warned me that I must never try to learn my father's identity. 'It carries with it a curse, that will fall on you, if you come to know the truth.' An odd thing to say, but you know what a romantic Ariakan is. . . ."

The spoon fell from Steel's nerveless fingers. "What the—" Blinking, he put his hand to his forehead. "I feel so strange . . ."

Suddenly, his eyes focused. He drew in a breath. He tried to stand, but swayed on his feet. "What . . . have you done? . . . Traitor! No, I won't let—"

Lurching forward, he reached out a shaking hand, then fell across the table, sending the bowls flying. He made one last, feeble effort to rise, then collapsed there, unconscious.

"Steel!" Sara bent over him and brushed back the dark, curly hair from the handsome, stern face. "Oh, my son . . ."

Tanis hurried from behind the curtain, Caramon on his heels.

"He's out cold and will be for some time by the looks of it. Well, Caramon, what do you think?" Tanis studied the young man's features.

"He's Kit's son, there's no doubt about that."

"Yes, you're right there," Tanis said quietly. "The father?"

"I don't know." Caramon's face wrinkled in intense concentration. "It could be Sturm. When I first set eyes on him, I almost thought it was Sturm. I . . . I was fairly taken aback! But, then, after that, all I saw was Kit." The big man shook his head. "At least there's no elf blood in him, Tanis."

Tanis had never truly suspected as much. And so he was surprised to find himself relieved . . . and some part of him disappointed.

"No, he is not my son, that much is certain," Tanis said aloud to Caramon. "I didn't think it likely anyway. Ariakan might have taken the boy if he had elven blood—there are dark elves, after all—but I doubt it. Does Ariakan know the truth, do you think?" Tanis looked at Sara questioningly.

"He might. That would be one reason he's never told Steel his father's name, warned him not to ask, added some old wives' tale about the curse."

"Old wives generally know what they're talking about," Tanis said. "Curses can take many forms. The young man's going to be in for an unpleasant shock, if nothing else."

"And he's going to be furious when he wakes up," Caramon pointed out. "I doubt if he'll even listen to us, much less believe anything we tell him. This is hopeless, Sara. Your plan won't work—"

"It can. It must! I will not lose him!" She glared at them fiercely. "You saw him. You heard him! He is not totally given over to evil. He might change his mind. Please, help me! Help him! Once we get him away from here, away from this dark influence—once he sees the High Clerist's Tower and remembers . . ."

"Very well. We'll try," Tanis said. "After all, we've come this far. I'll take one arm—"

"This is my work, Tanis." Caramon shouldered him aside.

Accustomed to carrying barrels of ale on his broad back, Caramon picked the young man up bodily and heaved him effortlessly over a broad shoulder. Steel's head and flaccid arms dangled in front, his long hair practically brushing the ground. Grunting, Caramon settled the young man more securely, then nodded.

"Let's go."

Sara flung a cloak over Steel, grabbed a cloak for herself and her dragon rider helm. Opening the door a crack, she peered out. The rain had ceased for the moment, and the stars shone. The constellation of the Dark Queen, very near, gleamed with ominous brilliance. Storm clouds were massing again on the horizon.

Sara motioned, and they hastened out. They met no one until they neared the stables, then ran almost headlong into a knight in black armor.

He glanced at Steel and smiled coolly. "Another casualty? The young men threw themselves into their training this night. The clerics will earn their keep today." Saluting, the knight went about his business.

The fortress was quiet, most of the men either resting after the night's endeavors or, as the knight had said, recovering from their wounds. Several dragons kept watch, perched atop the tall towers. Guards walked the battlements, probably more for the sake of training and discipline than because they actually feared assault. Ariakan had nothing to fear. Not now. Not yet. Few knew he was here, or what he plotted.

But now I know, Tanis realized uneasily. I can carry the warning, except that it may already be too late. Traitor, Steel called Sara. Is she? Has she really done that much damage to their cause? He thought back to what she'd said that very night. Her main goal was to keep Steel safe. To do that, she had served evil in silence for over ten years. She had broken that silence at last, but only out of desperation, only to save the young man from the final, irrevocable commitment.

They reached the cleared area. Sara put her hand to the brooch she wore on her breast. A blue dragon appeared in the sky, soaring toward them.

"If you can summon dragons," said Tanis, following up on this thoughts, "you could have escaped this place long ago."

"You are right." Sara hovered near Steel, hanging limply in Caramon's grasp. "But I would have had to go alone. He would have refused to come with me. I couldn't leave him here by himself. My influence is all that has kept him walking in the light."

"But you could have warned someone. The Knights of Solamnia might have been able to stop Ariakan." Tanis gestured at the mighty fortress. "Now, he is too strong."

"What would your knights have done?" Sara demanded. "Come with their dragons? Their lances? And what would that have accomplished? Ariakan and the knights would have fought to the death, all our deaths. No, I couldn't risk it. Back then, I still had hope. Someday, Steel might see how evil they are. He might agree to come with me. . . . But now . . . " She shook her head bleakly.

The blue dragon landed on the ground near them. Flare was agitated at the sight of Steel's seemingly lifeless form, but Sara quieted the dragon with a few softly spoken words of explanation. Flare still appeared dubious, but the blue obviously trusted Sara and was extremely solicitous of Steel. The dragon never took its eyes off the young man, as Caramon secured him in the saddle, then wedged himself in uncomfortably behind.

Sara approached the dragon. Tanis laid his hand over hers, halting her.

"We'll do what you ask, Sara Dunstan, but the final decision will rest with Steel. Unless you plan to lock him up in a cellar and throw away the key," he added dryly.

"This will work," she insisted.

Tanis kept hold of her wrist. "Sara, if it doesn't, you've lost him. He'll never forgive you for this act, for betraying him, betraying the knighthood. You know that, don't you?"

She stared at the lifeless form of her son, her face as cold and unlovely as the black lily brooch. Tanis saw, then, the true strength of the woman who had dwelt in this dark prison for so many dark years.

"I know," she said, and pulled herself up onto the dragon.

Chapter Eight

The High Clerist's Tower

"What have you done, Mother?" the young paladin demanded furiously.

Awakening in the mountains, on a windswept promontory overlooking the High Clerist's Tower, Steel was groggy and disoriented at first, but realization, then anger, soon burned away the potion-induced mists.

"I want to give you a chance to reconsider what you are doing," Sara told him.

She did not plead or beg; she was not a pathetic figure. She was calm and dignified and, as the two faced each other, Tanis saw a resemblance that was not born in the blood, but sprang from long years of mutual respect and affection.

Whatever clay the father and mother had brought into this world, it was Sara who had formed and molded it.

Steel swallowed any bitter recriminations or angry words. Instead he turned his dark-eyed gaze on Tanis and Caramon.

"Who are these men?"

"They are friends of your father," Sara replied.

"So that's what this is about," Steel said, favoring both Tanis and Caramon with a cold and haughty stare.

Magnificent in his youth and strength, retaining his pride and his composure when his head must have been swimming and his mind groping about in befuddled confusion, Steel won the grudging admiration of both men.

The blue dragon sniffed the air, shook her head, and snarled. Silver dragons, favored by the Knights of Solamnia, occasionally patrolled the skies above the tower. None could be seen in the skies this early, but the blue obviously scented something she didn't like.

Sara calmed Flare and led her into a large opening in the rocks, where the dragon would be at least partially hidden from view—the main reason she had chosen this particular landing site. The three men remained standing on the rock ledge, regarding each other in uncomfortable silence.

Steel looked ill, was unsteady on his feet, but he would obviously sooner die than admit to weakness, and so neither Tanis nor Caramon made any offer of assistance or comfort.

Caramon nudged Tanis.

"Do you remember the autumn the war started, right after we'd left Solace with Goldmoon and Riverwind? We ran afoul of draconians and Sturm was wounded. Blood covered his face. He could barely stand, let alone walk, and yet he never said a word of complaint, refused to stop . . ."

"Yes," said Tanis quietly, looking at the young man. "I remember." The memory was very vivid, just now.

Steel—aware that he was under scrutiny, if not discussion—turned proudly away.

Tanis eyed the dark paladin's black armor—hideously adorned with symbols of death—and wondered gloomily just how he and the others were supposed to march into the High Clerist's Tower. And, as if this wasn't trouble enough, when Sara emerged from the cave, Tanis knew at a glance that there was more.

"What is it, Sara? What's wrong?"

Caramon cast a nervous glance at the sky. "Not a patrol—"

"Flare claims that we were followed," Sara said in a low voice, not looking at Steel. "That knight . . . he must have suspected something."

"Great, just great!" Tanis muttered. "How many?"

Sara shook her head. "One blue with a single rider. He's not here now. He returned to the fortress . . . once he found out where we were bound . . ."

"But the Knights of Takhisis will come for us," said Steel with a cool and triumphant smile. He turned to Sara. "We can leave now, Mother, before any harm is done. Leave these two old fossils to their moldy memories."

Sighing, he touched her cheek gently. "I know what you're trying to do, Mother, but it won't work. Nothing will make me change my mind. Let us go back home. I'll see to it that Lord Ariakan doesn't blame you. I will tell my lord this mad scheme was my idea. A dare, taken over wine and dice, to spit on the High Clerist's Tower—"

Caramon made a rumbling sound, deep in his chest. "Mind how you talk, boy," he growled. "Your father's blood is red on those stones. His body lies inside."

Steel was obviously taken aback. He regained his composure swiftly, however, and shrugged. "So my father died in the assault—"

"He died defending the tower," said Tanis, observing the young man intently, "and the knighthood."

"He is honored among all Ansalon," Caramon added. "His name, like Huma's, is spoken with reverence."

"That name is Sturm. Sturm Brightblade," said Sara softly. "And that is the name you bear, Steel."

The young man had gone white. He stared at them all in disbelief that rapidly darkened to suspicion. "I don't believe you."

"To tell you the truth," Tanis said, treading on Caramon's foot to warn him to keep silent, "neither do we. This woman here"—he gestured at Sara—"came to us with some wild tale of a liaison between your mother and a man who was our friend, a liaison of which you were the unwitting product. We refused to believe her, and so we told her to bring you here to prove it."

"Why?" Steel demanded, sneering. "What will this prove?"

"Good question, Tanis," Caramon said under his breath. "What will this prove?"

Tanis looked at Sara for the answer.

Take my son inside the tower, her eyes begged him. Let him see the knights. He will remember how he honored them in his childhood. I know he will. My stories will come back to him.

"I wish to Paladine I had your faith, mistress," Tanis said into his beard. He scratched his chin, trying to think up some excuse. This whole scheme was beginning to make less and less sense, becoming more and more dangerous.

Aloud, he said the first thing that came to mind, "There's a jewel that hangs around your father's neck. It was buried with him. The star jewel is magical. It was given to him by an elven queen, Alhana Starbreeze. This jewel will . . . "

"Will what?" Steel mocked him. "Dissolve when I enter the sacred chamber."

"It will tell us the truth," Tanis snapped, irritated by this arrogant youngster. "Believe me, I don't like this any more than you do. What? What's that you say, Caramon?"

"The elf jewel is just a love token. It won't . . . "

"You're right, my friend," Tanis interrupted him loudly. "It is a wondrous jewel. Very magical."

"This is a trick," said Steel. He put his hand to his sword belt, forgetting that he'd taken off his sword. It was back in his mother's house. Flushing, he clenched his fists. "You intend to take me prisoner. Once we get to the tower, you'll hand me over to the knights. That's your plan, isn't it, Mother?"

"No, Steel!" Sara cried. "I never meant that, truly. Neither do these men. If you decide, after all this, to return to Storm's Keep, we will do nothing to stop you. The decision will be yours, Steel."

"I pledge you, by my honor and my life, that this is not a trick. I will guard you as if you were my own son," Tanis said quietly.

"Me, too, Nephew." Caramon nodded, then rested his hand on the hilt of his sword. "You're my flesh and blood. You have my word. I swear by my own children—your cousins."

Steel laughed. "You'll fight in my defense. Thank you, but I doubt if the day will come when I need the services of two soft, middle-aged—" He paused, suddenly struck by what he'd heard. "Nephew. Cousins." His dark eyes narrowed. "Who are you?"

"Your uncle, Caramon Majere," Caramon replied with dignity. "And this is Tanis Half-Elven."

Steel eyed Caramon speculatively, curiously. "My mother's half-brother." The dark-eyed gaze shifted to Tanis. "And one of her lovers, according to Lord Ariakan." The young man's lip curled.

Tanis's skin burned. It's over and done, past and gone, he reminded himself. Kitiara's been dead these many years. I love Laurana. I do, with all my heart and soul. I haven't thought of Kit in all these years, and now a flash of the eye, a turn of the head, her crooked grin, and it all comes back to me. My shame, my indiscretion. Our youth . . . our joy . . .

"So you two are here to save me from myself," Steel was saying, with bitter sarcasm.

"We only want to give you another option," said Tanis, shoulders hunched against the raw and biting wind, against the equally biting memories. "As Sara says, the final decision will be yours."

"That's why we fought the war, Nephew," Caramon added. "To ensure that people had choices."

"Nephew." Steel smiled, and it was meant to be a sneering and arrogant smile. But his lips trembled before he could tighten them, and there was, for the space of a faltering heartbeat, a glimpse of the face of an unhappy, lonely child.

It was then, in that moment, that Tanis came to truly believe that this young man was Sturm's son. In that expression of bleak pride and anguish, Tanis saw again the young knight who had grown up during a time when the Knights of Solamnia were themselves hated and reviled, when he'd been despised, made to feel ashamed of his birthright.

Sturm had known what it was to be different from others. He had used his pride as a shield against hatred and prejudice. That shield of pride had been heavy to carry in the beginning, but Sturm had learned to ease pride's weight with forbearance and compassion. This dark paladin bore the shield's weight eagerly, willingly, and it had left cruel marks on him.

Tanis opened his mouth, almost spoke his thoughts aloud, then he reconsidered. No poor words of mine will penetrate that shield, that dark, cruel armor. He is Sturm's son, yes, but Kitiara's son, too, a child of unholy darkness and hallowed light.

"You owe both these gentlemen an apology, Steel," Sara was sternly berating the young man. "They have proven their mettle in battle, something you have yet to do. It is not for you to speak to them with disrespect."

Steel's handsome face flushed at his mother's chiding, but he had been raised in a strict school. "I do apologize, sirs," he said stiffly. "I have heard of your exploits during the war. You may find this difficult to believe," he added with a grim smile, "but we who serve Queen Takhisis have been taught to honor you."

Tanis did indeed find this hard to believe, didn't like to consider the implications. "Then you have been taught to honor your father's deeds—"

"If Sturm Brightblade is my father," Steel countered. "I have been taught to admire his heroic death—one who stood alone against many enemies. And I have also been taught to honor the memory of my mother, Kitiara, the Dragon Highlord who slew him."

That remark effectively silenced everyone. Caramon shuffled his big feet, coughed, and stared down at the ground. Tanis heaved an exasperated sigh and ran his hand through his hair. A curse if Steel found out who his father was—so Ariakan had told the young paladin. Tanis was beginning to believe it. He couldn't for the life of him see how anything good could come out of this unhappy situation.

Steel turned his back on them all. Walking over to the cliff's edge, he gazed down with interest on the High Clerist's Tower.

"I'm sorry, Sara," Tanis said in an undertone. "I'll say this for the last time. Your scheme isn't going to work. Nothing we say or do is going to make any difference to him. Steel is right. The two of you should leave now. Go back to your home."

The woman's shoulders slumped. She closed her eyes and put a trembling hand to her lips. Tears slid down the careworn face. She couldn't speak, but nodded her head.

"C'mon, Caramon," Tanis said. "We've got to get off this mountain before dark—"

"Wait a minute," Steel said abruptly. He turned around, then stalked over to stand in front of Sara. Putting his hand on her chin, he turned her face to the sunlight. "You're crying," he said softly, and there was wonder in his voice. "All these years, I've never seen you cry."

He would have known how to defend himself against a battalion of knights, but his mother's tears disarmed him completely.

"Do you truly want me to go through with this . . . folly?" he asked, frustrated, helpless, bewildered.

Sara's face brightened. Eagerly, she clung to him. "Oh, yes, Steel. Please! Do this for me."

Tanis and Caramon stood silently by, waiting.

Steel gazed at her, his face a battlefield, revealing the struggle waging within. Then, with a dark, sidelong glance at the two older men, he said coldly, "I will accompany you, sirs—for her sake."

Turning on his heel, he walked to the edge of the ledge, leapt lightly onto another rock ledge below it, and started down the mountainside, picking his way among the tangle of rocks with the nimble dexterity and strength of youth.

Caught flat-footed by the unexpected move, Tanis hurried after, but his elegant and expensive boots—meant for walking his estate, not climbing mountains—slipped on a patch of gravel. He lost his balance and might have tumbled down the cliff had not a strong hand grasped the collar of his tunic and dragged him back.

"Take it slow, my friend," said Caramon. "We've a long way to go, and this isn't going to be easy on either our boots or our bones." He nodded down at Steel, whose dark curls could barely be seen among the boulders. "Let our young friend go it alone awhile. He needs time to think. His mind must feel about like that creek there."

Water, white-frothed and bubbling, swirled and eddied among the rocks, occasionally finding itself stranded in dark pools, then freeing itself to plunge on in a headlong rush to its final destination, the eternal sea.

"He'll be cooler when he reaches the bottom," Caramon finished.

"We won't," Tanis grumbled. The sun was hot on the cliff face. He was already sweating beneath his leather armor. Resting his hand on Caramon's arm, he smiled at the big warrior. "You're a wise man, my friend."

Caramon, looking embarrassed, shrugged. "I dunno. I've got three boys of my own, that's all."

Tanis heard words unspoken.

"Let's go," he said abruptly. He looked back at Sara.

"I'll wait for you here," she said, standing in front of the cave. "Flare's upset. It would never do to leave her alone. She might follow Steel."

Tanis nodded and started down the mountainside again, this time moving more slowly, taking more care.

"The gods bless you for this," Sara called fervently.

"Yes, well, one of the gods is likely going to bless us," Tanis muttered.

He didn't care to think which one.

Chapter Nine

Black Lily, White Rose

"The fortress, known as the High Clerist's Tower, was built by Vinas Solamnus, founder of the Knights of Solamnia, during the Age of Might. The fortress guards the Westgate Pass, leading into and out of one of the major cities of Ansalon, the city of Palanthas.

"After the Cataclysm, which many people mistakenly blamed on the Knights of Solamnia, the High Clerist's Tower was practically deserted, abandoned by the knights, who were in hiding for their lives. During the War of the Lance, the tower was reoccupied and was crucial to the defense of Palanthas and the surrounding countryside. Astinus has recorded the heroic deeds of those who fought and held the tower. You can find the record in the great Library of Palanthas, under the title *Dragons of Winter Night*.

"In that book, you will read of Sturm Brightblade, who died, facing alone the terror of the dragons. Thus it runs:

" 'Sturm faced east. Half-blinded by the sun's brilliance, Sturm saw the dragon as a thing of blackness. He saw the creature dip in its flight, diving below the level of the wall, and he realized the blue was going to come up from beneath, giving its rider the room needed to attack. The other two dragon riders held back, watching, waiting to see if their lord required help finishing this insolent knight.

" 'For a moment the sun-drenched sky was empty, then the dragon burst up over the edge of the wall, its horrifying scream splitting Sturm's eardrums, filling his head with pain. The breath from its gaping mouth gagged him. He staggered dizzily, but managed to keep his feet as he slashed out with his sword. The ancient blade struck the dragon's left nostril. Black blood spurted into the air. The dragon roared in fury.

" 'But the blow was costly. Sturm had no time to recover.

" 'The Dragon Highlord raised her spear, its tip flaming in the sun. Leaning down, she thrust it deep, piercing through armor, flesh, and bone.' "

Steel cast a smug glance at the two men accompanying him. He observed the effect of his recitation on each of them.

"Good god." His uncle's jaw sagged, the big man's round and somewhat stupid (so Steel thought scornfully) face was dumbstruck. The half-elf was eyeing the dark paladin grimly.

"You have a good memory," Tanis remarked.

"It is requisite, so my lord Ariakan teaches, for a warrior to know his enemy," Steel returned. He did not mention that it was his mother, Sara, who had first told him the tale, long ago, when he was a child.

Tanis's eyes shifted their gaze to one of the high walls near the central tower. "On that battlement, your father died. If you go up there, you can still see his blood on the stones."

Steel glanced up, out of curiosity, if nothing more. The wall was not empty these days. Knights walked it, keeping ceaseless vigilance, for, though the War of the Lance was over, Solamnia was not at peace. Yet, as Steel looked, the knights suddenly vanished, left only one, standing alone, knowing he was doomed to die, accepting his death with resignation, believing it was necessary, hoping it would serve to rally the disorganized and demoralized knights to fight on.

Steel saw flame and the bright sun, saw black blood and the red flowing over silver armor. His heart beat faster, with a secret pride. He had always loved this story, one reason he could recite it with such accuracy. Was that because it held some deeper meaning, some meaning only his soul recognized? . . .

Steel was suddenly conscious of the two men, standing quietly at his side.

Of course not. Don't be a fool, Steel berated himself. You're playing into their hands. It's just a story, nothing more.

He shrugged. "I see a wall. Let's get on with this."

They had come down out of the hills on the west side of the High Clerist's Tower. A short distance away from where they crouched, hiding in the brush, a wide causeway led to the main tower entrance. Below that entrance was the Chamber of Paladine, where Sturm Brightblade and the other knights who had fallen during the tower's defense lay buried.

All the Knights and would-be Knights of Takhisis had spent many hours studying the layout of the High Clerist's Tower, a layout provided them by Ariakan, who had been imprisoned here.

But it is one thing to look at a drawing, and quite another to look at the structure itself. Steel was impressed. He hadn't pictured the fortress quite this big, quite this imposing. He made haste to banish the feeling of awe, however, and began to count the number of men walking the battlements, the number standing guard at the main gate. Such information would be useful to his lord.

The causeway was always heavily traveled, and this morning was no different from any other. A knight, his lady wife, and several pretty daughters, rode slowly past them. Various tradesmen were bringing in wagon loads of food and casks of ale and wine. A regiment of knights on horseback, accompanied by their squires and pages, cantered out of the gate, on their way to fight bands of marauding hobgoblins or draconians, or maybe just to parade the streets of Palanthas in an impressive show of force. Steel noted what weapons they carried and the size of their baggage train.

Ordinary citizens were leaving and arriving, some with business dealings, some coming to seek charity, others coming to complain of dragons raiding their villages.

A group of grinning kender—chained together, hand and foot—were being marched out of the tower by grim-faced knights, who relieved the indignant "borrowers" of all their possessions before turning them loose outside the fortress walls.

"You don't see Tas, do you?" Caramon was peering intently at the kender, as they ran, giggling, past him.

"Paladine forbid!" said Tanis fervently. "We've got enough trouble."

"Just how do you propose we get inside?" Steel asked coolly. He'd seen—as had both the men—the knights guarding the main entrance stop and question every person who sought admittance.

"They let the kender in," Caramon pointed out.

"No, they didn't," Tanis returned. "You know the old saying, 'If a rat can get in, so can a kender.' You wouldn't fit in through a kender hole anyway, Caramon."

"That's true," said the big man, unperturbed.

"I've got an idea," Tanis said. He held out the blue cloak to Steel. "Put this on over your armor. Keep behind Caramon. I'll engage the knights at the gate in conversation and you two slip in past me . . ."

"No," said Steel.

"What do you mean, 'No'?" Tanis was exasperated.

"I won't hide myself or my allegiance. I won't creep in like . . . like a kender." Steel's voice was filled with scorn. "The knights will admit me as I am, knowing who and what I am, or not at all."

Tanis's expression hardened. He was about to argue, when Caramon interrupted him by an outburst of laughter.

"I don't find this particularly amusing," Tanis snapped.

Caramon choked, then cleared his throat. "I'm sorry, Tanis, but, by the gods, Steel sounded so like Sturm, I couldn't help myself. Do you remember that time in the inn, when we found the blue crystal staff, and all those goblins and Seeker guards were coming up the stairs, ready to tie us to the stake and burn us? And we were all running for our lives, hoping to escape through the kitchen, except Sturm.

"He just sat at the table, calmly drinking his ale. 'What?' he said, when you told him to run. 'Flee? From this rabble?' My nephew's face, when he said that about the knights letting him in, put me in mind of Sturm that night."

"Your nephew's face puts me in mind of a lot of things," Tanis said grimly, "like how Sturm and his stubbornness and his honor nearly got us killed more than once."

"We loved him for it," said Caramon softly.

"Yes." Tanis sighed. "Yes, I did, though there were times, like now, when I could have wrung his knightly neck."

"Look at it this way, Half-Elven," Steel said in a mocking tone, "you could take this as a sign from your god, the great Paladine. If Paladine wants me inside, he'll see to it that I get in."

"Very well, young man, I'll take your challenge. I'll trust in Paladine. Perhaps, as you say, this will be a sign. But"—Tanis held up a warning finger—"don't say a word, no matter what I say. And don't do anything to cause trouble."

"I won't," Steel said, with ice-hard dignity and disdain. "My mother's up in those hills with a blue dragon, remember? If anything happens to me, Lord Ariakan will take out his rage on her."

Tanis was regarding the young man intently. "Yes, we loved him for it," he said, beneath his breath.

Steel pretended he didn't hear. Turning his face toward the High Clerist's Tower, he climbed up out of the brush and stepped onto the causeway. He assumed his uncle and the half-elf would follow.

Tanis and Caramon flanked the dark paladin, one on each side of him, as they proceeded down the broad road leading to the tower's main gate. Caramon had his hand on the hilt of his sword, a grim and threatening expression on his face. Tanis kept close watch on those who passed them, waiting tensely for the expression of loathing, shocked horror—the outcry that would bring down on them a squadron of knights.

Steel walked tall and proud, the cold and handsome face impassive. If he was at all nervous, he was keeping it to himself.

Few, however, spared them a glance. Most of those who traveled this road were absorbed with their own private worries and concerns. And who would notice three armed men in this bastion of armed men? The only ones who did take note of them were the pretty young women accompanying their knightly father to the tower. They smiled at the handsome young knight in admiration, did everything short of tumbling out of their carriage to attract Steel's attention.

Tanis was extremely puzzled by this. Did the symbols of terror and death the dark paladin wore plainly on his person no longer have any effect on people? Had the Solamnians forgotten the dread power of the Dark Queen? Or were they just mindlessly, stupidly complacent?

Tanis, glancing at Steel, saw the young man's lip curl in scorn. He was finding this amusing.

Tanis quickened his pace. There was still the main gate to pass.

The half-elf had thought up and then discarded several arguments for allowing a Knight of Takhisis to enter the stronghold of Paladine. He had at last been forced to admit to himself that there could be no logical argument. As a last resort, he would use his standing as a renowned hero and respected government official to bully his way inside.

Wishing that he was decked out in his full ceremonial regalia, instead of his worn, albeit comfortable, traveling clothes, Tanis put on his you'll-do-what-I-say-and-like-it mask and strode up to the knights guarding the main gate.

Caramon and Steel came to a halt about a pace behind. Steel's face was hard, his dark eyes opaque, head thrown back in defiance.

One of the knights on guard duty stepped forward to meet them. His gaze swept over them with mild and friendly curiosity.

"Your names, gentle sirs," said the knight courteously. "And please state your business."

"I am Tanis Half-Elven." Tanis was so pent up, the words came out in an explosive bark, practically a shout. Forcing himself to calm down, he added in softer tones, "This is Caramon Majere . . ."

"Tanis Half-Elven and the famous Caramon Majere!" The young knight was impressed. "I am honored to meet you, sirs." In an undertone, he said to a cohort, "It's Tanis Half-Elven. Run and fetch Sir Wilhelm."

Probably the lord knight in charge of the gate.

"Please, there's no need to make a fuss," Tanis urged hastily, with what he hoped sounded like becoming modesty. "My friends and I are here on a pilgrimage to the Chamber of Paladine. We simply want to pay our respects, nothing more."

The young knight's face immediately assumed an expression of grave sympathy. "Yes, of course, my lord." His gaze shifted from Caramon, who glowered and appeared ready to take on the fortress single-handedly, then the knight looked at Steel.

Tanis tensed. He could already picture it. The young guard's astonishment changing to fury, the ringing trumpet call that would sound the alarm, bring down the portcullis, surround them with swords . . .

"I see you are a Knight of the Crown, sir, like myself," the young knight was saying . . . and he was saying it to Steel! The Solamnic Knight touched his breastplate, on which was the symbol of the lowest of the ranks of the Knights of Solamnia. He gave Steel the knight's salute on meeting a comrade, a lifting of the gloved hand to the helm. "I am Sir Reginald. You don't look familiar, Sir Knight. Where did you take your training?"

Tanis blinked, stared. Were they letting the nearsighted into the knighthood these days? He looked at Steel, saw black armor adorned with the Dark Queen's emblems: lily, axe, skull. Yet the Solamnic Knight was smiling and treating Steel as if they'd been barracks mates.

Had Steel cast some sort of spell on the knight? Was it possible? Tanis looked at him sharply, then relaxed. No, Steel was obviously as confused about what was going on as Tanis. Defiance had seeped out of the young man. He looked dazed and a little foolish.

Caramon's mouth hung wide open. A sparrow could have flown in and nested there, and he wouldn't have noticed.

"Where did you take your training, sir?" the knight asked again, in a friendly fashion.

"K-kendermore," Tanis said the first thing that came into his head.

The young knight was immediately sympathetic. "Ah, rough duty, I hear. I'd rather patrol Flotsam myself. Is this your first visit to the tower? I have an idea." The knight turned to Tanis. "After you've paid your respects in the Chamber of Paladine, why don't you hand over your friend to me? I'm off duty in half an hour. I'll take him all around the tower, show him our defenses, fortifications—"

"I don't believe that would be a good idea!" Tanis gasped. He was shaking, sweating beneath the leather armor. "We . . . we're expected in Palanthas. Our wives are waiting for us, aren't they, Caramon?"

Caramon took the hint. His mouth snapped shut. He managed to mumble something incoherent about Tika.

"Perhaps another time," Tanis added regretfully. He stole a glance at Steel, thinking that the young man must be getting quite a laugh out of all this.

Steel was shaken, pale, his eyes wide. He seemed to be having trouble breathing.

Well, thought Tanis, that's what happens when you brush up against a god.

Sir Wilhelm arrived and took charge of them at once. He was, Tanis was sorry to note, one of the old-time, pompous, set-in-the-saddle type of knights; the kind who let the Oath and the Measure do his thinking for him. He was the type of knight Sturm Brightblade had always detested. Fortunately, there were far fewer of Sir Wilhelm's sort these days than there had been in the past. A pity some god—or goddess—had put him in their path.

And, of course, Sir Wilhelm was insisting on personally accompanying them to the tomb.

"Thank you, my lord." Tanis attempted to rid himself of the man. "But this is a very poignant moment for us, as you can imagine. We would prefer to be by ourselves . . ."

Impossible! (Harumph) Sir Wilhelm would never permit it. (Harumph) The famous Tanis Half-Elven and the famous Caramon Majere and their young friend, a Knight of the Crown, paying his first visit to the Chamber of Paladine. No, no, (Harumph, harumph) this called for a full escort of knights!

Sir Wilhelm rounded up his escort, six knights, all armed. Forming them into ranks, he himself led the way to the Chamber of Paladine, marching with slow and solemn step, as though leading a funeral procession.

"Maybe he is," Tanis said into his beard. "Ours."

He glanced at Caramon. The big man shrugged unhappily. They had no choice but to follow decorously along behind.

The knights headed for two closed iron doors marked with the symbol of Paladine. Beyond those doors, a narrow staircase led down into the sepulcher.

Steel edged alongside Tanis. "What did you do back there?" he demanded, speaking in a low voice, his distrustful gaze divided between the half-elf beside him and the knights marching ahead of him.

"Me? Nothing," Tanis returned.

Steel didn't believe him. "You're not some sort of mage, are you?"

"No, I'm not," Tanis answered testily. They weren't out of this yet, not by a long shot. "I don't know what happened, except I could suppose that you got your sign!"

Steel was pale. The awe—and the fear—was plain on his face. Tanis relented toward the young man. Oddly enough, he found himself liking him.

"I know how you feel," Tanis told him, speaking softly. The knights had come to the iron doors and were handing out torches to light the way down the dark staircase. "I once confronted Her Dark Majesty. Do you know what I wanted to do? I wanted to fall down on my knees and worship her."

Tanis shivered at the memory, though it had happened years ago. "Do you understand what I'm saying? Queen Takhisis is not my god, but she is a god. I'm just a poor, puny mortal. How could I help but revere her?"

Steel made no answer. He was thoughtful, stern, withdrawn to some inner core of himself. Paladine had given the young knight the sign he'd mockingly demanded. What meaning did it hold for him—if any?

The iron doors swung open. The knights, marching with solemn tread, began to descend the stairs.

Chapter Ten

"My Honor is My Life"

The half-elf's explanation made sense to Steel. Paladine was a god—a weak and sniveling god, compared to his opposite, the Dark Queen, but a god nonetheless. It was right and proper for Steel to feel awed in Paladine's presence—if that's what had truly happened back there at the gate.

Steel even tried to laugh at the incident—it was too funny, these pompous knights leading their most feared enemy around by the hand.

The laughter died on his lips.

They had begun to descend the steps that led into the sepulcher—a place of awful majesty, holy and sacred. Here lay the bodies of many brave men, among them Sturm Brightblade.

Est Sularus oth Mithas. My Honor is My Life.

Steel heard a voice, deep and resonant, repeat those words. He looked quickly around, to see who had spoken.

No one had. All walked silently down the stairs, voices muted in respect and reverence.

Steel knew who had spoken. He knew himself to be in the presence of the god, and the young man was daunted.

Steel's challenge to Tanis had been made out of sheer bravado, made in order to quell the sudden aching longing that seared Steel's soul, the longing to know himself. Part of Steel wanted desperately to believe that Sturm Brightblade—noble, heroic, tragic knight—was truly his father. Another part was appalled.

A curse if you find out, Ariakan had warned him.

Yes, so it would be, but . . . to know the truth!

And therefore, Steel had challenged the god, dared Paladine to tell him.

It seemed the god had taken the young man's dare.

His heart subdued, Steel's soul bowed down in worship.

The Chamber of Paladine was a large rectangular room lined with stone coffins that held the heroes of the ancient past and the more recent dead of the War of the Lance.

Following the entombment of the bodies of Sturm Brightblade and the other knights who had fallen defending the tower, the iron doors to the chamber were shut and sealed. If the tower fell into enemy hands, the bodies of the dead would not be desecrated.

A year after the war had ended, the knights broke the seals, opened the chamber, and made it a place of pilgrimage, as they had done with Huma's Tomb. The Chamber of Paladine had been rededicated; Sturm Brightblade was made a national hero. Tanis had been present that day, as had his wife, Laurana; Caramon and Tika; Porthios and Alhana—rulers of Silvanesti and Qualinesti, the elven nations; and the kender, Tasslehoff Burrfoot. Raistlin Majere, Master of the Tower of High Sorcery in Palanthas and already turned to darkness, had not come, but he had sent a message of respect for his old comrade and friend.

The bodies of the dead had been laid unceremoniously on the floor during the dark days of the war. At this ceremony, they were given proper and seemly burial. A special catafalque had been built to hold Sturm's body. Made of marble and carved with images of the knight's heroic exploits, the catafalque stood in the very center of the chamber. Sturm's body lay on it, not entombed.

Some sort of magic had kept the body from decay these twenty-some years. No one was certain, but most believed the magic emanated from the elven jewel, given to him in love by Alhana Starbreeze. The jewel was a token exchanged between lovers; it was not supposed to have any such powerful arcane properties. But, then, love works its own magic.

Tanis had not visited the chamber since that day. That solemn occasion had been far too painful and blessed for him to repeat. Now he had returned, but he didn't feel either solemn or blessed. Looking around the room, with its ancient coffins, covered with dust, the catafalque standing in the center, Tanis felt trapped. If anything went wrong, they were a long way from the stairs, the iron doors, and escape.

"Nothing will go wrong," Tanis said to himself. "Steel will look on the body of his father, and he'll either be affected by it or he won't. Personally, I don't expect this to have any effect on him. As near as I can judge, that young man is well on his way to the Abyss. But, then, what do I know? I never expected us to get this far."

Sir Wilhelm, looking as sorrowful as if he were burying his own kin, led the way to the catafalque. The six knights formed ranks around it—three on either side. Sir Wilhelm stood at stiff attention at the head of the bier.

Tanis approached the catafalque. He looked on the face of his friend—the face that seemed as one with the carved marble, yet held the remembrance of life; a thing the cold stone could never emulate. Tanis forgot Steel; he felt peace surround him. He no longer grieved for his friend; Sturm had died as he had lived—with honor and courage.

It did Tanis good to see the knight's untroubled sleep. Tanis's fretful worries over his own son, over the hectic political situations, the brooding threat of war, all vanished. Life was good, sweet; but there was a greater good waiting.

Sturm Brightblade lay on his marble bier, his hands folded over the hilt of an antique sword—his father's sword. He was clad in his father's armor. The star jewel, shining with the light of love, gleamed on his breast. A dragonlance lay alongside him. Next to it was a wooden rose, carved by the hands of a grieving old dwarf, now sleeping his own restful sleep. Beside the rose, encapsulated in crystal, was a white feather, a final gift of a loving kender.

Tanis knelt on one knee beside the body. His head level with the knight's, Tanis spoke to his friend softly in Elvish. "Sturm, honorable, gentle, noble heart. I know you have forgiven Kitiara for what she did to you, for her treachery, her deceit—more painful for you than the spear she finally used to slay you. This young man is her son, far too much her son, I fear.

"Yet, there is, I think, something of you in him, my friend. Now that I stand here, I believe that you truly are his father. I see the resemblance in your features, but, stronger than physical evidence, I see you in this young man's spirit, in his dauntless courage, in his nobility of character, in the compassion for others that he counts as a mark against himself.

"Your son is in danger, Sturm. The Dark Queen draws him near, whispering her words of seduction, promising him glory that must surely end in ultimate defeat. He needs your help, my friend, if such help is possible for you to grant. I regret disturbing your peaceful slumber, but I am asking you, Sturm, to do whatever you can to draw your son away from the dark path he now walks."

Tanis stood up. Brushing his hand across his eyes, he looked over at Caramon.

The big man knelt on the opposite side of the catafalque. "I'd give up my life for my children," he said, in a quiet voice, "if I thought that would save them from danger. I know that you'll . . . Well, you'll do what's right, Sturm. You always did."

With this somewhat enigmatic request, Caramon stood up. Turning his back, he snuffled loudly, then wiped his eyes and nose on his shirt sleeve.

Tanis looked at Steel. The young man had held back. He stood alone, away from the knights, away from the catafalque, though he stared at the body with dark and burning eyes. He continued to stand, unmoving. His face, pale and cold and hard, was the exact copy of the face of the slumbering knight. Both might well have been carved out of marble.

"So much for that," Tanis said to himself. "Poor Sara. Still, she tried."

Sighing, he took a step forward. It was time to leave.

Suddenly Steel made a convulsive lunge for the marble catafalque.

"Father!" he cried brokenly, and it wasn't the man's voice who spoke, but the voice of the child, bereft, alone.

Steel's hands closed over the cold hands of the corpse.

A flash of white light, a light pure and radiant, cold and awful, surged through all present, left them paralyzed and half-blind.

Tanis rubbed his eyes, trying to knead out the vibrant afterimage, trying frantically to see through a bursting of fiery red and vivid yellow spots. Elven eyesight is keen, and elven eyes adjust better to darkness and to light than do human eyes. Or perhaps, in this instance, it was the eyes of the heart that saw clearer than those of the head.

Sturm Brightblade stood in the chamber.

So real was the vision—if vision it was—that Tanis very nearly called out his friend's name, very nearly reached out to once again clasp his friend's hand. Something kept the half-elf silent. Sturm's gaze was fixed on his son, and in it was sorrow, understanding, love.

Sturm spoke no word. He reached to his breast, clasped his hand over the star jewel. The dazzling white light was briefly diminished. Sturm reached out to his son.

Steel stared at his father; the young man was more livid than the corpse.

Sturm's hand touched Steel on the breast. The light of the jewel flared.

Steel put his hand swiftly to his breast, fumbled for something there, and closed his hand over it. White light pulsed briefly in Steel's grasp, welled through his fingers, then the light was darkness. Steel thrust whatever had been in his hand inside his armor.

"Sacrilege!" Sir Wilhelm gave a hoarse cry of outrage and fury, then drew his sword from its scabbard.

At last, the fiery halo disappeared. Tanis could see clearly and the sight unnerved and appalled him.

The body of Sturm Brightblade was gone. The corpse had disappeared. All that remained was the helm, the shining antique armor, and the ancient sword, lying on the bier.

"We have been deceived!" Sir Wilhelm was thundering. "This man is not one of us! He is not a Solamnic Knight. He is a servant of the Dark Queen! A minion of evil! Seize him! Slay him!"

"The magic jewel!" another knight cried. "It's gone! He has stolen it! The jewel must be on his person!"

"Take him! Search him!" Sir Wilhelm howled. Brandishing his sword, he leapt for Steel.

Weaponless, Steel reached instinctively for the nearest blade at hand. He grabbed the sword—his father's sword—from atop the catafalque. Bringing the blade up, he easily blocked Sir Wilhelm's wild downward slash. The young man threw the older knight backward, to fall with a clatter of armor among the ancient, dust-covered coffins.

The other knights closed in. Strong and skilled as he was, Steel could never hope to fight off seven at once.

Tanis drew his sword. Leaping over the catafalque, he jumped down beside Steel.

"Caramon! Guard his back!" Tanis yelled.

Caramon stood gaping. "Tanis! I thought I saw—"

"I know! I know!" Tanis shouted. "I saw it, too!" He had to do something to jolt the big man from his dazed wonderment. "Caramon, you took an oath! You swore you'd protect Steel like your own son."

"So I did," Caramon said with dignified gravity. Picking up the knight nearest him, who happened to block his way, the big man flung the knight bodily aside. Drawing his sword, Caramon put his back to Steel's.

"You don't have to do this for me," Steel gasped through bloodless lips. "I don't need you to fight my battles!"

"I'm not doing this for you," Tanis returned. "I'm doing this for your father."

Steel stared at him, suspicious, disbelieving.

"I saw what happened," Tanis said simply. "I know the truth."

He pointed at the dark paladin's breastplate, the armor decorated with the foul insignia of the Dark Queen. And shining from beneath it was a glimmer of white light.

Relief flooded Steel's face—the young man must have been wondering if what had happened had truly happened or if he were going mad. Immediately, he recollected himself, his face hardened. Steel was, once again, one of Takhisis's Knights. He turned grimly to face his foes.

The Solamnic Knights stood with swords drawn, but did not immediately pursue the attack. Tanis Half-Elven was a powerful force in the land, and Caramon Majere a respected and popular hero. The knights looked uneasily to their commander for orders.

Sir Wilhelm was struggling to regain his feet. For him, the answer was obvious. "The other two have been subverted by evil! They are all the servants of the Dark Queen. Seize all three!"

The knights leapt to the attack. Steel fought well; he was young, skilled, and had been waiting for just such a contest all his life. His eyes gleamed and his blade flashed in the torchlight. But the young Knights of Solamnia were his equals. Now that they could see the evil in their midst, their eyes shone with a holy light; they were defending their honor, avenging sacrilege. Four of them surrounded Steel, intent on capturing him alive, determined to wound him, not kill him.

Blades clashed. Bodies heaved and shoved. Soon, Steel was bleeding from a gash across his forehead. Two of the knights were also blooded, but they fought with renewed strength and fervor. They backed Steel up against the catafalque.

Tanis did what he could to help, but he hadn't wielded a sword in anger in many years. Caramon was huffing and wheezing and grunting, sweat rolling off the big man's head. He was getting in one blow to his opponent's six, but Caramon—with his size and strength—always managed to make that one blow count. His sword rang like a hammer falling on an anvil.

All three were trying to fight their way through to the stairs, but the knights were equally intent on cutting off this escape route. Fortunately, Sir Wilhelm had not thought of sending one of the knights for reinforcements. Probably he was hoping for the glory of capturing the Dark Queen's paladin himself. Either that, or he didn't dare risk reducing the size of his small force.

"If we can make it up the stairs," Tanis said to Caramon, as the two fought side-by-side, "we can rush the main gate. There were only two guards there. And after that . . ."

"Let's just . . . get that far!" Caramon was leaning on the side of the catafalque, still fighting gamely, though the big man was gasping for breath. "Damn heavy . . . chain mail!"

Tanis could no longer see Steel; he was encircled by a wall of silver armor. But Tanis could hear the ring of the young man's sword and could tell, by the numerous fresh wounds on the Knights of Solamnia, that Steel was still battling. He would keep fighting until they cut him down. He would never let himself be taken alive.

He wouldn't disgrace the memory of his father.

Every muscle in Tanis's body ached. Fortunately, his opponent, a young knight, was in such awe of the great hero that he was fighting only half-heartedly. Sir Wilhelm was looking exasperated. This battle should have been over by now. He glanced at the stairs. Now he was going to raise the alarm, shout for reinforcements.

If that happened, they were doomed.

"Sturm Brightblade," Tanis said softly, "you got us into this. The least you can do is help get us out!"

The iron doors, decorated with Paladine's symbol, stood open at the top of the stairs. It might have been a freakish prank of nature, or it might have been the breath of the god. Suddenly, a great gust of wind blasted through the door, blew out the torches as if they'd been candles, and plunged the tomb into darkness. Lifting the dust of centuries, the wind tossed dirt into the faces of the Solamnic Knights.

Sir Wilhelm, in the act of drawing a deep breath to call for help, sucked in a great cloud of dust. He began to choke and cough. The knights staggered around blindly, their eyes filled with grit, their mouths coated.

Oddly, the dust didn't affect Tanis. He located Steel in the darkness by the faint white light gleaming from beneath his breastplate. Grabbing hold of the young paladin, who was raising his sword over his suddenly disadvantaged foe, Tanis yelled in the young man's ear.

"Let's get out of here!"

He thought for a minute he was going to face an argument—Sturm would have argued—but then Steel flashed Tanis a grin—a crooked grin, Kitiara's crooked grin. Sword in hand, he ran for the stairs. Tanis found Caramon by the sound of heavy breathing.

Resting his hand on the big man's shoulder, Tanis said, "The stairs, our only chance. Can you make it?"

Caramon nodded—too spent to talk—and started lumbering after Steel. On his way past the catafalque, Tanis rested his hand lightly, briefly, on the antique armor.

"Thank you, my friend," Tanis whispered.

They clamored up the staircase. Bursting through the iron doors, Steel headed for the main gate. The fire of battle shone in his dark eyes. Tanis caught hold of him and nearly pulled the eager young man off his feet. Steel glared at him in fury and struggled to free himself.

Tanis held the young man fast. "Caramon, the doors!"

Caramon grabbed hold of the iron doors, swung them shut, then glanced hurriedly around for something to keep them shut. Several heavy marble blocks being used in repair work stood nearby. Heaving and grunting, Caramon shoved one of the blocks against the doors, just as footsteps could be heard stumbling up the stairs. A blow hit the iron doors, but they didn't budge.

Blows and muffled shouts came from inside the Chamber of Paladine. It would be only a matter of moments before someone heard.

"Now, we go," said Tanis to the young man. "Try to look as if nothing has happen— Oh, forget it."

Caramon was red in the face, huffing and puffing like an enraged bull. Tanis's shirt sleeves hung in ribbons around his left arm; he was bleeding from a wound he never knew he'd taken. Steel's head was bloodied, his armor dented and scratched.

And, Tanis thought, I have the feeling no one will ever again mistake a Knight of Takhisis for a Knight of Solamnia.

He was right. The three had no sooner reached the main gate when there came a trumpet call behind them. It was the alarm, the call to arms. The knights guarding the gate jumped to action, immediately began to take defensive measures.

Within moments, the gate would be shut, secured.

"Run for it!" Tanis ordered. "And keep running," he said to Steel.

They made a wild and desperate dash for the closing gates. The knights on duty took one look at Steel and, drawing their swords, rushed to stop him.

Lightning breath crackled outside the gate. The tip of a gigantic blue wing could be seen swooping past. Civilians caught outside were screaming about dragons. Panic-stricken, the frightened people stampeded the entrance, hampering both the knights' attack and their ability to shut the gate.

Tanis and Caramon joined the melee. It took them both to drag away Steel, who had turned to slash at an opposing knight.

Outside the tower, the blue dragon, Flare, was flying low over the heads of the terrified crowd, sending people tumbling into the ditches. Occasionally, the dragon increased the panic by blasting holes in the ground and the fortress walls with her lightning breath.

"Sara!" Tanis yelled, waved his arm.

Sara guided the dragon to the ground. She reached out a hand, pulled Tanis onto the saddle. He, in turn, caught hold of the still-battling Steel and, with Caramon's help from behind, managed to heave the young man up onto the dragon's back. Caramon jumped on last. Sara shouted a command, and Flare soared into the sky.

The knights ran out of the fortress, shouting and cursing, in Paladine's name, those who had committed the heinous act of desecrating the sacred tomb. Arrows flew from the bowmen posted on the walls. Tanis was more worried about the silver dragons, who guarded the fortress, and who had taken to the air when the trumpet had sounded.

But either the silver dragons had no desire to fight a blue and break the uneasy truce that existed among the dragons at this time, or the silvers, too, were being held back by an immortal hand. They eyed Flare balefully, but let her fly away in safety.

Perched on the back of a blue dragon, Tanis glanced down at the arrows, now whistling harmlessly beneath them.

"How," he wondered gloomily, "am I ever going to explain all this?"

Chapter Eleven

ᖰIS ᖴATᕼER'S SWORD

At Tanis's suggestion, Flare flew for the foothills of the Khalkist Mountains, still a no-man's-land, where they could rest in safety and figure out what to do next.

None of them spoke during the journey. Sara cast frequent worried glances at Steel. Tanis had explained, in a few brief words, some—not all—of what had occurred in the chamber. It would be up to Steel to tell her fully and completely what had happened to him.

Sara asked Steel about it, several times, but the young man didn't answer. He didn't even seem to hear her. He sat staring out into the deep blue sky, his gaze abstracted, eyes dark and fathomless, his thoughts unreadable.

At length Sara gave up and concentrated on flying. She chose a suitable landing place, a wide clearing surrounded by a thick forest of pine trees.

"We'll camp here for the night," Tanis said. "We can all use the sleep. Then, in the morning, we'll decide what to do, where to go."

Sara agreed.

Steel said nothing. He hadn't spoken a word since they had left the High Clerist's Tower. Immediately on landing, he jumped lightly from the dragon's back and took off for the forest. Sara was going to follow, but Caramon stopped her.

"Let him go," he said gently. "He needs time to think. A lot has happened to that young man. The person who went into that chamber isn't the same one who came out."

"Yes, I suppose you're right," Sara said with a sigh. She stood staring into the woods, her hands twisting together nervously. "Will he . . . Has this changed his mind, do you think?"

"Only he knows that," Tanis said.

Sara sighed again, then glanced at him anxiously. "Is there any doubt in your mind that he is the son of Sturm Brightblade?"

"None whatsoever," Tanis answered firmly.

Sara smiled. Looking more hopeful, she went to settle the dragon down for the night.

"Just what did happen back there in the chamber, Tanis?" Caramon asked in a low voice, as they set about building a small cooking fire. "Did I really see what I thought I saw?"

Tanis pondered. "I don't know for certain, Caramon. I'm not that sure myself. There was a blinding light, and my eyes were dazzled, but I could swear I saw Sturm standing there. He held out his hand, and the next thing I knew, the elven jewel was hanging around Steel's neck."

"Yeah, that's what I saw, too." Caramon pondered. "Still, it could have been a trick. Maybe he did steal it—"

"I don't think so. I saw the look on his face. Steel was the most startled person in that chamber. He stared at the jewel in amazement, then he grabbed hold of it and hid it beneath his armor. Trust your heart, Caramon. Sturm gave Steel the jewel and his sword. He gave them both to his son."

"What will he do with them—an elven love token and the sword of a Knight of Solamnia? Surely, he won't go back to that horrid place now?"

"That's up to him," Tanis said quietly.

"And if he does decide to stay, what do we do with him? And his mother?" Caramon asked. "I can't very well take them home with me. I'll be lucky if the sheriff and his men aren't waiting for me on the inn steps when I get back. Not to mention the fact that Ariakan will be out looking for his lost paladin. Maybe you—"

"I'm going to have to do some fast talking to keep from getting arrested myself," Tanis said, with a wry smile. He scratched his beard and turned the matter over in his mind. "We could take Steel and Sara to Qualinesti," he decided at last. "They'd both be safe there. Not even Lord Ariakan would dare follow them into the elven kingdom. Alhana would let Steel in, once she saw the jewel, heard his story."

Caramon shook his head. "Won't be much of a life for that young man, will it? Living among the elves. No offense, Tanis, but you and I both know how they'll treat him. I don't suppose the Solamnic Knights would let him into the knighthood?"

"I hardly think so," Tanis said dryly.

"Then what will he do? Become a mercenary? Sell his sword to the highest bidder? An aimless drifter . . ."

"What were we, my friend?" Tanis asked him.

"We were wanderers," Caramon said, after a moment's profound thought. "But Sturm Brightblade wasn't."

Steel was gone all afternoon. Tanis slept. Caramon—always thinking about where his next meal was coming from—went fishing. He caught some trout in a nearby stream. Adding pine nuts and wild onions he found growing in the forest, he wrapped the trout in the wet leaves and cooked the fish on rocks heated in the fire.

By sunset, Sara was growing exceedingly anxious. She was about to send Flare to search for the young man when he appeared, walking out of the shadows of the trees. Saying nothing, Steel squatted down by the fire. He laid the sword, sheathed in its ancient scabbard, in the grass at his side. Then he helped himself to the fish.

Tanis waited for Sara to ask her son the question she had been longing to ask him ever since his escape from the tower. But now either she was afraid to hear the answer or else she was waiting for him to broach the subject, because she kept silent. Her fond and loving gaze never left him, however.

He concentrated on the food, appeared to be avoiding his mother's eyes. Tanis had the feeling the young man's decision had been made. Steel was wondering, perhaps, how to tell her.

The meal continued in silence, until Caramon, looking skyward, touched Tanis's arm.

"Company," Caramon said.

Tanis stood up swiftly. Off toward the west, from the direction of Palanthas, four dragons veered and wheeled against the red and orange streaks of the dying sun.

"Damn! And here we sit, all cozy in front of a fire! You'd think we were on a picnic! I've been away from this sort of thing for too long, my friend," Tanis said ruefully.

"Douse that," Caramon ordered.

Steel was already doing so, flinging dirt on the fire to keep it from smoking.

"What kind of dragons are they? Can you see?" Caramon was squinting. He tried to sound hopeful. "Maybe Solamnic Knights, out on patrol."

"Knights, all right, but not Solamnic," Tanis said grimly.

"Those are blue dragons," Sara agreed, with certainty.

Her own blue dragon was restive, stamping its feet, lashing its tail. Well-disciplined, the beast was keeping quiet, not calling out to its mates, as it would have been inclined to do otherwise. But it was obvious the dragon had recognized its fellows and couldn't understand why it wasn't being permitted to join them.

Steel watched the dragons. "Half-Elven, you know these parts. Is there some town nearby, within walking distance?"

Sara clasped her hands together, her eyes bright with joy.

Tanis considered. "There's a village of hill dwarves at the base of the mountain. I should say it's about a day's journey from here. The dwarves trade with Palanthas. Caravans come and go all the time."

"Excellent," Steel said, keeping his gaze on the distant blues. "I didn't want to leave you stranded. I'm taking Flare with me."

The joy drained from Sara's eyes; the blood drained from her face.

"They're searching for me, of course," the young man continued briskly. "I'll fly to join them. You will be safe here. My return should satisfy Lord Ariakan. He'll call off the pursuit."

Sara gave a low, anguished cry.

Steel looked at her and paled, but the firm resolve on his face did not weaken. He shifted his gaze back to the two men.

"I have decided to keep the sword," Steel said defiantly, as if he expected an argument. "It is old-fashioned, admittedly, but I have never seen a sword so well-constructed."

Tanis nodded and faintly smiled. "The blade is yours, by right. Your father gave it to you. Care for his sword well, Steel Brightblade. The blade is accustomed to being treated with respect. Its lineage is long and proud."

"According to your father," Caramon said, "the sword will break only if the one who wields it breaks first."

"The blade never broke when Sturm carried it," Tanis added, "not even at the end."

Steel was obviously overcome. The dark eyes shimmered with unshed tears. His hands gently, reverently clasped the hilt, decorated with the rose and the crown. "It is a fine weapon," he said in a low, husky voice. "I will give it the care and honor it deserves, you may be sure of that."

He will keep the sword, Tanis thought, but what of the jewel he wears around his neck? Does he have it still? Or did he rid himself of it in the forest? What will he say about that?

Nothing, apparently.

Steel was continuing. "I want to thank you, Tanis Half-Elven, and you, Caramon Majere, for fighting at my side. I know that you've let yourselves in for serious trouble, maybe even danger, for my sake. I won't forget it." He drew the sword, held it up before him. "With my father's blade, I offer honor to you both."

He gave them each the knight's salute. Then, thrusting the sword carefully into its battered scabbard, he turned, at last, to Sara.

Despairing, she stretched out her arms to him. "Steel—"

He took hold of her, embraced her, held her close.

"You promised it would be my decision, Mother."

"Steel, no! How can you? After what you saw, after what happened!" Sara began to weep.

Gently, but firmly, Steel broke free of her loving grip. "Take care of her, won't you, Uncle?" he said softly, to Caramon. "Keep her safe."

"I will, Nephew." Caramon took hold of Sara and drew her away.

Turning on his heel, the young man ran for the blue dragon. Flare was eager, waiting. Steel leapt onto the dragon's back. The creature spread its wings.

Sara broke loose from Caramon's grip and ran to her son.

"You're doing this for my sake! Don't, please, don't!"

His handsome face was cold and hard, stern and implacable. He looked away from her, stared out into the setting sun.

"A curse, Lord Ariakan said. A curse if I discovered the truth." He sighed, then, glancing down, said coldly, "Stand back, Mother. I wouldn't want you to get hurt."

Caramon caught hold of the weeping Sara and pulled her out of the way of the dragon's great wings.

Steel spoke a word. Flare soared into the air. The dragon circled them once. They could see the young man's face—white against the blue wings.

And perhaps it was Tanis's imagination or maybe a trick of the dying sunlight, but he thought he saw an argent flash, as from an elven jewel, in the young man's hand.

The blue dragon disappeared into the darkening sky, heading north.

Chapter Twelve

His Mother's Blood

The winds blew fiercely on Storm's Keep. Waves lashed the rocks, broke across them in torrents of spray and foam. Lightning flared in the dark clouds; thunder rumbled, shook the foundations of the fortress. It was midnight.

The clear notes of a trumpet shattered the darkness. Lord Ariakan stood in the center of the courtyard of Storm's Keep, surrounded by a circle of knights. Torches sputtered and flickered in the rain. The knights' black armor glistened. The black lily of violent death adorned each black breastplate, the flower's severed stem entwined around a bloody axe. Black cloaks, trimmed in blue, white or red—depending on the knight's order—whipped about their armored bodies, but did little to protect them from the driving rain.

The Knights of Takhisis reveled in the rain, reveled in the storm. It was a mark of their goddess's favor. Soon, the young man to be invested into the knighthood would—if the high priestess deemed him worthy—emerge from the temple, where he had spent the day in vigil and in prayer.

In deep-voiced unison, the knights began to chant Her Dark Majesty's praises.

Inside the temple, in deathly silence, Steel Brightblade lay prostrate, in full armor, on the floor before the dark altar. He had spent the day lying on the chill, dank stone, abasing himself before his goddess. The temple was empty, except for him; none were permitted to disturb the knight's vigil.

At the sound of the trumpet call, a woman emerged from the thick black curtains in back of the obsidian altar. The woman was old and bent. Her hair was gray and worn long, straggling down over her crooked shoulders. She walked with slow steps, shuffled across the stone floor. Her eyes were red-rimmed, shrewdly intelligent. She wore the black robes and dragon necklace of a high priestess of Takhisis.

A favorite of the Dark Queen's, the priestess had immense power. It was whispered that, years ago, she had participated in the dread ceremonies that had produced draconians from the stolen eggs of the good dragons. There was not a knight on Storm's Keep, Lord Ariakan among them, who did not tremble at the old woman's look, her touch.

She came to stand before the young knight, who lay with his face pressed against the stones, his dark hair streaming about him, gleaming blue-black in the light of the altar candles. On the altar, awaiting the Dark Queen's blessing, was his helm, fashioned in the shape of a hideous, grinning skull, and his breastplate, with its lily and its axe. But not his sword, as was customary.

"Rise," said the priestess.

Weak from fasting and from lying, encased in chain mail, on the cold floor, Steel rose stiffly and awkwardly to his knees. His head remained bowed. Not daring to lift his eyes to the holy priestess, he clasped his hands before him.

She observed him closely, then, reaching out a clawlike hand, she placed her fingers beneath his chin. The nails dug into his flesh. He flinched at her touch, which was far colder than the stones. She raised his face to the light, to her scrutiny.

"You now know the name of your father?"

"Yes, Holiness," Steel said steadfastly, "I do."

"Say it. Speak it before the altar of your queen."

Steel swallowed, his throat constricted. He hadn't thought this would be so difficult.

"Brightblade," he whispered.

"Again."

"Brightblade." His voice rang out, defiantly proud.

The priestess was not displeased, it seemed.

"Your mother's name."

"Kitiara Uth Matar." Again, this time fiercely, with pride.

The priestess nodded.

"A worthy lineage. Steel Uth Matar Brightblade, do you hereby dedicate your body, your heart, your soul to Her Dark Majesty, Takhisis, Queen of Darkness, Dark Warrior, Dragon Queen, She-of-Many-Faces?"

"I do so," Steel answered calmly.

The priestess smiled a secret, dark smile.

"Body and heart and soul, Steel Uth Matar Brightblade?" she repeated.

"Yes, of course," he answered, troubled. This was not part of the ritual, as he had been taught. "Why should you doubt me?"

In answer, the priestess took hold of a slender, steel chain that encircled the young man's neck. She tugged on the chain, drew forth its ornament.

An elven jewel, carved in the shape of a star, pale and gleaming, hung from the steel chain.

"What is this?" the priestess hissed.

Steel shrugged, tried to laugh. "I stole it from the corpse of my father, at the same time I stole his sword. The knights were furious. I struck fear into their hearts!"

His words were bold, but they echoed too loudly, hollow and discordant, in the silence of the temple.

The priestess placed her fingertip gingerly on the jewel.

A flash of white light, a sizzling sound.

The priestess snatched her hand back with a shrill cry of pain.

"It is an artifact of good!" She spat the word. "I cannot touch it. No one who is a true servant of Her Dark Majesty could touch that cursed jewel. Yet you, Steel Brightblade, wear it with impunity."

Steel, deathly pale, stared at her in dismay. "I'll forsake it! I'll take it off," he cried. His hand closed over the jewel, shrouding its brilliant light in darkness. "It's just a bauble. It means nothing to me!"

He made ready to yank the jewel from its silver chain.

The priestess stopped him.

"Wear the cursed jewel. It is the Dark Queen's wish and pleasure that you do so. May it serve to remind you of this warning. Think of my words every time you look upon the jewel, Steel Brightblade. She-of-Many-Faces has many eyes. She sees all. There is nothing you can hide from her.

"Your heart is hers, your body is hers. But not your soul. Not now. . . .

"But it will be." The priestess pressed her wrinkled face so near the young man's that he felt her fetid breath hot upon his cheek. "And, in the meantime, Steel Uth Matar Brightblade, you will be of inestimable value to your queen."

The dry and withered lips kissed Steel upon his brow.

Shivering, sweating, he forced himself to hold still beneath the awful touch.

"Your helm and breastplate lie upon the altar. Both have been blessed by the Dark Queen. Stand, Sir Knight, and put them on."

Steel stared at the priestess in astonishment, then dawning joy. The priestess, with that secret smile, turned and left him. Parting the black curtains, she disappeared back into the innermost regions of the temple.

Two boys, in their teens, entered through the front temple doors. From now on, the younger would be his page, the older his squire. They stood silently, respectfully, waiting to assist the knight with his armor. Both boys gazed at Steel with admiration and envy, no doubt dreaming of their own future investiture, seeing it embodied in him.

Shaking, barely able to stand, Steel reverently approached the altar. One hand, his right, rested on the black breastplate, adorned with the death lily. The other hand, his left, stole to the jewel around his neck. His eyes closed. Tears burned beneath the lids. Angrily, he started, once again, to the rip the jewel from his neck.

His hand slid from it, fell limply upon the altar.

The trumpet call sounded, twice more.

In the courtyard of Storm's Keep, Lord Ariakan stood, waiting to knight the dark paladin with his father's sword.

Steel Uth Matar Brightblade, Knight of the Lily, son of Sturm Brightblade, Knight of the Crown, son of Dragon Highlord Kitiara Uth Matar.

Lifting the helm, with its skull-like grin, Steel placed it on his head. Then, kneeling before the altar, he offered a grateful prayer to his queen, Takhisis.

Rising proudly, extending his arms, he motioned for his squire to buckle on the black and shining breastplate.

11

Always the son
in that oldest of stories,
sport of the blood
in its natural turning,
the charmed one, least likely
to end up heroic,
captures the crown
and the grail and the princess.
Suddenly, out of the shires of concealment
the least likely son
perseveres and arises
after veiling his heart
through the hooded night,
and his unmasked glory
of grail and of jewelry
effaces the moment
before the beginning of stories,
when the galvanic heartbeat
contended with ice and illusion,
when the world was a country
of mirrors and brothers,
and harmony broke
on the long effacement of days.

It is brothers like these
whom poetry touches,
who are handy with visions
instead of with swords,
whose pale light is hidden
in the cloud of their knowing.
But for each who emerges
past wounds and obscurity,
for each who negotiates
bramble and dragon and wizard,
there is another forever forgotten
conceded and wed
to the language of brothers,
lost in the bloodline
of sword and money
in the old palindrome of the spirit.

It is brothers like these
that the poets sing,
for their baffled courage
and the water's solace
for the one in the bramble
and the failed inheritance,
it is for these
that the ink is drying,
it is for these
that the angels come.

The Legacy

Chapter One

Caramon stood in a vast chamber carved of obsidian. It was so wide, its perimeter was lost in shadow, so high its ceiling was obscured in shadow. No pillars supported it. No lights lit it. Yet light there was, though none could name its source. It was a pale light, white—not yellow. Cold and cheerless, it gave no warmth.

Though he could see no one in the chamber, though he could hear no sound disturb the heavy silence that seemed centuries old, Caramon knew he was not alone. He could feel the eyes watching him as they had watched him long ago, and so he stood stolidly, waiting patiently until they deemed it time to proceed.

He guessed what they were doing, and he smiled, but only inwardly. To those watching eyes, the big man's face remained smooth, impassive. They would see no weakness in him, no sorrow, no bitter regret. Though memory was reaching out to him, its hand was warm, its touch gentle. He was at peace with himself, and had been for twenty-five years.

As if reading his thoughts—which, Caramon supposed, they might well have been—those present in the vast chamber suddenly revealed themselves. It was not that the light grew brighter, or a mist lifted, or the darkness parted, for none of that happened. Caramon felt more as though he were the one who had suddenly entered, though *he* had been standing there upwards of a quarter hour. The two robed figures that appeared before him were a part of this place just like the white, magical light, the ages-old silence. He wasn't—he was an outsider and would be one forever.

"Welcome once again to our tower, Caramon Majere," said a voice.

Caramon bowed, saying nothing. He couldn't—for the life of him— remember the man's name.

"Justarius," the man said, smiling pleasantly. "Yes, the years have been long since we last met, and our last meeting was during a desperate hour. It is small wonder you have forgotten me. Please, be seated." A heavy, carved, oaken chair materialized beside Caramon. "You have journeyed long and are weary, perhaps."

Caramon started to state that he was just fine, that a journey like this was nothing to a man who had been over most of the continent of Ansalon in his younger days. But at the sight of the chair with its soft, inviting cushions, Caramon realized that the journey *had* been rather a long one—longer than he remembered it. His back ached, his armor appeared to have grown heavier, and it seemed that his legs just weren't holding up their end of things anymore.

Well, what do you expect, Caramon asked himself with a shrug. I'm the proprietor of an inn now. I've got responsibilities. Someone's got to sample the cooking. . . . Heaving a rueful sigh, he sat down, shifting his bulk about until he was settled comfortably.

"Getting old, I guess," he said with a grin.

"It comes to all of us," Justarius answered, nodding his head. "Well, most of us," he amended, with a glance at the figure who sat beside him. Following his gaze, Caramon saw the figure throw back its rune-covered hood to reveal a familiar face—an elven face.

"Greetings, Caramon Majere."

"Dalamar," returned Caramon steadily with a nod of his head, though the grip of memory tightened a bit at the sight of the black-robed wizard. Dalamar looked no different than he had years ago—wiser, perhaps, calmer and cooler. At ninety years of age, he had been just an apprentice magic-user, considered little more than a hot-blooded youth as far as the elves were concerned. Twenty-five years mattered no more to the long-lived elves than the passing of a day and night. Now well over one hundred, his cold, handsome face appeared no older than a human of thirty.

"The years have dealt kindly with you, Caramon," Justarius continued. "The Inn of the Last Home, which you now own, is one of the most prosperous in Krynn. You are a hero—you and your lady wife both. Tika Majere is well and undoubtedly as beautiful as ever?"

"More," Caramon replied huskily.

Justarius smiled. "You have five children, two daughters and three sons—"

A sliver of fear pricked Caramon's contentment. No, he said to himself inwardly, they have no power over me now. He settled himself more solidly in his chair, like a soldier digging in for battle.

"The two eldest, Tanin and Sturm, are soldiers of renown"—Justarius spoke in a bland voice, as though chatting with a neighbor over the fence. Caramon wasn't fooled, however, and kept his eyes closely on the wizard—"bidding fair to outdo their famous father and mother in deeds of valor on the field. But the third, the middle child, whose name is—" Justarius hesitated.

"Palin," said Caramon, his brows lowering into a frown. Glancing at Dalamar, the big man saw the dark elf watching him intently with slanted, inscrutable eyes.

"Palin, yes." Justarius paused, then said quietly, "It would seem he follows in the footsteps of his uncle."

There. It was out. Of course, that's why they had ordered him here. He had been expecting it, or something like it, for a long time now. Damn them! Why couldn't they leave him alone! He never would have come, if Palin hadn't insisted. Breathing heavily, Caramon stared at Justarius, trying to read the man's face. He might as well have been trying to read one of his son's spellbooks.

Justarius, head of the Conclave of Wizards, was the most powerful magic-user in Krynn. The red-robed wizard sat in the great stone chair in the center of the semicircle of twenty-one chairs. An elderly man, his gray hair and lined face were the only outward signs of aging. The eyes were as shrewd, the body appeared as strong—except the crippled left leg—as when Caramon had first met the archmage twenty-five years ago.

Caramon's gaze went to the mage's left leg. Hidden beneath the red robes, the man's injury was noticeable only to those who had seen him walk.

Aware of Caramon's scrutiny, Justarius's hand went self-consciously to rub his leg, then he stopped with a wry smile. Crippled Justarius may be, Caramon thought, chilled, but only in body. Not in mind or ambition. Twenty-five years ago, Justarius had been the leading spokesman only of his own order, the Red Robes, those wizards in Krynn who had turned their backs against both the evil and the good to walk their own path, that of neutrality. Now he ruled over all the wizards in the world, presumably—the White Robes, Red Robes, and the Black. Since magic is the most potent force in a wizard's life, he swears fealty to the conclave, no matter what private ambitions or desires he nurses within his own heart.

Most wizards, that is. Of course, there had been Raistlin . . .

Twenty-five years ago.

Par-Salian of the White Robes had been head of the conclave then. Caramon felt memory's hand clutch him more tightly still.

"I don't see what my son has to do with any of this," he said in an even, steady voice. "If you want to meet my boys, they are in that room you magicked us into after we arrived. I'm sure you can magic them in here anytime you want. So, now that we have concluded social pleasantries— By the way, where is Par-Salian?" Caramon demanded suddenly, his gaze going around the shadowy chamber, flicking over the empty chair next to Justarius.

"He retired as head of the conclave twenty-five years ago," Justarius said gravely, "following the . . . the incident in which you were involved."

Caramon flushed, but said nothing. He thought he detected a slight smile on Dalamar's delicate elven features.

"I took over as head of the conclave, and Dalamar was chosen to succeed LaDonna as head of the Order of Black Robes in return for his dangerous and valiant work during—"

"The incident." Caramon growled. "Congratulations," he said.

Dalamar's lip curled in a sardonic smile. Justarius nodded, but it was obvious he was not to be distracted from the previous topic of discussion.

"I would be honored to meet your sons," Justarius said coolly, "Palin in particular. I understand that the young man is desirous of becoming a mage someday."

"He's studying magic, if that's what you mean," Caramon said gruffly. "I don't know how seriously he takes it, or if he plans to make it his livelihood, as you seem to imply. He and I have never discussed it—"

Dalamar snorted derisively at this, causing Justarius to lay his hand on the dark elf's black-robed arm.

"Perhaps we have been mistaken in what we have heard of your son's ambition, then?"

"Perhaps you have," Caramon returned coolly. "Palin and I are close," he added in a softer voice. "I'm certain he would have confided in me."

"It is refreshing to see a man these days who is honest and open about his love for his sons, Caramon Majere," began Justarius mildly.

"Bah!" Dalamar interrupted. "You might as well say it is refreshing to see a man with his eyes gouged out!" Snatching his arm from the old wizard's grasp, he gestured at Caramon. "You were blind to your brother's dark ambition for years, until it was almost too late. Now you turn sightless eyes to your own son—"

"My son is a good boy, as different from Raistlin as the silver moon is from the black! He has no such ambition! What would you know of him anyway, you . . . you outcast?" Caramon shouted, rising to his feet in anger. Though well over fifty, the big man had kept himself in relatively good condition through hard work and training his sons in the arts of battle. His hand went reflexively to his sword, forgetting as he did so, however, that in the Tower of High Sorcery he would be as helpless as a gully dwarf facing a dragon. "And speaking of dark ambition, you served your master well, didn't you, Dalamar? Raistlin taught you a lot, perhaps more than we know—"

"And I bear the mark of his hand upon my flesh still!" Dalamar cried, rising to his feet in turn. Ripping his black robes open at the neck, he bared his breast. Five wounds, like the marks of five fingers, were visible on the dark elf's smooth skin. A thin trickle of blood trailed down each, glistening in the cold light of the Chamber of Wizards. "For twenty-five years, I've lived with this pain. . . ."

"And what of my pain?" Caramon asked in a low voice, feeling memory's hand dig sharp nails into his soul. "Why have you brought me here? To cause my wounds to open and bleed as well as your own!"

"Gentlemen, please," said Justarius softly. "Dalamar, control yourself. Caramon, please sit down. Remember, you two owe your lives to each other. This establishes a bond between you that should be respected."

The old man's voice penetrated the shouts that still echoed in the vast chamber, its cool authority silencing Caramon and calming Dalamar. Clasping his torn robes together with his hand, the dark elf resumed his seat next to Justarius.

Caramon, too, sat down, ashamed and chagrined. He had sworn that he would not let this happen, that these people would have no power to shake him. And already he'd lost control. Trying to assume a relaxed expression, he leaned back in the chair. But his hand clenched the hilt of his sword.

"Forgive Dalamar," Justarius said, his hand once again on the dark elf's arm. "He spoke in haste and anger. You are right, Caramon. Your son, Palin, *is* a good man—I think we must say *man* and not *boy*. He is, after all, twenty—"

"Just turned twenty," Caramon muttered, eyeing Justarius warily.

The red-robed archmage waved it aside. "And he is, as you say, different from Raistlin. How not? He is his own person, after all, born to different parents, under different, happier circumstances than faced you and your twin. From all we hear, Palin is handsome, likeable, strong, and fit. He does not have the burden of ill health to bear, as did Raistlin. He is devoted to his family, especially his two elder brothers. They, in turn, are devoted to him. Is all this true?"

Caramon nodded, unable to speak past the sudden lump in his throat.

Looking at him, Justarius's mild gaze suddenly became sharp and penetrating. He shook his head. "But in some ways you *are* blind, Caramon. Oh, not as Dalamar said"—Caramon's face went red with anger—"not the way you were blinded to your brother's evil. This is the blindness that afflicts all parents, my friend. I know." Justarius smiled and gave rueful shrug. "I have a daughter . . ."

Glancing at Dalamar out of the corner of his eye, the archmage sighed. The handsome elf's lips twitched in a hint of a smile. He said nothing, however, simply sat staring into the shadows.

"Yes, we parents can be blind," Justarius murmured, "but that is neither here nor there." Leaning forward, the archmage clasped his hands together. "I see you growing impatient, Caramon. As you guessed, we have called you here for a purpose. And, I'm afraid it does have something to do with your son, Palin."

This is it, Caramon said to himself, scowling, his sweating hand clenching and unclenching nervously around the hilt of his sword.

"There is no easy way to say this, so I will be blunt and direct." Justarius drew a deep breath; his face became grave and sorrowful, touched with a shadow of fear. "We have reason to believe that the young man's uncle—your twin brother, Raistlin—is *not* dead."

Chapter Two

"This place shivers my skin!" Tanin muttered, with a sideways glance at his youngest brother.

Slowly sipping a cup of tarbean tea, Palin stared into the flames of the fire, pretending not to have heard Tanin's remark, which he knew was addressed to him.

"Oh, in the name of the Abyss, would you sit down!" Sturm said, tossing pieces of bread at his brother. "You're going to walk yourself right through the floor, and the gods only know what's beneath us."

Tanin merely frowned, shook his head, and continued his pacing.

"Reorx's beard, Brother!" Sturm continued almost incomprehensibly, his mouth full of cheese. "You'd think we were in a draconian dungeon instead of what might pass for a room in one of the finest inns in Palanthas itself! Good food, great ale—" he took a long pull to wash down the cheese —"and there'd be pleasant company if you weren't acting like such a doorknob!"

"Well, we aren't in one of the finest inns in Palanthas," said Tanin sarcastically, stopping in his pacing to catch a hunk of thrown bread. Grinding it to bits in his hand, he tossed it on the floor. "We're in the Tower of High Sorcery in Wayreth. We've been spirited into this room. The damn doors are locked, and we can't get out. We have no idea what these wizards have done with Father, and all you can think of is cheese and ale!"

"That's not *all* I'm thinking of," Sturm said quietly with a nod of his head and a worried glance at their little brother, who was still staring into the fire.

"Yeah," Tanin snapped gloomily, his gaze following Sturm's. "I'm thinking of him, too! It's *his* fault we're here in the first place!" Moodily kicking a table leg as he walked past, Tanin resumed his pacing. Seeing his little brother flinch at his older brother's words, Sturm sighed and returned to his sport of trying to hit Tanin between the shoulder blades with the bread.

Anyone observing the older two young men (as someone was at this very moment) might have taken them for twins, though they were—in reality—a year apart in age. Twenty-four and twenty-three respectfully, Tanin and Sturm (named for Caramon's best friend, Tanis Half-Elven, and the heroic Knight of Solamnia, Sturm Brightblade) looked, acted, and even thought alike. Indeed, they often played the part of twins and enjoyed nothing so much as when people mistook one for the other.

Big and brawny, each young man had Caramon's splendid physique and his genial, honest face. But the bright red curls and dancing green eyes that wreaked such havoc among the women the young men met came directly from their mother, who had broken her share of hearts in her youth. One of the beauties of Krynn as well as a renowned warrior, Tika Waylan had grown a little plumper since the days when she bashed draconians over the head with her skillet. But heads still turned when Tika waited tables in her fluffy, low-necked white blouse, and there were few men who left the Inn of the Last Home without shaking their heads and swearing that Caramon was a lucky fellow.

The green eyes of young Sturm were not dancing now, however. Instead, they glinted mischievously as, with a wink at his younger brother—who wasn't watching—Sturm rose silently to his feet and, positioning himself behind the preoccupied Tanin, quietly drew his sword. Just as Tanin turned around, Sturm stuck the sword blade between his brother's legs, tripping him and sending him to the floor with a crash that seemed to shake the very foundation of the tower.

"Damn you for a lame-brained gully dwarf!" roared Tanin. Clambering to his feet, he leapt after his brother, who was scrambling to get out of the way. Tanin caught him and, grabbing hold of the grinning Sturm by the collar of his tunic, sent him sprawling backward into the table, smashing it to the floor. Tanin jumped on top of his brother, and the two were engaged in their usual rough-and-tumble antics, which had left several barrooms in Ansalon in shambles, when a quiet voice brought the tussle to a halt.

"Stop it," said Palin tensely, rising from his chair by the fire. "Stop it, both of you! Remember where you are!"

"I remember where I am," Tanin said sulkily, gazing up at his youngest brother.

As tall as the older two young men, Palin was well-built. Given to study rather than swordplay, however, he lacked the heavy musculature of the two warriors. He had his mother's red hair, but it was not fiery red, being nearer a dark auburn. He wore his hair long—it flowed to his shoulders in soft waves from a central part on his forehead. But it was the young man's face—his face and his hands—that sometimes haunted the dreams of his mother and father. Fine-boned, with penetrating, intelligent eyes that always seemed to be seeing right through one, Palin's face had the look of his uncle, if not his features. Palin's hands were Raistlin's, however. Slender, delicate, the fingers quick and deft, the young man handled the fragile spell components with such skill that his father was often torn between watching with pride and looking away in sadness.

Just now, the hands were clenched into fists as Palin glared grimly at his two older brothers lying on the floor amid spilled ale, pieces of bread, crockery, a half-eaten cheese, and shards of broken table.

"Then try to behave with some dignity, at least!" Palin snapped.

"I remember where I am," Tanin repeated angrily. Getting to his feet, he walked over to stand in front of Palin, staring at him accusingly. "And I remember who brought us here! Riding through that accursed wood that damn near got us killed—"

"Nothing in Wayreth Forest will hurt you," Palin returned, looking at the mess on the floor in disgust. "As I'd have told you if you'd only listened. This forest is controlled by the wizards in the tower. It protects them from unwanted intruders. We have been invited here. The trees let us pass without harm. The voices you heard whispered only the fears in your own heart. It's magic—"

"You listen, Palin," Tanin interrupted in what Sturm always referred to as his Elder Brother voice. "Why don't you just drop all this magic business? You're hurting Father and Mother—Father most of all. You saw his face when we rode up to this place! The gods know what it must have cost him to come back here."

Flushing, Palin turned away, biting his lip.

"Oh, lay off the kid, will you, Tanin?" Sturm said, seeing the pain on his younger brother's face. Wiping ale from his pants, he somewhat shamefacedly began trying to put the table back together—a hopeless task, considering most of it was in splinters.

"You had the makings of a good swordsman once, Little Brother," Tanin said persuasively, ignoring Sturm and putting his hand on Palin's shoulder. "C'mon, kid. Tell whoever's out there"—Tanin waved his hand somewhat vaguely—"that you've changed your mind. We can leave this cursed place, then, and go home—"

"We have no idea why they asked us to come here," Palin retorted, shaking off his brother's hand. "It probably has nothing to do with me! Why should it?" he asked bitterly. "I'm still a student. It will be years before I am ready to take my test . . . thanks to Father and Mother," he muttered beneath his breath. Tanin did not hear it, but the unseen observer did.

"Yeah? And I'm a half-ogre," retorted Tanin angrily. "Look at me when I'm talking, Palin—"

"Just leave me alone!"

"Hey, you two—" Sturm the peacemaker started to intervene when the three young men suddenly realized they were not alone in the room.

All quarrels forgotten, the brothers acted instantly. Sturm rose to his feet with the quickness of a cat. His hand on the hilt of his sword, he joined Tanin, who had already moved to stand protectively in front of the unarmed Palin. Like all magic-users, the young man carried neither sword nor shield nor wore armor. But his hand went to the dagger he wore concealed beneath his robes, his mind already forming the words of the few defensive spells he had been allowed to learn.

"Who are you?" Tanin asked harshly, staring at the man standing in the center of the locked room. "How did you get in here?"

"As to how I got here"—the man smiled expansively—"there are no walls in the Tower of High Sorcery for those who walk with magic. As for who I am, my name is Dunbar Mastersmate, of Northern Ergoth."

"What do you want?" Sturm asked quietly.

"Want? Why—to make certain you are comfortable, that is all," Dunbar answered. "I am your host—"

"You? A magic-user?" Tanin gaped, and even Palin seemed slightly startled.

In a world where wizards are noted for having more brains than brawn, this man was obviously the exception. Standing as tall as Tanin, he had a barrel of a chest that Caramon might well have envied. Muscles rippled beneath the shining black skin of his bare chest. His arms looked as though he could have picked up the stalwart Sturm and carried him about the room as easily as if he had been a child. He was not dressed in robes, but wore bright-colored, loose-fitting trousers. The only hint that he might have been a wizard at all came from the pouches that hung at his waist and a white sash that girdled his broad middle.

Dunbar laughed, booming laughter that set the dishes rattling.

"Aye," he said, "I am a magic-user." With that, he spoke a word of command, and the broken table, leaping to its legs, put itself back together with incredible speed. The ale vanished from the floor, and the cracked pitcher mended and floated up to rest on the table, where it was soon foaming with brew again. A roasted haunch of venison appeared, as did a loaf of fragrant bread, along with sundry other delicacies that caused Sturm's mouth to water and cooled even Tanin's ardor, though they did not allay his suspicions.

"Seat yourselves," said Dunbar, "and let us eat. Do not worry about your father," he added, as Tanin was about to speak. "He is in conference about important matters with the heads of the other two orders. Sit down! Sit down!" He grinned, white teeth flashing against his black skin. "Or shall I make you sit down. . . ?"

At this, Tanin let loose the hilt of his sword and pulled up a chair, though he did not eat but sat watching Dunbar warily. Sturm fell to with a good appetite, however. Only Palin remained standing, his hands folded in the sleeves of his white robes.

"Please, Palin," said Dunbar more gently, looking at the young man, "be seated. Soon we will join your father, and you will discover the reason you have been brought here. In the meanwhile, I ask you to share bread and meat with me."

"Thank you, master," Palin said, bowing respectfully.

"Dunbar, Dunbar . . ." The man waved his hand. "You are my guests. We will not stand on formalities."

Palin sat down and began to eat, but it was obvious he did so out of courtesy only. Dunbar and Sturm more than made up for him, however, and soon even Tanin was lured from his self-imposed role of protector by the delicious smells and the sight of the others enjoying themselves.

"You . . . you said the heads of the other orders, mast—Dunbar," Palin ventured. "Are you—"

"Head of the Order of White Robes. Yes." Dunbar tore off a hunk of bread with his strong teeth and washed it down with a draft of ale, which he drank at one long swallow. "I took over when Par-Salian retired."

"Head of the order?" Sturm looked at the big man in awe. "But—what kind of wizard are you? What do you do?"

"I'll wager it's more than pulling the wings off bats," Tanin mumbled through a mouthful of meat.

Palin appeared shocked, and frowned at his older brother. But Dunbar only laughed again. "You're right there!" he said with an oath. "I am a sea wizard. My father was a ship's captain and his father before him. I had no use for captaining vessels. My skills lay in magic, but my heart was with the sea, and there I returned. Now I sail the waves and use my art to summon the wind or quell the storm. I can leave the enemy becalmed so that we may outrun him, or I can cast bursting flame onto his decks if we attack. And, when necessary"—Dunbar grinned—"I can take my turn at the bilge pump or turn the capstan with the best of them. Keeps me fit." He pounded himself on his broad chest. "I understand you two"—he looked at Sturm and Tanin—"have returned from fighting the minotaurs who have been raiding the coast up north. I, too, have been involved in trying to stop those pirates. Tell me, did you—?"

The three were soon deeply involved in discussion. Even Tanin warmed to the subject, and was soon describing in vivid detail the ambush that had stopped the minotaurs from leveling the city of Kalaman. Dunbar listened attentively, asking intelligent questions, making comments, and appearing to enjoy himself very much.

But though the wizard's shrewd gaze was concentrated on the warrior brothers, his attention was in truth on the youngest.

Seeing the three deep in conversation and himself apparently forgotten, Palin thankfully gave up all pretense of eating and went back to staring into the fire, never noticing Dunbar watching him.

The young man's face was pale and thoughtful, the slender hands twisted together in his lap. So lost in his thoughts was he that his lips moved and, though he did not speak aloud, one other person in the room heard the words.

"Why have they brought me here? Can they read the secrets of my heart? Will they tell my father?"

And, finally, "How can I hurt him, who has suffered so much already?"

Nodding to himself as if he had found the answer to some unasked question, Dunbar sighed and turned his complete attention back to fighting minotaurs.

Chapter Three

"You're wrong," said Caramon calmly. "My brother is dead."

Raising his eyebrows, Justarius glanced at Dalamar, who shrugged. Of all the reactions they had been prepared for, this calm refutal had not been one of them, apparently. His expression grave, seeming uncertain what to say, Justarius looked back at Caramon.

"You talk as though you have proof."

"I have," said Caramon.

"May I ask what?" Dalamar inquired sarcastically. "The Portal to the Abyss closed, after all—closed *with your brother's help*—leaving him trapped on the other side." The dark elf's voice dropped. "Her Dark Majesty would not kill him. Raistlin prevented her entry into this world. Her rage would know no bounds. She would take delight in tormenting him eternally. *Death* would have been Raistlin's salvation."

"And so it was," said Caramon softly.

"Sentimental drivel—" Dalamar began impatiently, but Justarius once again laid his hand upon the dark elf's arm, and the black-robed mage lapsed into seething silence.

"I hear certainty in your voice, Caramon," Justarius said earnestly. "You have knowledge, obviously, that we do not. Share this with us. I know this is painful for you, but we face a decision of grave importance, and this may influence our actions."

Caramon hesitated, frowning. "Does this have something to do with my son?"

"Yes," Justarius replied.

Caramon's face darkened. His gaze went to his sword, his eyes narrowed thoughtfully, his hand absently fingering the hilt. "Then I will tell you," he said, speaking reluctantly, yet in a firm, low voice, "what I have never told anyone—not my wife, not Tanis, not anyone." He was silent a moment more, collecting his thoughts. Then, swallowing and brushing his hand across his eyes, keeping his gaze on the sword, he began. "I was numb after . . . after what happened in the tower in Palanthas. I couldn't think. I didn't want to think. It was easier to go through the day like a sleepwalker. I moved, I talked, but I didn't feel. It was easy." He shrugged. "There was a lot to do to keep me occupied. The city was in ruins. Dalamar"—he glanced briefly at the dark elf—"was nearly dead, Revered Daughter Crysania hurt badly. Then there was Tas—stealing that floating citadel." In spite of himself, Caramon smiled, remembering the antics of the merry kender. But the smile soon faded. Shaking his head, he continued.

"I knew that someday I'd have to think about Raistlin. I'd have to sort it out in my mind." Raising his head, Caramon looked at Justarius directly. "I had to make myself understand what Raistlin was, what he had done. I came to face the fact that he was evil, truly evil, that he had jeopardized the entire world in his lust for power, that innocent people had suffered and died because of him."

"And for this, of course, he was granted salvation!" Dalamar sneered.

"Wait!" Caramon raised his hand, flushing. "I came to realize something else. I loved Raistlin. He was my brother, my twin. We were close—no one knows how close." The big man could not go on, but stared down at his sword, frowning, until, drawing a shaking breath, he raised his head again. "Raistlin did some good in his life. Without him, we couldn't have defeated the dragonarmies. He cared for those who . . . who were wretched, sick . . . like himself. But even that, I know, wouldn't have saved him at the end." Caramon's lips pressed together firmly as he blinked back his tears. "When I met him in the Abyss, he was near victory, as you well know. He had only to reenter the portal, draw the Dark Queen through it, and then he would be able to defeat her and take her place. He would achieve his dream of becoming a god. But in so doing, he would destroy the world. My journey into the future showed that to me—and I showed the future to him. Raistlin would become a god—but he would rule over a dead world. He knew then that he couldn't return. He had doomed himself. He knew the risks he faced, however, when he entered the Abyss."

"Yes," said Justarius quietly. "And, in his ambition, he chose freely to take those risks. What is it you are trying to say?"

"Just this," Caramon returned. "Raistlin made a mistake, a terrible, tragic mistake. And he did what few of us can do—he had courage enough to admit it and try to do what he could to rectify it, even though it meant sacrificing himself."

"You have grown in wisdom over the years, Caramon Majere. What you say is convincing." Justarius regarded Caramon with new respect, even as the archmage shook his head sadly. "Still, this is a question for philosophers to argue. It is not proof. Forgive me for pressing you, Caramon, but—"

"I spent a month at Tanis's, before I went home," Caramon continued as if he hadn't heard the interruption. "It was in his quiet, peaceful home that I thought about all this. It was there that I first had to come to grips with the fact that my brother—my companion since birth, the person that I loved better than anyone else on this world—was gone. Lost. For all I knew, trapped in horrible torment. I . . . I thought, more than once, about taking the edge off my pain with dwarf spirits again." Caramon closed his eyes, shuddering. "One day, when I didn't think I could live anymore without going mad, I went into my room and locked the door. Taking out my sword, I looked at it, thinking how easy it would be to . . . to escape. I lay on my bed, fully intending to kill myself. Instead, I fell into an exhausted sleep. I don't know how long I slept, but when I woke up, it was night. Everything was quiet, Solinari's silver light shone in the window, and I was filled with a sense of inexpressible peace. I wondered why . . . and then I saw him."

"Saw who?" Justarius asked, exchanging quick glances with Dalamar. "Raistlin?"

"Yes."

The faces of the two wizards grew grim.

"I saw him," said Caramon gently, "lying beside me, asleep, just like when . . . when we were young. He had terrible dreams sometimes. He'd wake, weeping, from them. I'd comfort him and . . . and make him laugh. Then he'd sigh, lay his head on my arm, and fall asleep. That's how I saw him—"

"A dream!" Dalamar scoffed.

"No." Caramon shook his head resolutely. "It was too real. I saw his face as I see yours. I saw his face as I had seen it last, in the Abyss. Only now the terrible lines of pain, the twisted marks of greed and evil were gone, leaving it smooth and . . . at rest—like Crysania said. It was the face of my brother, my twin . . . not the stranger he'd become." Caramon wiped his eyes again. "The next day, I was able to go home, knowing that everything was all right. . . . For the first time in my life, I believed in Paladine. I knew that he understood Raistlin and judged him mercifully, accepting his sacrifice."

"He has you there, Justarius," boomed a voice from out of the shadows. "What do you say to faith like that?"

Looking around quickly, Caramon saw four figures materialize out of the shadows of the vast chamber. Three he recognized and, even in this grim place, with its storehouse of memories, his eyes blurred again, only these were tears of pride as he looked upon his sons. The older two, armor clanking and swords rattling, appeared somewhat subdued, he noticed. Not unusual, he thought grimly, considering all they had heard about the tower, both in legend and family history. Then, too, they felt about magic the way he himself felt—both disliked and distrusted it. The two stood protectively, as usual, one on each side of Caramon's third son, their younger brother.

It was this youngest son that Caramon looked at anxiously as they entered. Dressed in his white robes, Palin approached the head of the conclave with his head bowed, his eyes on the floor, as was proper for one of his low rank and station. Having just turned twenty, he wasn't even an apprentice yet and probably wouldn't be until he was twenty-five at least. That is the age when magic-users in Krynn may choose to take the Test—the grueling examination of their skills and talents in the Art, which all must pass before they can acquire more advanced and dangerous knowledge. Because magicians wield such great power, the Test is designed to weed out those who are unskilled or who do not take their art seriously. It does this very effectively—failure means death. There is no turning back. Once a young man or woman of any race—elven, human, ogre—decides to enter the Tower of High Sorcery with the intent of taking the Test—he or she commits body and soul to the magic.

Palin seemed unusually troubled and serious, just as he had on their journey to the tower—almost as if he were about to take the Test himself. But that's ridiculous, Caramon reminded himself sternly. The boy is too young. Granted, Raistlin took the Test at this age, but that was because the conclave needed him. Raistlin was strong in his magic, excelling in the Art, and—even so—the Test had nearly killed him. Caramon could still see his twin lying on the bloodstained stone floor of the tower. . . . He clenched his fist. No! Palin is intelligent, he is skilled, but he's not ready. He's too young.

"Besides," Caramon muttered beneath his breath, "give him a few more years, and he may decide to drop this notion. . . ."

As if aware of his father's worried scrutiny, Palin raised his head slightly and gave him a reassuring smile. Caramon smiled back, feeling better. Maybe this weird place had opened his son's eyes.

As the four approached the semicircle of chairs where Justarius and Dalamar sat, Caramon kept a sharp eye on them. Seeing that his boys were well and acting as they were supposed to act (his oldest two tended to be a bit boisterous on occasion), the big man finally relaxed and studied the fourth figure, the one who had spoken to Justarius about faith.

He was an unusual sight. Caramon couldn't remember having seen anything stranger, and he'd traveled most of the continent of Ansalon. This man was from Northern Ergoth, that much Caramon could tell by the black skin—the mark of that seafaring race. He was dressed like a sailor, too, except for the pouches on his belt and the white sash around his waist. His voice was that of one accustomed to shouting commands over the crashing of waves and the roaring of wind. So strong was this impression that Caramon glanced around somewhat uncertainly. He wouldn't have been the least surprised to see a ship under full sail materialize behind him.

"Caramon Majere, I take it," the man said, coming over to Caramon, who had risen awkwardly to his feet. Gripping Caramon's hand with a firmness that made the big man open his eyes wide, the man grinned and introduced himself. "Dunbar Mastersmate of Northern Ergoth, head of the Order of White Robes."

Caramon gaped. "A mage?" he said wonderingly, shaking hands.

Dunbar laughed. "Exactly your sons' reaction. Yes, I've been visiting with your boys instead of doing my duty here, I'm afraid. Fine lads. The oldest two have been with the knights, I understand, fighting minotaurs near Kalaman. We came close to meeting there. That's what kept me so long." He glanced in apology at Justarius. "My ship was in Palanthas for repairs to damage taken fighting those same pirates. I am a sea wizard," Dunbar added by way of explanation, noticing Caramon's slightly puzzled look. "By the gods, but your boys take after you!" He laughed, and, reaching out, shook Caramon's hand again.

Caramon grinned back. Everything would be all right, now that these wizards understood about Raistlin. He could take his boys and go home.

Caramon suddenly became aware that Dunbar was regarding him intently, almost as if he could see the thoughts in his mind. The wizard's face grew serious. Shaking his head slightly, Dunbar turned and walked across the chamber with rapid, rolling strides, as though on the deck of his ship, to take his seat to the right of Justarius.

"Well," said Caramon, fumbling with the hilt of his sword, his confidence shaken by the look on the wizard's face. All three were staring at him now, their expressions solemn. Caramon's face hardened in resolve. "I guess that's that. You've heard what I've had to say about . . . about Raistlin. . . ."

"Yes," said Dunbar. "We *all* heard, some of us—I believe—for the first time." The sea wizard glanced meaningfully at Palin, who was staring at the floor.

Clearing his throat nervously, Caramon continued. "I guess we'll be on our way."

The wizards exchanged looks. Justarius appeared uncomfortable, Dalamar stern, Dunbar sad. But none of them said anything. Bowing, Caramon turned to leave and was just motioning to his sons when Dalamar, with an irritated gesture, rose to his feet.

"You cannot go, Caramon," the dark elf said. "There is still much to discuss."

"Then say what you have to say!" Caramon stated angrily, turning back around to face the wizards.

"I will say it, since these two"—he cast a scathing glance at his fellow wizards—"are squeamish about challenging such devoted faith as you have proclaimed. Perhaps they have forgotten the grave danger we faced twenty-five years ago. I haven't." His hand strayed to the torn robes. "I never can. My fears cannot be dispelled by a 'vision,' no matter how touching." His lip curled derisively. "Sit down, Caramon. Sit down and hear the truth these two fear to speak."

"I do not fear to speak it, Dalamar." Justarius spoke in rebuking tones. "I was thinking about the story Caramon related, its bearing upon the matter—"

The dark elf snorted, but—at a piercing look from his superior—he sat back down, wrapping his black robes around him. Caramon remained standing, however, frowning and glancing from one wizard to the other. Behind him, he heard the jingle of armor as his two older boys shifted uncomfortably. This place made them nervous, just as it did him. He wanted to turn on his heel and walk out, never returning to the tower that had been the scene of so much pain and heartbreak.

By the gods, he'd do it! Let them try to stop him! Caramon clasped the hilt of his sword and took a step backward, glancing around at his sons. The two older boys moved to leave. Only Palin remained standing still, a grave, thoughtful expression on his face that Caramon could not read. It reminded him of someone, though. Caramon could almost hear Raistlin's whispering voice, *"Go if you want to, my dear brother. Lose yourself in the magical Forest of Wayreth, as you most surely will without me. I intend to remain . . ."*

No. He would not hear his son say those words. Flushing, his heart constricting painfully, Caramon seated himself heavily in the chair. "Say what you have to say," he repeated.

"Almost thirty years ago, Raistlin Majere came to this tower to take his test," Justarius began. "Once inside the tower, taking his test, he was contacted by—"

"We know that," Caramon growled.

"Some of us do," Justarius replied. "Some of us do not." His gaze went to Palin. "Or at least, they do not know the entire story. The Test was difficult for Raistlin—it is difficult for all of us who take it, isn't it?"

Dalamar did not speak, but his pale face went a shade paler, and the slanted eyes were clouded. All traces of laughter had vanished from Dunbar's face. His gaze went to Palin, and he almost imperceptibly shook his head.

"Yes," Justarius continued softly, absently rubbing his leg with his hand as though it pained him. "The Test is difficult, but it is not impossible. Par-Salian and the heads of the orders would not have granted Raistlin permission to take it—as young as he was—if they had not deemed it likely that he would succeed. And he would have! Yes, Caramon! There is not a doubt in my mind or in the minds of any who were present that day and witnessed it. Your twin had the strength and the skill to succeed on his own. But he chose the easy way, the sure way—he accepted the help of an evil wizard, the greatest of our orders who ever lived—Fistandantilus.

"Fistandantilus," Justarius repeated, his eyes on Palin. "His magic having gone awry, he died at Skullcap Mountain. But he was powerful enough to defeat death itself. His spirit survived on another plane, waiting to find a body it could inhabit. And it found that body. . . ."

Caramon sat silently, his eyes fixed on Justarius, his face red, his jaw muscles stiff. He felt a hand on his shoulder and, glancing up, saw Palin, who had come to stand behind him. Leaning down, Palin whispered, "We can go, Father. I'm sorry. I was wrong to make you come. We don't have to listen . . ."

Justarius sighed. "Yes, young mage, you do have to listen, I am afraid. You must hear the truth!"

Palin started, flushing at hearing his words repeated. Reaching up, Caramon gripped his son's hand reassuringly. "We know the truth," he growled. "That evil wizard took my brother's soul! And you mages let him!"

"No, Caramon!" Justarius's fist clenched, and his gray brows drew together. "Raistlin made a deliberate choice to turn his back upon the light and embrace the darkness. Fistandantilus gave him the power to pass the Test and, in exchange, Raistlin *gave* Fistandantilus part of his life-force in order to help the lich's spirit survive. *That* is what shattered his body—not the Test. Raistlin said it himself, Caramon! 'This is the sacrifice I made for my magic!' How many times have you heard him say those words!"

"Enough!" Scowling, Caramon stood up. "It was Par-Salian's fault. No matter what evil my twin did after that, you mages started him down the path he eventually walked." Motioning to his sons, Caramon turned upon his heel and walked rapidly from the chamber, heading for what he hoped (in this strange place) was the way out.

"No!" Justarius rose unsteadily to his feet, unable to put his full weight upon his crippled left leg. But his voice was powerful, thundering through the chamber. "Listen and understand, Caramon Majere! You must, or you will regret it bitterly!"

Caramon stopped. Slowly, he turned around, but only halfway. "Is this a threat?" he asked, glaring at Justarius over his shoulder.

"No threat, at least not one we make," Justarius said. "Think, Caramon! Don't you see the danger? It happened once. It can happen again!"

"I don't understand," Caramon said stubbornly, his hand on his sword, still considering.

Like a snake uncoiling to strike, Dalamar leaned forward in his chair. "Yes, you do!" His voice was soft and lethal. "You understand. Don't ask for us to tell you details, for we cannot. But know this—by certain signs we have seen and certain contacts we have made in realms beyond this one, we have reason to believe that Raistlin lives—much as did Fistandantilus. He seeks a way back into this world. He needs a body to inhabit. And you, his beloved twin, have thoughtfully provided him with one—young, strong, and already trained in magic."

Dalamar's words sank into Caramon's flesh like poisoned fangs. "Your son . . ."

Chapter Four

Justarius resumed his seat, easing himself into the great stone chair carefully. Smoothing the folds of his red robes about him with hands that looked remarkably young for his age, he spoke to Caramon, though his eyes were on the white-robed young man standing at his father's side. "Thus you see, Caramon Majere, that we cannot possibly let your son—Raistlin's nephew—continue to study magic and take the Test without first making certain that his uncle cannot use this young man to gain entry back into the world."

"Especially," added Dunbar gravely, "since the young man's loyalties to one particular order have yet to be established."

"What do you mean?" Caramon frowned. "Take the Test? He's a long way from taking the Test. And as for his loyalties, he chose to wear the White Robes—"

"You and Mother chose that I wear the White Robes," Palin said evenly, his eyes staring straight ahead, avoiding his father. When only hurt silence answered him, Palin made an irritated gesture. "Oh, come now, Father. You know as well as I do that you wouldn't have considered letting me study magic under any other conditions. I knew better than to even ask!"

"But the young man must declare the allegiance that is in his heart. Only then can he use the true power of his magic. And he must do this during his test," Dunbar said gently.

"Test! What is this talk of the Test! I tell you, he hasn't even made up his mind whether or not to take the damn thing. And if I have anything to say about it—"

Caramon stopped speaking abruptly, his gaze going to his son's face. Palin stared at the ground, his cheeks flushed, his lips pressed tightly together.

"Well, never mind that," Caramon muttered, drawing a deep breath. Behind him, he could hear his other two sons shuffling nervously, the rattle of Tanin's sword, Sturm's soft cough. He was acutely aware, too, of the wizards watching him, especially of Dalamar's cynical smile. If only he and Palin could be alone! He'd have a chance to explain. Caramon sighed. It was something they should have talked about before this, he supposed. But he kept hoping. . . .

Turning his back on the wizards, he faced his son. "What other loyalty would you choose, Palin?" he asked belatedly, trying to make amends. "You're a good person, Son! You enjoy helping people, serving others! White seems obvious. . . ."

"I don't know whether I enjoy serving others or not," Palin cried impatiently, losing control. "You thrust me into this role, and look where it has gotten me! You admit yourself that I am not as strong or skilled in magic as my uncle was at my age. That was because he devoted his life to study! He let nothing interfere with it. It seems to me a man must put the magic first, the world second. . . ."

Closing his eyes in pain, Caramon listened to his son's words, but he heard them spoken by another voice—a soft, whispering voice, a shattered voice: *a man must put the magic first, the world second. By doing anything else, he limits himself and his potential*—

He felt a hand grasp his arm. "Father, I'm sorry," Palin said softly. "I would have discussed it with you, but I knew how much it would hurt you. And then there's Mother." The young man sighed. "You know Mother. . . ."

"Yes," said Caramon in a choked voice, reaching out and grasping his son in his big arms, "I know your mother." Clearing his throat, he tried to smile. "She might have thrown something at you—she did me once—most of my armor, as I recall. But her aim is terrible, especially when it's someone she loves."

Caramon couldn't go on for a moment, but stood holding his son. Looking over his shoulder at the wizards, he asked harshly, "Is this necessary right now? Let us go home and talk about it. Why can't we wait—"

"Because this night there is a rare occurrence," Justarius answered. "The silver moon, the black, and the red are all three in the sky at the same time. The power of magic is stronger this night than it has been in a century. If Raistlin has the ability to call upon the magic and escape the Abyss—it could be on a night like this."

Caramon bowed his head, his hand stroking his son's auburn hair. Then, his arm around Palin's shoulder, he turned to face the wizards, his face grim.

"Very well," he said huskily, "what do you want us to do?"

"You must return with me to the tower in Palanthas," said Dalamar. "And there, we will attempt to enter the portal."

"Let us ride as far as the Shoikan Grove with you, Father," Tanin pleaded.

"Yes!" added Sturm eagerly. "You'll need us, you know you will. The road between here and Palanthas is open—the knights see to that—but we've had reports from Porthios of draconian parties lying in ambush—"

"I am sorry to disappoint you, warriors," said Dalamar, a slight smile upon his lips, "but we will not be using the roads between here and Palanthas. Conventional roads, that is," he amended.

Both the young men looked confused. Glancing warily at the dark elf, Tanin frowned as though he suspected a trick.

Palin patted Tanin's arm. "He means magic, my brother. Before you and Sturm reach the front entryway, Father and I will be standing in Dalamar's study in the Tower of High Sorcery in Palanthas—the tower my uncle claimed as his own," he added softly. Palin had not meant anyone to hear his last words, but—glancing around—he caught Dalamar's intense, knowing gaze. Flushing in confusion, the young man fell silent.

"Yes, that's where we'll be," muttered Caramon, his face darkening at the thought. "And you two will be on your way home," he added, eyeing his older sons sternly. "You have to tell your mother—"

"I'd rather face ogres," said Tanin gloomily.

"Me, too," Caramon said with a grin that ended in a sigh. Leaning down suddenly to make certain his pack was cinched tightly, he kept his face carefully in the shadows. "Just make certain she's not standing where she can get hold of the crockery," he said, keeping his voice carefully light.

"She knows me. She's been expecting this. In fact, I think she knew when we left," Palin said, remembering his mother's tender hug and cheery smile as she stood at the door to the inn, waving at them with an old towel. Glancing behind him as they had been riding out of town, Palin recalled seeing that towel cover his mother's face, Dezra's arms going around her comfortingly.

"Besides," said Caramon, standing up to glare at his older two sons, his tone now severe, "you both promised Porthios you'd go to Qualinesti and help the elves handle those draconian raiding parties. You know what Porthios is like. It took him ten years to even speak to us. Now he's showing signs of being friendly. I won't have sons of mine going back on their word, especially to that stiff-necked elf. No offense," he said, glancing at Dalamar.

"None taken," said the dark elf. "I know Porthios. And now—"

"We're ready," interrupted Palin, an eager look on his face as he turned to Dalamar. "I've read about this spell you're going to cast, of course, but I've never seen it done. What components do you use? And do you inflect the first syllable of the first word, or the second? My master says—"

Dalamar coughed gently. "You are giving away our secrets, young one," he said in smooth tones. "Come, speak your questions to me in private." Placing his delicate hand upon Palin's arm, the dark elf drew the young man away from his father and brothers.

"Secrets?" said Palin, mystified. "What do you mean? It doesn't matter if they hear—"

"That was an excuse," Dalamar said coldly. Standing in front of the young man, he looked at Palin intently, his eyes dark and serious. "Palin, don't do this. Return home with your father and brothers."

"What do you mean?" Palin asked, staring at Dalamar in confusion. "I can't do that. You heard Justarius. They won't let me take my test or even keep on studying until we know for certain that Raistlin is . . . is . . ."

"Don't take the Test," Dalamar said swiftly. "Give up your studies. Go home. Be content with what you are."

"No!" Palin said angrily. "What do you take me for? Do you think I'd be happy entertaining at country fairs, pulling rabbits out of hats and golden coins out of fat men's ears? I want more than that!"

"The price of such ambition is great, as your uncle discovered."

"And so are the rewards!" Palin returned. "I have made up my mind . . ."

"Young one"—Dalamar leaned close to the young man, placing his cold hand upon Palin's arm. His voice dropped to a whisper so soft that Palin wasn't certain he heard its words spoken or in his mind—"why do you think they are sending you—truly?" His gaze went to Justarius and Dunbar, who were standing apart, conferring together. "To somehow enter the portal and find your uncle—or what's left of him? No"—Dalamar shook his head—"that is impossible. The room is locked. One of the Guardians stands constant watch with instructions to let no one in, to kill any who tries. *They* know that, just as they *know* Raistlin lives! They are sending you to the tower—*his* tower—for one reason. Do you recall the old legend about using a young goat to net a dragon?"

Staring at Dalamar in disbelief, Palin's face suddenly drained of all color. Licking his ashen lips, he tried to speak, but his mouth was too dry, his throat tight.

"I see you understand," Dalamar said coolly, folding his hands in the sleeves of his black robes. "The hunter tethers the young goat in front of the dragon's lair. While the dragon devours the goat, the hunters sneak up on him with their nets and their spears. They catch the dragon. Unfortunately, it is a bit late for the goat. . . . Do you still insist on going?"

Palin had a sudden vision of his uncle as he had heard of him in the legends: facing the evil Fistandantilus, feeling the touch of the bloodstone upon his chest as it sought to draw out his soul, suck out his life. The young man shivered, his body drenched in chill sweat. "I am strong," he said, his voice cracking. "I can fight as *he* fought—"

"Fight him? The greatest wizard who ever lived? The archmage who challenged the Queen of Darkness herself and nearly won?" Dalamar laughed mirthlessly. "Bah! You are doomed, young man. You haven't a prayer. And you know what I will be forced to do if Raistlin succeeds!" Dalamar's hooded head darted so near Palin that the young man could feel the touch of breath on his cheek. "I must destroy him—I *will* destroy him. I don't care whose body he inhabits. That's why they're giving you to me. *They* don't have the stomach for it."

Unnerved, Palin took a step back from the dark elf. Then he caught himself, and stood still.

"I . . . understand," he said, his voice growing firmer as he continued. "I told you that once. Besides, I don't believe my uncle would harm me in . . ."

the way you say."

"You don't?" Dalamar appeared amused. His hand moved to his chest. "Would you like to see what harm your uncle is capable of doing?"

"No!" Palin averted his eyes, then, flushing, he added lamely, "I know about it. I've heard the story. You betrayed him—"

"And this was my punishment." The dark elf shrugged. "Very well. If you are determined—"

"I am."

"—then I suggest you bid farewell to your brothers—a final farewell, if you take my meaning. For I deem it unlikely that you will meet again in this life."

The dark elf was matter-of-fact. His eyes held no pity, no remorse. Palin's hands twitched, his nails dug into his flesh, but he managed to nod firmly.

"You must be careful what you say." Dalamar glanced meaningfully at Caramon, who was walking over to Justarius. "Your brothers mustn't suspect. *He* mustn't suspect. If he knew, he would prevent your going. Wait"— Dalamar caught hold of the young man—"pull yourself together."

Swallowing, trying to moisten a throat that was parched and aching, Palin pinched his cheeks to bring the color back and wiped the sweat from his brow with the sleeve of his robe. Then, biting his lips to keep them steady, he turned from Dalamar and walked over to his brothers.

His white robes rustled around his ankles as he approached them. "Well, Brothers," he began, forcing himself to smile, "I'm always standing on the porch of the inn, waving good-bye to you two, going off to fight something or other. Looks like it's my turn now."

Palin saw Tanin and Sturm exchange swift, alarmed glances, and he choked. The three were close; they knew each other inside out. How can I fool them? he thought bitterly. Seeing their faces, he knew he hadn't.

"My brothers," Palin said softly, reaching out his hands. Clasping hold of both of them, he drew them near. "Don't say anything," he whispered. "Just let me go! Father wouldn't understand. It's going to be hard enough for him as it is."

"I'm not sure *I* understand," Tanin began severely.

"Oh, shut up!" Sturm muttered. "So we don't understand. Does it matter? Did our little brother blubber when you went off to your first battle?" Putting his big arms around Palin, he hugged him tightly. "Good-bye, kid," he said. "Take care of yourself and . . . and . . . don't be gone . . . long. . . ." Shaking his head, Sturm turned and walked hurriedly away, wiping his eye and muttering something about "those damn spell components make me sneeze!"

But Tanin, the oldest, remained standing beside his brother, staring at him sternly. Palin looked up at him pleadingly, but Tanin's face grew grim. "No, Little Brother," he said. "You're going to listen."

Dalamar, watching the two closely, saw the young warrior put his hand on Palin's shoulder. He could guess what was being said. The dark elf saw Palin drawn away, shaking his head stubbornly, the young man's features hardening into an impassive mask that Dalamar knew well. The wizard's hand went to the wounds in his chest. How like Raistlin the young man was! Like, yet different, as Caramon had said, as different as the white moon and the black. . . . The dark elf's thoughts were interrupted when he noticed that Caramon had observed the conversation between his two sons, and was taking a step toward them. Quickly, Dalamar interceded. Walking over to Caramon, he placed his slender hand on the big man's arm.

"You have not told your children the truth about their uncle," Dalamar said as Caramon glanced at him.

"I've told them," Caramon retorted, his face flushing, "as much as I thought they should know. I tried to make them see both sides of him. . . ."

"You have done them a disservice, particularly one of them," Dalamar replied coldly, his glance going to Palin.

"What could I do?" Caramon asked angrily. "When the legends started about him—sacrificing himself for the sake of the world, daring to go into the Abyss to rescue Lady Crysania from the clutches of the Dark Queen— what could I say? I told them how it was. I told them the true story. I told them that he lied to Crysania, that he seduced her in spirit, if not in body, and led her into the Abyss. And I told them that, at the end, when she was of no more use to him, he abandoned her to let her die alone. *I* told them. Tanis has told them. But they believe what they want to believe. . . . We all do, I guess," Caramon added with an accusing glance at Dalamar. "I notice you mages don't go out of your way to refute those stories!"

"They've done us good," Dalamar said, shrugging his slender shoulders. "Because of the legends about Raistlin and his 'sacrifice,' magic is no longer feared, we wizards no longer reviled. Our schools are flourishing, our services in demand. The city of Kalaman has actually invited us to build a new Tower of High Sorcery there." The dark elf smiled bitterly. "Ironic, isn't it?"

"What?"

"By his failure, your brother succeeded in what he set out to accomplish," Dalamar remarked, his smile twisting. "In a way, he *has* become a god. . . ."

"Palin, I insist on knowing what's going on." Tanin laid his hand on Palin's shoulder.

"You heard them, Tanin," Palin hedged, nodding toward Justarius, who was talking with his father. "We're going to travel to the Tower of High Sorcery in Palanthas, where the portal is located, and . . . and look in. . . . That's all."

"And I'm a gully dwarf!" growled Tanin.

"Sometimes you think like one," Palin snapped, losing his patience and thrusting his brother's arm away.

Tanin's face flushed a dull red. Unlike the easygoing Sturm, Tanin had inherited his mother's temper along with her curls. He also took his role of Elder Brother seriously, too seriously sometimes to Palin's mind. But it's only because he loves me, the young man reminded himself.

Drawing a deep breath, he sighed and, reaching out, clasped his brother by the shoulders. "Tanin, you listen to me for a change. Sturm's right. I didn't 'blubber' when you went off to battle that first time. At least not when you could see me. But I cried all night, alone, in the darkness. Don't you think I know that each time you leave may be the last time we ever see each other? How many times have you been wounded? That last fight, that minotaur arrow missed your heart by only two fingerbreadths."

Tanin, his face dark, stared down at his feet. "That's different," he muttered.

"As Grandpa Tas would say, 'A chicken with its neck wrung is different from a chicken with its head cut off, but does it matter to the chicken?' " Palin smiled.

Tanin shrugged and tried to grin. "I guess you're right." He put his hands on Palin's shoulders, looking intently into his brother's pale face. "Come home, kid! Give this up!" he whispered fiercely. "It isn't worth it! If anything happened to you, think of what it would do to Mother . . . and Father. . . ."

"I know," Palin said, his eyes filling despite all his best efforts to prevent it. "I have thought of that! I must do this, Tanin. Try to understand. Tell Mother I . . . I love her very much. And the little girls. Tell them I'll . . . I'll bring them a present, like you and Sturm always do . . ."

"What? A dead lizard?" Tanin growled. "Some moldy old bat's wing?"

Wiping his eyes, Palin smiled. "Yeah, tell 'em that. You better go. Dad's watching us."

"Watch yourself, Little Brother. And him." Tanin glanced at his father. "This will be pretty tough on him."

"I know." Palin sighed. "Believe me, I know."

Tanin hesitated. Palin saw one more lecture, one more attempt to dissuade him, in his brother's eyes.

"Please, Tanin," he said softly. "No more."

Blinking rapidly and rubbing his nose, Tanin nodded. Cuffing his little brother on the cheek and ruffling the auburn hair, Tanin walked across the shadowy chamber to stand near the entryway with Sturm.

Palin watched him walk away, then, turning, he went the opposite direction, toward the front of the great hall, to bid his parting respects to the two wizards.

"So Dalamar has spoken to you," Justarius said as the young man came to stand before him.

"Yes," said Palin grimly. "*He* has told me the truth."

"Has he?" Dunbar asked suddenly. "Remember this, young one. Dalamar wears the Black Robes. He is ambitious. Whatever he does, he does because he believes it will ultimately benefit him."

"Can you two deny what he told me is true? That you are using me as bait to trap my uncle's spirit if it still lives?"

Justarius glanced at Dunbar, who shook his head.

"Sometimes you have to look for the truth here, Palin," Dunbar said in answer, reaching out his hand to touch Palin gently on the chest, "in your heart."

His lip curled in derision, but Palin knew what respect he must show two such high-ranking wizards, so he simply bowed. "Dalamar and my father are waiting for me. I bid you both farewell. The gods willing, I will return in a year or two for my test, and I hope I will have the honor of seeing you both again."

Justarius did not miss the sarcasm, nor the bitter, angry expression on the young man's face. It made him recall another bitter, angry young man, who had come to this tower almost thirty years ago. . . .

"May Gilean go with you, Palin," the archmage said softly, folding his hands in the sleeves of his robes.

"May Paladine, the god you are named for, guide you, Palin," Dunbar said. "And consider this," he added, a smile creasing his black face, "in case you never see the old sea wizard again. You may learn that, by serving the world, you serve yourself best of all."

Palin did not reply. Bowing again, he turned and left them. The chamber seemed to grow darker as he walked back across it. He might have been alone; he could see no one for a moment, not his brothers, not Dalamar or his father . . . but as the darkness deepened, the white of his robes gleamed more brightly, like the first star in the evening sky.

For an instant, fear assailed Palin. Had they all left him? Was he alone in this vast darkness? Then he saw a glint of metal near him—his father's armor, and he breathed a sigh of relief. His steps hurried and, as he came to stand beside his father, the chamber seemed to lighten. He could see the dark elf, standing next to Caramon, the elf's pale face all that was visible from the shadows of his black robes. Palin could see his brothers, could see them lift their hands in farewell. Palin started to raise his, but then Dalamar began chanting, and it seemed a dark cloud covered the light of Palin's robes, of Caramon's shining armor. The darkness grew thicker, swirling around them until it was so deep that it was a hole of blackness cut into the shadows of the chamber. Then there was nothing. The cold, eerie light returned to the tower, filling up the gap.

Dalamar, Palin, and Caramon were gone.

The two brothers left behind shouldered their packs and began the long, strange journey back through the magical Forest of Wayreth. Thoughts of breaking this news to their red-haired, fiery-tempered, loving mother hung around their hearts with the weight of dwarven armor.

Behind them, standing beside the great stone chairs, Justarius and Dunbar watched in grim silence. Then, each speaking a word of magic, they, too, were gone, and the Tower of High Sorcery at Wayreth was left to its shadows, and only memories walked the halls.

Chapter Five

"He came in the middle of a still black night," Dalamar said softly. "The only moon in the sky was one his eyes alone could see." The dark elf glanced at Palin from the depths of the black hood that covered the elf's head. "Thus runs the legend about your uncle's return to this tower."

Palin said nothing—the words were in his heart. They had been there, secretly, ever since he was old enough to dream. In awe, he looked up at the huge gates that barred the entrance, trying to imagine his uncle standing where he now stood, commanding the gates to open. And when they did. . . . Palin's gaze went further upward to the dark tower itself.

It was daylight in Palanthas. It had been midmorning when they had left the Tower of High Sorcery in Wayreth, hundreds of miles to the south. And it was midmorning still, their magical journey having taken them no more than the drawing of a breath. The sun was at its zenith, shining right above the tower. Two of the blood-red minarets atop the tower held a golden orb between them, like bloodstained fingers greedily grasping a coin. And the sun might well have been nothing more than a coin for all the warmth it shed, for no sunshine ever warmed this place of evil. The huge black stone edifice—torn from the bones of the world by magic spells—stood in the shadow of the spell-bound Shoikan Grove, a stand of massive oak trees that guarded the tower more effectively than if each tree had been a hundred knights-at-arms. So powerful was its dread enchantment that no one could even come near it. Unless protected by a dark charm, no one could enter and come out alive.

Turning his head, Palin glanced from the folds of his white hood at the grove's tall trees. They stood unmoving, though he could feel the wind from the sea blowing strong upon his face. It was said that even the terrible hurricanes of the Cataclysm had not caused a leaf to flutter in the Shoikan Grove, though no other tree in the city remained standing. A chill darkness flowed among the trunks of the oaks, reaching out with snaking tendrils of icy fog that slithered along the paved courtyard before the gates and writhed about the ankles of those who stood there.

Shivering with cold and a fear he could not control, a fear fed by the trees, Palin looked at his father with new respect. Driven by love for his twin, Caramon had dared enter the Shoikan Grove, and had very nearly paid for his love with his life.

He must be thinking of that, Palin thought, for his father's face was pale and grim. Beads of sweat stood upon his forehead. "Let's get out of here," Caramon said harshly, his eyes carefully avoiding the sight of the cursed trees. "Go inside, or something. . . ."

"Very well," replied Dalamar. Though his face was hidden once again by the shadows of his hood, Palin had the impression the dark elf was smiling. "Although there is no hurry. We must wait until nightfall, when the silver moon, Solinari, beloved of Paladine, the black moon, Nuitari, favored by the Dark Queen, and Lunitari, the red moon of Gilean, are in the sky together. Raistlin will draw upon the black moon for his power. Others—who might need it—may draw upon Solinari—if they choose. . . ." He did not look at Palin as he spoke, but the young man felt himself flush.

"What do mean—draw upon its power?" Caramon demanded angrily, grabbing hold of Dalamar. "Palin's not a mage, not yet. You said you would deal with everything—"

"I am aware of my words," Dalamar interrupted. He neither moved nor spoke, but suddenly Caramon snatched his hand back with a gasp of pain. "And I will deal with . . . what must be dealt with. But things strange and unexpected may happen this night. It is well to be prepared." Dalamar regarded Caramon coolly. "And do not interfere with me again. Come, Palin. You may need my assistance to enter these gates."

Dalamar held out his hand. Glancing back at his father, Palin saw his eyes fixed on him. Don't go in there, his anguished gaze pleaded. If you do, I will lose you. . . .

Lowering his own eyes in confusion, pretending he hadn't read the message that had been as clear as the very first words his father taught him, Palin turned away and laid his hand hesitantly upon the dark elf's arm. The black robes were soft and velvety to the touch. He could feel the hard muscles and, beneath, the fine, delicate bone structure of the elf, almost fragile to the touch, yet strong and steady and supportive.

An unseen hand opened the gates that had once, long ago, been made of fluted silver and gold but were now black and twisted, guarded by shadowy beings. Drawing Palin with him, Dalamar stepped through them.

Searing pain pierced the young man. Clutching his heart, Palin doubled over with a cry.

Dalamar stopped Caramon's advance with a look. "You cannot aid him," the dark elf said. "Thus the Dark Queen punishes those not loyal to her who tread upon this sacred ground. Hold on to me, Palin. Hold on to me tightly and keep walking. Once we are inside, this will subside."

Gritting his teeth, Palin did as he was told, moving forward with halting footsteps, both hands gripping Dalamar's arm.

It was well the dark elf led him on for, left on his own, Palin would have fled this place of darkness. Through the haze of pain, he heard soft words whisper, "Why enter? Death alone awaits you! Are you anxious to look upon his grinning face? Turn back, foolish one! Turn back. Nothing is worth this. . . ." Palin moaned. How could he have been so blind? Dalamar had been right . . . the price was too high. . . .

"Courage, Palin!" Dalamar's voice blended with the whispering words.

The tower was crushing Palin beneath the weight of its dark, magical power, pressing the life from his body. Still he kept walking, though he could barely see the stones beneath his feet through a blood-red film blurring his eyes. Was this how *he* felt when *he* first came? Palin asked himself in agony. But no, of course not. Raistlin had worn the Black Robes when he first entered the tower. *He* came in the fullness of his power, Master of Past and Present. *For him, the gates had opened. . . . All dark and shadowy things bowed in homage.* Thus went the legend. . . .

For him, the gates had opened. . . .

With a sob, Palin collapsed upon the threshold of the tower.

"Feeling better?" Dalamar asked as Palin raised himself dizzily from the couch on which he lay. "Here, a sip of wine. It is elven, a fine vintage. I have it 'shipped' to me from Silvanesti, unknown to the Silvanesti elves, of course. This was the first wine made following the land's destruction. It has a dark, faintly bitter taste—as of tears. Some of my people, I am told, cannot drink it without weeping." Pouring a glassful, Dalamar held the deep purple-hued liquid out to Palin. "I find, in fact, that even when I drink it, a feeling of sadness comes over me."

"Homesick," suggested Caramon, shaking his head as Dalamar offered him a glass. Palin knew by the tone of his father's voice that he was upset and unhappy, frightened for his son. He sat stolidly in his chair, however, trying to appear unconcerned. Palin cast him a grateful glance as he drank the wine, feeling its warming influence banish the strange chill.

Oddly enough, the wine *was* making him think about his home. "Homesick," Caramon had said. Palin expected Dalamar to scoff or sneer at this statement. Dark elves are, after all, "cast from the light" of elven society, banned from entering the ancient homelands. Dalamar's sin had been to take the Black Robes, to seek power in dark magic. Bound hand and foot, his eyes blindfolded, he had been driven in a cart to the borders of his homeland and there thrown out, never more to be admitted. To the elves, whose centuries-long lives are bound up in their beloved woods and gardens, to be dismissed from the ancestral lands is worse than death.

Dalamar appeared so cool and unfeeling about everything, however, that Palin was surprised to see a look of wistful longing and swift sorrow pass over the dark elf's face. It was gone as quickly as a ripple over quiet water, but he had seen it nonetheless. He felt less in awe of the dark elf. So something could touch him, after all.

Sipping the wine, tasting the faint bitterness, Palin's thought went to *his* home, the splendid house his father had built with his own hands, the inn that was his parents' pride and joy. He thought about the town of Solace, nestled among the leaves of the great vallenwood trees, a town he had left only to attend school, as must all young, aspiring magic-users. He thought of his mother, of the two little sisters who were the bane of his existence— stealing his pouches, trying to peek under his robes, hiding his spellbooks. . . . What would it be like—never seeing them again?

. . . never seeing them again . . .

Palin's hand began to tremble. Carefully, he set the fragile glass down upon the table near his chair, fearing he might drop it or spill his wine. He looked around hurriedly to see if either his father or Dalamar had noticed. Neither had, both being engaged in a quiet discussion near the window overlooking the city of Palanthas.

"You have never been back to the laboratory since?" Caramon was asking, his voice low.

Dalamar shook his head. He had removed the hood of his robes, and his long, silky hair brushed his shoulders. "I went back the week you left," he replied, "to make certain all was in order. And then I sealed it shut."

"So everything is still there," Caramon murmured. Palin saw his father's shrewd gaze turn to the dark elf, who was staring out the window, his face cold and expressionless. "It must contain objects that would grant tremendous power to a wizard, or so I would guess. What is in there?"

Almost holding his breath, Palin rose from his chair and crept silently across the beautiful, luxurious carpet to hear the dark elf's answer.

"The spellbooks of Fistandantilus, Raistlin's own spellbooks, his notes on herb lore and, of course, his staff—"

"His staff?" Palin asked suddenly.

Both men turned to look at the young man, Caramon's face grave, Dalamar's faintly amused.

"You told me my uncle's staff was lost!" Palin said to his father accusingly.

"And so it is, young one," Dalamar answered. "The spell I put upon that chamber is such that even the rats do not come anywhere near it. None may enter on pain of death. If the famed Staff of Magius were at the bottom of the Blood Sea, it could not be more effectively lost to this world than it is now."

"There's one other thing in that laboratory," Caramon said slowly in sudden realization. "The Portal to the Abyss. If we can't get in the laboratory, how are we supposed to look inside the portal or whatever fool thing you wizards want me to do to prove to you my twin is dead?"

Dalamar was silent, twirling the thin-stemmed wineglass in his hand thoughtfully, his gaze abstracted. Watching him, Caramon's face flushed red in anger. "This was a ruse! You never meant it, any of you! What do mean, bringing us here? What do you want of me?"

"Nothing of you, Caramon," Dalamar answered coolly.

Caramon blenched. "No!" he cried in a choked voice. "Not my son! Damn you, wizards! I won't allow it!" Taking a step forward, he grabbed hold of Dalamar . . . and gasped in pain. Yanking his hand back, Caramon flexed it, rubbing his arm, which felt as though he had touched lightning.

"Father, please! Don't interfere!" murmured Palin, going to his father's side. The young man glanced angrily at Dalamar. "There was no need for that!"

"I warned him," Dalamar said, shrugging. "You see, Caramon, my friend, we cannot open the door from the outside." The dark elf's gaze went to Palin. "But there is one here for whom the door may open from the *inside*!"

Chapter Six

For me, the gates will open. . . .

Palin whispered the words to himself as he climbed the dark and winding stairs. Night had stolen upon Palanthas, sealing the city in darkness, deepening the perpetual gloom that hung about the Tower of High Sorcery. Solinari, the silver moon beloved of Paladine, shone in the sky, but its white rays did not touch the tower. Those inside gazed upon another moon, a dark moon, a moon only their eyes could see.

The stone stairs were pitch black. Though Caramon carried a torch, its feeble, wavering flame was overwhelmed by the darkness. He might have been holding a burning wisp of straw for all the light the torch shed. Groping his way up the stairs, Palin stumbled more than once. Each time, his heart pulsed painfully, and he pressed himself close against the chill, damp wall, closing his eyes. The core of the tower was a hollow shaft. The stairs ascended it in a dizzying spiral, protruding from the wall like the bones of some dead animal.

"You are safe, young one," Dalamar said, his hand on Palin's arm. "This was designed to discourage unwelcome intruders. The magic protects us. Don't look down. It will be easier."

"Why did we have to walk?" Palin asked, stopping to catching his breath. As young as he was, the steep climb had taken its toll. His legs ached; his lungs burned. He could only imagine what his father must be feeling. Even the dark elf appeared to be at a loss for breath, though Dalamar's face in the dim light was as cold and impassive as ever. "Couldn't we have used magic?"

"I will not waste my energies," Dalamar replied, "not on this night of all nights."

Seeing the slanted eyes observing him coolly, Palin said nothing, but began climbing again, keeping his eyes staring straight ahead and upward.

"There is our destination." Dalamar pointed. Looking up at the top of the stairs, Palin saw a small doorway.

For me, the gates will open. . . .

Raistlin's words. Palin's fear began to subside, and excitement surged through his blood. His steps quickened. Behind him, he heard Dalamar's light tread and his father's heavier, booted one. He could also hear Caramon's labored breathing, and felt a twinge of remorse.

"Do you want to rest, Father?" he asked, stopping and turning around.

"No," Caramon grunted. "Let's get this foolishness over with. Then we can go home."

His voice was gruff, but Palin heard a strange note in it, a note he had never heard before. Turning slowly around to face the door, Palin knew it for what it was—fear. His father was afraid. It wasn't just the dreadful climb, or the voices whispering of doom and despair. He was afraid of everything within this place. Palin knew then a secret feeling of joy—one his uncle must have known. His father—Hero of the Lance, the strongest man he knew, who could, even now, wrestle the brawny Tanin to the ground and disarm the skilled swordsman, Sturm—his father was frightened, frightened of the magic.

He is afraid, Palin realized, and I am not! Closing his eyes, Palin leaned back against the chill wall of the tower and, for the first time in his life, gave himself up to the magic. He felt it burn in his blood, caress his skin. The words it whispered were no longer of doom, but of welcome, of invitation. His body trembled with the ecstasy of the magic and, opening his eyes, Palin saw his exultation reflected in the dark elf's intense, glittering gaze.

"Now you taste the power!" Dalamar whispered. "Go forward, Palin, go forward."

Smiling to himself, cocooned in the warmth of his euphoria, Palin climbed the stairs rapidly, all fear forgotten. For him, the door would open. He had no doubts. Why or by whose hand, he did not speculate. It did not matter. Finally, he would be inside the ancient laboratory where some of the greatest magic upon Krynn had been performed. He would see the spell-books of the legendary Fistandantilus, the spellbooks of his uncle. He would see the great and terrible portal that led from this world into the Abyss. And he would see the famed Staff of Magius. . . .

Palin had long dreamt of his uncle's staff. Of all Raistlin's arcane trea-sures, this intrigued Palin most, perhaps because he had seen it portrayed so often in paintings or because it always figured prominently in legend and song. Palin even owned one such painting (he kept it wrapped in silk, hidden in his bedroom) of Raistlin in his black robes, the Staff of Magius in his hand, battling the Queen of Darkness.

If he had lived to teach me, and I had been worthy of him, perhaps he might have given me the staff, Palin thought wistfully every time he looked at the painting of the wooden staff with its golden dragon claw clutching a shining, faceted, crystal ball.

Now I will at least get to see it, perhaps even get to hold it! Palin shivered in delicious anticipation at the thought. And what else will we find in the laboratory? he wondered. What will we see when we look into the portal?

"All will be as my father said," Palin whispered, feeling a momentary pang. "Raistlin is at rest. It must be! Father would be hurt, so terribly hurt, otherwise."

If Palin's heart was whispering other words, the young man ignored them. His uncle was dead. His father had said so. Nothing else was possible; nothing else was to be wished for. . . .

"Stop!" hissed Dalamar, his hand closing about Palin's arm.

Starting, Palin halted. He had been so lost in his thoughts, he had scarcely noticed where he was. Now he saw that they had come to a large landing, located directly below the laboratory door. Looking up the short flight of stairs that led to it, Palin drew in his breath with a gasp. Two cold, white eyes stared at them out of the darkness—eyes without a body, unless the darkness itself was their flesh and blood and bone. Falling back a step, Palin stumbled into Dalamar.

"Steady, young one," the dark elf commanded, supporting Palin. "It is the Guardian."

Behind them, the torchlight wavered. "I remember them," Caramon said hoarsely. "They can kill you with a touch. . . ."

"Living beings," came the specter's hollow voice, "I smell your warm blood. I hear your hearts beating. Come forward. You awaken my hunger!"

Shoving Palin to one side, Dalamar stepped in front of him. The white eyes glistened for an instant, then lowered in homage.

"Master of the Tower. I did not sense your presence. It has been long since you have visited this place."

"Your vigil remains undisturbed?" Dalamar asked. "None have tried to enter?"

"Do you see their bones upon these floors? For surely you would, if any had dared disobey your command."

"Excellent," Dalamar said. "Now, I give you a new command. Give me the key to the lock. Then stand aside, and let us pass."

The white eyes flared open, a pale, eager light shining from them.

"That cannot be, Master of the Tower."

"Why not?" Dalamar asked coolly. His hands folded in the sleeves of his black robes, he glanced at Caramon as he spoke.

"Your command, master, was to 'Take this key and keep it for all eternity. Give it to no one,' you said, 'not even myself. And from this moment on, your place is to guard this door. No one is to enter. Let death be swift for those who try.' Thus were your words to me, master, and—as you see—I obey them."

Dalamar nodded his hooded head. "Do you?" he murmured, taking a step forward. Palin caught his breath, seeing the white eyes glow even more brightly. "What will you do if I come up there?"

"Your magic is powerful, master," said the specter, the disembodied eyes drifting nearer Dalamar, "but it can have no effect on me. There was only one who had *that* power—"

"Yes," said Dalamar irritably, hesitating, his foot upon the first stair.

"Do not come closer, master," the being warned, though Palin could see the eyes shining with a lust that brought sudden visions of cold lips touching his cringing flesh, drinking away his life. Shuddering, he wrapped his arms around his shivering body and sagged back against the wall. The warm feeling was gone, replaced by the chill of this horrible creature, the chill of death and disappointment. He felt nothing inside now, just empty and cold. Perhaps I will give it up. It isn't worth it. Palin's head drooped. Then his father's hand was on his shoulder, his father's voice echoing his thoughts.

"Come, Palin," Caramon said wearily. "This has all been for nothing. Let's go home—"

"Wait!" The gaze of the disembodied eyes shifted from the dark elf to the two figures that huddled behind him. "Who are these? One I recognize—"

"Yes," said Caramon, his voice low, "you've seen me before."

"*His* brother," murmured the specter. "But who is this? The young one? Him I do *not* know. . . ."

"C'mon, Palin," Caramon ordered gruffly, casting a fearful glance at the eyes. "We've got a long journey—"

Caramon's arm encircled Palin's shoulders. The young man felt his father's gentle urging and tried to turn away, but his gaze was fixed on the specter, which was staring at him strangely.

"Wait!" the specter commanded again, its hollow voice ringing through the darkness. Even the whispers fell silent at its command. "Palin?" it murmured softly, speaking questioningly, it seemed, to itself . . . or to someone else. . . .

A decision was reached, apparently, because the voice became firm. "Palin. Come forward."

"No!" Caramon grasped his son.

"Let him go!" Dalamar ordered, glancing around with a furious look. "I told you this might happen! It is our chance!" He gazed coldly at Caramon. "Or are you afraid of what you might find?"

"I am not!" Caramon returned in a choked voice. "Raistlin is dead! I have seen him at peace! I don't trust you mages! You're not going to take my son from me!"

Palin could feel his father's body trembling near his. He could see the anguish in his father's eyes. Compassion and pity stirred within the young man. There was a brief longing to stay safe within his father's strong, sheltering arms, but these feelings were burned away by a hot anger that surged up from somewhere inside of him, an anger kindled by the magic.

"Did you give Tanin a sword then bid him break it?" Palin demanded, pulling free of his father's grip. "Did you give Sturm a shield and tell him to hide behind it? Oh, I know!" Palin snapped, seeing Caramon, his face flushed, about to speak. "*That* is different. *That* is something *you* understand. You've never understood me, have you, Father? How many years was it before I persuaded you to let me go to school, to study with the master who had taught my uncle? When you finally relented, I was the oldest beginning student there! For years, I was behind the others, working to catch up. And all the time, I could sense you and mother watching me anxiously. I could hear you talking at night, saying that maybe I'd outgrown this 'fancy.' *Fancy!*" Palin's voice grew agonized. "Can't you see? The magic is my *life*! My *love*!"

"No, Palin, don't say that!" Caramon cried, his voice breaking.

"Why not? Because I sound like my uncle? You never understood him, either! You aren't intending to let me take the Test, are you, Father?"

Caramon stood without moving, refusing to answer, staring grimly into the darkness.

"No," said Palin softly. "You aren't. You're going to do everything in your power to stop me. Maybe even this!" The young man turned to look at Dalamar suspiciously. "Maybe this is some foul stew you and your friends here have cooked up to feed to me so that I'll quit! It gives you all the perfect excuse! Well, it won't work." Palin's cold gaze went from Dalamar to his father. "I hope you choke on it!"

Stepping past the dark elf, Palin put his foot upon the first step, his eyes on the specter, which floated above him.

"Come, Palin"—a pallid hand appeared from nowhere, beckoning—"come closer."

"*No!*" Caramon screamed in rage, jumping forward.

"I will do this, Father!" Palin took another step.

Caramon reached out to grasp his son. There came a spoken word of magic, and the big man was frozen to the stone floor. "You must not interfere," Dalamar said sternly.

Glancing back, Palin saw his father—tears streaming down his face—still struggling in impotent fury to break free of the spell that bound him. For a moment, Palin's heart misgave him. His father loved him. . . . No. Palin's lips tightened in resolution. All the more reason for letting me go. I will prove to him I am as strong as Tanin and Sturm. I will make him proud of *me* as he is proud of them. I will show him I am not a child, needing his protection.

Palin saw Dalamar start to ascend the stairs behind him. But then the dark elf himself came to a halt as two more pairs of disembodied eyes suddenly materialized out of the darkness and ranked themselves around him.

"What is this?" Dalamar demanded furiously. "Do you dare stop me— the Master of the Tower?"

"There is only one true Master of the Tower," the Guardian said softly. "He who came to us long ago. For him, the gates opened."

As the Guardian spoke, it held out its pallid hand. A silver key lay within its skeletal palm.

"Palin!" Dalamar shouted, fear and anger tightening his voice. "Don't enter alone! You know nothing of the Art! You have not taken the Test! You cannot fight him! You could destroy us all!"

"Palin!" Caramon begged in agony. "Palin, come home! Can't you understand? I love you so much, my son! I can't lose you—not like I lost him. . . ."

The voices dinned in his ears, but Palin didn't hear them. He heard another voice, a soft, shattered voice whispering in his heart. *Come to me, Palin! I need you! I need your help . . .*

A thrill tingled in his blood. Reaching out, Palin took the key from the specter and, his hand shaking with fear and excitement, finally managed to insert the silver key into the ornate silver lock.

There was a sharp click. Placing the tips of his five fingers on the oaken panel, Palin gave a gentle push.

For him, the door opened.

Chapter Seven

Palin entered the dark laboratory, slowly, exultantly, his body shaking in excitement. He glanced back to see if Dalamar was behind him (to gloat a little, if the truth must be told) when the door slammed shut. There was a click, a snap. Sudden fear assailed Palin, trapped alone in the darkness. Frantically, he groped for the silver door handle, his fingers trying desperately to fit the key in the lock—a key that vanished in his hand.

"Palin!" On the other side of the door, he heard his father's frantic shout, but it sounded muffled and far away. There was a scuffling sound outside the door, muttered words of chanting, and then a thud, as though something heavy had smote it.

The thick oaken door shivered, and light flared from beneath it.

"Dalamar's cast a spell," Palin said to himself, backing up. The thud was probably his father's broad shoulder. Nothing happened. From somewhere behind him, Palin noticed a faint light beginning to glow in the laboratory. His fear diminished. Shrugging, the young man turned away. Nothing they did could open that door. He knew that, somehow, and he smiled. For the first time in his life, he was doing something on his own, without father or brothers or master around to "help." The thought was exhilarating. Sighing with pleasure, Palin relaxed and looked around, a tingle of joy surging through his body.

He had heard this chamber described to him only twice—once by Caramon and once by Tanis Half-Elven. Caramon never spoke about what had happened that day in this laboratory, the day his twin had died. It had been only after much pleading on Palin's part that his father had told him the story at all—and then only in brief, halting words. Caramon's best friend, Tanis, had been more elaborate, though there were parts of the bittersweet tale of ambition, love, and self-sacrifice about which not even Tanis could talk. Their descriptions had been accurate, however. The laboratory looked just as Palin had pictured it in his dreams.

Walking slowly inside, examining every detail, Palin held his breath in reverent awe.

Nothing and no one had disturbed the great chamber in twenty-five years. As Dalamar had said, no living being had dared enter it. Gray dust lay thick on the floor—no skittering mice feet had disturbed its drifted surface—as smooth and trackless as newfallen snow. The dust sifted from the window ledges where no spider spun its web, no bat flapped its leathery wings in anger at being awakened.

The size of the chamber was difficult to determine. At first, Palin had thought it small, logic telling him it couldn't be very large, located as it was at the top of the tower. But the longer he stayed, the larger the chamber seemed to grow.

"Or is it me that grows smaller?" Palin whispered. "I am not even a mage. I don't belong here," said his mind. But his heart answered, *You never really belonged anywhere else. . . .*

The air was heavy with the odors of mildew and dust. There lingered still a faint spicy smell, familiar to the young man. Palin saw the light glint off rows of jars filled with dried leaves, rose petals, and other herbs and spices lining one wall—spell components. There was another smell, too, this one not so pleasant—the smell of decay, of death. The skeletons of strange and unfamiliar creatures lay curled at the bottoms of several large jars on the floor or the huge, stone table. Remembering rumors of his uncle's experiments in creating life, Palin gave them a glance and looked hurriedly away.

He examined the stone table, with its runes and polished surface. Had it really been dragged from the bottom of the sea as legend told? Palin wondered, running his fingers lovingly over the smooth top, leaving behind a spidery trail in the dust. His hand touched the high stool next to the table. He could picture his uncle sitting here, working, reading. . . .

Palin's gaze went to the rows of spellbooks lining shelf after shelf along one entire wall of the chamber. His heart beat faster as he approached them, recognizing them from his father's description. The ones with the nightblue bindings and silver runes were the books of the great archmage, Fistandan-tilus. A whispering chill flowed from them. Palin shivered and stopped, afraid to go nearer, though his hands twitched to touch them.

He dared not, however. Only mages of the highest ranking could even open the books, much less read the spells recorded therein. If he tried it, the binding would burn his skin, just as the words would burn his mind—eventually dri-ving him mad. Sighing with bitter regret, Palin turned his gaze to another row of other spellbooks, these black with silver runes—his uncle's.

He was wondering if he should try to read, wondering what would hap-pen if he did, and was just starting to examine them closer when he noticed, for the first time, the source of the light illuminating the laboratory.

"His staff . . ." he whispered.

It stood in a corner, leaning against a wall: the Staff of Magius. Its magical crystal burned with a cold, pale light, like the light from Solinari, Palin thought. Tears of longing filled his eyes and ran, unheeded, down his cheeks. Blinking them back so that he could see, hardly daring to breathe, fearful that the light might go out in an instant, he drew nearer the staff.

Given to Raistlin by the wizard Par-Salian when the young mage had successfully completed his test, the staff possessed untold magical power. It could cast light at a word of command, Palin recalled. According to legend, however, no hand but his uncle's could touch the staff or the light would extinguish.

"But my father held it," Palin said softly. "He used it—with my dying uncle's help—to close the portal and prevent the Dark Queen from entering the world. Then the light went out and nothing anyone said could make it glow again."

But it was glowing now. . . .

His throat dry and aching, his heart beating so that it made him short of breath, Palin reached out a trembling hand toward the staff. If the light failed, he would be left alone, trapped, in the smothering darkness.

His fingertips brushed the wood.

The light gleamed brightly.

Palin's cold fingers closed around the staff, grasping it firmly. The crystal burned brighter still, shedding its pure radiance over him; his white robes glowed molten silver. Lifting the staff from its corner, Palin looked at it in rapture and saw, as he moved it, that its beam grew concentrated, sending a shaft of light into a distant corner of the laboratory—a corner that had pre-viously stood in deepest darkness.

Walking nearer, the young man saw the light illuminate a heavy curtain of purple velvet hanging from the ceiling. The tears froze on Palin's face, and a chill shook his body. He had no need to pull the golden, silken cord that hung beside the velvet, no need to draw aside those curtains to know what lay behind.

The portal.

Created long ago by wizards greedy for knowledge, the portals had led them to their own doom—into the realms of the gods. Knowing what terrible consequences this could have for the unwary, the wise among all three orders of wizards came together and closed them as best they could, decreeing that only a powerful archmage of the Black Robes and a holy cleric of Paladine acting together could cause the portal to open. They believed, in their wisdom, that this unlikely combination could never come about. But they had not counted on love.

So Raistlin was able to persuade Crysania, the Revered Daughter of Paladine, to act with him to open the portal. He had entered and challenged the Queen of Darkness, thinking to rule in her stead. The consequences of such ambition in a human would have been disastrous—the destruction of the world. Knowing this, his twin brother, Caramon, had risked all to enter the Abyss and stop Raistlin. He had done so, but only with his twin's assistance. Realizing his tragic mistake, Raistlin had sacrificed himself for the world—according to legend. He closed the portal, preventing the queen from entering, but at a dreadful cost. He himself was trapped upon the other side of this dread doorway.

Palin came nearer and nearer the curtain, drawn to it against his will. Or was he? Was it fear making his steps falter and his body shake—or excitement?

And then he heard that whispering voice again, *Palin . . . help . . .*

It came from beyond the curtain!

Palin closed his eyes, and he leaned weakly upon the staff. No! It couldn't be! His father had been so certain. . . .

Through his closed eyelids, the young man saw another light begin to glow, coming from in front of him. Fearfully, he opened his eyes and saw the light radiating from around and above and beneath the curtain. A multicolored light, it welled out in a dreadful rainbow.

Palin . . . help me . . .

Palin's hand closed of its own volition over the golden drawstring. He had no conscious thought of moving his fingers, yet found himself holding on to the cord. Hesitating, he looked at the staff in his hand, then glanced back behind him at the door leading into the laboratory. The thudding had stopped, and no lights flashed. Perhaps Dalamar and his father had given up. Or perhaps the Guardians had attacked them. . . .

Palin shivered. He should go back, abandon this. It was too dangerous. He wasn't even a mage! But as the thought crossed his mind, the light from the crystal atop the staff dimmed—or so it seemed to him.

No, he thought resolutely. I must go on. I must know the truth!

Gripping the drawstring with a palm wet with sweat, he pulled it hard, watching, holding his breath as the curtain slowly lifted, rising upward in shimmering folds.

The light grew more and more brilliant as the curtain rose, dazzling him. Raising his hand, shading his eyes, Palin stared in awe at the magnificent, fearful sight. The portal was a black void surrounded by five metallic dragon heads. Carved by magic into the likeness of Takhisis, Queen of

Darkness, their mouths gaped open in a silent scream of triumph, each head glowing green, blue, red, white, or black.

The light blinded Palin. He blinked painfully and rubbed his burning eyes. The dragon heads shone only more brilliantly, and now he could hear them each began to chant.

The first, *From darkness to darkness, my voice echoes in the emptiness.*

The second, *From this world to the next, my voice cries with life.*

The third, *From darkness to darkness, I shout. Beneath my feet, all is made firm.*

The fourth, *Time that flows, hold in your course.*

And finally, the last head, *Because by fate even the gods are cast down, weep ye all with me.*

A magical spell, Palin realized. His vision blurred, and tears streamed down his cheeks as he attempted to see through the dazzling light into the portal. The multicolored lights began to whirl madly, spinning around the outside of the great, gaping, twisting void within the center of the portal.

Growing dizzy, Palin clutched the staff and kept his gaze on the void within. The darkness moved! It began to swirl, circling around an eye of deeper darkness within its center, like a maelstrom without substance or form. Round . . . and round . . . and round . . . sucking the air from the laboratory up in its mouth, sucking up the dust, and the light of the staff. . . .

"No!" Palin cried, realizing in horror that it was sucking him in as well! Struggling, he fought against it, but the force was irresistible. Helpless as a babe trying to stop his own birth, Palin was drawn inside the dazzling light, the writhing darkness. The dragon's heads shrieked a paean to their Dark Queen. Their weight crushed Palin's body, then their talons pulled him apart, limb by limb. Fire burst upon him, burning his flesh from his bones. Waters swirled over him; he was drowning. He screamed without sound, though he could hear his voice. He was dying, and he was thankful he was dying, for the pain would end.

His heart burst.

Chapter Eight

Everything stopped. The light, the pain. . . .

Everything was silent.

Palin was lying facedown, the Staff of Magius still clutched in his hand. Opening his eyes, he saw the light of the staff shining silver, gleaming cold and pure. He felt no pain, his breathing was relaxed and normal, and his heartbeat steady, his body whole and unharmed. But he wasn't lying on the floor of the laboratory. He was in sand! Or so it seemed. Glancing around, slowly rising to his feet, he saw that he was in a strange land—flat, like a desert, with no distinguishing features of any type. It was completely empty, barren. The landscape stretched on and on endlessly as far as he could see. Puzzled, he looked around. He had never been here before, yet it was familiar. The ground was an odd color—a kind of muted pink, the same color as the sky. His father's voice came to him, *As though it was sunset or somewhere in the distance, a fire burned. . . .*

Palin closed his eyes to blot out the horror of realization as fear surged over him in a suffocating wave, robbing him of breath or even the power to stand.

"The Abyss," he murmured, his shaking hand holding the staff for support.

"Palin—" The voice broke off in a choked cry.

Palin's eyes flared open, startled at hearing his name, alarmed by the sound of desperation in the voice.

Turning around, stumbling in the sand, the young man looked in the direction of that terrible sound and saw, rising up before him, a stone wall where no wall had been only seconds previously. Two undead figures walked toward the wall, dragging something between them. The "something" was human, Palin could see, human and living! It struggled in its captors' grasp, as though trying to escape, but resistance was useless against those whose strength came from beyond the grave.

The three drew nearer the wall, which was, apparently, their destination, for one pointed to it and laughed. The human ceased his struggles for a moment. Lifting his head, he looked directly at Palin.

Golden skin, eyes the shape of hourglasses . . .

"Uncle?" Palin breathed, starting to take a step forward.

But the figure shook its head, making an almost imperceptible movement with one of its slender hands as though saying, "Not now!"

Palin realized suddenly that he was standing out in the open, alone in the Abyss, with nothing to protect him but the Staff of Magius—a staff whose magic he had no idea how to use. The undead, intent upon their struggling captive, had not noticed him yet, but it would be only a matter of time. Frightened and frustrated, Palin looked about hopelessly for someplace to hide. To his amazement, a thick bush sprang up out of nowhere, almost as if he had summoned it into being.

Without stopping to think why or how it was there, the young man ducked swiftly behind the bush, covering the crystal on the staff with his hand in an attempt to keep its light from giving him away. Then he peered cautiously out into the pinkish, burning land.

The undead had hauled their captive to the wall that stood in the middle of the sand. Manacles appeared on the wall at a spoken word of command. Hoisting their captive up into the air with their incredible strength, the undead fastened Raistlin to the wall by his wrists. Then, with mocking bows, they left him there, hanging from the wall, his black robes stirring in the hot breeze.

Rising to his feet, Palin started forward again when a dark shadow fell across his vision, blinding him more completely than the brilliant light, filling his mind and soul and body with such terror and fear that he could not move. Though the darkness was thick and all encompassing, Palin saw things within it—he saw a woman, more beautiful and desirable than any other woman he had ever seen before in his life. He saw her walk up to his uncle, he saw his uncle's manacled fists clench. He saw all this, yet all around him was such darkness as might have been found on the floor of the deepest ocean. Then Palin understood. The darkness was in his mind, for he was looking upon Takhisis—the Queen of Darkness herself.

As he watched, held in place by awe and horror and such reverence as made him want to kneel before her, Palin saw the woman change her form. Out of the darkness, out of the sand of the burning land, rose a dragon. Immense, its wingspan covered the land with shadow, its five heads writhed and twisted upon five necks, and its five mouths opened in deafening shrieks of laughter and of cruel delight.

Palin saw Raistlin's head turn away involuntarily, the golden eyes closed as though unable to face the sight of the creature that leered above him. Yet the archmage fought on, trying to wrench himself free of the manacles, his arms and wrists torn and bleeding from the futile effort.

Slowly, delicately, the dragon lifted a claw. With one swift stroke, she slit open Raistlin's black robes. Then, with almost the same, delicate movement, she slit open the archmage's body.

Palin gasped and shut his eyes to blot out the dreadful sight, but it was too late. He had seen it, and he would see it always in his dreams, just as he would hear his uncle's agonized cry forever. Palin's mind reeled, and his knees went limp. Sinking to the ground, he clasped his stomach, retching.

Then, through the haze of sickness and terror, Palin was aware of the queen and knew that she was suddenly aware of him! He could sense her searching for him, listening, smelling. . . . He had no thought of hiding. There was nowhere he could go where she would not find him. He could not fight, could not even look up at her. He didn't have the strength. He could only crouch in the sand, shivering in fear, and wait for the end.

Nothing happened. The shadow lifted, Palin's fear subsided.

Palin . . . help . . . The voice, ragged with pain, whispered in the young man's mind. And, horribly, there was another sound, the sound of liquid dripping, of blood running. . . .

"No!" The young man moaned, shaking his head and burrowing into the sand as though he would bury himself. There came another gurgling cry, and Palin retched again, sobbing in horror and pity and disgust at himself for his weakness. "What can I do? I am nothing. I have no power to help you!" he mumbled, his fist clenching around the staff that he held still. Holding it near him, he rocked back and forth, unable to open his eyes, unable to look.

"Palin—" the voice gasped for breath, each word causing obvious pain— "you must be . . . strong. For your own . . . sake as well as . . . mine."

Palin couldn't speak. His throat was raw and aching; the bitter taste of bile in his mouth choked him.

Be strong. For his sake . . .

Slowly, gripping the staff, Palin used it to pull himself to his feet. Then, bracing himself, feeling the touch of the wood cool and reassuring beneath his hand, he opened his eyes.

Raistlin's body hung limply from the wall by its wrists, the black robes in tatters, the long white hair falling across his face as his head lolled forward. Palin tried to keep his eyes focused on his uncle's face, but he could not. Despite himself, his gaze went to the bloody, mangled torso. From chest to groin, Raistlin's flesh had been ripped apart, torn asunder by sharp talons, exposing living organs. The dripping sound Palin heard was the sound of the man's lifeblood, falling drop by drop into a great stone pool at his feet.

The young man's stomach wrenched again, but there was nothing left to purge. Gritting his teeth, Palin kept walking forward through the sand toward the wall, the staff aiding his faltering footsteps. But when Palin reached the gruesome pool, his weak legs would support him no longer. Fearing he might faint from the horror of the dreadful sight, he sank to his knees, bowing his head.

"Look at me . . ." said the voice. "You . . . know me . . . Palin?"

The young man raised his head reluctantly. Golden eyes stared at him, their hourglass pupils dilated with agony. Bloodstained lips parted to speak, but no words came. A shudder shook the frail body.

"I know you . . . Uncle. . . ." Doubling over, Palin began to sob, while in his mind, the words screamed at him. "Father lied! He lied to me! He lied to himself!"

"Palin, be strong!" Raistlin whispered. "You . . . can free me. But you must . . . be quick. . . ."

Strong . . . I must be strong. . . .

"Yes." Palin swallowed his tears. Wiping his face, he rose unsteadily to his feet, keeping his gaze on his uncle's eyes. "I—I'm sorry. What must I do?"

"Use . . . the staff. Touch the locks around . . . my wrists. . . . Hurry! The . . . queen . . ."

"Where—where is the Dark Queen?" Palin stammered. Stepping carefully past the pool of blood, he came to stand near his uncle and, reaching up, touched the glowing crystal of the staff to the first of the manacles that held Raistlin bound to the wall.

Exhausted, near death, his uncle could speak no longer, but his words came to Palin's mind. *Your coming forced her to leave. She was not prepared to face one such as you. But that will not last long. She will return. Both of us . . . must be gone. . . .*

Palin touched the other manacle and, freed of his chains, Raistlin slumped forward, his body falling into the arms of the young man. Catching hold of his uncle, his horror lost in his pity and compassion, Palin gently laid the torn, bleeding body on the ground.

"But how can you go anywhere?" Palin murmured. "You are dying. . . ."

Yes, Raistlin answered wordlessly, his thin lips twisting in a grim smile. *In a few moments, I will die, as I have died countless mornings before this. When night falls, I will return to life and spend the night looking forward to the dawn, when the queen will come and tear my flesh, ending my life in tortured pain once more.*

"What can I do?" Palin cried helplessly. "How can I help you?"

"You are helping already," Raistlin said aloud, his voice growing stronger. His hand moved feebly. "Look . . ."

Reluctantly, Palin glanced down at his uncle's terrible wound. It was closing! The flesh was mending! The young man stared in astonishment. If he had been a high-ranking cleric of Paladine, he could have performed no greater miracle. "What is happening? How—?" he asked blankly.

"Your goodness, your love," whispered Raistlin. "So might my brother have saved me if he had possessed the courage to enter the Abyss himself." His lip curled in bitterness. "Help me stand . . ."

Palin swallowed, but said nothing as he helped the archmage rise to his feet. What could he say? Shame filled his soul, shame for his father. Well, he would make up for it.

"Give me your arm, Nephew. I can walk. Come, we must reach the portal before the queen returns."

"Are you sure you can manage?" Palin put his arm around Raistlin's body, feeling the strange, unnatural heat that radiated from it warm his own chilled flesh.

"I must. I have no choice." Leaning upon Palin, the archmage gathered his torn black robes about him, and the two walked forward as fast as they could through the shifting sand toward where the portal stood in the center of the red-tinged landscape.

But before he had gone very far, Raistlin stopped, his frail body wracked by coughing until he gasped for air.

Standing beside him, holding him, Palin looked at his uncle in concern. "Here," he offered. "Take your staff. It will aid your steps—"

Raistlin's hourglass eyes went to the staff in the young man's hand. Reaching out his slender, golden-skinned hand, he touched the smooth wood, stroking it lovingly. Then, looking at Palin, he smiled and shook his head.

"No, Nephew," he said in his soft, shattered voice. "The staff is yours, a gift from your uncle. It would have been yours someday," he added, speaking almost to himself. "I would have trained you myself, gone with you to watch the Test. I would have been proud . . . so proud . . ." Then, he shrugged, his gaze going to Palin. "What am I saying? I *am* proud of you, my nephew. So young, to do this, to enter the Abyss—"

As if to remind them where they were and the danger they were in, a shadow fell upon them as of dark wings, hovering overhead.

Palin looked up fearfully. Then his gaze went to the portal that seemed farther away than he remembered. He gasped. "We can't outrun her!"

"Wait!" Raistlin paused for breath, color coming back to his face. "We don't need to run. Look at the portal, Palin. Concentrate on it. Think of it as being right in front of you."

"I don't understand." Palin looked at Raistlin, confused.

"Concentrate!" the archmage snarled.

The shadow was growing increasingly dark. Looking at the portal, Palin tried to do as he was told, but he kept seeing his father's face, the dragon ripping his uncle's flesh. . . . The shadow over them grew still darker, darker than night, as dark as his own fear.

"Don't be afraid." His uncle's voice came to him through the darkness. "Concentrate."

The disciplined training in magic came to Palin's aid. Thus was he forced to concentrate on the words to a spell. Closing his eyes, the young man shut everything out—his fear, his horror, his sorrow—and envisioned the portal in his mind, standing directly before him.

"Excellent, young one," came Raistlin's soft voice.

Palin blinked, startled. The portal was right where he had envisioned it, just a step or two away.

"Don't hesitate," Raistlin instructed, reading the young man's mind. "The way back is not difficult, not like coming through. Go ahead. I can stand on my own. I will follow. . . ."

Palin stepped inside, feeling a slight sensation of dizziness and a momentary blindness, but it passed quickly. Looking around, he drew a deep breath of relief and thankfulness. He was standing in the laboratory once more. The portal was behind him, though he had no clear remembrance of how he walked through it, and beside the portal he saw his uncle. But Raistlin was not looking at him. His eyes were on the portal itself, a strange smile played on his thin lips.

"You are right! We must close it!" Palin said suddenly, thinking he knew his uncle's mind. "The queen will come back into the world—"

Raising the staff, the young man stepped forward. A slender, golden-skinned hand closed over his arm. Its grip hurt; the touch burned him. Catching his breath, biting his lip from the pain, Palin looked at his uncle in confusion.

"All in good time, my dear nephew," whispered Raistlin, "all in good time. . . ."

Chapter Nine

Raistlin drew the young man nearer, smiling slightly as Palin flinched, noting the look of pain in the green eyes. Still Raistlin held him, regarding him searchingly, studying the features, probing the depths of his soul.

"There is much of myself in you, young one," Raistlin said, reaching up to brush back a lock of hair that had fallen across Palin's pale face. "More of me than of your father. And he loves you best for that, doesn't he? Oh, he is proud of your brothers"—Raistlin shrugged, as the young man started to protest—"but you he cherishes, protects. . . ."

Flushing, Palin broke free of Raistlin's grip. But he might have spared his energy. The archmage held him fast—with his eyes, not his hands.

"He'll smother you!" Raistlin hissed. "Smother you as he did me! He will prevent you from taking the Test. You know that, don't you?"

"He—he doesn't understand," Palin faltered. "He's only trying to do what he thinks—"

"Don't lie to me, Palin," Raistlin said softly, placing his slender fingers on the young man's lips. "Don't lie to yourself. Speak the truth that is in your soul. I see it in you so clearly! The hatred, the jealousy! Use it, Palin! Use it to make you strong—as I did!"

The golden-skinned hand traced over the bones of Palin's face—the firm, strong chin, the clenched jaw, the smooth, high cheekbones. Palin trembled at the touch, but more still at the expression in the burning, hourglass eyes. "You should have been *mine*! My son!" Raistlin murmured. "I would have raised you to power! What wonders I would have shown you, Palin. Upon the wings of magic we would have flown the world—cheered the winner of the fights for succession among the minotaurs, gone swimming with the sea elves, battled giants, watched the birth of a golden dragon. . . . All this could have been yours, *should* have been yours, Palin, if only they—"

A fit of coughing checked the archmage. Gasping, Raistlin staggered, clutching his chest. Catching hold of him in his strong arms, Palin led his uncle to a dusty, cushioned chair that stood near the portal. Beneath the dust he could discern dark splotches on the fabric—as though it had, long ago, been stained with blood. In his concern for his uncle, Palin thought little of it. Raistlin sank down into the chair, choking, coughing into a soft, white cloth that Palin drew from his own robes and handed to him. Then, leaning the staff carefully against the wall, the young man knelt beside his uncle.

"Is there something I can do? Something I can get for you? That herbal mixture you drank." His glance went to the jars of herbs on a shelf. "If you tell me how to fix it—"

Raistlin shook his head. "In time . . ." he whispered as the spasm eased. "In time, Palin." He smiled wearily, his hand reaching out to rest on the young man's head. "In time. I will teach you that . . . and so much more! How they have wasted your talent! What did they tell you, young one? Why did they bring you here?"

Palin bowed his head. The touch of those slender fingers excited him, yet he caught himself cringing, squirming beneath their burning caress. "I came— They said . . . you would try . . . to take . . ." He swallowed, unable to continued.

"Ah, yes. Of course. That is what those idiots would think. I would take your body as Fistandantilus tried to take mine. What fools! As if I would deprive the world of this young mind, of this power. The two of us . . . There will be two of us, now. I make you my apprentice, Palin." The burning fingers stroked the auburn hair.

Palin raised his face. "But," he said in amazement, "I am of low rank. I haven't taken the Test—"

"You will, young one," Raistlin murmured, exhaustion plain upon his face. "You will. And with my help, you will pass easily, just as I passed with the help of another . . . Hush. Don't speak anymore. I must rest." Shivering, Raistlin clutched his tattered robes about his frail body. "Bring me some wine and a change of clothes, or I will freeze to death. I had forgotten how damp this place was." Leaning his head back against the cushions, Raistlin closed his eyes, his breath rattling in his lungs.

Palin stood slowly, casting an uneasy glance behind him.

The five heads of the dragon around the portal still glowed, but their colors were faded, less brilliant. Their mouths gaped open, but no sound came out. It seemed to Palin, though, that they were waiting, biding their time. Their ten eyes, glittering with some secret, inner knowledge, watched him. He looked inside the portal. The red-tinged landscape stretched into the distance. Far away, barely discernible, he could see the wall, the pool of blood beneath it. And above it, the dark, winged shadow. . . .

"Uncle," Palin said, "the portal. Shouldn't we—?"

"Palin," said Raistlin softly, "I gave you a command. You will learn to obey my commands, apprentice. Do as I bid."

As Palin watched, the shadow grew darker. Like a cloud covering the sun, the wings cast a chill of fear over his soul. He started to speak again, but at that moment glanced back at Raistlin.

His uncle's eyes appeared to be closed, but Palin caught a slit of gold gleaming beneath the lids, like the eyes of a lizard. Biting his lower lip, the young man turned hastily away. He took hold of the staff, used its light to search the laboratory for that which his uncle had requested.

Dressed once more in soft black velvet robes, Raistlin stood before the portal, sipping a glass of elven wine that Palin had discovered in a carafe far back in a corner of the laboratory. The shadow over the land within had now grown so dark that it seemed night had fallen over the Abyss. But no stars shone, no moons lit that dread darkness. The wall was the only object visible, and it glowed with its own horrid light. Raistlin stared at it, his face grim, his eyes haunted by pain.

"Thus she reminds me of what will happen should she catch me, Palin," he said. "But, no, I am not going back." Looking around, the archmage glanced at the young man. Raistlin's eyes glittered within the depths of his black hood. "I had twenty-five years to consider my mistakes. Twenty-five years of unbearable agony, of endless torment. . . . My only joy, the only thing that gave me strength to meet each morning's torture was the shadow of you I saw in my mind. Yes, Palin"—smiling, Raistlin reached out and drew the young man nearer—"I have watched you all these years. I have done what I could for you. There is a strength—an inner strength—in you that comes from me! A burning desire, a love for the magic! I knew, one day, you would seek me out to learn how to use it. I knew *they* would try to stop you. But they could not. Everything they did to prevent your coming must only bring you closer. Once in here, I knew you would hear my voice. You would free me. And so I made my plans . . ."

"I am honored that you take this interest in me," Palin began. His voice broke, and he cleared his throat nervously. "But you must know the truth. I—I didn't seek you out to . . . to gain power. I heard your voice, pleading for help, and I—I came because . . ."

"You came out of pity and compassion," Raistlin said with a twisted smile. "There is still much of your father in you. That is a weakness that can be overcome. As I told you, Palin. Speak the truth—to yourself. What did you feel upon entering this place? What did you feel when you first touched the staff?"

Palin tried to look away from his uncle. Though the laboratory was chill, he was sweating beneath his robes. Raistlin held him tightly, however, forcing the young man to look into the golden, glittering eyes.

And there see a reflection of himself. . . . Was what he said true? Palin stared at the image in the archmage's eyes. He saw a young man, dressed in robes whose color was indeterminate, now white, now red, now darkening. . . .

The arm Raistlin held jerked spasmodically within the archmage's grasp.

He can feel my fear, Palin realized, trying to control the tremors that shook his body.

Is it fear? the golden eyes asked. Is it fear? Or exultation?

Palin saw the staff he held in his hand reflected in those eyes. He stood within the pool of its bright light. The longer he held the staff, the more he could sense the magic within it—and within himself. The golden eyes shifted in their gaze slightly, and Palin followed them. He saw the black-bound spellbooks standing upon the shelf. He felt once again the thrill he had experienced upon entering the laboratory, and he licked his dry, parched lips like a man who had been wandering long in a vast desert and who had, at last, found the cool water to ease his burning thirst. Looking back at Raistlin, he saw himself as in a mirror, standing before the archmage dressed in black robes.

"What—what are your plans?" Palin asked hoarsely.

"Very simple. As I said, I had long years to consider my mistake. My ambition was too great. I dared become a god—something mortals are not meant to do—as I was painfully reminded every morning when the Dark Queen's talon ripped my flesh."

Palin saw the thin lip curl for a moment and the golden eyes glint. The slender hand clenched in anger and remembered agony, its grip tightening painfully around the young man's arm. "I learned my lesson," Raistlin said bitterly, drawing a rasping, shuddering breath. "I have trimmed my ambition. No longer will I strive to be a god. I will be content with the world." Smiling sardonically, he patted Palin's hand. "We will be content with the world, I should say."

"I—" The words caught in Palin's throat. He was dazed with confusion and fear and a wild rush of excitement. Glancing back at the portal, however, he felt the shadow cover his heart. "But, the queen? Shouldn't we shut it?"

Raistlin shook his head. "No, apprentice."

"No?" Palin looked at him in alarm.

"No. This will be my gift to her, to prove my loyalty—admittance to the world. And the world will be her gift to me. Here she will rule and I . . . I will serve." Raistlin bit the words with his sharp teeth, his lips parted in a tight, mirthless grin. Sensing the hatred and the anger surging through the frail body, Palin shuddered.

Raistlin glanced at him. "Squeamish, Nephew?" He sneered, letting loose of Palin's arm. "The squeamish do not rise to power—"

"You told me to speak the truth," Palin said, shrinking away from Raistlin, relieved that the burning touch was gone, yet longing—somehow—to gain it back. "And I will. I'm frightened! For us both! I know I am weak—" He bowed his head.

"No, Nephew," said Raistlin softly, "not weak, just young. And you will always be afraid. I will teach you to master your fear, to use its strength. To make it serve you, not the other way around."

Looking up, Palin saw a gentleness in the archmage's face, a gentleness few in the world had ever seen. The image of the young man in the black robes faded from the glittering, golden eyes, replaced by a yearning, a hunger for love. Now it was Palin who reached out and clasped hold of Raistlin's hand. "Close the portal, Uncle!" the young man pleaded. "Come home and live with us! The room my father built for you is still there, in the inn. My mother has kept the plaque with the wizard's mark on it! It is hidden in a chest of rosewood, but I've seen it. I've held it and dreamt of this so often! Come home! Teach me what you know! I would honor you, revere you! We could travel, as you said. Show me the wonders your eyes have seen. . . ."

"Home." The word lingered on Raistlin's lips as though he were tasting it. "Home. How often I dreamt of it"—his golden-eyed gaze went to the wall, shining with its ghastly light—"especially with the coming of dawn. . . ."

Then, glancing at Palin from within the shadows of his hood, Raistlin smiled. "Yes, Nephew," he said softly. "I believe I will come home with you. I need time to rest, to recover my strength, to rid myself of . . . old dreams." Palin saw the eyes darken with remembered pain.

Coughing, Raistlin motioned the young man to help him. Carefully, Palin leaned the staff against the wall and assisted Raistlin to the chair. Sinking into it weakly, Raistlin gestured for the young man to pour him another glass of wine. The archmage leaned his head back wearily into the cushions. "I need time . . ." he continued, moistening his lips with the wine. "Time to train you, my apprentice. Time to train you . . . and to train your brothers."

"My brothers?" Palin repeated in astonishment.

"Why, yes, young one." Amusement tinged Raistlin's voice as he looked at the young man standing by his chair. "I need generals for my legions. Your brothers will be ideal—"

"Legions!" Palin cried. "No, that's not what I meant! You must come live at home with us in peace. You've earned it! You sacrificed yourself for the world—"

"*I?*" Raistlin interrupted. "I sacrificed myself for the world?" The archmage began to laugh—dreadful, fearful laughter that set the shadows of the laboratory dancing in delight like dervishes. "Is that what they say of me?" Raistlin laughed until he choked. A coughing fit seized him, this one worse than the others.

Palin watched helplessly as his uncle writhed in pain. The young man could still hear that mocking laughter dinning in his ears. When the spasm passed, and he could breathe, Raistlin lifted his head and, with a weak motion of his hand, beckoned Palin near.

Palin saw blood upon the cloth in his uncle's hand and upon Raistlin's ashen lips. Loathing and horror came over the young man, but he drew nearer anyway, compelled by a terrible fascination to kneel beside his uncle.

"Know this, Palin!" Raistlin whispered, speaking with an effort, his words barely audible. "I sacrificed . . . *myself* . . . for . . . *myself!*" Sinking back into his chair, he gasped for breath. When he could move, he reached out a shaking, bloodstained hand and caught hold of Palin's white robes. "I saw . . . what I must . . . become . . . if I succeeded. *Nothing!* That . . . was . . . all. Dwindle . . . to . . . nothing. The world . . . dead. . . . This way"—his hand gestured feebly at the wall, the gruesome pool beneath it; his eyes gleamed feverishly—"there was . . . still . . . a chance . . . for me . . . to return . . . ."

"No!" Palin cried, struggling to free himself from Raistlin's grasp. "I don't believe you!"

"Why not?" Raistlin shrugged. His voice grew stronger. "You told them yourself. Don't you remember, Palin? 'A man must put the magic first, the world second. . . .' That's what you said to them in the tower. The world doesn't matter to you any more than it does to me! Nothing matters—your brothers, your father! The magic! The power! That's all that means anything to either of us!"

"I don't know!" Palin cried brokenly, his hands clawing at Raistlin's. "I can't think! Let me go! Let me go. . . ." His fingers fell nervelessly from Raistlin's wrists, his head sank into his hands. Tears filled his eyes.

"Poor young one," Raistlin said. Laying his hand on Palin's head, he drew it gently into his lap and stroked the auburn hair soothingly.

Wracking sobs tore at Palin's body. He was bereft, alone. Lies, all lies! Everyone had lied to him—his father, the mages, the world! What did it matter, after all? The magic. That was all he had. His uncle was right. The burning touch of those slender fingers; the soft black velvet, wet with his tears, beneath his cheek; the smell of rose petals and spice. . . .That would be his life. . . . That and this bitter emptiness within, an emptiness that all the world could not fill . . . .

"Weep, Palin," Raistlin said softly. "Weep as I wept once, long, long ago. Then you will realize, as I did, that it does no good. No one hears you, sobbing in the night alone."

Palin lifted his tearstained face suddenly, staring into Raistlin's eyes.

"At last you understand." Raistlin smiled. His hand stroked back the wet hair from Palin's eyes. "Get hold of yourself, young one. It is time for us to go, before the Dark Queen comes. There is much to be done—"

Palin regarded Raistlin calmly, though the young man's body still shuddered from his sobs, and he could see his uncle only through a blur of tears. "Yes," he said. "At last I understand. Too late, it seems. But I understand. And you are wrong, Uncle," he murmured brokenly. "Someone *did* hear you crying in the night. My father."

Rising to his feet, Palin brushed his hand across his eyes, keeping his gaze steadfastly on his uncle. "I am going to close the portal."

"Don't be a fool!" Raistlin said with a sneer. "I won't let you! You know that!"

"I know," said Palin, drawing a shivering breath. "You will stop me—"

"I will kill you!"

"You will . . . kill me. . . ." Palin continued, his voice faltering only slightly. Turning around, he reached out for the Staff of Magius, which stood against the desk beside Raistlin's chair. The light of the crystal beamed white and cold as his hand closed over it.

"What a waste!" Raistlin hissed, twisting out of his chair. "Why die in such a meaningless gesture? For it will be meaningless, I assure you, my dear nephew. I will do all I planned. The world will be mine! You will be dead—and who will know or care?"

"You will," said Palin in a low voice.

Turning his back on his uncle, Palin walked with firm, steady steps to stand before the portal. The shadow was deeper and darker, making the wall within the Abyss stand out by hideous contrast. Palin could feel the evil now, feel it seeping through the portal like water flowing into a wrecked ship. He thought of the Dark Queen, able to enter the world at last. Once more, the flames of war would sweep across the land as the forces of good rose to stop her. He saw his father and mother die by his uncle's hand, his brothers fall victim to their uncle's magic. He saw them dressed in dragon scale armor, riding evil dragons into battle, leading troops of hideous beings spawned of darkness.

No! With the help of the gods, he would stop this if he could. But, raising the staff, Palin realized helplessly that he hadn't the vaguest idea how to close the portal. He could sense the power in the staff, but he could not control it. Raistlin was right—what a stupid, meaningless gesture.

Behind him, Palin heard his uncle laugh. It wasn't mocking laughter this time, however. It was bemused, almost angry.

"This is senseless, Palin! Stop! Don't make me do this!"

Drawing a deep breath, Palin tried to concentrate his energy and his thoughts upon the staff. "Close the portal," he whispered, forcing himself to think about nothing else, though his body quivered with fear. It was not a fear of dying, he could tell himself that with quiet pride. He loved life, never so much as now, he realized. But he could leave it without regret, though the thought of the grief that his death would cause those who loved him filled him with sorrow. His mother and father would know what he had done, however. They would understand, no matter what his uncle said.

And they'll fight you, Palin knew. They will fight you and your Dark Queen as they fought once before. You will not win.

Palin gripped the staff, his hand sweating, his body trembling. He wasn't afraid of dying. He was afraid of . . . of the pain.

Would it hurt . . . very much . . . to die?

Shaking his head angrily, the young man cursed himself for a coward and stared hard at the portal. He had to concentrate! To put death out of his mind. He must make fear serve him! Not master him. There was a chance, after all, that he might close the portal before his uncle . . . before . . .

"Paladine, help me," said Palin, his gaze going to the silvery light gleaming atop the staff with steadfast, unwavering brilliance in the shadowy darkness.

"Palin!" Raistlin shouted harshly. "I warn you—"

Lightning crackled from Raistlin's fingertips. But Palin kept his eyes upon the staff. Its light grew brighter, shining with a radiance whose beauty and clarity eased Palin's last fears.

"Paladine," he murmured.

The name of the god mercifully obliterated the sound of magical chanting Palin heard rising behind him.

The pain was swift, sudden . . . and soon over.

Chapter Ten

Raistlin stood alone in the laboratory, leaning upon the Staff of Magius. The light of the staff had gone out. The archmage stood in darkness as thick as the dust that lay, undisturbed, upon the stone floor, upon the spellbooks, upon the chair, upon the drawn, heavy curtain of purple velvet.

Almost as deep as the darkness was the silence of the place.

Raistlin stilled his breathing, listening to the silence. The sound of no living being disturbed it—neither mouse nor bat nor spider—for no living being dared enter the laboratory, guarded by those whose vigilance would last unto the end of the world and beyond. Almost Raistlin thought he could hear one sound—the sound of the dust falling, the sound of time passing. . . .

Sighing wearily, the archmage raised his head and looked into the darkness, broke the ages-long silence. "I have done what you wanted of me," he cried. "Are you satisfied?"

There was no answer, only the gently sifting dust drifting down into the perpetual night.

"No," Raistlin murmured. "You cannot hear me. And that is just as well. Little did you think, Dalamar, that when you conjured my illusion for this purpose, you would conjure *me*! Oh, no, apprentice"—Raistlin smiled bitterly—"do not pride yourself. You are good, but not that good. It was not your magic that woke me from my long sleep. No, it was something else. . . ." He paused, trying to remember. "What did I tell the young man?

'A shadow on my mind'? Yes, that's what it was.

"Ah, Dalamar, you are lucky." The archmage shook his hooded head. For a brief moment, the darkness was lit by a fierce glint in the golden eyes, gleaming with their inner flame. "If he had been what I was, you would have found yourself in sad straits, dark elf. Through him, I could have returned. But as his compassion and his love freed me from the darkness into which I cast myself, so it binds me there still."

The light of the golden eyes faded as the darkness returned.

Raistlin sighed. "But that is all right," he whispered, leaning his head against the staff that supported him. "I am tired, so very tired. I want to return to my sleep." Walking across the stone floor, his black robes rustling about his ankles, his soft, unheard footsteps leaving no trail at all in the thick dust, the archmage came to stand before the velvet curtain. Placing his hand on it, he stopped and looked around the laboratory that he could not see except in his memories, in his mind.

"I just want you to know," Raistlin cried, "that I didn't do this for you, mages! I didn't do it for the conclave. I didn't do it for my brother! I had one more debt to pay in my lifetime. Now I have discharged it. I can sleep in peace."

In the darkness, Raistlin could not see the staff he leaned upon, but he didn't need to. He knew every curve of the wood, every tiny imperfection in the grain. Lovingly he caressed it, his delicate fingers touching the golden dragon's claw, running over each facet of the cold, dark crystal it held. Raistlin's eyes stared into the darkness, stared into the future he could glimpse by the light of the black moon.

"He will be great in the Art," he said with quiet pride. "The greatest that has yet lived. He will bring honor and renown to our profession. Because of him, magic will live and flourish in the world." The archmage's voice lowered. "Whatever happiness and joy was in my life, Palin, came from the magic.

"To the magic, I give you. . . ."

Raistlin held the staff an instant longer, pressing the smooth wood against his cheek. Then, with a word of command, he sent it from him. It vanished, swallowed up by the endless night. His head bowed in weariness, Raistlin laid his hand upon the velvet curtain and sank again into sleep, becoming one with the darkness and the silence and the dust.

Chapter Eleven

Palin came slowly to consciousness. His first reaction was one of terror. The fiery jolt that had burned and blasted his body had not killed him! There would be another. Raistlin would not let him live. Moaning, Palin huddled against the cold stone floor, waiting fearfully to hear the sound of magical chanting, to hear the crackle of sparks from those thin fingertips, to feel once again the searing, exploding pain. . . .

All was quiet. Listening intently, holding his breath, his body shivering in fear, Palin heard no sound.

Cautiously, he opened his eyes. He was in darkness, such deep darkness that nothing whatever was visible, not even his own body.

"Raistlin?" Palin whispered, raising his head cautiously from the damp stone floor. "Uncle?"

"Palin!" a voice shouted.

Palin's heart stilled in fear. He could not breathe.

"Palin!" the voice shouted again, a voice filled with love and anguish.

Palin gasped in relief and, falling back against the stone floor, sobbed in joy.

He heard booted footsteps clambering up stairs. Torchlight lit the darkness. The footsteps halted, and the torchlight wavered as though the hand holding it shook. Then the footsteps were running, the torchlight burned above him.

"Palin! My son!" and Palin was in his father's arms.

"What have they done to you?" Caramon cried in a choked voice as he lifted his son's body from the floor and cradled it against his strong breast.

Palin could not speak. He leaned his head against his father's chest, hearing the heart beating rapidly from the exertion of climbing the tower stairs, smelling the familiar smells of leather and sweat, letting—for one last moment—his father's arms shelter and protect him. Then, with a soft sigh, Palin raised his head and looked into his father's pale, anguished face.

"Nothing, Father," he said softly, gently pushing himself away. "I'm all right. Truly." Sitting up, he looked around, confused. "But where are we?"

"Out—outside that . . . that place," Caramon growled. He let go of his son, but watched him dubiously, anxiously.

"The laboratory," murmured Palin, puzzled, his gaze going to the closed door and the two, white, disembodied eyes that hovered before it.

The young man started to stand.

"Careful!" said Caramon, putting his arm around his son again.

"I told you, Father. I'm all right," Palin said firmly, shaking off his father's help and getting to his feet without assistance. "What happened?" He looked at the sealed laboratory door.

The two eyes of the specter stared back at him unblinking, unmoving.

"You went in . . . there," Caramon said, his brow creasing into a frown as his gaze shifted to the sealed door as well. "And . . . the door slammed shut! I tried to get in . . . Dalamar cast some sort of spell on it, but it wouldn't open. Then more of those . . . those *things*"—he gestured at the eyes with a scowl—"came and I . . . I don't remember much after that. When I came to, I was with Dalamar in the study. . . ."

"Which is where we will return now," said a voice behind them, "if you will honor me by sharing my breakfast."

"The only place we're going now," said Caramon in a stern, low voice as he turned to face the dark elf, who had materialized behind them, "is home.

And no more magic!" he snarled, glaring at Dalamar. "We'll walk, if need be. Neither my son nor I are ever coming back to one of these cursed towers again—"

Without a glance at Caramon, Dalamar walked past the big man to Palin, who was standing silently next to his father, his hands folded in the sleeves of his white robes, his eyes downcast as was proper in the presence of the high-ranking wizard.

Dalamar reached out his hands and clasped the young man by the shoulders.

"*Quithain, Magus,*" the dark elf said with a smile, leaning forward to kiss Palin on the cheek as was the elven custom.

Palin stared at him in confusion, his face flushed. The words the elf had spoken tumbled about in his mind, making little sense. He spoke some Elvish, learned from his father's friend, Tanis. But, after all that had happened to him, the language went right out of his head. Frantically, he struggled to remember, for Dalamar was standing in front of him, looking at him, grinning.

"*Quithain . . .*" Palin repeated to himself. "Means . . . congratulations. Congratulations, *Magus* . . ."

He gasped, staring at Dalamar in disbelief.

"What does it mean?" demanded Caramon, glaring at the dark elf. "I don't understand—"

"He is one of us now, Caramon," said Dalamar quietly, taking hold of Palin's arm and escorting him past his father. "His trials are over. He has completed the Test."

"We are sorry to have put you through this again, Caramon," Dalamar said to the big warrior.

Seated opposite the ornately carved desk in the dark elf's luxuriously appointed study, Caramon flushed, his brow still lined with the signs of his concern and fear and anger.

"But," Dalamar continued, "it was fast becoming apparent to all of us that you would do your best to prevent your son from taking the Test."

"Can you blame me?" Caramon asked harshly. Rising to his feet, he walked over to the large window and stared out into the dark shadows of the Shoikan Grove below him.

"No," said Dalamar, "we could not blame you. And so we devised this way of tricking you into it."

Scowling angrily, Caramon turned, jabbing his finger at Dalamar. "You had no right! He's too young! He might have died!"

"True," said Dalamar softly, "but that is a risk we all face. It is a risk you take every time you send your older sons to battle. . . ."

"This is different." Caramon turned away, his face dark.

Dalamar's gaze went to Palin, who sat in a chair, a glass of untasted wine in his hand. The young mage was staring dazedly around as though he could still not believe what had occurred.

"Because of Raistlin?" Dalamar smiled. "Palin is truly gifted, Caramon, as gifted as his uncle. For him, as for Raistlin, there could have been only one choice—his magic. But Palin's love for his family is strong. He would have made the choice, and it would have broken his heart."

Caramon bowed his head, clasping his hands behind him.

Palin, hearing a muffled choke behind him, set his wine glass down and, rising to his feet, walked over to stand beside his father.

Reaching out his hand, Caramon drew his son close. "Dalamar's right," the big man said huskily. "I only wanted what was best for you and—and I was afraid . . . afraid I might lose you to the magic as I lost him. . . . I—I'm sorry, Palin. Forgive me."

Palin's answer was to embrace his father, who wrapped both his great arms around the white-robed mage and hugged him tight.

"So you passed! I'm proud of you, Son!" Caramon whispered. "So proud—"

"Thank you, Father!" Palin said brokenly. "There is nothing to forgive. I understand at last—" The rest of the young mage's words were squeezed from him by his father's hug. Then, with a clap on the back, Caramon let his boy go and returned to staring out the window, frowning down at the Shoikan Grove.

Turning back to Dalamar, Palin looked at the dark elf, puzzled.

"The Test," he said hesitantly. "It—it all seems so real! Yet, I'm here. . . . Raistlin didn't kill me . . ."

"Raistlin!" Caramon glanced around in alarm, his face pale.

"Be at ease, my friend," Dalamar said, raising his slender hand. "The Test varies for each person who takes it, Palin. For some, it is very real and can have real and disastrous consequences. Your uncle, for example, barely survived an encounter with one of my kind. Justarius's test left him crippled in one leg. But, for others, the Test is only in the mind." Dalamar's face grew tense, his voice quivered in remembered pain. "That, too, can have its effects, sometimes worse than the others . . ."

"So—it was all in my mind. I didn't go into the Abyss? My uncle wasn't really there?"

"No, Palin," Dalamar said, regaining his composure. "Raistlin is dead. We have no reason to believe otherwise, despite what we told you. We do not know for certain, of course, but we believe that the vision your father described is a true one, given to him by Paladine to ease his grief. When we told you we had signs that Raistlin was still alive, that was all part of the ruse to bring you here. There have been no such signs. If Raistlin lives today, it is only in our legends. . . ."

"And our memories," Caramon muttered from the window.

"But he seemed so real!" Palin protested. He could feel the soft black velvet beneath his fingertips; the burning touch of the golden-skinned hands; the cool, smooth wood of the Staff of Magius. He could hear the whispering voice, see the golden, hourglass eyes, smell the rose petals, the spice, the blood. . . .

Lowering his head, he shivered.

"I know," said Dalamar with a soft sigh. "But it was only illusion. The Guardian stands before the door, which is still sealed. It will be, for all eternity. You never even went inside the laboratory, much less the Abyss."

"But I saw him enter—" Caramon protested.

"All part of the illusion. I alone saw through it. I helped create it, in fact. It was designed to be very real to you, Palin. You will never forget it. The Test is meant not only to judge your skill as a magic-user but, more importantly, to teach you something about yourself. You had two things to discover—the truth about your uncle, and the truth about yourself."

Know the truth about yourself . . . Raistlin's voice echoed.

Palin smoothed the fabric of his white robes with his hands. "I know now where my loyalties lie," he said softly, remembering that bitter moment standing before the portal. "As the sea wizard said, I will serve the world and, in so doing, serve myself."

Smiling, Dalamar rose to his feet. "And now, I know you are eager to return to your home and your family, young mage. I will detain you no longer. I almost regret that you did not make another choice, Palin," the dark elf said with a shrug. "I would have enjoyed having you as my apprentice. But you will make a worthy adversary. I am honored to have been a part of your success." Dalamar extended his hand.

"Thank you," said Palin, flushing. Taking Dalamar's hand in his, he clasped it gratefully. "Thank you . . . for everything."

"Yeah," mumbled Caramon, leaving the window to come stand beside his son. He, too, gripped Dalamar's hand in his, the elf's slender fingers completely engulfed in the big man's grip. "I—I guess I will let you use . . . that magic of yours . . . to send us back to Solace. Tika'll be worried sick—"

"Very well," Dalamar said, exchanging smiles with Palin. "Stand close together. Farewell, Palin. I will see you at the Tower of Wayreth."

There came a soft knock upon the door.

Dalamar frowned. "What is it?" he asked irritably. "I gave instructions that we were not to be disturbed!"

The door opened by itself, apparently. Two white eyes gleamed from out of the darkness. "Forgive me, master," said the specter, "but I have been instructed to give the young mage a parting gift."

"Instructed? By whom?" Dalamar's eyes flashed. "Justarius? Has he dared set foot in my tower without my permission—"

"No, master," said the specter, floating into the room. The chill gaze went to Palin. Slowly the specter approached the young mage, its fleshless hand outstretched. Caramon moved swiftly to stand in front of his son.

"No, Father," said Palin firmly, putting a restraining hand on his father's sword arm. "Stand aside. It means me no harm. What is it you have for me?" the young mage asked the specter, who came to a halt only inches from him.

In answer, the fleshless hand traced an arcane symbol in the air. The Staff of Magius appeared, held fast in the skeletal fingers.

Caramon gasped and took a step backward. Dalamar regarded the specter coldly. "You have failed in your duties!" The dark elf's voice rose in anger. "By our Dark Queen, I will send you to the eternal torment of the Abyss for this!"

"I have not failed in my duty," the Guardian replied, its hollow tone reminding Palin fearfully of the realm he had entered—if only in illusion. "The door to the laboratory remains locked and spellbound. The key is here, as you can see." The Guardian held out its other hand, showing a silver key lying in the bony palm. "All is as it was, undisturbed. No living being has entered."

"Then who—" Dalamar began in fury. Suddenly, his voice dropped, and his face went ashen. "No living being . . ." Shaken, the dark elf sank back into his seat, staring at the staff with wide eyes.

"This is yours, Palin, as was promised," the specter said, handing the staff to the young mage.

Reaching out, Palin took hold of the staff with a shaking hand. At his touch, the crystal on the top flared into light, blazing with a cool, clear radiance, filling the dark room with a bright, silvery light.

"A gift from the true Master of the Tower. With it," the specter added in its chill tones, "goes his blessing."

The white eyes lowered in reverence, then they were gone.

Holding the staff in his hand, Palin looked wonderingly at his father.

Blinking rapidly, Caramon smiled through his tears. "Let's go home," he said quietly, putting his arm around his son.

]]]

The mythologists tell you
how the journey takes place
in a landscape of spirit.
But there is also a highway,
dusty and palpable,
and washed-out bridges
that harbor a navy of trolls,
overpriced inns full of vermin,
and signposts half twisted
by vandals and travelers
searching for something to do.

This is the road
out of which the myth rises
when suddenly bridges
most suspect and ramshackle
waver and gable with light.
It is then you are saying
this must be the answer
the crossroad is more than a crossroad
the wayside numinous
littered with symbols.

That is the story
when the bridge collapses,
when your abstracted ankle
twists in the rutted road.
It is the tale
that the trolls choose always,
for the danger of myth
is in too much meaning.

Sometimes the stars
or the steepled cloud
is sufficient in gas or vapor,
the road is dust
leading out of belief
and the markers are stone upon stone.

It is then, in the fundamental time,
your travel lies waiting before you.
It is the long house
of all mythology,
what they cannot explain
nor explain away.
It is where journeys begin.

"Wanna Bet?"

forward

(Or Afterword, As The Case May Be)

"A fine mage you are," muttered Tanin, standing on the dock, watching the ship sail away. "You should have known all along there was something strange about that dwarf!"

"Me?" Palin retorted. "*You* were the one that got us mixed up in the whole thing to begin with! 'Adventures always start in such places as this,' " the young magic-user said, mimicking his older brother's voice.

"Hey, guys," began Sturm in mollifying tones.

"Oh, shut up!" Both brothers turned to face him. "It was *you* who took that stupid bet!"

The three brothers stood glaring at each other, the salt breeze blowing the red curling hair of the two eldest into their eyes and whipping the white robes of the youngest about his thin legs.

A ringing shout, sounding over the dancing waters, interrupted them.

"Farewell, lads! Farewell! It was a nice try. Perhaps we'll do it again someday!"

"Over my dead body!" All three brothers muttered fervently, raising their hands and waving halfheartedly, sickly grins on their faces.

"That's *one* thing we can all agree on," said Sturm, beginning to chuckle. "And I know another." The brothers turned thankfully away from the sight of the sailing vessel lumbering through the waters.

"And that is . . . ?"

"That we never tell another living soul about this, as long as we live!" Sturm's voice was low. The other two brothers glanced about at the spectators standing on the docks. They were looking at the ship, laughing. Several, glancing at the brothers, pointed at them with stifled giggles.

Grinning ruefully, Tanin held his right hand out in front of him. Sturm placed his right hand on his brother's, and Palin put his right hand over the other two.

"Agreed," each said solemnly.

Chapter One

Dougan Redhammer

"Adventures always start in such places as this," said Tanin, regarding the inn with a satisfied air.

"You can't be serious!" Palin said, horrified. "I wouldn't stable my horse in this filthy place, let alone stay here myself!"

"Actually," reported Sturm, rounding the corner of the building after an inspection tour, "the stables are clean compared to the inn, and they smell a damn sight better. I say we sleep there and send the horses inside."

The inn, located on the docks of the seaside town of Sancrist, was every bit as mean and ill-favored in appearance as those few patrons the young men saw slouching into it. The windows facing the docks were small, as though staring out to sea too long had given them a perpetual squint. Light from inside could barely filter through the dirt. The building itself was weather- and sand-blasted and crouched in the shadows at the end of the alley like a cutpurse waiting for his next victim. Even the name, *The Spliced Jib*, had an ominous sound.

"I expected Little Brother to complain," Tanin remarked sourly, dismounting and glaring at Sturm over the pommel of his saddle. "He misses his white linen sheets and Mama tucking him in at night. But I expected better of you, Sturm Majere."

"Oh, I've no objection," Sturm said easily, sliding off his horse and beginning to untie his pack. "I was just making an observation. We don't have much choice anyway," he added, withdrawing a small leather pouch and shaking it. Where there should have been the ring of steel coins, there was only a dismal clunk. "No linen sheets tonight, Palin," he said, grinning at his younger brother, who remained seated disconsolately upon his horse. "Think of tomorrow night, though—staying at Castle Uth Wistan, the guests of Lord Gunthar. Not only white linen but probably rose petals strewn about the bed as well."

"I don't expect white linen," Palin returned, nettled. "In fact, bed sheets at all would be a pleasant change! And I'd prefer sleeping in a bed where the mattress wasn't alive!" Irritably, he scratched himself under the white robes.

"A warrior must get used to such things," Tanin said in his worldly-wise Elder Brother voice, which made Palin long to toss him in the horse trough. "If you are attacked by nothing worse than bedbugs on your first quest, you may count yourself lucky."

"Quest?" Palin muttered bitterly, sliding down off his horse. "Accompanying you and Sturm to Castle Uth Wistan so that you can join the knighthood. This isn't a quest! It's been like a kender outing, and both you and Father knew it would be when you decided I could go! Why, the most danger we've been in since we left home was from that serving wench who tried to cut off Sturm's ears with a butcher knife!"

"It was a mistake anyone could make," Sturm muttered, flushing. "I keep telling you!—I intended to grab her mugs. She was what you might call a buxom girl and when she leaned over me holding the tray, I wasn't exactly paying attention to what I was doing—"

"Oh, you were paying attention, all right!" Palin said grimly. "Even when she came at you with a knife, we had to drag you out of there! And your eyes were the size of your shield."

"Well, at least I'm interested in such things," Sturm said irritably. "Not like some people I could mention, who seem to think themselves too good—"

"I have high standards!" retorted Palin. "I don't tumble for every 'buxom' blonde who jiggles in my direction—"

"Stop it, both of you!" Tanin ordered tiredly. "Sturm, take the horses around and see that they're brushed down and fed. Palin, come with me."

Palin and Sturm both looked rebellious, and Tanin's tone grew stern. "Remember what Father said."

The brothers remembered. Sturm, still grumbling, grabbed the horses' reins in his hand and led them to the stables. Palin swallowed a barbed comment and followed his brother.

Although quick-tempered like his mother, Tanin appeared to have inherited few other qualities from his parents. Instead, he was in temperament more like the man in whose honor he had been named—his parents' dearest friend, Tanis Half-Elven. Tanin idolized his name-father and did his best to emulate his hero. Consequently, the twenty-four-year-old young man took his role as leader and eldest brother quite seriously. This was fine with one younger brother. The fun-loving Sturm was almost the epitome of his father, having inherited Caramon's jovial, easygoing nature.

Disliking to take responsibility himself, Sturm generally obeyed Tanin without question. But Palin, just twenty-one, possessed the keen mind and intellect of his uncle, the powerful, tragic archmage Raistlin. Palin loved his brothers, but he chafed under what he considered Tanin's overbearing leadership and was irritated beyond measure by Sturm's less than serious outlook on life.

This was, however, Palin's "first quest"—as Tanin never failed to remind him at least once an hour. A month had gone by since the young mage had taken the grueling Test in the Tower of High Sorcery in Palanthas. He was now an accepted member of the order of wizards on Krynn. But somehow that didn't satisfy him. He felt let down and depressed. For years, his greatest goal had been passing the Test, a goal that, once attained, would open countless doors.

It hadn't opened one. Oh, admittedly Palin was a young mage. He had little power yet, being able to cast only minor spells. Ideally, he would apprentice himself to some skilled archmage, who would take over his tutelage. But no archmage had requested his services, and Palin was shrewd enough to know why.

His uncle, Raistlin, had been the greatest wizard ever to have lived. He had taken the Black Robes of evil and challenged the Queen of Darkness herself, intending to rule the world—an attempt that ended in his death. Though Palin wore the White Robes of good, he knew that there were those in the order who did not trust him and who, perhaps, never would. He carried his uncle's staff—the powerful Staff of Magius, given to him under mysterious circumstances in the Tower of High Sorcery at Palanthas. Rumors were already buzzing among the conclave as to how Palin could have acquired the staff. It had, after all, been locked in a room sealed with a powerful curse. No, whatever he accomplished, Palin knew deep within himself, he would accomplish as his uncle had—studying, working, and fighting alone.

But that was in the future. For the time being, he supposed, he must be content to travel with his brothers. His father, Caramon, who, with his own twin brother, Raistlin, had been a hero in the War of the Lance, was adamant on that point. Palin had never been out in the world. He'd been sheltered by his books, immersed in his studies. If he went on this journey to Sancrist, he was to submit to Tanin's authority, placing himself under his brothers' guidance and protection.

Palin swore a sacred oath to his father to obey his brothers, just as Tanin and Sturm swore to protect him. In point of fact, their deep love and affection for each other made the oath superfluous—as Caramon knew. But the big man was also wise enough to know that this first outing together would put a strain on brotherly love. Palin, the most intelligent of the brothers, was eager to prove himself—eager to the point of foolhardiness.

"Palin has to learn the worth of other people, to respect them for what they know, even if they're not as quick-thinking as he is," Caramon said to Tika, remembering with regret the twin who had never learned that lesson. "And Sturm and Tanin have to learn to respect him, to realize that they can't solve every problem with a whack of their swords. Above all, they've got to learn to depend on each other!" The big man shook his head. "May the gods go with them."

He was never to know the irony of that prayer.

It appeared, at the beginning of the journey, that none of these lessons was going to be learned easily. The two older boys had decided privately (certainly not mentioning this to their father) that this trip was going to "make a man" of their scholarly sibling.

But their views as to what constituted "manhood" didn't accord with Palin's. In fact, as far as he could see, "being a man" meant living with fleas, bad food, worse ale, and women of dubious character—something Palin considered pointing out when Tanin muttered, "Act like a man!" out of the corner of his mouth as he and Palin entered the inn.

But Palin kept his mouth shut. He and his brothers were entering a strange inn, located in what was reputedly a rough part of Sancrist. The young mage had learned enough to know that their very lives might depend on presenting a unified front to the world.

This the brothers, despite their differences, managed quite successfully. So successfully, in fact, that they had met with no trouble whatsoever on the long trip northward from Solace. The oldest two brothers were big and brawny, having inherited Caramon's girth and strength. Experienced campaigners, they bore their battle scars proudly, and wore their swords with practiced ease. The youngest, Palin, was tall and well built, but had the slender body of one accustomed to studying rather than to wielding weapons. Any who might consider him an easy mark, however, could look into the young man's handsome, serious face, note the intense, penetrating gaze of the clear eyes, and think twice about interfering with him.

The Staff of Magius that Palin carried might have had something to do with this as well. Made of plain wood, adorned with a faceted crystal held fast in a dragon's claw made of gold, the staff gave no outward, visible sign of being magical. But there was a dark, unseen aura around it, perhaps associated with its late master, that viewers invariably perceived with a sense of uneasiness.

Palin kept the staff near him always. If he wasn't holding it, the staff rested near him, and he often reached out to touch it reassuringly.

This night, as on other nights, the sight of Tanin and Palin entering the inn did not particularly impress those within, except for one party. Seated at a grubby booth in a corner, this group immediately began to jabber among themselves, whispering and pointing. The whispering increased, growing even more excited, when Sturm came in and joined his brothers. Several members of the group nudged a person who was sitting nearest the wall, his face hidden in deep shadows.

"Aye, I see, I see!" grumbled the man. "You think they'll do, do you?"

The others at the table nodded and chattered among themselves enthusiastically. Smaller than the man in the shadows, they were just as hidden. Muffled to the eyebrows in brown robes, their features and even their hands and feet were indistinguishable.

The person in the corner gave the young men a shrewd, appraising scrutiny. The brown-robed creatures continued to jabber. "Shut up, you buggers," the man growled irritably. "You'll attract their notice."

Those in the brown robes immediately hushed, falling into a silence so deep they might have all tumbled into a well. Naturally, this startling silence caused everyone in the common room of the inn to turn and stare at them, including the three young men.

"Now you've done it!" snarled the man from the shadows. Two of the brown-robed creatures hung their heads, though a third seemed inclined to argue. "Be quiet! I'll handle this!"

Leaning forward into the light, he gave the three young men an amiable smile from the depths of a full, glossy black beard and, raising his mug, said cheerfully, "Dougan Redhammer, at your service, young gents. Will you take a drink with an old dwarf?"

"That we will, and with pleasure," Tanin said politely.

"Let me out," grunted the dwarf to the brown-robed creatures, who were so packed into the booth it was impossible to tell how many of them there might have been. With much groaning and swearing and "ouch, that's my foot, you widget brain" and "mind my beard, gear-head," the dwarf emerged—somewhat flushed and panting—from the back of the booth. Carrying his mug and calling for the innkeep to bring "my private stock," Dougan approached the table where the young men had taken seats.

The others in the inn, sailors and local residents for the most part, returned to their own conversations—the subjects of which appeared to Palin to be of a sinister nature, judging from the grim and ill-favored expressions on their faces. They had not welcomed the brothers nor did they seem interested in either the dwarf or his companions. Several cast scowling glances at Dougan Redhammer. This didn't disconcert the dwarf in the least. Pulling up a high stool that compensated for his short stature, the stout and flashily dressed (at least for a dwarf) Dougan plopped himself down at the brothers' table.

"What'll you have, gentlemen?" asked the dwarf. "The spirits of my people? Ah, you're men of taste! There's nothing better than the fermented mushroom brew of Thorbardin."

Dougan grinned at the brothers expansively as the innkeeper shuffled to the table, carrying three mugs in his hand. Putting these down, he thumped a large clay bottle stoppered with a cork in front of the dwarf. Dougan pulled the cork and inhaled the fumes with a gusty sigh of contentment that caused Sturm's mouth to water in anticipation.

"Aye, that's prime," said the dwarf in satisfaction. "Hand your mugs round, gents. Don't be shy. There's plenty for all and more where this came from. I don't drink with strangers, though, so tell me your names."

"Tanin Majere, and these are my brothers, Sturm and Palin," said Tanin, sliding his mug over willingly. Sturm's was already in the dwarf's hand.

"I'll have wine, thank you," Palin said stiffly. Then he added in an undertone, "You know how Father feels about that stuff." Tanin responded with an icy glare and Sturm laughed.

"Aw, loosen up, Palin!" Sturm said. "A mug or two of dwarf spirits never hurt anyone."

"Right you are there, lad!" said Dougan roundly. " 'Tis good for what ails you, my father was wont to say. This marvelous elixir'll mend broken head or broken heart. Try it, young wizard. If your father be the Hero of the Lance, Caramon Majere, then he lifted a glass or two in his day, if all the tales I've heard about him be true!"

"I'll have wine," Palin repeated, coldly ignoring his brothers' elbow-nudging and foot-kicking.

"Probably best for the young lad," said Dougan with a wink at Tanin. "Innkeep, wine for the youngster here!"

Palin flushed in shame, but there was little he could say, realizing he'd said more than enough already. Embarrassed, he took his glass and hunched down in his white robes, unable to look around. He had the feeling that everyone in the inn was laughing at him.

"So, you've heard of our father?" Tanin asked abruptly, changing the subject.

"Who hasn't heard of Caramon Majere, Hero of the Lance?" said Dougan. "Here's to his health!" Lifting his mug, the dwarf took a long pull of the spirits, as did both Tanin and Sturm. When the three set the mugs down, there was no sound for the moment except slight gaspings for air. This was followed by three satisfied belches.

"Damn good!" said Sturm huskily, wiping his streaming eyes.

"I've never had better!" Tanin swore, drawing a deep breath.

"Drink up, lad!" said the dwarf to Palin. "You'll surely drink a toast to your own father, won't you?"

"Of course he will, won't you, Palin?" said Tanin, his voice dangerously pleasant.

Palin obediently took a sip of his wine, drinking to his father's health. After that, the others quickly ignored him, becoming absorbed in conversation about the parts of the world each had been in recently and what was transpiring where. Palin, unable to take part in the conversation, fell to studying the dwarf. Dougan was taller than most dwarves the young man had known and, although he called himself "old," he couldn't have been much over one hundred years, an age considered to be just suitably mature for a dwarf. His beard was obviously his pride and joy; he stroked it often, never failing to draw attention to it when possible. Shining black, it grew thick and luxuriant, tumbling over his chest and down past his belt. His hair, too, was as black and curly as his beard and he wore it almost as long. Like most dwarves, he was rotund and probably hadn't seen his feet below his round belly in years. Unlike most dwarves, however, Dougan was dressed in a flamboyant style that would have well become the lord of Palanthas.

Outfitted in a red velvet jacket, red velvet breeches, black stockings, black shoes with red heels, and a silk shirt with puffy sleeves—a shirt that might once have been white but was now stained with dirt, spirits, and what may have been lunch—Dougan was an astonishing sight. He was remarkable, too, in other ways. Most dwarves are somewhat surly and withdrawn around members of other races, but Dougan was jovial and talkative and altogether the most engaging stranger the brothers had come across on their travels. He, in his turn, appeared to enjoy their company.

"By Reorx," said the dwarf admiringly, watching Tanin and Sturm drain their mugs, "but you are lads after my own heart. It's a pleasure to drink with real men."

Sturm grinned. "There are not many who can keep up with us," he boasted, motioning the dwarf to pour the spirits. "So you better have a care, Dougan, and slow down."

"Slow down! Look who's talking!" The dwarf roared so loudly that all eyes in the common room turned on them, including the eyes of the small creatures in the brown robes. "Why, there isn't a human alive who can outdrink a dwarf with his own brew!"

Glancing at Sturm, Tanin winked, though he kept his face solemn. "You've just met two of them, Dougan Redhammer," he said, leaning back in his chair until it creaked beneath his weight. "We've drunk many a stout dwarf under the table and were still sober enough, Sturm and I, to guide him to his bed."

"And I," returned Dougan, clenching his fist, his face turning a fiery red beneath the black beard, "have drunk ten stout humans under the table and not only did I lead them to their beds, I put their nightclothes on them and tidied up their rooms to boot!"

"You won't do that to us!" vowed Tanin.

"Wanna bet?" roared the dwarf, with a slight slur.

"A wager, then?" cried Sturm.

"A wager!" shouted Dougan.

"Name the rules and the stakes!" Tanin said, sitting forward.

Dougan stroked his beard thoughtfully. "I'll match you lads one on one, drink for drink—"

"Ha!" Sturm burst out laughing.

"—drink for drink," continued the dwarf imperturbably, "until your beardless chins hit the floor."

"It'll be your beard and not our chins that hits the floor, dwarf," Sturm said. "What stakes?"

Dougan Redhammer pondered. "The winner has the very great satisfaction of assisting the losers to their beds," he said, after a pause, twirling a long moustache around his finger.

"And loser pays the tabs for all," added Tanin.

"Done," said the dwarf, with a grin, holding out his hand.

"Done," said Tanin and Sturm together. Each shook Dougan's hand, then the dwarf turned to Palin, his hand outstretched.

"I want no part of this!" Palin said emphatically, glaring at his brothers. "Tanin," he said in a low voice, "think of our funds. If you lose, we—"

"Little Brother," Tanin interrupted, flushing in anger, "next journey, remind me to leave you home and bring along a cleric of Paladine! We'd get preached at less and probably have more fun."

"You have no right to talk to me that way!" Palin snapped.

"Ah, it must be all three of you," Dougan interrupted, shaking his head, "or the bet's off. There's no challenge in a dwarf outdrinking two humans. And it must be dwarf spirits. Why, the lad might as well be drinking his mother's milk as that elf water!" (*Elf water*—a name dwarves use for wine, which they can't abide.)

"I won't drink that—" Palin began.

"Palin"—Tanin's voice was stern and cold—"you are shaming us! If you can't have some fun, go to your room!"

Angrily, Palin started to rise, but Sturm caught hold of the sleeve of his robes.

"Aw, come on, Palin," his brother said cheerfully. "Relax! Reorx's beard! Father's not going to walk through that door!" He tugged at Palin's sleeve until his brother slowly resumed his seat. "You've been studying too hard. Your brain's gone all cobwebby. Here, try some. That's all we ask. If you don't like it, then we won't say any more about it."

Shoving a full mug over to his brother, Sturm leaned close and whispered in Palin's ear, "Don't make Tanin mad, all right? You know how he sulks, and we'll have to put up with him from here to Lord Gunthar's. Big Brother's got your own best interests at heart. We both do. We just want to see you have a little fun, that's all. Give it a try, huh?"

Glancing at Tanin, Palin saw that his brother's face was grim and unhappy. Maybe Sturm's right, Palin thought. Maybe I should relax and have some fun. Tanin was more than half serious when he said that about leaving me home. He's never talked that way before. It's just that I've been wanting them to take me seriously, to quit treating me like a kid. Maybe I *have* gone too far. . . .

Forcing a laugh, Palin lifted the mug. "To my brothers," he said huskily, and was pleased to see Tanin's green eyes brighten and Sturm's face break into a broad grin. Putting the mug to his lips, Palin took a drink of the infamous brew known as dwarf spirits.

The taste wasn't bad. It was pleasant, in fact, a kind of dark and earthy flavor that brought visions of the dwarves' underground home of Thorbardin to his eyes. Rolling it on his tongue, Palin nodded in pleased surprise and swallowed. . . .

The young mage wondered suddenly if a fireball had exploded in his head. Flames shot through his mouth. Fire burst out his ears and nose, roared down his throat, and seared his stomach. He couldn't breathe, he couldn't see. He was going to die, he knew it . . . any moment . . . here, in this filthy, gods-forsaken tavern. . . .

Someone—Palin had the vague impression it was Sturm—was pounding him on the back and, at last, he was able to gasp for air.

"I do enjoy seeing a man enjoy his liquor," said Dougan earnestly. "My turn now. A drink to the young mage!" Putting his mug to his lips, the dwarf tilted his head back and drained it in one long swallow. When he reappeared, his eyes were watery and his large, bulbous nose bright red. "Ahhh!" he breathed, blinking back his tears and wiping his mouth with the end of his beard.

"Hear, hear," cried both Sturm and Tanin, raising their mugs. "A drink to our brother, the mage!" They, too, drained their mugs, not quite as fast as the dwarf, but without stopping for breath.

"Thank you," said Palin, deeply moved. Cautiously, he took another gulp. The effect wasn't so awful the second time. In fact, it was pleasurable. Palin took another drink, then another, and finally drained the mug. Setting it down on the table amid cheers from his brothers and Dougan, the young man felt warm and good all over. His blood tingled in his veins. Tanin was looking at him with approval and pride; Sturm was filling his mug again. Dougan downed two more mugs in a row, Sturm and Tanin drank theirs, and then it was Palin's turn again. He lifted the mug to his lips. . . .

Palin was smiling, and he couldn't quit smiling. He loved Tanin and Sturm better than anyone else in the world, and he told them so, until he broke down and cried on Sturm's broad shoulder. But no! There was someone else he loved—that was the dwarf. He staggered to his feet and went round the table to shake the dwarf's hand. He even made a speech. Fast friends . . . firm friends, like his father and his father's friend . . . old Flint, the dwarf . . . He went back to his chair, only there seemed to be four chairs now, instead of just one. Picking one, Palin sat down, missed and would have ended up on the floor if Tanin hadn't caught him. He drank another mug, watching his brothers and his new friend with tears of affection streaming down his face.

"I tell you, lads"—Dougan's voice seemed to Palin to come from a long distance away—"I love you like my own sons. And I must say, I think you've had a wee bit more to drink than you can handle."

"Naw!" Sturm cried indignantly, pounding his hand on the table.

"We can keep up with you," Tanin muttered, breathing heavily, his face beefy red.

"Damnrigh'," said Palin, striking the table—or he would have if the table hadn't suddenly and unaccountably leapt out of the way.

And then Palin was lying on the floor, thinking this was an interesting place to be, much safer than up there in four chairs, with tables jumping around. . . . Glancing around blearily, he saw his staff on the floor beside him. He reached out, caressed it lovingly.

"*Shirak*!" he slurred, and the crystal atop the staff burst into light. He heard some commotion at this; high, shrill voices jabbering and chattering somewhere in the background. Palin giggled and couldn't quit giggling.

From high above, Dougan's voice came floating down to him. "Here's to our beds," said the dwarf, "and a sound night's sleep!" And if there was a sinister note in the gruff voice or more than a trace of triumphant laughter, Palin discounted it. The dwarf was his friend, a brother to him. He loved him like a brother, his dear brothers . . .

Palin laid his head on the floor, resting his cheek on the staff's cool wood. Shutting his eyes, he slipped away into another world—a world of small creatures in brown robes, who lifted him up and ran away with him. . . .

Chapter Two

A Really Bad Hangover

The world heaved and shivered, and Palin's stomach heaved and his skin shivered in agreement, misery loving company. Rolling over on his side, he was violently sick, and he wondered as he lay on whatever it was he was lying on—he couldn't open his eyes to see; they felt all gummed together—how long it would take him to die and end this suffering.

When he could be sick no more and when it seemed that his insides might actually stay inside, Palin lay back with a groan. His head was beginning to clear a little, and he realized suddenly, when he tried to move, that his hands were tied behind his back. Fear shot through his muzzy brain, its cold surge blowing away the mists of the dwarf spirits. He couldn't feel his feet, and he dimly realized that cords tied around his ankles had cut off his circulation. Gritting his teeth, he shifted his position slightly and wiggled his toes inside his soft leather boots, wincing as he felt the tingling of returning blood.

He was lying on a wooden plank, he noticed, feeling it beneath him with his hands. And there was a peculiar motion to the plank, it was rocking back and forth in a manner most unsettling to Palin's aching head and churning stomach. There were strange noises and smells, too—wood creaking, an odd whooshing and gurgling, and, every so often, a tremendous roaring and thudding and flapping above his head that sounded like a stampede of horses or, Palin thought with a catch in his throat, his father's description of attacking dragons. Cautiously, the young mage opened his eyes.

Almost instantly, he shut them again. Sunlight streaming through a small, round window pierced his brain like an arrow, sending white-hot pain bouncing around the backs of his eyeballs. The plank rocked him this way and that, and Palin was sick again.

When he recovered sufficiently to think he might not die in the next ten seconds—a matter of extreme regret—Palin braced himself to open his eyes and keep them open.

He managed, but at the cost of being sick again. Fortunately or unfortunately, there was nothing left inside him to lose, and it wasn't long before he was able to look around. He was on a plank, as he had surmised. The plank had been built into a curved wooden wall of a small room and was obviously intended as a crude bed. Several other planks lined the walls of the oddly shaped room, and Palin saw his two brothers lying unconscious on these, bound hand and foot as he was. There was no other furniture in the room, nothing but a few wooden chests, which were sliding along the wooden floor.

Palin had only to look out the small, round window on the wall across from him to confirm his worst fears. At first, he saw nothing but blue sky and white clouds and bright sunlight. Then the plank on which he was lying dropped—it seemed—into a chasm. The wooden chests scraped across the floor, running away past him. Blue sky and clouds vanished, to be replaced by green water.

Shutting his eyes once more, Palin rolled over to ease his cramped muscles, pressing his aching head against the cool, damp wood of the crude bed.

Or perhaps he should say "berth." That's the nautical term, isn't it? he thought to himself bitterly. That's what you call a bed on a ship. And what will they call us on the ship? Galley slaves? Chained to the oars, subject to the overmaster with his whip, flaying the flesh from our backs. . . .

The motion of the ship changed, the sea chests skittered along the floor in the opposite direction, sky and clouds leapt back into the window, and Palin knew he was going to be sick again.

"Palin . . . Palin, are you all right?"

There was an anguished tone in the voice that brought Palin to consciousness. Painfully, he once again opened his eyes. He must have slept, he realized, though how he could have done so with this throbbing in his head and the queasy state of his stomach he had no idea.

"Palin!" The voice was urgent.

"Yes," said Palin thickly. It took an effort to talk; his tongue felt and tasted as though gully dwarves had taken up residence in his mouth. The thought made his stomach lurch, and he abandoned it hurriedly. "Yes," he said again, "I'm . . . all right. . . ."

"Thank Paladine!" groaned the voice, which Palin recognized now as Tanin's. "By the gods, you looked so pale, lying there, I thought you were dead!"

"I wish I was," Palin said feelingly.

"We know what you mean," said Sturm—a very subdued and miserable Sturm, to judge by the sound.

Twisting around, Palin was able to see his brothers. If I look as bad as they do, he thought, no wonder Tanin believed I was dead. Both young men were pale beneath their tan skin, their pallor had a faint greenish tinge, and there was ample evidence on the deck below that both had been extremely sick. Their red curls were tangled and wet and matted, their clothes soaked. Both lay on their backs, their hands and feet tied with rough leather thongs. Tanin had a large bruise on his forehead and, in addition, his wrists were cut and bleeding. He had obviously been trying to free himself and failed.

"This is all my fault," said Tanin glumly, with another groan as nausea welled up inside of him. "What a fool I was, not to see this coming!"

"Don't give yourself all the credit, Big Brother," said Sturm. "I went right along with you. We should have listened to Palin—"

"No, you shouldn't have," Palin mumbled, closing his eyes against the sight of the sea and sky constantly shifting places in the porthole. "I was being a superior, self-righteous twit, as both of you tried to point out." He was silent a moment, trying to decide if he was going to be sick or not. Finally, he thought he wasn't and added, "We're in this together now, anyway. Either of you know where we are and what's going on?"

"We're in the hold of a ship," Tanin said. "And, from the sounds of it, they've got some great beast chained up there."

"A dragon?" Palin asked quietly.

"Could be," Tanin answered. "I remember Tanis describing the black dragon that attacked them in Xak Tsaroth. He heard a gurgling noise and a hissing, like water boiling in a kettle. . . ."

"But why would anyone chain up a dragon on a ship?" argued Sturm weakly.

"All kinds of reasons," Palin muttered, "most of them nasty."

"Probably keeps slaves like us in line. Palin," said Tanin in a low voice, "can you do anything? To free us, I mean? You know, your magic?"

"No," said Palin bitterly. "My spell components are gone—not that I could get to them if I had them, since my hands are tied. My staff—*My staff!*" he recalled with a pang. Fearfully, he struggled to sit up, glanced around, then breathed a sigh of relief. The Staff of Magius stood in a corner, leaning up against the hull of the ship. For some reason, it did not move when the ship listed, but remained standing perfectly still, seemingly unaffected by the laws of nature. "My staff might help, but the only thing I know how to make it do," he admitted shamefacedly, "is give light. Besides," he added, lying wearily back down, "my head aches so I can barely remember my name, much less a magic spell."

The young men were silent, each thinking. Tanin struggled against his bonds once more, then gave it up. The leather had been soaked with water and had tightened when it dried so that it was impossible for the big man to escape.

"So, it looks like we're prisoners in this wretched hole—"

"Prisoners?" called a booming voice. "Losers, maybe. But prisoners, never!"

A trapdoor in the ceiling opened, and a short, stocky figure in bright red velvet with black curling hair and beard poked his head through. "My guests you are!" cried Dougan Redhammer lustily, peering at them through the hatch. "And fortunate beyond all humans, because I have chosen you to accompany me on my grand quest! A quest that will make you famous throughout the world! A quest that will make that minor adventure your parents were involved in seem like a kender scavenger hunt!" Dougan leaned so far through the hatch that his face became quite red with the exertion and he almost tumbled through upside down.

"We're not going on any quest of yours, dwarf!" Tanin said with an oath. And, for once, both Palin and Sturm were in full agreement.

Leering down at them through the hatch, Dougan grinned. "Wanna bet?"

"You see, lads, it's a matter of honor."

Throwing down a rope ladder, Dougan—somewhat perilously—climbed down into the hold of the ship, his journey being hampered by the fact that he couldn't see his feet for his great belly. Reaching the deck, he rested a moment from his labors, removing a lace-covered handkerchief from the sleeve of his coat and using it to mop his perspiring face.

"I tell you, lads," he said solemnly, "I'm feeling a bit under myself. By Reorx, but you can drink! Just like you said." Stumbling slightly as the deck listed beneath him, the dwarf pointed at Sturm. "You, especially! I swear by my beard"—he stroked it—"that I saw two of yourself, lad, and I was workin' on four before your eyes rolled back in your head and you crashed to the floor. Shook the foundations of the inn, you did. I had to pay damages."

"You said you were going to cut us loose," Tanin snarled.

"That I did," Dougan muttered, drawing a sharp knife from his belt. Making his way around the sea chests, he began to saw away industriously at the leather thongs that bound Tanin's wrists.

"If we aren't prisoners," Palin asked, "then why are we bound hand and foot?"

"Why, laddie," said the dwarf, looking around at Palin with an injured air, "it was for your own safety! I had only your welfare at heart! You were so enthusiastic when you saw we were carrying you aboard this fine vessel, that we had to restrain your enthusiasm—"

"Enthusiasm!" Tanin snorted. "We were out cold!"

"Well, no, actually, you weren't," Dougan admitted. "Oh, he was." The dwarf jerked his head back at Palin. "Sleeping like he was in his mother's arms. But you two, as I saw the moment I clapped eyes on you, lads, are grand fighters. Perhaps you were wondering how you got that bit of a clout on your head—"

Tanin said nothing, simply glared at the dwarf. Sitting up, the young man gingerly put his hand to his forehead, where there was a lump the size of an egg.

"Enthusiasm," said the dwarf solemnly, going over to cut Sturm loose. "That's one reason I chose you for my quest."

"The only quest I'd consider going on with you is to see you in the Abyss!" Tanin retorted stubbornly.

Lying back, Palin sighed. "My dear brother," he said wearily, "has it occurred to you that we have little choice in the matter? We're on a ship, miles away from land"—he glanced at Dougan, who nodded assent—"and completely at the mercy of this dwarf and his crew of cutthroats. Do you think he would release us from our bonds if we had the slightest chance of escaping?"

"Intelligent lad," said the dwarf approvingly, cutting Palin's ropes as Sturm sat up stiffly, rubbing his wrists. "But then, he's a mage. And they're all intelligent, at least so's I've heard. So intelligent," continued Dougan cunningly, "that I'm certain he'll think twice about casting any spells that might come to mind. A sleep spell, for example, might be very effective and give my *cutthroat* crew a rest, but can you three sail the ship? Besides," he continued, seeing Palin's grim expression, "as I said before—it's a matter of honor. You lost the bet, fair and square. I kept my part, I put you to bed. Now you must keep yours." Dougan's grin made the ends of his moustache curl upward. He stroked his beard in satisfaction. "You must pay the tab."

"I'll be damned if I'm going to pay!" Tanin snarled. "I'll yank your black beard out by its roots!"

Tanin's voice literally shook with anger, and Palin cringed, watching helplessly as his hot-tempered brother made a lunge for the grinning dwarf—and fell flat on his face in the muck and filth.

"There, there, lad," said Dougan, helping Tanin stagger to his feet. "Get your sea legs first, then you can yank out my beard—if you refuse to honor your bet. But from what I've heard of Caramon Majere, I'd be disappointed indeed to see his sons turn out to be welshers."

"We're no welshers!" said Tanin sulkily, leaning weakly against the berth and clinging to it with both hands as the ship rocked out from underneath him. "Though some might say the bet was rigged, we'll pay it just the same! What do you want of us?"

"To accompany me on my quest," said the dwarf. "Where we're bound is perilous in the extreme! I need two strong, skilled fighters, and a wizard always comes in handy."

"What about your crew?" Sturm asked. Carefully, he edged himself off his berth and dropped to the deck just as the ship listed, sending him crashing backward into the hull.

Dougan's grinning face went abruptly sober. He glanced up above, where the strange roaring sound could be heard again, mingled this time, Palin noted, with shrieks and cries. "Ah, my . . . um . . . crew," said the dwarf, shaking his head sadly. "They're . . . well, best you come see for yourselves, lads."

Turning on the heel of his fancy shoes, Dougan made for the rope ladder, stumbling awkwardly as the ship canted off in the other direction. "Ouch! That reminds me," he said, cursing and rubbing his leg where he had come up against one of the roving sea chests. "We stowed your equipment in here." He thumped on the lid. "Swords, shield, armor, and such like. You'll be needing them where we're headed!" he added cheerfully.

Catching hold of the swinging rope ladder, the dwarf scrambled up it and pulled himself through the hatch. "Don't be long!" they heard him shout.

"Well, what do we do now?" Sturm asked, standing up cautiously, only to fall forward with the motion of the ship. The young man's face was decidedly green; beads of sweat stood on his forehead.

"We get our swords," Tanin said grimly, stumbling toward the sea chests.

"And we get out of this foul place," said Palin. He covered his nose and mouth with the hem of his sleeve. "We need fresh air, and I for one want to see what's going on up there."

"Wanna bet?" Tanin mocked.

Smiling ruefully, Palin managed to make his way to the Staff of Magius, which was still standing up against the hull. Whether it was any magical property of the staff, or whether just holding it gave him confidence, the young mage felt better the moment his hand wrapped around the smooth wood.

"Think of the danger this staff has seen and led its masters through safely," Palin whispered to himself. "Magius held it as he fought at Huma's side. My uncle held it as he entered the Abyss to face the Dark Queen. This situation probably doesn't bother it at all."

Gripping the staff in his hand, Palin started up the rope ladder.

"Hold on there, Little Brother," Tanin said, catching Palin's sleeve. "You don't know what's up there. You admitted yourself you weren't feeling up to spellcasting. Why don't you let Sturm and me go ahead?"

Palin stopped, looking at Tanin in pleased astonishment. His older brother had not ordered him, as he would have done earlier. He could almost hear him, "Palin, you fool! You wait below. Sturm and I will go first." Tanin had spoken to him respectfully, presented his argument logically, and then left it up to Palin to decide.

"You're right, Tanin," Palin said, stepping back away from the ladder—only it was back a little farther than he had intended as the swaying ship threw him off balance once again. Sturm caught hold of him and the three stood, waiting for the ship to right itself. Then, one by one, they climbed up the rope ladder.

Sturm's strong hand hauled Palin up on deck. Thankfully, the young mage breathed the fresh air, blinking in the bright sunlight and doing his best to ignore the throbbing in his head. His eyes were just adjusting to the glare when he heard the roaring behind him—a frightful sound, a combination of howling, shrieking, creaking, and hissing. The deck below his feet thrummed and shivered. Alarmed, he started to turn and face whatever horrible beast was attacking when he heard Tanin cry, "Palin, look out!"

His brother's weight struck Palin, knocking him off his feet and onto the deck just as something dark and awful thundered overhead with a wild flapping noise.

"You all right?" Tanin asked anxiously. Standing up, he offered Palin his hand. "I didn't mean to hit you quite so hard."

"I think you broke every bone in my body!" Palin wheezed, trying to catch his breath. He stared at the prow of the ship, where the thing was disappearing over the edge. "What in the name of the Abyss was that?" He looked at Dougan. The dwarf was also, somewhat shamefacedly, picking himself up off the deck.

His face as red as his velvet breeches, Dougan was brushing off bits of wood, strands of rope, and sea foam when he was suddenly surrounded by a horde of jabbering, small creatures endeavoring to help him.

"Ahoy there!" Dougan roared irritably, flapping his hands at the creatures. "Stand off! Stand off, I say! Get back to your tasks!"

Obediently, the creatures ran off, though more than a few took a second or two to eye the three brothers. One even approached Palin, an eager hand stretched out to touch the Staff of Magius.

"Get back!" Palin cried, clutching the staff to him.

Sniffing, the creature retreated, but its bright eyes lingered hungrily on the staff as it returned to whatever it was it had been doing.

"Gnomes!" said Sturm in awe, lowering his sword.

"Uh, yes," muttered Dougan, embarrassed. "My . . . um . . . crew of cutthroats."

"The gods help us!" Tanin prayed fervently. "We're on a gnome ship."

"And that thing that makes such a terrible racket?" Palin was almost afraid to ask.

"That's the . . . uh . . . sail," Dougan mumbled, wringing water out of his beard. He made a vague gesture with his hand. "It'll be back again in a few minutes, so . . . um . . . be prepared."

"What in the Abyss is a dwarf doing on a gnome ship?" Tanin demanded.

Dougan's embarrassment increased. "Ah, well, now," he muttered, twirling his long moustache around his index finger. "That's a bit of a story, now. Perhaps I'll have time to tell you—"

Balancing himself on the heaving deck with the aid of the staff, Palin looked out to sea. An idea had occurred to him, and his heart was beginning to sink at about the same rate it appeared this vessel was sinking. The sun was behind them, they were heading west, riding on a gnome ship with a dwarf captain. . . .

"The Graygem!" Palin murmured.

"Aye, laddie!" Dougan cried, clapping the young mage on the back. "You've womped the lizard in the gullet, as the gully dwarves say. *That* is the reason I'm on this . . . um . . . somewhat unique vessel and *that*" continued Dougan, rocking back on his feet, his belly thrust out in front of him, "is my quest!"

"What is?" asked Tanin suspiciously.

"My brothers," said Palin, "it appears we are bound on a voyage in search of the legendary lost Graygem of Gargath."

"Not 'in search of'," Dougan corrected. "I have found it! We are on a quest to end all quests! We're going to *recover* the Graygem and—ahoy, lads, look out." Casting an uneasy glance behind him, Dougan threw himself down on the deck.

"Here comes the sail," he grunted.

Chapter Three

The Miracle

The gnomish sailing vessel was a true technological wonder. (The wonder being, as Sturm said, that it managed to stay afloat, much less actually sail!) Years in design (longer years in committee) and centuries of craftsmanship later, the gnome ship was the terror of the high seas. (This was quite true. Most ships fled in terror at the sight of the gnome flag—a golden screw on a field of puce—but this was because the steam-generating boilers had an unfortunate habit of exploding. The gnomes claimed to have once attacked and sunk a minotaur pirate ship. The truth of the matter was that the minotaurs, rendered helpless by laughter, had negligently allowed their ship to drift too close to the gnomes who, in panic, released the pressurized air stored in casks used to steer the vessel. The resulting blast blew the minotaurs out of the water and the gnomes off course by about twenty miles.)

Let other races mock them, the gnomes knew that their ship was years ahead of its time in practicality, economy, and design. Just because it was slower than anything on the water—averaging about half a knot on a good day with a strong wind—didn't bother the gnomes. (A committee is currently working on this problem and is confidently expected to come up with a solution sometime in the next millennium.)

The gnomes knew that all ships had sails. This was requisite, in their opinion, of a ship being a ship. The gnomes' ship had a sail, therefore. But the gnomes, upon studying vessels built by other, less intelligent races, considered it a waste of space to clutter the deck with masts and ropes and canvas and an additional waste of energy hoisting sails up and down in an effort to catch the wind. The gnome ship, therefore, used one gigantic sail that not only caught the wind but, in essence, dragged the wind along with it.

It was this sail that gave the ship its revolutionary design. An enormous affair of billowing canvas with a beam the size of ten stout oaks, the sail rested upon three greased wooden rails, one on each side of the ship and one down the middle. Huge cables, running the length of the ship and driven by steam generated by a giant boiler down below, operated this miracle of modern naval technology, pulling the sail along the greased wooden rail at a high rate of speed. The sail, moving from front to back, manufactured its own wind as it roared along and thus propelled the ship on its course.

When the sail had completed its impressive sweep across the deck and reached the ship's stern . . . (There *was* one tiny problem. It was impossible to turn the ship around. Therefore the stern looked just like the prow. The gnomes had solved this slight hitch in design by fixing the sail so that it could go either forward or backward, as needed, and had given the ship two figureheads—buxom gnome maidens, one on each end, each holding screws in their hands and staring out to sea with resolute intensity.). . . . Where were we? Ah yes. When the sail reached the stern, it rolled itself up neatly and traveled under the ship through the water until it reached the prow. Here it leapt out of the water, unfurled itself, and thundered along the deck once more.

At least, that is what the sail did on the drawing board and in numerous gnomish bathtubs. In actuality, the gears that controlled the winding-up mechanism rusted almost immediately in the salt water, and the sail often hit the water either completely or partially open. In this manner it swept under the ship, creating a tremendous drag that occasionally pulled the vessel back farther than it had gone forward. This small inconvenience was considered to be fully outweighed, however, by an unlooked-for bonus. When the open sail came up from the sea, it acted as a net, hauling in schools of fish. As the sail lifted up over the prow, fish rained down upon the deck, providing lunch, dinner, and the occasional concussion if one had the misfortune to be struck by a falling tuna.

The ship had no tiller, there being nowhere for a tiller to go, since the boat had, in essence, two prows and no stern. Nothing daunted, the gnomes designed their vessel to be steered by the use of the aforementioned pressurized air casks. Located at each side of the hull, these were kept filled with air by giant, steam-driven bellows. (We said earlier that it was impossible to turn the ship around. We were in error. The gnomes had discovered that the ship *could* be turned by means of releasing the air in both casks simultaneously. This caused the ship to revolve, but at such an alarming rate that most of the crew was flung overboard and those that remained could never afterward walk a straight line. These unfortunates were promptly hired by the gnome Street Designers Guild.)

The name of this remarkable vessel was *The Great Gnome Ship of Exploration and Questing Made of Wooden Planks Held Together by the Miracle of Gnome Glue* (of which the less said the better) *Instead of that Paltry Human Invention the Nail Which We Have Designed More Efficiently Anyway and Driven by Steam Created by Bringing Water to a Rapid Boil* and so forth and so on, the full name taking up several volumes of text in the gnomes' library. This name, or rather a shortened version, was carved upon the hull and, when the gnomes ran out of room, the deck as well.

Needless to say, traveling upon the *Miracle* (the shorter human version of the name) was not conducive to either peace of mind or keeping one's dinner down. The ship wallowed in the water like a drunken sea elf when the sail was underneath it, surged forward with a stomach-wrenching jolt when the sail was sweeping along the deck, and rocked sickeningly when the sail hit the water from behind. The bilge pumps were at work constantly (due to the wonders of gnome glue). Fortunately, the gnomes were heading in a straight direction—due west—so that it was not necessary to turn the ship, thus avoiding the need to open the air casks (a thrill akin to being caught in a cyclone)—a blessing rather lost upon Tanin, Sturm, and Palin (though Dougan assured them solemnly that they should thank their respective gods for it!).

Night was falling. The sun sank into the sea in a blaze of red, as though trying to outshine the gaudily dressed dwarf. Crouching miserably on the foredeck, the brothers were glad to see night come. They had spent a wretched day, forced to duck every time the sail raced overhead. In addition, they were pelted by fish and drenched with water streaming down from the sail. Seasick and hung over, there was little for them to eat except fish (plenty of that) and some sort of gnome biscuit that looked suspiciously like the miracle glue. To take their minds off their troubles and prepare them for the quest ahead, Dougan proposed to tell them the story of the Graygem of Gargath.

"I know that story," Tanin said sullenly. "Everyone on Krynn knows that story! I've heard it since I was a child."

"Ah, but do you know the *true* story?" Dougan asked, gazing at them intently with his bright, dark eyes.

No one replied, being unable to hear themselves think as the sail—with much flapping of canvas and creaking of winches—leapt out of the water and hurtled along the deck. Fish flopped about their feet, the gnomes hopping here and there after them. The sail's traversal along the deck was punctuated by shrieks and screams as certain unlucky gnomes forgot to duck and were swept overboard by the beam. Since this happened almost every time the sail made a pass, several gnomes were stationed permanently along the sides of the ship to yell "Gnome overboard!" (which they did with great gusto) and heave their floundering fellows life-saving devices (which also doubled as anchors when in port).

"How should we know whether or not it's the true story?" Tanin said grumpily when he could be heard again.

"I know that there are differing accounts depending on whether one hears the tale from a dwarf or any other race," Palin added.

Dougan appeared extremely uncomfortable. "Aye, lad," he said, "and there you've touched on a sore point. But, for now, you go ahead and tell it, young mage. Tell it as you heard it. I assume you've studied it, since it involves the bringing of magic into the world."

"Very well," said Palin, rather pleased and flattered at being the center of attention. Hearing that the human was going to tell their favorite story, many gnomes left their duties (and fish chasing) to settle down around Palin, regarding the mage with varying expressions ranging from eager assurance that he was going to get it wrong to downright suspicion that he might accidentally get it right.

"When the gods awakened from chaos and gained control over chaos, the Balance of the Universe was established and chaos subdued. The pendulum of time swung between good and evil, with neutrality watching to see that neither grew stronger. It was at this time that the spirits of the races first began to dance among the stars, and the gods decided to create a world for these races to inhabit.

"The world was forged, but now the gods fought over the spirits of the races. The gods of good wanted to give the races power over the physical world, nurturing them toward good. The gods of evil wanted to enslave the races, forcing them to do their evil bidding. The gods of neutrality wanted to give the races physical power over the world, but with the freedom to choose between evil and good. Eventually, the latter course was decided upon, the gods of evil believing that they would have little trouble gaining the upper hand.

"Three races were born, then—the elves, beloved of the gods of good; the ogres, willing slaves of the gods of evil; and the humans, the neutrals, who—of all the races—had the shortest life span and therefore were easily drawn to one side or the other. When these races were created, the god Reorx was given the task of forging the world. He chose some humans to help him in this task, since they were the most willing workers. But Reorx soon grew angry at the humans. Many were greedy and worked only to gain wealth, taking little pride in what they created. Some sought to cheat, others stole. Furious, Reorx cursed his followers, turning them into gnomes—small creatures doomed—I don't really mean *doomed*," Palin interrupted himself hastily, seeing the gnomes begin to frown—"I mean . . . uh . . . *blessed* to be tinkers"—the gnomes smiled—"and to spend their entire lives tinkering with mechanical devices that would never, er, I mean, rarely work. . . ."

The sail rumbled overhead, and Palin paused thankfully.

"Getonwiththegoodpart!" shouted the gnomes, who always speak extremely fast and jamtheirwordstogether. Deciding that this was excellent advice (once he understood it), Palin continued.

"Soon after this, Reorx was tricked by one of the evil gods into taking the vast power of chaos and forging it into a gem. It is generally believed that the god behind this was Hiddukel, god of corrupt wealth—"

"No, lad." Dougan sighed. "It was Morgion."

"Morgion?" repeated Palin in astonishment.

"Aye, the god of decay. But I'll go into that later." The dwarf waved his hand. "Carry on."

"At any rate," continued Palin, somewhat confused, "Reorx made the

Graygem and set it into the moon, Lunitari the Red, the moon sacred to the gods of neutrality."

The gnomes were all grinning; their favorite part was coming up.

"During this time, the gnomes had built a great invention, designed to take them off the world and out into the stars. This invention lacked only one thing to make it operational and that was a force to propel it. Looking into the sky at night, the gnomes saw the Graygem shining from the heart of Lunitari and knew, instantly, that if they could capture the power of chaos that resided in the Graygem, it would drive their invention."

Much nodding of heads and wise looks among the gnomes. Sturm yawned. Tanin stood up and leaned over the railing, where he was quietly sick.

"One extremely gifted gnome built an extension ladder that actually worked. It carried him up to the moon and there, with a net he had brought along for the purpose, he captured the Graygem before the gods were aware of him. He brought the gem down to the world below, but there it escaped him and sailed off to the west, passing over the lands and trailing chaos behind. Chaos entered the world in the form of magic. Beasts and creatures were transformed by the gem in its passing, becoming wondrous or hideous as the gem chose.

"A band of gnomes followed the Graygem across the sea, hoping still to catch it and claim it for their own. But it was a human, a man named Gargath, who trapped the stone and held it in his castle by certain newly acquired magical means. Reaching the castle, the gnomes could see the light of the Graygem illuminating the countryside. They demanded that Gargath give the stone up. He refused. The gnomes threatened war"— shouts and cheers among the gnomes here—"Gargath welcomed the battle. He built a high wall all around the castle to protect it and the gem. There was no way the gnomes could get over the wall, so they left, vowing, however, to return."

"Hear! Hear!" cried the gnomes.

"A month later, a gnome army arrived at Castle Gargath with a huge, steam-powered siege engine. It reached the wall of the castle, but broke down just short of its goal. The gnomes retreated with heavy losses. Two months later, the gnomes returned with an even larger steam-powered siege engine. This engine plowed into the first, caught fire, and burned. The gnomes retreated with even heavier losses. Three months later, the gnomes were back with a humongous, steam-powered siege engine. It lumbered over the ashes of the first two siege engines and was thundering toward the wall when the drive mechanism broke down. The engine, with a mighty groan, toppled over on its side, smashing down the wall. Although not quite what they'd had in mind, the gnomes were delighted."

More cheering.

"But, as they rushed through the breach in the wall, a steel gray light beamed forth from the stone, blinding everyone. When Lord Gargath could see again, he saw—to his astonishment—that the gnomes were fighting among themselves!"

Frowns here and cries of "Liar! We were misquoted!"

"One faction of gnomes was demanding that they be given the Graygem to carve up and turn into wealth. The other faction demanded that they be given the Graygem to take apart and see how it worked.

"As the two sides fought, their aspect changed. . . . Thus were born the races of the dwarves, who carve rock and think constantly of wealth; and kender, driven by their insatiable curiosity to roam the world. The Graygem escaped during the confusion and was last seen heading westward, a party of gnomes and Lord Gargath in pursuit. And that," finished Palin, somewhat out of breath, "is the story of the Graygem—unless you ask a dwarf, that is."

"Why? What do the dwarves say?" demanded Tanin, looking at Dougan with a somewhat sickly grin.

Dougan fetched up a sigh that might have come from the tips of his black shoes. "The dwarves have always maintained that *they* are the chosen of Reorx, that he forged their race out of love, and that gnomes and kender came about from trial and error until he got it right." Boos. The gnomes appeared highly indignant, but were instantly subdued by Dougan, whirling around and fixing them with a piercing stare. "According to the dwarves, Reorx created the Graygem to give them as a gift and it was stolen by the gnomes." More boos, but these hushed immediately.

"Well, it seems to me," said Sturm, with another yawn, "that the only one who knows the true story is Reorx."

"Not quite, lad," said Dougan, looking uncomfortable. "For, you see, I know the true story. And that is why I'm on this quest."

"Which is right, then?" asked Tanin, with a wink at Palin.

"Neither," said Dougan, appearing even more uncomfortable. His head drooped down, his chin buried itself in his beard, while his hands fumbled at the golden buttons on his sopping-wet velvet coat. "You . . . uh . . . you see," he mumbled, making it extremely difficult for anyone to hear him over the splashing of the sea and the flapping of fish on the deck, "Reorx . . . uh . . . losttheGraygeminagameofbones."

"What?" asked Palin, leaning forward.

"Helostit," muttered the dwarf.

"I still didn't hear—"

"HE LOST THE DAMN GEM IN A GAME OF BONES!" Dougan roared angrily, lifting his face and glaring around him. Terrified, the gnomes immediately scattered in all directions, more than a few getting conked on the head by the sail as it whizzed past. "Morgion, god of decay and disease, tricked Reorx into making the gem, knowing that if chaos were loosed in the world, his evil power would grow. He challenged Reorx to a game, with the Graygem as the stakes and . . ." The dwarf fell silent, scowling down at his shoes.

"He gambled it in away in a *bones game?*" Sturm finished in amazement.

"Aye, lad," said Dougan, sighing heavily. "You see, Reorx has one little flaw.

Just a tiny flaw, mind you, otherwise he is as fine and honorable a gentleman as one could hope to meet. But"—the dwarf heaved another sigh—"he does love his bottle, and he does love a good wager."

"Oh, so you know Reorx, do you?" Sturm said with a yawn that cracked his jaws.

"I'm proud to say so," said Dougan seriously, stroking his beard and curling his moustache. "And, with his help, I've managed after all these years to locate the Graygem. With the assistance of these lads here"—he smote a passing gnome on the shoulder, completely bowling the little fellow over—"and with the help of you three fine young men, we'll recover it and . . . and . . ." Dougan stopped, seeming confused.

"And?"

"And return it to Reorx, naturally," the dwarf said, shrugging.

"Naturally," Tanin responded. Glancing over at Sturm, who had fallen asleep on the deck, the big man caught a gnome in the act of making off with his brother's helm. "Hey!" cried Tanin angrily, collaring the thief.

"Ijustwantedtolookatit!" whined the gnome, cringing. "Iwasgoingto-giveitbackhonest. You see," he said, talking more slowly as Tanin released his grip, "we have developed a revolutionary new design in helms. There are just a few problems with it, such as getting it off one's head, and I—"

"Thank you, we're not interested," Tanin growled, yanking the helm away from the gnome, who was admiring it lovingly. "C'mon, Little Brother," he said, turning to Palin. "Help me get Sturm to bed."

"Where is bed?" Palin asked tiredly. "And, no, I'm not going back into that foul-smelling hold again."

"Me either," Tanin said. He looked around the deck and pointed. "That lean-to-looking thing over there seems to be about the best place. At least it'll be dry."

He indicated several wooden planks that had been skillfully and ingeniously fit together to form a small shelter. Leaning against the hull, the planks were beneath the sail as it rumbled past, and protected those lying within from water and falling fish.

"It is," said Dougan smugly. "That's *my* bed."

"It *was* your bed," returned Tanin. Leaning down, he shook Sturm. "Wake up! We're not going to carry you! And hurry up, before that god-cursed sail decapitates us."

"What?" Sturm sat up, blinking drowsily.

"You can't do this!" roared the dwarf.

"Look, Dougan Redhammer!" Tanin said, bending down and staring the dwarf grimly in the eye. "I'm hung over, seasick, and I haven't had anything to eat all day. I've been doused with water, hit by fish, run over by a sail, and bored to death by kids' bedtime stories! I don't believe you, I don't believe your stupid quest." Tanin paused, seething, and raised a finger, shaking it at the dwarf's nose. "I'm going to sleep where I want to sleep, and tomorrow, when I'm feeling better, I swear by the gods I'm going to make these little bastards turn this ship around and take us back home!"

"And if I stop you?" Dougan threatened with a leer, not at all disconcerted by Tanin's rage.

"Then there'll be a new figurehead on whichever end of this stupid boat is the front!" Tanin hissed through clenched teeth. "And it'll have a long, black beard!" Angrily, the big man stalked over to the lean-to and ducked inside. Sleepily, Sturm followed.

"If I were you, dwarf," Palin added, hurrying after them, "I'd keep out of his way! He's quite capable of doing what he says."

"Is he, lad? I'll keep that in mind," the dwarf replied, tugging thoughtfully at his beard.

The shelter was crammed with the dwarf's possessions—most of which appeared to be gaudy clothes. These Palin shoved unceremoniously out onto the deck with his foot. Tanin stretched out on the deck, Sturm collapsed next to him, and both were asleep almost as quickly as if their younger brother had cast a spell over them. Palin lay down in the small remaining space, hoping sleep would come to him as swiftly.

But he was not the campaigner his brothers were. Sturm could sleep in full armor on the sands of a desert while Tanin had been known to snore blissfully as lightning cut down a tree standing next to him. Soaked to the skin, shivering with cold, Palin lay on the deck and gave himself up to misery. He was hungry, but every time he thought of food, his stomach lurched. His muscles ached from the sickness; the bitter taste of salt water filled his mouth. He thought with longing of his bed at home; of clean, sweet-smelling sheets; of hours of peaceful study, sitting beneath the sheltering limbs of the vallenwood, his spellbook in his lap.

Closing his eyes, Palin tried to keep back the tears of homesickness, but it engulfed him like a wave. Reaching out his hand, he touched the Staff of Magius. And suddenly the memory of his uncle came to him. From where? Palin had no idea. Raistlin had died long before Palin was born. Perhaps it was from the staff . . . or maybe he was recalling some tale of his father's, and it had become real to him now in his weakened state. Whatever the reason, Palin saw Raistlin clearly, lying on the ground in a dismal, rainswept forest. Huddled in his red robes, the mage was coughing, coughing until it seemed he could never draw breath again. Palin saw blood upon the ashen lips, saw the frail body wracked by pain. But he heard him speak no word of complaint. Softly, Palin approached his uncle. The coughing ceased; the spasm eased. Lifting his head, Raistlin looked directly into Palin's eyes. . . .

Bowing his head in shame, Palin drew the staff nearer to him, resting his cheek upon its cool, smooth wood and, relaxing, fell into sleep. But he thought he heard, in the final moment before he slipped over the edge of unconsciousness, the voice of the dwarf, and he thought he saw a head peering into the lean-to.

"I've a deck of cards here, lads. . . . What do you say? High card sleeps here tonight? . . ."

Chapter Four

The Isle of Gargath

Tanin was quite capable of carrying out his threat to take over the ship, though just how he was going to force the gnomes to sail it was another matter entirely. During the night, the gnomes, just as firmly determined to continue the voyage, began to organize a supply of weapons. Since most of these weapons were of gnomish design, there was every possibility that they would do as much or more damage to the wielder as to the intended victim, and thus the outcome of the battle—two warriors and a mage against numerous gnomes and a dwarf—was open to question.

The question was, fortunately, never answered. The next morning the brothers were awakened by a tremendous crash, the heart-stopping sound of splintering wood, and the somewhat belated cry of "Land ho!"

Staggering to their feet, they made their way out of the lean-to and across the deck, not an easy task since it was listing steeply to port.

"What is it? What's happened? Where are we?" demanded Tanin, rubbing his eyes.

"We've arrived!" announced Dougan, smoothing his beard in satisfaction. "Look!" He made a grand, sweeping gesture toward what was—at this time—the prow. "The Isle of Gargath."

The brothers looked. At first all they could see was a confused mass of split sail, dangled ropes, broken beams, and gnomes waving their hands, arguing furiously, and shoving each other about. The motion of the ship through the water had ceased, due, no doubt, to the presence of a cliff, which had bashed in the figurehead, part of the hull, and snapped the sail in two.

His face grim, Tanin made his way through the wreckage, followed by Sturm and Palin, several bickering gnomes, and the dwarf. Reaching the prow, he clung to the side and stared out past the cliff face toward the island. The sun was rising behind them, shedding its bright light upon a stretch of sandy beach that curved out of sight to the north, vanishing in a patch of gray fog. Strange-looking trees with thin, smooth trunks that erupted in a flourish of frondlike leaves at the top surrounded the beach. Beyond the wide, sandy strip, towering above the trees and the cliff face upon which the boat now rested, was a gigantic mountain. A cloud of gray smoke hung over it, casting a pall upon the beach, the water, and the ship.

"The Isle of Gargath," Dougan repeated triumphantly.

"Gargath?" Palin gaped. "You mean—"

"Aye, laddie. The lord himself followed the Graygem, if you remember, when it escaped. He built a ship and sailed after it as it vanished over the western horizon, and that was the last anyone on Ansalon ever heard of him. His family figured he had dropped off the edge of the world. But, a few years back, I happened to be drinking with a group of minotaurs. One thing led to another, there was a game, as I recall, and I won this map off them." Reaching into the pocket of his red velvet coat (now much the worse for wear and salt water), Dougan pulled out a piece of parchment and handed it to Tanin.

"It's a minotaur map, all right," Tanin said, setting it down on the listing rail and smoothing it out, trying to keep his balance at the same time. Sturm lurched over to see, and Palin crowded next to him, bracing himself on the Staff of Magius. Though it was written in the uncouth language of the man-beasts, the map was drawn with the precision and skill for which minotaurs are grudgingly renowned by the civilized races of Krynn. There was no mistaking the continent of Ansalon or, much farther to the west, a tiny island with the word "Gargath" written out to the side.

"What does that mean," Sturm asked, pointing to an ominous-looking symbol next to the island, "that thing that looks like a bull's head with a sword stuck through it?"

"That?" repeated Dougan, shrugging nonchalantly. Snatching the map from Tanin, he rolled it up hastily. "Some minotaur doodle, no doubt—"

"The minotaur 'doodle' for danger," Palin said grimly. "Isn't that right?"

Dougan flushed, thrusting the map back into his pocket. "Well, now, laddie, I believe you may be on to something there, although I personally don't put much stock in what those savage creatures might take it into their heads to draw—"

"Those 'savage creatures' have marked this island with their strongest warning!" Palin interrupted. "No minotaur ship will land anywhere bearing that mark," he added, turning to his brothers.

"And there are few things in this world or the next that minotaurs fear," Tanin said, staring at the island, his face dark.

"What more proof do you need?" asked Dougan in a soft voice, following Tanin's gaze; the dwarf's dark, bright eyes were filled with hunger. "The Graygem is here! It is its power the minotaurs feel and fear!"

"What do you think, Palin?" Tanin turned to his youngest brother. "You're the magic-user. Surely you can sense it."

Once again, Palin felt the thrill of pleasure, seeing his older brothers, the two people he looked up to in this world most with the exception of his father—or maybe even more than his father—looking at him respectfully, awaiting his judgment. Gripping the Staff of Magius, Palin closed his eyes and tried to concentrate and, as he did so, a chill feeling clutched his heart with fingers of ice, spreading its cold fear through his body. He shuddered and opened his eyes to find Tanin and Sturm regarding him anxiously.

"Palin—your face! You're as pale as death. What is it?"

"I don't know. . . ." Palin faltered, his mouth dry. "I felt something, but what I'm not sure. It wasn't danger so much as a lost and empty feeling, a feeling of helplessness. Everything around me was spinning out of control. There was nothing I could do to stop it—"

"The power of the gem," Dougan said. "You felt it, young mage! And now you know why it must be captured and returned to the gods for safe-keeping. It escaped man's care before; it will escape again. The gods only know," the dwarf added sorrowfully, "what mischief it has wreaked upon the inhabitants of this wretched island."

Wagging his black beard, Dougan held out a trembling hand to Tanin. "You'll help me, lads, won't you?" he asked in heartfelt, pleading tones, so different from his usual braggadocio that Tanin was caught off guard, his anger punctured. "If you say no," continued Dougan, hanging his head, "I'll understand. Though I *did* win the wager, I guess it was wrong of me to get you drunk and take you prisoner when you were weak and helpless."

Tanin chewed his lip, obviously not welcoming this reminder.

"And I swear by my beard," said the dwarf solemnly, stroking it, "that if you say the word, I'll have the gnomes take you back to Ansalon. As soon as they get the ship repaired, that is."

"*If* they get the ship repaired!" Tanin growled at last. (This appeared unlikely. The gnomes were paying no attention whatsoever to the ship, but were arguing among themselves about who was supposed to have been on watch, who was supposed to be reading the gnomes' own map, and the committee that had drawn up the map in the first place. It was later decided that, since the cliff hadn't been marked on the map, it wasn't there. Having reached this conclusion, the gnomes were able to get to work.)

"Well, what do you two say?" Tanin turned to his brothers.

"I say that since we're here, we ought to at least take a look around," Sturm said in low tones. "If the dwarf is right and we could retrieve the Graygem, our admittance into the knighthood would be assured! As he said, we'd be heroes!"

"To say nothing of the wealth we might obtain," Tanin muttered. "Palin?"

The young mage's heart beat fast. Who knows what magical powers the Graygem possesses? he thought suddenly. It could enhance *my* power, and I wouldn't need any great archmage to teach me! I might become a great archmage myself, just by touching it or . . . Palin shook his head. Raising his eyes, he saw his brothers' faces. Tanin's was ugly with greed, Sturm's twisted with ambition. My own face—Palin put his hand on it—what must it look like to them? He glanced down at his robes, and saw their white color faded to dirty gray. It might just be from the salt water, but it might be from something else. . . .

"My brothers," he said urgently, "listen to us! Think what you just said! Tanin, since when did you ever go in search of wealth and not adventure!"

Tanin blinked, as if waking from a dream. "You're right! Wealth! What am I talking about? I never cared that much for money—"

"The power of the Graygem is speaking," Dougan cried. "It's beginning to corrupt you, as it corrupted others." His gaze went to the gnomes. The shoving and pushing had escalated into punching and tossing one another overboard.

"I say we should at least investigate this island," Palin said in a low voice so that the dwarf would not overhear. He drew his brothers closer. "If for no other reason than to find out if Dougan's telling the truth. If he is, and if the Graygem *is* here, and if we could be the ones to bring it back . . ."

"Oh, it's here!" Dougan said, eagerly poking his black-bearded face into their midst. "And when you bring it back, lads, why, the stories they tell of your famous father will be nothing compared to the legends they'll sing of you! And you'll be rescuing the poor people of this island from their sad fate," continued the dwarf in solemn tones.

"People?" Tanin said, startled. "You mean this place is inhabited?"

"Yes, there are people here," the dwarf said with a gusty sigh, though he was eyeing the brothers shrewdly.

"He's right," said Sturm, staring intently at the beach. "There are people on Gargath. And it doesn't look to me, Dougan Redhammer, like they want to be rescued!"

Tanin, Palin, Sturm, and the dwarf were ferried across the water from the *Miracle* by a party of gnomes in a dinghy. Bringing along the dinghy on board the *Miracle* had been the dwarf's idea, and the gnomes were enchanted with something so practical and simple. The gnomes had themselves designed a lifeboat to be attached to the *Miracle*. Roughly the same weight and dimensions as the ship itself, the lifeboat had been left behind, to be studied by a committee.

As the boat drew nearer to shore, surging forward with the waves and the incoming tide, the brothers could see the welcoming party. The rising sun glinted off spears and shields carried by a crowd of men who were awaiting their arrival on the beach. Tall and muscular, the men wore little clothing in the balmy clime of the island. Their skin was a rich, glistening brown, their bodies adorned with bright beads and feathers, their faces stern and resolute. The shields they carried were made of wood and painted with garish designs, the spears handmade as well—wooden with stone tips.

"Honed nice and sharp, you can believe me," said Sturm gloomily. "They'll go through flesh like a knife through butter."

"We're outnumbered at least twenty to one," Tanin pointed out to Dougan, who was sitting in the prow of the boat, fingering a battle-axe that was nearly the size of the dwarf.

"Bah! Primitives!" said Dougan contemptuously, though Palin noted the dwarf's face was a bit pale. "First sight of steel, they'll bow down and worship us as gods."

The "gods'" arrival on the beach was something less than majestic. Tanin and Sturm did look quite magnificent in their bright steel armor of elven make and design—a gift from Porthios and Alhana of the United Elven Kingdoms. The breastplates glittered in the morning sun; their helms gleamed brightly. Climbing out of the boat, they sank to their shins in the sand and, within minutes, were both firmly mired.

Dougan, dressed in his suit of red velvet, demanded that the gnomes take him in to shore, so he would not ruin his clothes. The dwarf had added to his costume a wide-brimmed hat decorated with a white plume that fluttered in the ocean breeze, and he was truly a wonderful sight, standing proudly in the prow of the boat with his axe at his side, glaring sternly at the warriors drawn up in battle formation on the beach. The gnomes obeyed his injunction to the letter, running the boat aground on the beach with such force that Dougan tumbled out headfirst, narrowly missing slicing himself in two with his great battle-axe.

Palin had often imagined his first battle—fighting at the side of his brothers, combining steel and magic. He had spent the journey to shore committing the few spells he knew to memory. As they drew toward land, his pulse raced with what he told himself was excitement, not fear. He was prepared for almost any eventuality . . . with the exception of helping a cursing, sputtering, irate dwarf to his feet; trying to dislodge his brothers from the wet sand; and facing an army of silent, grim, half-naked men.

"Why don't they attack us?" Sturm muttered, floundering about in the water, trying to keep his balance. "They could cut us to ribbons!"

"Maybe they have a law that prohibits them from harming idiots!" snapped Tanin irritably.

Dougan had managed, with Palin's help, to stagger to his feet. Shaking his fist, he sent the gnomes on their way back to the ship with a parting curse, then turned and, with as much dignity as he could bluster, stomped across the beach toward the warriors. Tanin and Sturm followed more slowly, hands on the hilts of their swords. Palin came after his brothers more slowly still, his white robes wet and bedraggled, the hem caked with sand.

The warriors waited for them in silence, unmoving, their faces expressionless as they watched the strangers approach. But Palin noticed, as he drew near, that occasionally one of the men would glance uneasily back into the nearby jungle. Observing this happening more than once, Palin turned his attention to the trees. After watching and listening intently for a moment, he drew nearer Tanin.

"There's something in those trees," he said in an undertone.

"I wouldn't doubt it," Tanin growled. "Probably another fifty or so warriors."

"I don't know," Palin said thoughtfully, shaking his head. "The warriors appear to be nervous about it, maybe even—"

"Shush!" Tanin ordered sharply. "This is no time to talk, Palin! Now keep behind Sturm and me, like you're supposed to!"

"But—" Palin began.

Tanin flashed him a look of anger meant to remind the young man who was in charge. With a sigh, Palin took up his position behind his brothers. But his eyes went to the jungle and he again noticed that more than one of the warriors allowed his gaze to stray in that direction as well.

"Hail!" cried Dougan, stumping through the sand to stand in front of the warrior who, by standing out slightly in front of his fellows, appeared to be the chief. "Us gods!" proclaimed the dwarf, thumping himself on the chest. "Come from Land of Rising Sun to give greeting to our subjects on Isle of Gargath."

"You're a dwarf," said the warrior glumly, speaking excellent Common. "You've come from Ansalon, and you're probably after the Graygem."

"Well . . . uh . . . now . . ." Dougan appeared flustered. "That's . . . uh . . . a good guess, lad. We are, as it happens, mildly interested in . . . uh . . . the Graygem. If you'd be so good as to tell us where we might find it—"

"You can't have it," said the warrior, sounding depressed. He raised his spear. "We're here to stop you."

The warriors behind him nodded unenthusiastically, fumbling with their spears and clumsily falling into some sort of ragged battle formation. Again, Palin noticed many of them looking into the jungle with that same nervous, preoccupied expression.

"Well, we're going to take it!" Tanin shouted fiercely, apparently trying to drum up some enthusiasm for the conflict. "You'll have to fight us to stop us."

"I guess we will," mumbled the chief, hefting his spear in halfhearted fashion.

Somewhat confused, Tanin and Sturm nevertheless drew their swords, as Dougan, his face grim, lifted his axe. The words to a spell chant were on Palin's lips, and the Staff of Magius seemed to tremble with eagerness in his hand. But Palin hesitated. From all he'd heard, battles weren't supposed to be like this! Where was the hot blood? The ferocious hatred? The bitter determination to die where one stood rather than give an inch of ground?

The warriors shuffled forward, prodding each other along. Tanin closed on them, his sword flashing in the sun, Sturm at his back. Suddenly, a cry came from the jungle. There was movement and a rustling sound, more cries, and then a yelp of pain. A small figure dashed out of the trees, running headlong across the sand.

"Wait!" Palin yelled. "It's a child!"

The warriors turned at the sound. "Damn!" muttered the chief, tossing his shield and spear into the sand in disgust. The child—a little girl of about five—ran to the warrior and threw her arms around his legs. At that moment, another child, older than the first, came running out of the woods in pursuit.

"I thought I told you to keep her with you!" the chief said to the older child, a boy, who came dashing up.

"She bit me!" said the boy accusingly, exhibiting bloody marks on his arm.

"You're not going to hurt my daddy, are you?" the little girl asked Tanin, glaring at him with dark eyes.

"N-no," stuttered Tanin, taken aback. He lowered his sword. "We're just"—he shrugged, flushing scarlet—"talking. You know, man talk."

"Bless my beard!" exclaimed the dwarf in awe. More children were running from the jungle—children of all ages, from toddlers who could barely make their way across the sand to older boys and girls of about ten or eleven. The air was filled with their shrill voices.

"I'm bored. Can we go home?"

"Lemme hold the spear!"

"No, it's my turn! Dad said—"

"Apu said a bad word!"

"Did not!"

"Did so!"

"Look, Daddy! That short, fat man with the hair on his face! Isn't he ugly?"

Glancing at the strangers in deep embarrassment, the warriors turned from their battle formation to argue with their children.

"Listen, Blossom, Daddy's just going to be a little longer. You go back and play—"

"Apu, take your brothers back with you and *don't* let me hear you using language like that or I'll—"

"No, dear, Daddy needs the spear right now. You can carry it on the way home—"

"Halt!" roared the dwarf. Dougan's thunderous shout cut through the confusion, silencing warrior and child alike.

"Look," said Tanin, sheathing his sword, his own face flushed with embarrassment, "we don't want to fight you, especially in front of your kids."

"I know," the chief said, chagrined. "It's always like that. We haven't had a good battle in two years! Have you ever"—he gave Tanin a pained look—"tried to fight with a toddler underfoot?"

Profoundly perplexed, Tanin shook his head.

"Takes all the fun out of it," added another warrior as one child swarmed up his back and another bashed him in the shins with his shield.

"Leave them at home with their mothers, then, where they belong," said Dougan gruffly.

The warriors' expression grew grimmer still. At the mention of their mothers, several of the children began to cry.

"We can't," stated a warrior.

"Why not?" demanded Dougan.

"Because their mothers are gone!"

"It all started two years ago," said the chief, walking with Dougan and the brothers back to the village. "Lord Gargath sent a messenger to us, demanding ten maidens be paid him in tribute or he'd unleash the power of the Graygem." The warrior's gaze went to the volcano in the distance, its jagged top barely visible amid the shifting gray clouds that surrounded it. Forked lightning streaked from the cloud, and thunder rumbled. The chief shivered and shook his head. "What could we do? We paid him his tribute. But it didn't stop there. The next month, here came the messenger again. Ten more maidens, and more the month following. Soon, we ran out of maidens, and then the lord demanded our wives. Then he sent for our mothers! Now"—the chief sighed—"there isn't a woman left in the village!"

"All of them!" Sturm gaped. "He's taken *all* of them!"

The chief nodded in despair, and the child in his arms wailed in grief. "And not only us. It happened to every tribe on the island. We used to be a fierce, proud people," the chief added, his dark eyes flashing. "Our tribes were constantly at war. To win honor and glory in battle was what we lived for. To die fighting was the noblest death a man could find! Now, we lead lives of drudgery—"

"Our hands in dishwater instead of blood," said another, "mending clothes instead of cracking skulls."

"To say nothing of what *else* we're missing, without the women," added a third with a meaningful look.

"Well, why don't you go get them back!" Tanin demanded.

The warriors, to a man, looked at him with undisguised horror, many glancing over their shoulders at the smoking volcano, expressions of terror on their faces, as if fearing they might be overheard.

"Attack the powerful Lord Gargath?" asked the chief in what was practically a whisper. "Face the wrath of the Graygem's master? No!" He shuddered, holding his child close. "At least now our children have one parent."

"But if all the tribes fought together," Sturm argued, "that would be . . . how many men? Hundreds? Thousands?"

"If there were millions, we would not go up against the Master of the Graygem," said the chief.

"Well, then," said Dougan sharply, "why did you try to stop us back there on the beach? Seems to me you would be only too glad to rid yourselves of the thing!"

"Lord Gargath ordered us to fight any who tried to take it," said the chief simply.

Reaching their village—a scattering of thatched huts that had seen better days—the warriors dispersed, some taking children to bed, others hurrying to look into steaming pots, still others heading for a stream with baskets loaded with clothes.

"Dougan," said Tanin, watching all this in astonishment almost too great for words, "this doesn't make any sense! What's going on?"

"The power of the Graygem, lad," said the dwarf solemnly. "They're deep under its spell and can no longer see anything rationally. I'll lay ten to one that it's the Graygem keeping them from attacking Lord Gargath. But us, now"— the dwarf looked at the brothers cunningly—"we're not under its spell."

"Not yet," mentioned Palin.

"And therefore we stand a chance of defeating him! After all, how powerful can he be?"

"Oh, he could have an army of a couple thousand men or so," said Sturm.

"No, no," said Dougan hastily. "If he did, he would have just sent the army to attack the villages, kill the men, and carry off the women. Lord Gargath is using the power of the Graygem because that's all he's got! We must act quickly, though, lads, because its power will grow on us the longer we stay near its influence."

Tanin frowned, considering. "How do we get the Graygem, then?" he asked abruptly. "And what do we do with it after we've got it? It seems to me, we'll be in worse danger than ever!"

"Ah, leave that to me!" said Dougan, rubbing his hands. "Just help me to get it, lads."

Tanin kept on frowning.

"And think of the women—poor things," the dwarf continued sadly, "held in thrall by this wicked lord, forced to submit to his evil will. They'll undoubtedly be grateful to the brave men who rescue them. . . ."

"He's right," said Sturm in sudden resolve. "It is our duty, Tanin, as future Knights of Solamnia, to rescue the women."

"What do you say, Little Brother?" asked Tanin.

"It is my duty as a mage of the White Robes to help these people," Palin said, feeling extremely self-righteous. "*All* these people," he added.

"Plus it's a matter of honor, lad," Dougan said solemnly. "You *did* lose the bet. And it will be a few days before the gnomes have the ship repaired. . . ."

"And the women will probably be *very* grateful!" struck in Sturm.

"All right, we'll go!" said Tanin. "Though I'd rather face a dragon than fight the power of some sort of weird rock."

"Ha, ha, dragon!" repeated the dwarf, with a sickly grin that Tanin was too preoccupied to notice.

The brothers and the dwarf walked up to the chief, who was hanging laundry out to dry and keeping an anxious eye on the stew pot to see that it didn't boil over.

"Listen to me, men!" Tanin called loudly, motioning the warriors of the village to gather around him. "My brothers and the dwarf and I are going to go to the castle of this Lord Gargath to take the Graygem. Would any of you like to come along?"

Glancing at each other, the warriors shook their heads.

"Well, then," Tanin continued in exasperation, "will any of you go with us as our guide? You can come back when we reach the castle."

Again, the warriors shook their heads.

"Then we'll go alone!" Tanin said fiercely. "And we will return with the Graygem or leave our lives in that castle!"

Spinning on his heel, the big man stalked out of the camp, his brothers and the dwarf marching behind. As they left, however, they encountered dark looks from the warriors and heard muttered comments. More than a few shook their fists at them.

"They certainly don't look pleased," Tanin said. "Especially since we're the ones facing all the danger. What is it they're saying?"

"I think it's just occurred to them that the women will probably be *very* grateful," Dougan answered in a low voice.

Chapter Five

A Matter of Honor

Sturm later maintained that Tanin should have realized what was going on and kept the dwarf out of the game that night. Tanin retorted that Sturm should keep his mouth shut since he slept through the whole thing. But Palin reminded them both that they were all under the influence of the

Graygem at the time, so it probably wouldn't have made any difference anyway.

They had walked all day, moving easily through the thick jungle, following a trail that had obviously been there for years. The major problem was the heat, which was intense. Sturm and Tanin soon took off their armor and packed it away and finally convinced Palin to strip off his white robes, though he protested long against wandering the wilderness clad only in his undergarments.

"Look," said Tanin, finally, after Palin was on the verge of collapse, his robes dripping with sweat, "there aren't any women to see you, that much we know. Hang your spell bags around your waist. We can always get dressed again before we reach the next village." Palin reluctantly agreed and, other than taking some ribbing from Sturm about his skinny legs, was thankful he did so. The jungle grew steamier as the sun rose higher. Intermittent rain showers cooled the brothers and the dwarf occasionally, but in the end served only to increase the humidity.

Dougan, however, steadfastly refused to shed so much as his broad-brimmed hat, maintaining that the heat was nothing to a dwarf and ridiculing the humans for their weakness. This he did with perspiration streaming down his face until it dripped off the ends of his moustache. He marched along with a defiant air, as if daring one of them to say something, and often grumbled that they were slowing him down. Yet Palin saw Dougan more than once, when he thought no one was looking, slump down on a rock, fan himself with his hat, and mop his face with his beard.

By the time they arrived at the next village, which was about a day's walk through the jungle, all of them—even the dwarf—were so limp and tired that they barely had the strength to put their clothes and their armor back on in order to make an impressive show. Word of their coming must have traveled in some mysterious way (Palin thought he knew, then, the reason for the strange drumbeats they'd been hearing), for they were met by the men of the village and the children. The men regarded them coldly (though more than a few eyes flashed at the sight of the elven armor), gave them food and drink, and indicated a hut where they could spend the night. Tanin made a stirring speech about storming Gargath Castle and asked for volunteers.

The only responses were dark looks, shuffling feet, and a muttered comment, "I can't. I've got a chicken stewing. . . ."

This being no more than they had expected, the brothers stripped off their armor and their clothes and went to bed. Their night's rest was unbroken, save for slapping at some sort of winged, carnivorous insect that apparently had a craving for human flesh, and one other incident.

Around midnight, Tanin was wakened by the dwarf, shaking his shoulder and loudly calling his name.

"Whasit?" mumbled Tanin sleepily, fumbling for his sword.

"Nay, lad, put your weapon away," said Dougan, hurriedly. "I just need to know something, lad. You and me and your brothers, we're comrades, aren't we?"

Tanin recalled, as well as he could recall anything, that the dwarf had seemed particularly anxious about this and had repeated the question several times.

"Yeah, comrades," Tanin muttered, rolling over.

"What's mine is yours, yours is mine?" persisted the dwarf, leaning over to look the young man in the face.

"Yeah, yeah." Tanin waved a hand, brushing away a feeding insect and the dwarf's beard at the same time.

"Thank you, lad! Thank you," said Dougan gratefully. "You won't regret it."

Tanin said later that the dwarf's last words, "You won't regret it," lingered ominously in his dreams, but he was too tired to wake up and ponder the situation.

As it was, he had plenty of time for pondering the next morning when he woke to find a spear point at his throat and several tall warriors standing over him. A quick glance showed him his brothers in similar circumstances.

"Sturm!" Tanin called, not daring to move and keeping his hands in plain sight. "Palin, wake up!"

His brothers woke quickly at the sound of alarm in his voice, and stared at their captors in sleepy surprise.

"Tanin," said Palin, keeping his voice even, "what's going on?"

"I don't know, but I'm going to find out!" Tanin angrily thrust the spear point aside. "What is this nonsense?" he asked, starting to stand up. The spear point was at his throat again, joined, this time, by two more—one at his chest, the other jabbing him in the back.

"Tell them that no matter how grateful the women are, it won't matter to us!" said Sturm, swallowing and trying in vain to inch backward. The spear followed him. "We're going to be knights! We've taken vows of celibacy. . . ."

"It's . . . uh . . . not the women, lad," muttered a shamefaced Dougan, entering the hut and thrusting his head in between the warriors. "It's . . . uh . . . a matter of honor . . . so to speak. The truth of it is, lads," the dwarf continued with a heart-rending sigh, "I got into a wee bit of a game last night."

"So?" grunted Tanin. "What has that got to do with us?"

"I'll explain," Dougan began, licking his lips, his eyes darting from one to the other of the brothers. "I threw the bones well the first hour or two. Won the chief's feather headdress *and* two cows. I was going to quit then, I swear it, but the old boy was upset and so what could I do but let him try to win them back? My luck was going that good, I bet it all on one toss, plus threw in my axe and my own hat as well."

Tanin looked at the dwarf's bare head. "You lost."

Dougan's shoulders slumped. "I didn't miss the other so much, but I couldn't do without my hat, now could I? So I bet all my money against the hat and—" He looked at Tanin wistfully.

"You lost that, too," Tanin muttered.

"Snake eyes," said the dwarf sadly.

"So now you've lost your money, your axe, and your hat."

"Not quite," Dougan hedged. "You see, I just couldn't do without my hat. . . . And I didn't have anything left that the old boy wanted, my jacket not fitting him. And you *did* say we were comrades, share and share alike—"

"When did you say that?" Sturm demanded, glaring at Tanin.

"I don't remember!" Tanin growled.

"So, I bet your armor," said the dwarf.

"You what?" Tanin roared in fury.

"The chief had taken a liking to it when he saw it on you last evening," continued Dougan rapidly. Even with five spears pointed directly at him, Tanin looked extremely formidable and extremely angry. "I bet your armor against my axe and hat, and I won." The dwarf looked smug.

"Thank Paladine!" breathed Tanin, relaxing.

"Then," said Dougan, looking uncomfortable, "since my luck was obviously turning, I decided to try for my money back. I bet the armor, my hat, and"—he pointed—"the magic staff against my money, the cows, and the axe."

This time it was Palin who, oblivious of the spears, sat forward, his face deathly pale, his lips ashen. "You bet . . . my staff!" He could scarcely speak. Reaching out a trembling hand, he grasped hold of the staff, which lay at his side even while he slept.

"Aye, lad," said Dougan, regarding him with wide-eyed innocence. "We're comrades. Share and share—"

"This staff," said Palin in a low, shaking voice, "belonged to my uncle, Raistlin Majere! It was a gift from him."

"Indeed?" Dougan appeared impressed. "I wish I had known that, lad," he said wistfully, "I would have wagered more—"

"What happened?" Palin demanded feverishly.

"I lost." Dougan heaved a sigh. "I've seen a man roll snake eyes twice in a game only once before and that was when I— Well, never mind."

"You lost my staff!" Palin seemed near fainting.

"And our armor?" Sturm shouted, veins swelling in his neck.

"Wait!" Dougan held up his hand hastily. The warriors with the spears, despite their weapons and their obvious advantage, were beginning to look a little nervous. "I knew how upset you lads would be, losing all your possessions like this, so I did the only thing I could. I wagered your swords."

This time the shock was so great that neither Tanin nor Sturm could speak, they simply stared at Dougan in stunned silence.

"I put up the swords and my battle-axe against the magic staff and my hat. I truly wish"—Dougan glanced at the shaken Palin—"that I'd known the staff belonged to Raistlin of the Black Robes. Even here, they've heard of him, and I likely could have gotten the chief to throw in the armor. As it was, he wasn't all that impressed with what he'd seen of the staff—"

"Get on with it!" Palin cried in a choked voice, clutching the staff close.

"I won!" Dougan spread his hands, then sighed again, only this was a sigh of ecstasy. "Ah, what a throw that was. . . ."

"So . . . I have my staff?" Palin asked timidly, brightening.

"We have our swords?" Tanin and Sturm began to breathe.

"Finding that my luck had shifted," the dwarf continued, plunging the brothers into gloom once more, "I decided to try for the armor again. Figuring what good were swords without armor, I bet the weapons and—" He gestured bleakly toward the warriors with the spears.

"You lost," Tanin said glumly.

"But I still have my staff?" Palin asked nervously.

"Aye, lad. I tried to use it to win back the swords, my axe, and the armor, but the chief didn't want it." Dougan shook his head, then gazed at Palin intently, a sudden, cunning expression twisting his face. "But if you were to tell him it belonged to the great Raistlin Majere, perhaps I could—"

"No!" snarled Palin, holding the staff close.

"But, lad," pleaded the dwarf, "my luck's bound to change. And we're comrades, after all. Share and share alike . . . "

"This is great!" said Sturm gloomily, watching the last of his armor being carried out of the hut. "Well, I guess there's nothing left to do now but go back to the ship."

"The ship?" Dougan appeared astonished. "When we're so close? Why, Lord Gargath's castle's only a day's march from here!"

"And what are we going to do when we get there?" Tanin demanded furiously. "Knock on the door in our underwear and ask him to lend us weapons so that we can fight him?"

"Look at it this way, Big Brother," Sturm pointed out, "he might drop over dead from laughter."

"How can you joke at a time like this?" Tanin raged. "And I'm not certain I'm ready to leave yet."

"Easy, my brothers," Palin said softly. "If all we lose from this fool quest is some weapons and armor, I'm beginning to think we can count ourselves lucky. I agree with Sturm, Tanin. We'd better head back for the ship before the day gets much hotter."

"That's easy for you to say!" Tanin retorted bitterly. "You've still got your precious staff!" He looked over to the chief's hut, where the old man was happily decking himself out in the bright armor, putting most of it on upside down. Then he cast a dark glance at the contrite Dougan. "I suppose Palin's right," Tanin said grudgingly, glaring at the dwarf. "We should count ourselves lucky. We've had enough of this fool quest, dwarf. We're getting out of here before we lose anything else—like our lives!"

Turning, Tanin found himself, once again, facing a ring of spears and this time his own sword, held by a grinning warrior.

"Wanna bet, lad?" Dougan said cheerfully, twirling his moustache.

"I thought as much," Palin remarked.

"You're always thinking 'as much' when it's too late to do anything about it!" Tanin snapped.

"It was too late when we first set eyes on the dwarf," Palin said in low tones.

The three, plus Dougan, were being escorted down the jungle trail, spears at their backs. The castle of Lord Gargath loomed ahead of them. They could see it quite clearly now—a huge, misshapen building made entirely of shining gray marble. All three brothers had visited the Tower of High Sorcery in Wayreth Forest, and they had been impressed and over-awed by the magical aura that surrounded it. They felt a similar awe approaching this strange castle, only it was an awe mingled with the wild desire to laugh hysterically.

None of them could tell afterward describe Castle Gargath, since the appearance of the castle shifted constantly. First it was a massive fortress with four tall, stalwart towers topped by battlements. As they watched in amaze-ment, the towers swelled out and spiraled upward into graceful minarets. Then the minarets melted together, forming one gigantic dome that separated into four square towers once more. While all this was going on, turrets sprouted from the walls like fungi, windows blinked open and shut, a draw-bridge over a moat became a bower of gray roses over a still, gray pond.

"The power of the Graygem," Dougan remarked.

" 'The power of the Graygem,' " Tanin mimicked sarcastically. He shook his fist at the dwarf. "I'm getting so sick of hearing about that blasted rock that I—"

"I think I figured out what's going on," Palin interrupted.

"Well, what?" Sturm asked miserably. "They don't want us to go, appar-ently. Yet they threaten to kill us if we try to turn back! They take our clothes . . ." In addition to losing their armor and their weapons, he and Tanin had been stripped of their clothes; the chief having discovered that the armor chafed without anything underneath it. Sturm and Tanin, there-fore, were now approaching Gargath Castle clad only in loincloths (having coldly refused the offer of breastplates made of bone).

Palin and Dougan had been more fortunate, the mage having kept his robes and the dwarf his red velvet jacket and breeches (minus the hat). The reason for this leniency on the chief's part was, Palin suspected, Dougan's whispered remarks to the chief concerning the staff. Contrary to what the dwarf had anticipated, the fact that the staff had belonged to Raistlin Majere caused the chief to open his eyes wide in terror. Palin also suspected Dougan of continuing to try to drum up a game (the dwarf wanted his hat back badly), but the chief obviously wanted no part of an object of such evil. The members of the tribe kept a respectful distance from Palin after that, some waving chickens' feet in his direction when they thought he wasn't watching.

That didn't stop the warriors from marching him off down the trail at spear-point toward the castle with his brothers and the chagrined Dougan, however.

"Put yourself in the place of one of these warriors," said Palin, sweating in his hot robes but not daring to take them off for fear the warriors would grab them, too. "You are under the influence of the Graygem, which is literally chaos incarnate. You hate the Graygem more than anything, yet you are ordered to guard it with your life. Because of the Graygem, you've lost your women. Strangers come to take the Graygem and rescue your women, who will undoubtedly be grateful to their saviors. You don't want strangers saving your womenfolk, but you'd give anything to have your women back. You must guard the Graygem, but you'd do anything to get rid of it. Are you following me?"

"Sort of," Tanin said cautiously. "Go on."

"So you take the strangers," Palin finished, "and send them to the castle naked and weaponless, knowing they're bound to lose, yet hoping in your heart they'll win."

"That makes sense, in a weird sort of way," Sturm admitted, looking at Palin with undisguised admiration. "So, what do we do now?"

"Yes, Palin," Tanin said gravely. "I can fight minotaurs and draconians . . . I'd *rather* be fighting minotaurs and draconians," he added, breathing heavily, the heat and humidity taking their toll on the big man, "but I'm lost here. I can't fight chaos. I don't understand what's going on. If we're going to get out of this, it's up to you and your magic, Little Brother."

Palin's eyes stung with sudden tears. It had been worth it, he thought. It had been worth this whole insane adventure to know that he had finally won his brothers' respect and admiration and trust. It was something a man might willingly die to achieve . . . For a moment, he did not trust himself to speak, but walked on in silence, leaning on the Staff of Magius, which felt oddly cool and dry in the hot, humid jungle.

"I don't know what to do," he said after a moment when he had his voice back. "But if we're going to get out of this, it's up to *all* of us." Reaching out to his brothers, Palin hugged each of them unashamedly. "We're together, and that counts for much. Somehow, we'll make this come out right!"

Glancing over at the dwarf, Palin was disconcerted to find Dougan regarding him with a wolfish leer on the black-bearded face. The dwarf didn't say anything aloud but, giving Palin a wink, he formed words with his lips.

"Wanna bet?"

Chapter Six

Castle Gargath

It was nearing sundown when they reached the outer walls of Castle Gargath. The walls shifted aspect just like the castle. Sometimes they appeared to be built of bricks. When the group looked again, however, they were hedges, then iron bars. The change was so rapid that it made one dizzy to watch.

On reaching the base of the shifting walls, the warriors left them, despite another recruiting speech from Tanin. The speech was a halfhearted attempt at best. The fact that he was giving it practically naked lessened his enthusiasm, plus he was fairly certain it was bound to fail. Nonetheless, he made the attempt.

"Come with us! Show this evil lord that you are men! That you intend to stand up to him and fight! Show him you are willing to risk your lives in defense of your homes!"

Sure enough, the speech had not worked. The moment the shadow of the shifting castle walls fell over them, the warriors backed away, looking up at it in terror. Shaking their heads and muttering, they fled back into the jungle.

"At least leave us your spears?" Sturm pleaded.

That didn't work either.

"They need their spears," Tanin said, "to make certain we don't hightail it back to the ship."

"Aye, you're right, lad," said Dougan, peering into the trees. "They're out there, watching us. And there they'll stay until—" He stopped.

"Until what?" Palin demanded coldly. He could still see the dwarf's leer and hear the unspoken words, and he shivered in the jungle heat.

"Until they're certain we're not coming back. Right?" Sturm said.

"Now, laddie, we'll be coming back," Dougan said soothingly, stroking his beard. "After all, you have me with you. And we're comrades—"

"Share and share alike," Tanin and Sturm both said grumpily.

"The first thing we have to do is make some weapons," Tanin continued. Thick jungle vegetation grew all around them. Strange-looking trees of various types, festooned with hanging vines and brightly colored flowers, grew right up to within a foot of the wall. And there the vegetation stopped. "Not even plants come near this place," he muttered. "Palin, give me your knife."

"Good idea," said the young mage. "I'd forgotten about it." Rolling up his white sleeve, Palin fumbled at the dagger in its cunning leather thong, which held it to his forearm and was supposed to—at a flick of its owner's wrist—release the dagger and allow it to drop into Palin's hand. But the cunning thong was apparently more cunning that its master, for Palin couldn't get the dagger loose.

"Here," he said, flushing in embarrassment and holding out his arm to Tanin, "you get it."

Keeping his smile carefully concealed, Tanin managed to free the dagger, which he and Sturm used to cut off tree branches. These they honed into crude spears, working rapidly. Day was dying a lingering death, the light fading from the sky, leaving it a sickly gray color.

"Do you know anything of this Lord Gargath?" Tanin asked Dougan as he worked, whittling the point of the green stick sharp.

"No," said the dwarf, watching in disapproval. He refused to either make or carry a wooden spear. "A fine sight I'd look if I'm killed, standing before Reorx with a stick in my hand! Naw, I need no weapon but my bare hands!" the dwarf snarled. Now he was rubbing his chin, pacing back and forth beneath the strange walls that were now made of shining black marble. "I know nothing of this present Lord Gargath, save what I could find out from those cowards." Dougan waved his hand contemptuously at the long-gone warriors.

"What do they say?"

"That he is what you might expect of someone who has been under the influence of the Graygem for years!" Dougan said, eyeing Tanin irritably. "He is a wild man! Capable of great good or great evil, as the mood—or the gem—sways him. Some say," the dwarf added in low tones, switching his gaze to Palin, "that he is a wizard, a renegade, granting his allegiance to neither white, nor black, nor red. He lives only for himself—and the gem."

Shivering, Palin gripped his staff more tightly. Renegade mages refused to follow the laws and judgments of the Conclave of Wizards, laws that had been handed down through the centuries in order to keep magic alive in a world where it was despised and distrusted. All wizards, those who followed both the paths of good and of evil, subscribed to these laws. Renegades were a threat to everyone and, as such, their lives were forfeit.

It would be Palin's duty, as a mage of the White Robes, to try to reclaim the renegade or, if that failed, to trap him and bring him to the conclave for justice. It would be a difficult task for a powerful wizard of the White Robes, much less an apprentice mage. Those of the Black Robes had it easier. "You, my uncle, would have simply killed him," Palin murmured in a low voice, leaning his cheek against his staff.

"What do you think he's done with the women?" Sturm asked anxiously.

The dwarf shrugged. "Used them for his pleasure, tossed them into the volcano, sacrificed them in some unholy magic rite. How should I know?"

"Well, we're about as ready as we'll ever be, I guess," Tanin said heavily, gathering up a handful of spears. "These look like toys," he muttered. "Maybe the dwarf's right. If we're facing an evil wizard gone berserk, we might as well die fighting with dignity instead of like some kid playing at knights and goblins."

"A weapon's a weapon, Tanin," Sturm said matter-of-factly, taking a spear in his hand. "At least it gives us *some* advantage. . . ."

The three brothers and the dwarf approached the wall that was still changing its aspect so often it made them dizzy to watch it.

"I don't suppose there's any point trying to find a secret way in," Tanin said.

"By the time we found it, it'd likely be turning into the front door," Dougan agreed. "If we wait here long enough, there's bound to be an opening."

Sure enough, but not exactly the opening any of them anticipated.

One moment they were looking at a wall of solid stone ("Dwarvish make," remarked Dougan, admiringly), then it changed to a wall of water, thundering down around them out of nowhere, soaking them with its spray.

"We can get through this, I think!" Sturm cried above the noise of the waterfall. "I can see through it! The castle's on the other side!"

"Yes, and there's likely to be a chasm on the other side as well!" Tanin returned.

"Wait," said Palin. "*Shirak!*" He spoke the magic word to the staff and instantly the faceted crystal globe on top burst into light.

"Ah, I wish the chief had seen *that!*" said the dwarf wistfully.

Palin thrust the staff into the water, simply with the idea of being able to see something beyond it. To his amazement, however, the water parted the instant the staff touched it. Flowing down around the staff, it formed an archway that they could walk through, safe and dry.

"I'll be damned!" Tanin said in awe. "Did you know it would do that, Little Brother?"

"No," Palin admitted shakily, wondering what other powers Raistlin had invested into the staff.

"Well, thank Paladine it did," Sturm said, peering through the hole in the water. "All safe over here," he reported, stepping through. "In fact," he added as Palin and Tanin and Dougan—with a wide-eyed gaze of longing at the staff—followed, "it's grass!" Sturm, in wonderment, looked around in the gray gloom by the light of the staff. Behind them, the water changed again, this time to a wall of bamboo. Ahead of them stretched a long, smooth sward that rose up a gentle slope, leading to the castle itself.

"Now it's grass, but it's liable to change into a lava pit any moment," Palin pointed out.

"You're right, Little Brother," Tanin grunted. "We'd better run for it."

Run they did, Palin hiking up his white robes, the stout dwarf huffing and puffing along about three steps behind. Whether they truly made their destination before the sward had time to change into something more sinister or whether the sward was always a sward, they never knew. At any rate, they reached the castle wall just as night's black shadows closed in on them, and they were still standing on smooth, soft grass.

"Now all we need," said Sturm, "is a way inside—"

The blank wall of gray marble shimmered in the staff's light, and a small wooden door appeared, complete with iron hinges and an iron lock.

Hurrying forward, Tanin tugged at the lock.

"Bolted fast," he reported.

"Just when a kender would come in handy," Sturm said with a sigh.

"Kender! Bite your tongue!" Dougan muttered in disgust.

"Palin, try the staff," Tanin ordered, standing aside.

Hesitantly, Palin touched the brilliantly glowing crystal of the staff to the lock. The lock not only gave way, but it actually melted, forming a puddle of iron at Palin's feet.

"Lad," said the dwarf, swallowing, "your uncle must have been a remarkable man. That's all I can say."

"I wonder what else it can do?" Palin stared at the staff with a mixture of awe, pride, and frustration.

"We'll have to worry about that later! Inside," said Tanin, yanking open the door. "Sturm, you go first. Palin follow him. We'll use your staff for light. The dwarf and I'll be right behind you."

They found themselves crowded together on a flight of narrow, winding stairs that spiraled upward. Walls surrounded them on all sides, and they could see nothing save the stairs vanishing into darkness.

"You realize," said Palin suddenly, "that the door will—" Whirling around, he shone the light of the staff on a blank wall.

"Disappear," finished Tanin grimly.

"There goes our way out!" Shuddering, Sturm looked around. "These stairs could change! Any moment, we could be encased in solid rock!"

"Keep moving!" ordered Tanin urgently.

Running up the steep stairs as fast as they could, expecting to find themselves walking on anything from hot coals to a swinging bridge, they climbed up and up until, at last, the stout dwarf could go no farther.

"I've got to rest, lads," Dougan said, panting, leaning against a stone wall that was, unaccountably, remaining a stone wall.

"Nothing inside seems to be changing," Palin gasped, weary himself from the unaccustomed exercise. He looked with envy at his brothers. Their bronze-skinned, muscular bodies gleamed in the staff's light. Neither was even breathing hard.

"Palin, shine the light up here!" Sturm ordered, peering ahead.

His legs aching so that he thought he could never move them again, Palin forced himself to take another step, shining the staff's light around a corner of the stairwell.

"There's a door!" Sturm said softly, in triumph. "We've reached the top!"

"I wonder what's beyond it," Tanin said darkly.

He was interrupted by, of all things, a giggle. "Why don't you open it and find out?" called a laughing voice from the other side of the door. "It's not locked."

The brothers looked at each other. Dougan frowned. Palin forgot his aching body, forcing himself to concentrate on his spellcasting. Tanin's face tightened and his jaw muscles clenched. Gripping his spear, he thrust his way past Dougan and Palin to stand beside Sturm.

Cautiously, both warriors put their hands on the door.

"One, two, three," Sturm counted in a whisper.

On the count of three, he and Tanin threw their combined weight against the door, knocking it open and leaping through, spears at the ready. Palin ran after them, his hands extended, a spell of fire on his lips. Behind him, he could hear the dwarf roaring.

They were greeted with peals of merry laughter.

"Did you ever see," came the giggling voice, "such cute legs?"

The mist of battle rage clearing from his eyes, Palin stared around blankly. He was surrounded, literally, by what must have been hundreds of women. Beside him, he heard Sturm's sharp intake of breath, and he saw, dimly, Tanin lower his spear in confusion. From somewhere on the floor at his feet, he heard Dougan swearing, the dwarf having tripped over the stoop in his charge and fallen flat on his face. But Palin was too stunned, staring at his captors, to pay any attention to him.

An incredibly gorgeous, dark-haired and dark-eyed beauty approached Tanin. Putting her hand on his spear, she gently pushed it to one side. Her eyes lingered appreciatively on the young man's strong body, most of which—due to the loincloth—was on exhibit.

"My, my," said the young woman in a sultry voice, "did you know it was my birthday?"

More laughter sounded through the vast stone hall like the chiming of many bells.

"Just—just stay back," Tanin ordered gruffly, raising his spear and keeping the woman at bay.

"Well, of course," she said, raising her hands in mock terror. "If that's what you *really* want."

Tanin, his eyes still on the dark-haired beauty, fell back a pace to stand beside Palin. "Little Brother," he whispered, beads of sweat on his upper lip and trickling down his forehead, "are these women enchanted? Under some sort of spell?"

"N-no," stammered Palin, staring around him. "They . . . they don't appear to be. I don't sense any kind of magic, other than the force of the Graygem. It's much stronger here, but that's because we're closer to it."

"Lads," said the dwarf urgently, scrambling to his feet and thrusting himself between them, "we're in big trouble."

"We are?" Tanin asked dubiously, still holding the spear in front of him and noticing that Sturm was doing likewise. "Explain yourself, dwarf!" he growled. "What do you know about these women? They certainly don't appear to be prisoners! Are they banshees, vampires? What?"

"Worse," gasped the dwarf, mopping his face with his beard, his eyes staring wildly at the laughing, pointing females. "Lads, think! We're the first to enter this castle! These women probably haven't seen a man in two years!"

Chapter Seven

Our Heroes

Surrounded by hundreds of admiring women reaching out to touch them and fondle them, the confused and embarrassed "rescuers" were captured by kindness. Laughing and teasing them, the women led the brothers and the dwarf from the vast entry hall to a smaller room in the castle, a room filled with silken wall hangings and large, comfortable silk-covered couches. Before they knew quite what was happening, the men were being shoved down among the cushions by soft hands, the women offering them wine, sumptuous food, and delicacies of all sorts . . . *all* sorts.

"I think it's sweet, you came all this way to rescue us," purred one of the women, leaning against Sturm and running her hand over his shoulder. Long blond hair fell down her bare arm. She wore it tucked behind one ear, held back by a flower. Her gown, made of something gray and filmy, left very little to the imagination.

"All in a day's work," said Sturm, smiling. "We're going to be made Knights of Solamnia, you know," he added conversationally. "Probably for doing this very deed."

"Really? Tell me more."

But the blonde wasn't the least bit interested in the knights. She wasn't even listening to Sturm, Palin realized, watching his brother with growing irritation. The big warrior was rambling on somewhat incoherently about the Oath and the Measure, all the while fondling the silky blond hair and gazing into blue eyes.

Palin was ill at ease. The young mage felt a burning in his blood; his head buzzed—not an unusual sensation around such lovely, seductive females. He felt no desire for these women, however. They were strangely repulsive to him. It was the magic he sensed, burning within him. He wanted to concentrate on it, on his feeling of growing power. Thrusting aside a doe-eyed beauty who was trying to feed him grapes, Palin inched his way among the cushions to get nearer to Sturm, who was enjoying the attentions of the attractive blonde to the fullest.

"Sturm, what are you doing? This could be a trap, an ambush!" Palin said in an undertone.

"Lighten up for once, Little Brother," Sturm said mildly, putting his arm around the blonde and drawing her close. "Here, I'll put your mind at ease. Tell me," he said, kissing the blonde's rosy lips, "is this an ambush?"

"Yes!" She giggled, wriggling closer. "You're under attack, right now."

"There you are, Palin. No help for it. We're surrounded." Sturm kissed the girl's neck. "I surrender," he said softly, "unconditionally."

"Tanin?" Alarmed, Palin looked to his oldest brother for help, and was relieved to see the serious young man getting to his feet, despite all efforts of the dark-haired beauty to drag him back down beside her. The dwarf, too, was doing his best to escape.

"Get away! Leave me be, woman!" Dougan roared, slapping at the hands of a lithesome girl. Struggling up from among the cushions, the red-faced dwarf turned to face the women.

"What about Lord Gargath? Where is he?" the dwarf demanded. "Using you women to seduce us, then capture us, no doubt?"

"Lord Gargath? Hardly!" The dark-haired beauty who had been making much of Tanin laughed, as did the other women in the room. Shrugging her lovely shoulders, she glanced at the ceiling. "He's up there . . . somewhere," she said without interest, caressing Tanin's bare chest. The big man shoved her away, glancing nervously about the room.

"For once, you've made sense, dwarf. We better find this Gargath before he finds us. Come on." Tanin took a step toward a door at the end of the perfumed, candlelit chamber, but the dark-haired beauty caught hold of his arm.

"Relax, warrior," she whispered. "You don't need to worry about Lord Gargath. He won't bother you or anybody." She ran her fingers admiringly through Tanin's thick red curls.

"I'll see for myself," Tanin returned, but he sounded less enthusiastic.

"Very well, if you must." The woman sighed languorously, nestling her body against Tanin's. "But it's a waste of time—time that could be spent in much more pleasant pursuits. The dried up old wizard's been our prisoner now for two years."

"He's *your* prisoner?" Tanin gaped.

"Well, yes," said the blonde, looking up from nibbling at Sturm's ear. "He was such a boring old thing. Talking about pentagrams and wanting to know which of us were virgins and asking a lot of other personal questions. So we locked him in his old tower with his stupid rock." She kissed Sturm's muscular shoulder.

"Then who's been taking the women hostage all these months?" Palin demanded.

"Well, we did, of course," said the dark-haired beauty.

"You?" Palin said, stunned. He put his hand to his forehead and noticed his skin felt abnormally hot. He was dizzy, and his head ached. The room and everything in it seemed to be just slightly out of focus.

"This is a wonderful life!" said the blonde, sitting back and teasingly rebuffing Sturm's attempts to pull her down. "The Graygem provides all we need. We live in luxury. There is no work, no cooking and mending—"

"No children screaming—"

"No husbands coming back from battle, bleeding and dirty—"

"No washing clothes in the stream day after day—"

"No endless talks of war and bragging about great deeds—"

"We read books," said the dark-haired beauty. "The wizard has many in his library. We became educated, and we found out we didn't have to live that kind of life anymore. We wanted our sisters and our mothers to share our comfortable surroundings with us, so *we* kept up the ruse, demanding that hostages be brought to the castle until all of us were here."

"Bless my beard!" exclaimed the dwarf in awe.

"All we lack are some nice men, to keep us from being lonely at night," said the blonde, smiling at Sturm. "And now that's been taken care of, thanks to the Graygem. . . ."

"I'm going to go find Lord Gargath," said Palin, standing up abruptly. But he was so dizzy that he staggered, scattering cushions over the floor. "Are the rest of you coming?" he asked, fighting this strange weakness and wondering why his brothers didn't seem afflicted.

"Yes," said Tanin, extricating himself with difficulty from the dark-haired beauty's embrace.

"Count on me, lad," said Dougan grimly.

"Sturm?" said Palin.

"Just leave me here," said Sturm. "I'll act as . . . rear guard. . . ."

The women broke into laughter.

"Sturm!" Tanin repeated angrily.

Sturm waved his hand. "Go ahead, if you're so keen on talking to some moldy old wizard, when you could be here, enjoying . . . "

Tanin opened his mouth again, his brows coming together in anger. But Palin stopped him. "Leave this to me," the young mage said with a twisted smile. Setting the staff down carefully among the cushions, Palin lifted both hands and held them out, pointing at Sturm. Then he began to chant.

"Hey! What are you doing? Stop!" Sturm gasped.

But Palin continued chanting and began raising his hands. As he did so, Sturm's prone body rose into the air, too, until soon the young man was floating a good six feet off the floor.

"Wonderful trick! Show us some more!" called out the women, applauding.

Palin spoke again, snapped his fingers, and ropes appeared out of nowhere, snaking up from the floor to wrap themselves around Sturm's arms and legs. The women squealed in glee, many of them transferring their admiring gazes from the muscular Sturm—now bound hand and foot—to the mage who could perform such feats.

"G-good trick, Palin. Now put me down!" Sturm said, licking his lips and glancing beneath him nervously. There was nothing between him and the floor but air.

Pleased with himself, Palin left Sturm in the air and turned to Tanin. "Shall I bring him along?" he asked casually, expecting to see Tanin also regarding him with awe.

Instead, Palin found his older brother's brows furrowed in concern. "Palin," said Tanin in a low voice, "how did you do that?"

"Magic, my dear brother," Palin said, thinking suddenly how unaccountably stupid Tanin was.

"I know it was magic," Tanin said sharply. "And I admit I don't know much about magic. But I do know that only a powerful wizard could perform such a feat as that. *Not* one who just recently passed his test!"

Looking back at the levitated Sturm hovering helplessly in the air, Palin nodded. "You're right," he said proudly. "I performed a very advanced spell, without any assistance or aid! Not even the Staff of Magius helped me!" Reaching out, he took hold of the staff. The wood was cold to the touch, icy cold, almost painful. Palin gasped, almost dropping it. But then he noticed that the dizziness was easing. He felt his skin grow cool; the buzzing in his head diminished. "My magic!" he murmured. "The Graygem must be enhancing it! I've only been here a short while, and look what I can do! I have the power of an archmage. If I had the gem, I'd be as strong as my uncle! Maybe stronger!" His eyes glistened; his body began to tremble. "I'd use my power for good, of course. I would seize the tower at Palanthas from Dalamar and cleanse it of its evil. I would lift the curse from the Shoikan Grove, enter my uncle's laboratory." Thoughts and visions of the future came to him in a swirl of wild colors, so real and vivid he literally reeled at the sight.

Strong hands held him. Blinking, clearing the mist from his eyes, Palin looked down to see himself reflected in the bright, dark, cunning eyes of the dwarf. "Steady, laddie," said Dougan, "you're flying high, too high for one whose wings have just sprouted."

"Leave me alone!" Palin cried, pulling away from the dwarf's grip. "You want the gem yourself!"

"Aye, laddie," said Dougan softly, stroking his black beard. "And I have a right to it. I'm the *only* one who has a right to it, in fact!"

"Might makes right, dwarf," Palin said with a sneer. Picking up his staff, he started to walk toward the door. "Coming?" he asked Tanin coldly, "or must I bring you along as I'm carrying that great oaf!" Gesturing toward Sturm, he drew the young man toward him with a motion of his hand. Twisting his head, Sturm gazed back at Tanin in fear and alarm as he drifted through the air.

"Oh, no! Don't leave! Do some more tricks!" cried the women in dismay.

"Stop, young mage!" Dougan cried. "You're falling under the spell!"

"Palin!" Tanin's quiet voice cut through the buzzing in Palin's head and the laughter of the women and the shouts of the dwarf. "Don't listen to Dougan or me or anyone for a moment. Just listen to yourself."

"And what's *that* supposed to mean, my brother?" Palin scoffed. "Something wise that suddenly struck you? Did a brain finally make an appearance through all that muscle?"

He leered mockingly at Tanin, expecting—no, *hoping* that his brother would become angry and try to stop him. Then I'll *really* show him a trick or two! Palin thought.

But Tanin just stood there, regarding him gravely.

And then it was his uncle—Raistlin—regarding the young mage gravely . . . sadly, in disappointment.

"I—I—Name of the gods!" Palin faltered, putting his hand to his head. His cruel words came back to him. "Tanin, I'm sorry! I don't know what's come over me." Turning, he saw Sturm, hanging helplessly in the air. "Sturm!" Palin held out his hands. "I'm sorry! I'll let you go—"

"Palin, don't—!" Sturm began wildly, but it was too late.

The spell broken, the young man fell to the floor with a yell and a crash, to be instantly surrounded by the cooing and clucking women. It was a few moments before Sturm made his appearance again, his red hair tousled, his face flushed. Getting to his feet, he pushed the women aside and limped toward his brothers.

"I was wrong," Palin said, shivering. "I understand now. These women *are* being held in thrall . . . "

"Aye, lad," said Dougan. "Just as you were yourself. It's the power of the Graygem, trying to take hold of you, exploiting your weaknesses as it did theirs."

"By giving us what we want," Palin said thoughtfully.

"That's what we'll turn into, the longer we stay here," Tanin added. "Slaves of the Graygem. Don't you see, these women are guarding it just as effectively inside this castle as their men are outside. That's why nothing shifts in here. The Graygem's keeping it stable for them!"

The women began sidling nearer, reaching out their hands once more. "How boring . . . don't go . . . don't leave us . . . stupid rock . . ."

"Well, let's go find this Lord Gargath then," Sturm muttered, shamefaced. Try as he might, his gaze still strayed toward the blonde, who was blowing kisses at him.

"Take your spears," said Tanin, shoving aside the soft hands that were clinging to him. "These women might or might not be telling us the truth. That old wizard could be laughing at us right now."

"They said he was 'up there.' " Palin gazed at the ceiling. "But where? How do we get there?"

"Uh, I believe I know the way, laddie," Dougan said. "Just a hunch, mind you," he added hastily, seeing Tanin's dark look. "That door, there, leads upstairs . . . I think. . . ."

"Humpf." Tanin growled, but went to investigate the door, his brothers and the dwarf following behind.

"What did you mean, *you're* the only one who has a right to the Graygem?" Palin asked Dougan in an undertone.

"Did I say that?" The dwarf looked at him shrewdly. "Must have been the gem talking. . . ."

"Oh, please don't go!" cried the women.

"Never mind. They'll be coming back soon," predicted the dark-haired beauty.

"And when you do come back, maybe you can show us some more of those cute magic tricks," called the blonde to Palin politely.

Chapter Eight

Lord Gargath

Dougan was right. The door led to another flight of narrow stairs, carved out of the stone walls of the castle. It was pitch dark; the only light was the burning crystal atop the Staff of Magius. After another leg-aching climb, they came to a large wooden door.

"Would you look at that!" Sturm said, stunned.

"What in the name of the Abyss is it?" Tanin wondered.

It was a fantastic mechanism, sitting in front of the door. Barely visible in the shadows, it was made of iron and had all sorts of iron arms and gears and rope pulleys and winches extending from the stone floor up to the ceiling.

"Hold the light closer, Palin," Tanin said, stooping down beside it. "There's something in the center, surrounded by a bunch of . . . mirrors."

Cautiously, Palin held the light down near the device and the room was suddenly illuminated as if by a hundred suns. Tanin shrieked and covered his eyes with his hands. "I can't see a thing!" he cried, staggering back against the wall. "Move the staff! Move the staff!"

"It's a sundial!" Palin reported, holding the staff back and staring at the device in astonishment. "Surrounded by mirrors . . ."

"Ah," said Dougan triumphantly, "a gnome timelock."

"A timelock?"

"Aye, lad. You wait until the dial casts the shadow of the sun on the correct time, and the lock will open."

"But," pointed out Palin in confusion, "the way the mirrors are fixed, there could never be a shadow! It's always noon."

"Not to mention," added Tanin bitterly, rubbing his eyes, "that this place is pitch dark. There're no windows! How's the sun supposed to hit it?"

"Small design flaws," said the dwarf. "I'm sure it's in committee—"

"Meanwhile, how do we open the door?" Sturm asked, slumping back wearily against the wall.

"Too bad Tas isn't here," said Palin, with a smile.

"Tas?" Dougan scowled, whirling around. "You don't mean Tasslehoff Burrfoot? The kender?"

"Yes, do you know him?"

"No," the dwarf growled, "but a friend of mine does. This crazy dwarf sits under a tree near my for— near where I work, day in, day out, whittling his endless wood and muttering 'doorknob of a kender' this and 'doorknob of a kender' that."

"A friend?" Palin said, mystified. "Why that sounds like a story our father told about Flint—"

"Never you mind!" Dougan snapped irritably. "And quit talking about kender! We're in enough trouble as it is. Brrrrr." He shivered. "Makes my skin crawl . . ."

The faintest glimmering of understanding lit the confused darkness of Palin's mind. Dimly he began to see the truth. But though the light shone on his thoughts, they were such a confused jumble that he couldn't sort them out or even decide whether he should feel relieved or more terrified.

"Maybe we could break the mirrors," Tanin suggested, blinking in the darkness, trying to see beyond the sea of bright blue spots that filled his vision.

"I wouldn't," Dougan warned. "The thing's likely to blow up."

"You mean it's trapped?" Sturm asked nervously, backing away.

"No!" Dougan snapped irritably. "I mean it's made by gnomes. It's likely to blow up."

"If it did"—Tanin scratched his chin thoughtfully—"it would probably blow a hole in the door."

"And us with it," Palin pointed out.

"Just you, Little Brother," Sturm said helpfully. "We'll be down at the bottom of the stairs."

"We have to try, Palin," Tanin decided. "We have no idea how long before the power of the Graygem takes hold of us again. It probably won't be a big explosion," he added soothingly. "It isn't a very big device, after all."

"No, it just takes up the whole door. Oh, very well," Palin grumbled. "Stand back."

The warning was unnecessary. Dougan was already clambering down the stairs, Sturm behind him. Tanin rounded the corner of the wall, but stopped where he could see Palin.

Edging up cautiously on the device, Palin raised the end of the staff over the first mirror, averting his face and shutting his eyes as he did so. At that moment, however, a voice came from the other side of the door.

"I believe all you have to do is turn the handle."

Palin arrested his downward jab. "Who said that?" he shouted, backing up.

"Me," said the voice again in meek tones. "Just turn the handle."

"You mean, the door's not locked?" Palin asked in amazement.

"Nobody's perfect," said the voice defensively.

Gingerly, Palin reached out his hand and, after removing several connecting arms and undoing a rope or two, he turned the door handle. There was a click, and the door swung open on creaking hinges.

Entering the chamber with some difficulty, his robes having caught on a gear, Palin looked around in awe.

He was in a room shaped like a cone—round at the bottom, it came to a point at the ceiling. The chamber was lit by oil lamps, placed at intervals around the circular floor, their flickering flames illuminating the room as brightly as day. Tanin was about to step through the door past Palin, when his brother stopped him.

"Wait!" Palin cautioned, catching hold of Tanin's arm. "Look! On the floor!"

"Well, what is it?" Tanin asked. "Some sort of design—"

"It's a pentagram, a magic symbol," Palin said softly. "Don't step within the circle of the lamps!"

"What's it there for?" Sturm peered over Tanin's broad shoulders, while Dougan jumped up and down in back, trying to see.

"I think . . . Yes!" Palin stared up into the very top of the ceiling. "It's holding the Graygem! Look!" He pointed.

Everyone tilted back their heads, staring upward, except the dwarf, who was cursing loudly about not being able to see. Dropping down to his hands and knees, Dougan finally managed to thrust his head in between

Tanin's and Sturm's legs and peered upward, his beard trailing on the polished stone floor.

"Aye, laddie," he said with a longing sigh. "That's it! The Graygem of Gargath!"

Hovering in the air, below the very point of the cone, was a gray-colored jewel. Its shape was impossible to distinguish, as was its size, for it changed as they stared at it—first it was round and as big as a man's fist; then it was a prism as large as a man himself; then it was a cube, no bigger than a lady's bauble; then round again. . . . The jewel had been dark when they entered the room, not even reflecting the light from the lamps below. But now a soft gray light of its own began to beam from it.

Palin felt the magic tingle through him. Words to spells of unbelievable power flooded his mind. His uncle had been a weakling compared to him! He would rule the world, the heavens, the Abyss—

"Steady, Little Brother," came a distant voice.

"Hold onto me, Tanin!" Palin gasped, reaching out his hand to his brother. "Help me fight it!"

"It's no use," came the voice they had heard through the door, this time sounding sad and resigned. "You can't fight it. It will consume you in the end, as it did me."

Wrenching his gaze from the gray light that was fast dazzling him with its brilliance, Palin peered around the conical room. Looking across from where he stood, he could make out a tall, high-backed chair placed against a tapestry-adorned wall. The chair's back was carved with various runes and magical inscriptions, designed—apparently—to protect the mage who sat there from whatever beings he summoned forth to do his bidding. The voice seemed to be coming from the direction of the chair, but Palin could not see anyone sitting there.

Then, "Paladine have mercy!" the young man cried in horror.

"Too late, too late," squeaked the voice. "Yes, I am Lord Gargath. The wretched Lord Gargath! Welcome to my home."

Seated upon the chair's soft cushion, making a graceful—if despairing—gesture with its paw, was a hedgehog.

"You may come closer," said Lord Gargath, smoothing his whiskers with a trembling paw. "Just don't step in the circle, as you said, young mage."

Keeping carefully outside the boundaries of the flickering oil lamps, the brothers and Dougan edged their way along the wall. Above them, the Graygem gleamed softly, its light growing ever brighter.

"Lord Gargath," Palin began hesitantly, approaching the hedgehog's chair. Suddenly, he cried out in alarm and stumbled backward, bumping into Tanin.

"Sturm, to my side!" Tanin shouted, pushing Palin behind him and raising the spear.

The chair had vanished completely beneath the bulk of a gigantic black dragon! The creature stared at them with red, fiery eyes. Its great wings spanned the length of the wall. Its tail lashed the floor with a tremendous thud. When the dragon spoke, though, its voice held the same sorrow as had the hedgehog's.

"You're frightened," said the dragon wistfully. "Thank you for the compliment, but you needn't be. By the time I could attack you, I'd probably be a mouse or a cockroach.

"Ah, there! You see how it is," continued Lord Gargath in the form of a lovely young maiden, who put her head in her hands and wept dismally. "I'm constantly changing, constantly shifting. I never know from one moment to the next," snarled a ferocious minotaur, snorting in anger, "what I'm going to be."

"The Graygem has done this to you?"

"Yessssss," hissed a snake, coiling around upon itself on the cushion in agony. "Once I wasssss a wizzzzard like you, young one. Once I wassss . . . powerful and wealthy. This island and its people were mine," continued a dapper young man, sitting in the chair, a cold drink in his hand. "Care for some? Tropical fruit punch. Not bad, I assure you. Where was I?"

"The Graygem," Palin ventured. His brothers could only stare in silence.

"Ah, yes," burbled a toad unhappily. "My great-great-great—well, you get the picture—grandfather followed the damn thing, centuries ago, in hopes of retrieving it. He did, for a time. But his power failed as he grew old and the Graygem escaped. I don't know where it went, spreading chaos throughout the world. But *I* always knew that . . . someday . . . it would come within my grasp. And I'd be ready for it!" A rabbit, sitting up on its hind feet, clenched its paw with a stern look of resolve.

"Long years I study," said a gully dwarf, holding up a grubby hand. "Two years. I think two years." The gully dwarf frowned. "I make pretty design on floor. I wait. Two years. Not more than two. Big rock come! I catch . . .

"And I'd trapped the Graygem!" shrieked an old, wizened man with a wild cackle. "It couldn't escape me! At last, all the magic in the world would be mine, at my fingertips! And so it was, so it was," squeaked a red-eyed rat, chewing nervously on its tail. "I could have anything I wanted. I demanded ten maidens— Well, I was lonely," said a spider, curling its legs defensively. "You don't get a chance to meet nice girls when you're an evil mage, you know."

"And the Graygem took control of the women!" said Palin, growing dizzy again, watching the transformations of the wizard. "And used them against you."

"Yes," whinnied a horse, pacing back and forth restlessly in front of the chair. "It educated them and gave them this palace. *My* palace! It gives them everything! They never have to work. Food appears when they're hungry. Wine, whatever they want. . . . All they do is lounge around all day, reading elven poetry and arguing philosophy. God, I *hate* elven poetry!" groaned a middle-aged bald man. "I tried to talk to them, told them to make something of their lives! And what did they do? They shut me in here, with that!" He gestured helplessly at the stone.

"But the women are getting restless," Palin said, his thoughts suddenly falling into order.

"One can only take so much elven poetry," remarked a walrus, gloomily waving its flippers. "They want diversion—"

"Men . . . and *not* their husbands. No, that wouldn't suit the Graygem at all. It needs the warriors to guard the gem from the outside while the women guard it from inside. So, to keep the women happy, it brought—"

"Us!" said Tanin, rounding upon the dwarf in fury.

"Now, don't be hasty," Dougan said with a cunning grin. He glanced at Palin out of the corner of his eye. "You're very clever, laddie. You take after your uncle, yes, you do. Who was it guarding itself from, if you're so smart? What would it have to fear?"

"The one person who'd been searching for it for thousands and thousands of years," said Palin softly. Everything was suddenly very, very clear. "The one who made it and gambled it away. It has kept away from you, all these centuries, staying in one place until you got too close, then disappearing again. But now it is trapped by the wizard. No matter what it does, it can't escape. So it set these guards around itself. But you knew the women were unhappy. You knew the Graygem *had* to allow them to have what they wanted—"

"Good-looking men. They'd let no one else in the castle," said Dougan, twirling his moustache. "And, if I do say so myself, we fill the bill," he added proudly.

"But who is he?" said Sturm, staring from Palin to the dwarf in confusion. "*Not* Dougan Redhammer, I gather—"

"I know! I know!" shouted Lord Gargath, now a kender, who was jumping on the cushion of the chair. "Let me tell! Let me tell!" Leaping down, the kender ran over to embrace the dwarf.

"Great Reorx! Keep away from me!" roared Dougan, clutching his empty money pouch.

"You told!" The kender pouted.

"My god!" whispered Tanin.

"That about sums it up," Palin remarked.

Chapter Nine

Wanna Bet?

"Yes!" roared Dougan Redhammer in a thunderous voice. "I am Reorx, the Forger of the World, and I have come back to claim what is mine!"

Suddenly aware of the presence of the god, aware, now, of the danger it was in, the Graygem flared with brilliant gray light. Trapped by the magic of the wizard's symbol on the floor, it could not move, but it began to spin frantically, changing shape so fast that it was nothing more than a blur of motion to the eye.

The aspect of the wizard changed too. Once again, the black dragon burst into being, its great body obliterating the chair, its vast wingspan filling the cone-shaped room.

Palin glanced at it without interest, being much more absorbed in his own internal struggles. The Graygem was exerting all its energy, trying to protect itself. It was offering Palin anything, everything he wanted. Images flashed into his head. He saw himself as head of the Order of White Robes, he saw himself ruling the Conclave of Wizards. *He* was driving the evil dragons back into the Abyss! *He* was doing battle with the Dark Queen. All he had to do was kill the dwarf. . . .

Kill a god? he asked in disbelief.

I will grant you the power! the Graygem answered.

Looking around, Palin saw Sturm's body bathed in sweat, his eyes wild, his fists clenched. Even Tanin, so strong and unbending, was staring straight ahead, his skin pale, his lips tight, seeing some vision of glory visible only to himself.

Dougan stood in the center of the pentagram, watching them, not saying a word.

Palin held fast to the staff, nearly sobbing in his torment. Pressing his cheek against the cool wood, he heard words forming in his mind. *All my life, I was my own person. The choices I made, I made of my own free will. I was never held in thrall by anyone or anything; not even the Queen of Darkness herself! Bow to others in reverence and respect, but never in slavery, Nephew!*

Palin blinked, looking around as though awaking from a daze. He wasn't conscious of having heard the words, but they were in his heart, and he had the strength now to know their worth. *No!* he was able to tell the Graygem firmly, and it was then that he realized the black dragon behind him was undergoing similar torture.

"But I don't *want* to flay the skin from their bones!" the dragon whimpered. "Well, yes, I wouldn't mind having my island back the way it was. And ten maidens who would act like maidens and not turn into poets."

Looking at the dragon in alarm, Palin saw its red eyes gleaming feverishly. Acid dripped from its forked tongue, burning holes in the polished floor; its claws glistened. Spreading its wings, the dragon lifted itself into the air.

"Tanin! Sturm!" Palin cried, grasping hold of the nearest brother and shaking him. It was Tanin. Slowly the big man turned his eyes to his little brother, but there was no recognition in them.

"Help me, wizard!" Tanin hissed at him. "Help me slay the dwarf! I'll be the leader of armies. . . ."

"Dougan!" Palin ran to the dwarf. "Do something!" the young mage shouted wildly, waving his arms at the dragon.

"I am, laddie, I am," said Dougan calmly, his eyes on the Graygem.

Palin could see the black dragon's eyes watching him hungrily. The black wings twitched.

I'll cast a sleep spell, Palin decided in desperation, reaching into his pouches for sand. But as he drew it forth a horrible realization came to him. His fingers went limp, the sand trickled from them, spilling down upon the floor.

His magic was gone!

"No, please, no!" Palin moaned, looking up at the Graygem, which appeared to sparkle with a chaotic malevolence.

The wooden door to the room burst open, banging against the wall.

"We have come as you commanded us, Graygem!" cried a voice.

It was the voice of the dark-haired beauty. Behind her was the blonde, and behind them all the rest of the women, young and old alike. But gone were the diaphanous gowns and seductive smiles. The women were dressed in tiger skins. Feathers were tied in their hair, and they carried stone-tipped spears in their hands.

And now Tanin's voice rang out loudly as a trumpet call, "My troops! To my side! Rally round!" Raising his arm, he gave a battle cry and the women answered with a wild shout.

"Bring me wine!" cried Sturm, executing an impromptu dance. "Let the revelry begin!"

The blonde's eyes were on him and they burned with lust. Unfortunately, it was lust of the wrong kind. She raised her spear, her eyes looking to her leader—Tanin—for the order to attack.

"You promise me?" said the black dragon eagerly, its forked tongue flicking in and out of its dripping mouth. "No more gully dwarves? I didn't mind the rest so much, but I *won't* be changed into a gully dwarf again!"

"The world's gone mad!" Palin slumped back against the wall. He felt his strength and his sanity draining from him as the sand fell from his nerveless fingers. The chaos around him and the loss of his magic had overthrown his mind. He stared at the Staff of Magius and saw nothing more than a stick of wood, topped by a glistening bauble. He heard his brothers, one dispersing his troops for battle, the other calling for the pipers to strike up another tune. He heard the dragon's great wings creak and the intake of breath that would be released in a stream of acid. Shutting his eyes, Palin cast the useless staff away from him and turned his face to the wall.

"Halt!" thundered a voice. "Halt, I command you!"

Chaos whirled wildly an instant longer, then it slowed and finally wound down until all was silence and stillness in the room where before had been a blur of noise and motion. Dougan stood on the pentagram in the center of the room, his black beard bristling in anger. Raising his arm, he cried out, *"Reorx Drach Kalahzar!"* and a gigantic warhammer materialized in the dwarf's hand. The huge hammer glowed with a fierce red light that was reflected in Dougan's dark, bright eyes.

"Yes!" shouted the dwarf, staring up at the flaring Graygem. "I know your power! None better! After all, you are my creation! You can keep this chaos going eternally and you know that I cannot stop you. But you are trapped eternally yourself! You will never be free!"

The Graygem's light flickered an instant, as though considering Dougan's words. Then it began to pulse, brighter than before, and Palin's heart sank in despair.

"Wait!" Dougan cried, raising one hand, the other grasping the handle of the burning red warhammer. "I say we leave everything up to chance. I offer you . . . a wager!"

The Graygem appeared to consider; its light pulsed more slowly, thoughtfully.

"A wager?" the women murmured, lowering their spears.

"A wager," said the dragon in pleased tones, settling back down to the floor once more.

"A wager!" Palin muttered, wiping his sleeve across his sweating brow. "My god, that's what started all this!"

"We agree to it, " said the dark-haired beauty, striding forward, the shaft of her spear thumping against the floor as she walked. "What will be the stakes?"

Dougan stroked his beard. "These young men," he said finally, pointing at Tanin, Sturm, and Palin, "for yourselves. Freedom for the Graygem."

"What?" Both Tanin and Sturm came back to reality, staring around the room as though seeing it for the first time.

"You can't do this to us, dwarf!" Tanin shouted, lunging forward, but two of the larger and stronger women caught him and, with strength given them by the brightly burning Graygem, bound the struggling man's arms behind him. Two more took care of Sturm. No one bothered with Palin.

"If I lose the wager," Dougan continued imperturbably, "these young men will stay with you as your slaves. I'll break the magic spell that holds the gem trapped here and it will be free once more to roam the world. If I win, the Graygem is mine and these men will be released."

"We agree to the stakes," said the dark-haired beauty, after a glance at the Graygem. "And now what is the wager?"

Dougan appeared to consider, twirling his moustache round and round his finger. His gaze happened to rest on Palin, and he grinned. "That this young man"—he pointed at the mage—"will throw my hammer in the air and it will hang suspended, never falling to the floor."

Everyone stared at the dwarf in silence, considering. What was the angle? . . .

Then, "No! Dougan!" Palin cried frantically, pushing himself away from the wall. One of the women shoved him back.

"This young man?" The dark-haired beauty suddenly caught on. "But he is a magic-user—"

"Only a very young one," Dougan said hastily. "And he won't use his magic, will you, Palin?" the dwarf asked, winking at the young mage when the women weren't looking.

"Dougan!" Palin wrenched himself free from the woman's grasp and lurched across the floor, his knees so weak he could barely walk. "I can't! My magic—"

"Never say 'can't,' laddie," Dougan said severely. "Didn't your uncle teach you anything?" Once again, he winked at Palin.

It seemed the dark-haired beauty suddenly realized Palin's weakness, for she glanced about at her fellows and smiled in pleased fashion. "We accept your wager," she said.

"Dougan!" Palin cried desperately, grabbing hold of the dwarf, who was looking up at him with a sly grin. "Dougan! I *can't* use my magic! I don't have any! The Graygem drained it!" he whispered urgently in the dwarf's ear.

Dougan's face crumpled. "You don't say now, laddie," he muttered, glancing at the women and rubbing his bearded chin. "That's a shame, now," he said sadly, shaking his head. "A real shame. Are you sure?"

"Of course I'm sure!" Palin snapped.

"Well, give it your best shot, lad!" the dwarf said, clapping Palin on the arm with his hand. "Here you go!" He thrust the handle of the warhammer into Palin's hands. Feeling the unfamiliar touch, the hammer's red glow faded, turning an ugly, leaden gray.

Palin looked around helplessly at his brothers. Tanin regarded him gravely, his expression grim. Sturm averted his head, his big shoulders heaving in a sigh.

Swallowing, licking his dry lips, Palin wrapped his hands around the handle of the hammer, uncertain, even, how to hold the weapon. He tried to lift it. A groan escaped his lips—a groan echoed by his brothers.

"By Paladine!" Palin gasped. "I can barely move this thing, Dougan! How can I throw it?" Leaning closer, staring into the dwarf's eyes, the young man murmured, "You're a god. . . . I don't suppose . . ."

"Of course not, laddie!" The dwarf looked shocked. "It's a matter of honor! You understand . . ."

"Sure," Palin grunted bitterly.

"Look, lad," Dougan said, positioning Palin's hands. "It's not that difficult. You just hold the hammer like this . . . there. . . . Now, you pick it up and began spinning round and round in a circle. Your momentum will help you lift the hammer and, when you're going good, just give it a heave, like so. Nature will do the rest."

"Nature?" Palin appeared dubious.

"Yes," answered the dwarf gravely, smoothing his beard. "It's called Centrifug's Force or some such thing. The gnomes explained it to me."

"Great!" Palin muttered. "Gnomes!"

Drawing a deep breath, the young man lifted the hammer. A groan of pain escaped his lips, sweat stood out on his forehead from the strain, and he heard several of the women giggle. Gritting his teeth, certain that he had ruptured something inside him, Palin began to turn in a circle, the hammer in his hands. He was startled to notice that Dougan was right. The momentum of his motion made the hammer seem lighter. He was able to lift it higher and higher. But the handle began to slip in his sweaty palms. . . .

"He's losing it! Get down! Everyone!" Tanin called out, falling flat on his face. There was a clattering of spears as the women followed suit. Even the black dragon—seeing Palin spinning about in the center of the room, out of control, the hammer starting to glow a fiery red—crouched on the floor with a whimper, attempting to fold its wings over its head. Only the dwarf remained standing, his face split in a broad grin.

"I . . . can't . . . hold . . . it!" Palin cried and, with a gasp, he let the hammer fly.

The young mage fell to his knees, in too much pain and exhaustion to even bother looking to see what happened. But everyone else in the room, lying flat on the floor, raised their heads to watch the hammer. Round and round it whizzed, flying over the heads of the women, buzzing over Tanin and Sturm, whisking past the cowering dragon. Round and round it flew and, as it flew, it began to rise into the air. Dougan watched it placidly, his hands laced across his great belly.

Glowing now a fiery red, the hammer circled higher and higher and, as it rose, the Graygem's light began to waver in sudden fear. The hammer was aiming straight for it!

"Yes, my beauty," murmured Dougan, watching the hammer in satisfaction. "You forged it. Now, bring it home."

Desperately the Graygem sought to dim its light, realizing, perhaps, that it was its own power that was drawing the hammer to it. But it was too late. The hammer flew to the Graygem it had helped create as a lass flies to her lover's arms. There was a shattering sound and a blinding flare of red and gray light, so brilliant that even Dougan was forced to shade his eyes, and no one else could see anything for the dazzling radiance.

The two energies seemed to strive together, the red light and the gray, and then the gray began to dim. Peering upward, tears streaming from his eyes in the bright light, Palin thought he caught a glimpse of a gray, sparkling jewel tumbling from the air to land in Dougan's hand. But he couldn't be certain because, at that moment, the red glowing hammer fell from the air as well, plummeting straight down on top of them!

Clasping his aching arms over his head, Palin hugged the floor, visions of his head being split open and his brains splattering everywhere coming to him with vivid clarity. He heard a resounding clang. Timidly raising his head, he saw the hammer, glowing red in triumph, lying on the floor at Dougan's feet.

Slowly, trembling, Palin stood up, as did everyone else in the room. He was hurting and exhausted; Tanin had to come help him or he would have collapsed. But Palin smiled up at him as his big brother clasped him in his arms. "My magic's returned!" he whispered. "It's back!"

"I'm back, too," said a voice. Glancing around, Palin saw the dragon was gone. In its place, crouched on the floor, his hands over his head, was a thin, middle-aged wizard dressed in black robes. The wizard sat up, staring around him as if he couldn't believe it. "I'm back!" he cried out joyfully, patting his head and his neck and his shoulders with his hands. "No rabbit ears! No dragon's breath! No minotaur muscles! I'm me again!" He burst into tears.

"And you lost the bet, dwarf!" the dark-haired beauty cried out suddenly, getting to her feet. "The hammer fell!"

"Yes!" shouted the women. "You lost the bet! The men are ours!"

"Dougan . . ." growled Tanin ominously.

The women were closing in on them, eyes burning with the fire of love instead of the fire of battle.

Raising the hammer over his head, Dougan held up his arms. His face stern, his black eyes flashed as red as the glowing hammer. The voice that spoke was no longer the voice of the dwarf with the flashy clothes, but a voice as ancient as the mountains it had carved, as deep as the oceans it had poured.

"Women!" the god called out in stern tones. "Listen to me! The power of the Graygem over you is broken. Remember now your children and your husbands. Remember your brothers and your fathers! Remember your homes and those who love you and need you!"

One by one, the women looked around in dazed fashion, some putting their hands to their heads, some blinking in confusion.

"Where are we?" asked one.

"Why are we dressed like this?" asked another, staring at the tiger skin.

"How dare you?" cried the blonde, slapping Sturm across the face.

Only the dark-haired beauty seemed sad. Shaking her head, she said with a sigh, "I miss my family. And I remember the man I love and am betrothed to marry. But it will start all over again. The eternal wars. The fighting, the bleeding, the dying. . . ."

She turned to the god, only to find no one but a flashily dressed dwarf, who smiled at her in understanding.

"Think a moment, lassie," said Dougan kindly, patting her hand. "You've read the books, remember? And so have they." He pointed at the others. "You have knowledge now. No one can take that from you. Use it wisely, and you can stop the senseless wars. You and the others, with the help of your menfolk and your children, can make this island a paradise."

"I don't know who you are," the dark-haired beauty said, gazing at the dwarf in wonder, "but you are wise. We will do as you say. And we will honor you always, in our hearts and our prayers." (And so the islanders did, becoming the only humans, as far as anyone knows, to once again worship Reorx, the Forger of the World.)

Bending down, she kissed Dougan on his cheek. The dwarf's face flamed as red as his hammer.

"Go along with you now!" he said gruffly.

Arms linked around each other's waists, the women ran, laughing merrily, from the room, and the brothers soon heard their joyful voices outside the castle walls.

"As for you—" Dougan turned upon the black-robed wizard.

"Don't scold me!" begged Lord Gargath meekly. "I've learned my lesson. Truly. I will never have anything to do with gems as long as I live. You can believe me!" he said, glancing up at the empty ceiling with a shudder.

"And we'll expect to see you at the conclave," said Palin severely, retrieving the Staff of Magius. "You'll be a renegade no longer?"

"I'm looking forward to the next meeting!" Lord Gargath said eagerly. "Is there anything I can bring? A cake, perhaps? I make a marvelous devil's food. . . ."

Afterword

(This Time for Real)

Dougan and the brothers returned to the gnome ship without incident. In fact, the warriors were so happy to have their women back with them, their families once more united, that they gave back the armor and the swords. (The chief had decided the armor was too hot anyway, and he thought the sword a primitive weapon, compared to a spear.)

The gnomes had repaired the damage to the ship. Indeed, they discovered that having one end smashed in improved the steering immeasurably and they were quite excited at the prospect of returning home to Mount Nevermind and smashing in the prows (or sterns) of the remainder of the gnomish fleet.

One small incident marred an otherwise idyllic cruise (not counting constantly ducking the sail, being hit by falling fish, and wondering whether or not they were going to sink before they reached land, due to the leaking of the smashed-in prow . . . or stern . . .).

Dougan was lounging on the deck one night, contemplating the heavens (the planet Reorx was missing) when suddenly he was accosted by the three brothers.

"Sturm, get his arms!" Tanin ordered, leaping on the dwarf from behind. "Palin, if his beard so much as twitches, send him to sleep!"

"What is this outrage! How dare you?" Dougan roared, struggling in Sturm's strong grasp.

"We risked our lives for that rock," Tanin said grimly, glaring down at the red-faced dwarf. "And I want to see it."

"You've been putting us off for days," added Palin, standing beside his brother. "We at least want a look at it before you take it back to your forge or wherever."

"Let me loose!" Dougan swore an oath. "Or you'll see nothing ever again!"

Sturm, at a nod from Tanin, let go of the dwarf's arms. Dougan glanced around at them uncomfortably.

"The Graygem?" the brothers said, gathering around.

"Well, now, lads." The dwarf appeared highly uncomfortable. "That's going to be a bit of a problem."

"What do you mean?" Palin asked nervously, not liking the expression on the dwarf's face. "Is it so powerful that we can't look at it?"

"Nooo . . ." said Dougan slowly, his face flushing in the red light of Lunitari. "That's not it, exactly. . . ."

"Well, then, let's see it!" Tanin demanded.

"The . . . uh . . . the fact is, lads," stammered Dougan, winding his black beard around his finger, "that I've . . . I've misplaced it. . . ."

"Misplaced it!" Sturm said in amazement.

"The Graygem?" Palin glanced around the boat in alarm, fearing to see its gray light beaming out at them.

"Perhaps, 'misplaced' isn't quite the word," the dwarf mumbled. "You see, I got into this bones game, the night before we left the island and . . ." His voice trailed off miserably.

"You *lost* it!" Tanin groaned.

Palin and Sturm stared at the dwarf, too stunned to speak.

"Aye, lad." Dougan sighed heavily. "It was a sure thing, too. . . ."

"So the Graygem's loose in the world again," Palin murmured.

"I'm afraid so. After all, I *did* lose the original wager, if you will remember. But don't worry, laddie," said the dwarf, laying his hand on Palin's arm. "We'll get it back! Someday, we'll get it back!"

"What do you mean *we!*" Tanin growled.

"I swear by Paladine and by Gilean and by the Dark Queen and by all the gods in the heavens that if I ever in my life see you even looking my direction, dwarf, I will turn around and walk—no, run—the opposite way!" Sturm vowed devoutly.

"The same goes for me," said Palin.

"And me!" said Tanin.

Dougan looked at them, downcast for a moment. Then, a grin split the dwarf's face. His beady eyes glittered.

"Wanna bet?"

IV

The first sign of the change
is not the golden eye
nor the dangerous stature
the countenance of hill and desert,

instead it is the child's breath
the chill of water underground
the cry at night a memory of knives

and you startle
sit up in the bed and say
this is something I have made
somehow I have made this thing.

So you fear it away
let the night cover your dream
and the red moon wades
through a hundred journeys
jostled like blood
in the coded vein,

and then the arrivals
rending the edge of belief
a vacancy in play
the abstract smile
that has nothing to do
with whatever you did
and you know that your wishes
can never conceal
the long recollection of elsewhere.

The cuckoo's story, the supplanted nest
the egg left in care of unwary others.
Surely its child is alien, elfshot,
stolen by gypsies, forever another,
and yet, in the accident
of blood and adoption,
as it was in your time
and the time of your mothers,
forever and always your own.

So sing to the stranger this lullaby
Sing the inventions of family
    the fiction of brothers
    the bardic ruse of the father
Sing the mother concocted of reasons and light,
Sing to me, golden-eyed daughter.

Raistlin's Daughter

Margaret Weis and Dezra Despain

I first heard the legend of Raistlin's Daughter about five years after my twin's death. As you can imagine, I was extremely intrigued and disturbed by the rumors and did what I could to investigate. In this I was assisted by my friends—the old Companions—who had by this time scattered over most of Ansalon. We found versions of the legend in almost every part of Ansalon. It is being told among the elves of Silvanesti, the people of Solamnia, and the Plainsmen who have returned to Queshu. But we could find no verification of it. Even the kender Tasslehoff Burrfoot, who goes everywhere and hears everything (as kender do), could discover no first-hand information regarding it. The story is always told by a person who heard it from his aunt who had a cousin who was midwife to the girl . . . and so forth.

I even went so far as to contact Astinus the Historian, who records history as it passes before his all-seeing eyes. In this, my hope to hear anything useful was slim, for the Historian is notoriously close-mouthed, especially when something he has seen in the past might affect the future. Knowing this, I asked only for him to tell me whether or not the legend was true. Did my twin father a child? Does he or she live still on this world?

His response was typical of that enigmatic man, whom some whisper is the god Gilean himself. "If it is true, it will become known. If not, it won't."

I have agreed to allow the inclusion of the legend in this volume as a curiosity and because it might, in the distant future, have some bearing upon the history of Krynn. The reader should be forewarned, however, that my friends and I regard it as veritable gossip.

—Caramon Majere

Twilight touched the Wayward Inn with its gentle hand, making even that shabby and ill-reputed place seem a restful haven to those who walked or rode the path that led by its door. Its weather-beaten wood—rotting and worm-ridden when seen in broad daylight—appeared rustic in the golden-tinged evening. Its cracked and broken windowpanes actually sparkled as they caught the last rays of dying light, and the shadows hit the roof just right, so that no one could see the patches. Perhaps this was one reason that the inn was so busy this night—either that or the masses of gray, lowering clouds gathering in the eastern sky like a ghostly, silent army.

The Wayward Inn was located on the outskirts—if the magical trees deemed it so—of the Forest of Wayreth. If the magical trees chose otherwise, as they frequently did, the inn was located on the outskirts of a barren field where nothing anyone planted grew. Not that any farmer cared to try his luck. Who would want anything from land controlled, so it was believed by the archmages of the Tower of High Sorcery; by the strange, uncanny forest?

Some thought it peculiar that the Wayward Inn was built so close to the Forest of Wayreth (when the forest was in appearance), but then the owner—Slegart Havenswood—was a peculiar man. His only care in the world, seemingly, was profit—as he would say to anyone who asked. And there was always profit to be made from those who found themselves on the fringes of wizards' lands when night was closing in.

There were many this evening who found themselves in those straits, apparently, for almost every room in the inn was taken. For the most part, the travelers were human, since this was in the days before the War of the Lance, when elves and dwarves kept to themselves and rarely walked this world. But there were a few gully dwarves around; Slegart hired them to cook and clean up, and he was not averse to allowing goblins to stay in his place as long as they behaved themselves. There were no goblins this night, however, though there were some humans who might have been taken for goblins—so twisted and crafty were their faces. It was this large party that had taken several of Slegart's rooms (and there weren't many in the small, shabby place), leaving only two empty.

Just about the time when the first evening star appeared in the sky, to be almost immediately overrun by the advancing column of clouds, the door to the inn burst open, letting in a chill blast of air, a warrior in leather armor, and a mage in red robes. From his place behind the dirty bar, Slegart frowned. It was not that he disliked magic-users (rumor had it that his inn existed by the grace of the wizards of the tower), but that he didn't particularly like them staying in his place.

When the big warrior (and he was a remarkably big young man, as both Slegart and the others in the common room noted) slapped down a coin and said, "Dinner," Slegart's frown broadened immediately to a smile. When the big man added, "and a room for the night," however, the smile slipped.

"We're full up," growled Slegart, with a significant glance around the crowded common room. "Hunting moon tonight . . ."

"Bah!" The big warrior snorted. "There'll be no moon tonight, hunting or otherwise. That storm's goin' to break any moment now and, unless you're partial to hunting snowflakes, you won't shoot anything this night." At this, the big man glanced around the common room to see if any cared to dispute his remark. Noting the size of his shoulders, the well-worn scabbard he wore, and the nonchalant way his hand went to the hilt of his sword, even the rough-appearing humans began to nod their heads at his wisdom, agreeing that there would definitely be no hunting this night.

"At any rate," said the big man, returning his stern gaze to Slegart, "we're spending the night here, if we have to make up our beds by the fire. As you can see"—the warrior's voice softened, and his gaze went to the magic-user, who had slumped down at a table as near the fire as possible—"my brother is in no condition to travel farther this day, especially in such weather."

Slegart's glance went to the mage and, indeed, the man appeared to be on the verge of exhaustion. Dressed in red robes, with a hood that covered his head and left his face in shadow, the magic-user leaned upon a wooden staff decorated at the top with a golden dragon's claw holding a faceted crystal. He kept this staff by him always, his hand going to it fondly as if both to caress it and to reassure himself of its presence.

"Bring us your best ale and a pot of hot water for my twin," said the warrior, slapping another steel coin down upon the bar.

At the sight of the money, Slegart's senses came alert. "I just recollect"—he began, his hand closing over the coin and his eyes going to the warrior's leather purse where his ears could detect the chink of metal. Even his nose wrinkled, as though he could smell it as well—"a room's opened up on t'second floor."

"I thought it might," the warrior said grimly, slapping another steel piece down on the bar.

"One of my best," Slegart remarked, eyeing the warrior.

The big man grunted, scowling.

"It's goin' to be no fit night for man nor beast," added the innkeeper and, at that moment, a gust of wind hit the inn, whistling through the cracked windows and puffing flakes of snow into the room. At that moment, too, the red-robed mage began to cough—a wracking, choking cough that doubled the man over the table. It was difficult to tell much about the mage—he was cloaked and hooded against the weather. But Slegart knew he must be young, if he and this giant were, indeed, twins. The innkeeper was considerably startled, therefore, to catch a glimpse of ragged white hair straying out from beneath the hood and to note that the hand holding the staff was thin and wasted.

"We'll take it," the warrior muttered, his worried gaze going to his brother as he laid the coin down.

"What's the matter with 'im?" Slegart said, eyeing the mage, his fingers twitching near the coin, though not touching it. "It ain't catchin', is it?" He drew back. "Not the plague?"

"Naw!" The warrior scowled. Leaning nearer the innkeeper, the big man said in a low voice, "We've just come from the Tower of High Sorcery. He's just taken the Test. . . ."

"Ah," the innkeeper said knowingly, his gaze on the young mage not unsympathetic. "I've seen many of 'em in my day. And I've seen many like yourself"—he looked at the big warrior—"who have come here alone, with only a packet of clothes and a battered spellbook or two as all that remains. Yer lucky, both of you, to have survived."

The warrior nodded, though it didn't appear—from the haunted expression on his pale face and dark, pain-filled eyes—that he considered his luck phenomenal. Returning to the table, the warrior laid his hand on his brother's heaving shoulder, only to be rebuffed with a bitter snarl.

"Leave me in peace, Caramon!" Slegart heard the mage gasp as the innkeeper came to the table, bearing the ale and a pot of hot water on a tray. "Your worrying will put me in my grave sooner than this cough!"

The warrior, Caramon, did not answer, but sat down in the booth opposite his brother, his eyes still shadowed with unhappiness and concern.

Slegart tried his best to see the face covered by the hood, but the mage was huddled near the fire, the red cowl pulled low over his eyes. The mage did not even look up as the innkeeper laid the table with an unusual amount of clattering of plates and knives and mugs. The young man simply reached into a pouch he wore tied to his belt and, taking a handful of leaves, handed them carefully to his brother.

"Fix my drink," the mage ordered in a rasping voice.

Slegart, watching all this intently, was considerably startled to note that the skin that covered the mage's slender hand gleamed a bright, metallic gold in the firelight!

The innkeeper tried for another glimpse of the mage's face, but the young man drew back even further into the shadows, ducking his head and pulling the cowl even lower over his eyes.

"If the skin of 'is face be the same as the skin of 'is hand, no wonder he hides himself," Slegart reflected, and wished he had turned this strange, sick mage away—money or no money.

The warrior took the leaves from the mage and dropped them in a cup. He then filled it with hot water.

Curious in spite of himself, the innkeeper leaned over to catch a glimpse of the mixture, hoping it might be a magic potion of some sort. To his disappointment, it appeared to be nothing more than tea with a few leaves floating on the surface. A bitter smell rose to his nostrils. Sniffing, he started to make some comment when the door blew open, admitting more snow, more wind, and another guest. Motioning one of the slatternly barmaids to finish waiting on the mage and his brother, Slegart turned to greet the new arrival.

It appeared—from its graceful walk and its tall, slender build—to be either a young human male, a human female, or an elf. But so bundled and muffled in clothes was the figure that it was impossible to tell sex or race.

"We're full up," Slegart started to announce, but before he could even open his mouth, the guest had drifted over to him (it was impossible for him to describe its walk any other way) and, reaching out a hand remarkable for its delicate beauty, laid two steel coins in the innkeeper's hand (remarkable only for its dirt).

"A place by the fire this night," said the guest in a low voice.

"I do believe a room's opened up," announced Slegart to the delight of the goblinish humans, who greeted this remark with coarse laughs and guffaws. Even the warrior grinned ruefully and shook his head, reaching across the table to nudge his brother. The mage said nothing, only gestured irritably for his drink.

"I'll take the room," the guest said, reaching into its purse and handing two more coins to the grinning innkeeper.

"Very good. . . ." Noticing the guest's fine clothes, made of rich material, Slegart thought it wise to bow. "Uh, what name . . . ?"

"Do the room and I need an introduction?" the guest asked sharply.

The warrior chuckled appreciatively at this, and it seemed as if even the mage responded, for the hooded head moved slightly as he sipped his steaming, foul-smelling drink.

Somewhat at a loss for words, Slegart was fumbling about in his mind, trying to think of another way to determine his mysterious guest's identity, when the guest turned from him and headed for a table located in a shadowed corner as far from the fire as possible. "Meat and drink." It tossed the words over its shoulder in an imperious tone.

"What would Your . . . Your Lordship like?" Slegart asked, hurrying after the guest, an ear cocked attentively. Though the guest spoke Common, the accent was strange, and the innkeeper still couldn't tell if his guest was male or female.

"Anything," the guest said wearily, turning its back on Slegart as it walked over to the shadowy booth. On its way, it cast a glance at the table where the warrior, Caramon, and his brother sat. "That. Whatever they're having." The guest gestured to where the barmaid was heaping a wooden bowl full of some gray, coagulating mass and rubbing her body up against Caramon's at the same time.

Now, perhaps it was the way the mysterious guest walked or perhaps it was the way the person gestured or even perhaps the subtle sneer in the guest's voice when it noticed Caramon's hand reaching around to pat the barmaid on a rounded portion of her anatomy, but Slegart guessed instantly that the muffled guest was female.

It was dangerous journeying through Ansalon in those days some five years before the war. There were few who traveled alone, and it was unusual for women to travel at all. Those women who did were either mercenaries—skilled with sword and shield—or wealthy women with a horde of escorts, armed to the teeth. This woman—if such she was—carried no weapon that Slegart could see and if she had escorts, they must enjoy sleeping in the open in what boded to be one of the worst blizzards ever to hit this part of the country.

Slegart wasn't particularly bright or observant, and he arrived at the conclusion that his guest was a lone, unprotected female about two minutes after everyone else in the place. This was apparent from the warrior's slightly darkening face and the questioning glance he cast at his brother, who shook his head. This was also apparent from the sudden silence that fell over the "hunting" party gathered near the bar and the quick whispers and muffled snickers that followed.

Hearing this, Caramon scowled and glanced around behind him. But a touch on the hand and a softly spoken word from the mage made the big warrior sigh and stolidly resume eating the food in his bowl, though he kept his eyes on the guest, to the disappointment of the barmaid.

Slegart made his way back of the bar again and began wiping out mugs with a filthy rag, his back half-turned but his sharp eyes watching everything. One of the ruffians rose slowly to his feet, stretched, and called for another pint of ale. Taking it from the barmaid, he sauntered over to the guest's table.

"Mind if I sit down?" he said, suiting his action to his words.

"Yes," said the guest sharply.

"Aw, c'mon." Grinning, the ruffian settled himself comfortably in the booth across from the guest, who sat eating the gray gunk in her bowl. "It's a custom in this part of the country for innfellows to make merry on a night like this. Join our little party . . ."

The guest ignored him, steadily eating her food. Caramon shifted slightly in his seat, but, after a pleading glance at his brother, which was answered with an abrupt shake of the hooded head, the warrior continued his dinner with a sigh.

The ruffian leaned forward, reaching out his hand to touch the scarf the guest had wound tightly about her face. "You must be awful hot—" the man began.

He didn't complete his sentence, finding it difficult to speak through the bowl of hot stew dripping down his face.

"I've lost my appetite," the guest said. Calmly rising to her feet, she wiped stew from her hands on a greasy napkin and headed for the stairs. "I'll go to my room now, innkeeper. What number?"

"Number sixteen. You can bolt lock it from the inside to keep out the riff-raff," Slegart said, his mug-polishing slowing. Trouble was bad for business, cut into profits. "Serving girl'll be along to turn down the bed."

The "riffraff," stew dripping off his nose, might have been content to let the mysterious person go her way. There had been a coolness in the voice and the quick, self-possessed movement indicating that the guest had some experience caring for herself. But the big warrior laughed appreciatively at the innkeeper's remark, and so did the "hunting" party by the fire. Their laughter was the laughter of derision, however.

Casting his comrades an angry glance, the man wiped stew from his eyes and leapt to his feet. Overturning the table, he followed the woman, who was halfway up the stairs.

"I'll show you to yer room!" He leered, grabbed hold of her, and jerked her backward.

Caught off balance, the guest fell into the ruffian's arms with a cry that proved beyond a shadow of a doubt that she was, indeed, a female.

"Raistlin?" pleaded Caramon, his hand on the hilt of his sword.

"Very well, my brother," the mage said with a sigh. Reaching out his hand for the staff he had leaned against the wall, he used it to pull himself to his feet.

Caramon was starting to stand up when he saw his brother's eyes shift to a point just behind him. Catching the look, Caramon nodded slightly just as a heavy hand closed over his shoulder.

"Good stew, ain't it?" said one of the "hunting" party. "Shame to interrupt yer dinner over somethin' that ain't none of yer business. Unless, of course, you want to share some of the fun. If so, we'll let you know when it's your tur—"

Caramon's fist thudded into the man's jaw. "Thanks," the warrior said coolly, drawing his sword and twisting around to face the other thugs behind him. "I think I'll take my turn now."

A chair flung from the back of the crowd caught Caramon on the shoulder of his sword arm. Two men in front jumped him, one grabbing his wrist and trying to knock the sword free, the other flailing away with his fists. The mob—seeing the warrior apparently falling—surged forward.

"Get the girl, Raist! I'll take care of these!" Caramon shouted in muffled tones from beneath a sea of bodies. "Everything's . . . under . . . contr—"

"As usual, my brother," said the mage wryly. Ignoring the grunts and yells, the cracking of furniture and bone, Raistlin leaned on his staff and began climbing the stairs.

Though the girl was fighting her attacker with her fists, she apparently had no other weapon, and it was easy to see she must soon lose. The man's attention was fixed on dragging his struggling victim up the stairs, so he never noticed the red-robed mage moving swiftly behind him. There was a flash of silver, a quick thrust of the mage's hand, and the ruffian, letting loose of the girl, clutched his ribs. Blood welled out from between his fingers. For an instant he stared at Raistlin in astonishment, then tumbled past him, falling headlong down the stairs, the mage's dagger protruding from his side.

"Raist! Help!" Caramon shouted from below. Though he had laid three opponents low, he was locked in a vicious battle with a fourth, his movements decidedly hampered by a gully dwarf, who had crawled up his back and was beating him over the head with a pan.

But Raistlin was not able to go to his brother's rescue. The girl, weak and dizzy from her struggles, missed her step upon the stairs.

Letting go of his staff—which remained perfectly upright, standing next to him as though he were holding it—Raistlin caught the girl before she fell.

"Thank you," she murmured, keeping her head down. Her scarf had come undone in her struggles and she tried to wrap it around her face again. But Raistlin, with a sardonic smile and a deft movement of his skilled hands, snatched the scarf from the girl's head.

"You dropped this," he said coolly, holding the scarf out to her, all the while his keen eyes looking to see why this young woman hid her face from the sun. He gasped.

The girl kept her head down, even after losing the scarf, but, hearing the man's swift intake of breath, she knew it was too late. He had seen her. She checked the movement, therefore, looking up at the mage with a small sigh.

What she saw in his face shocked her almost as much as what he saw in hers.

"Who . . . what kind of human are you?" she cried, shrinking away from him.

"What kind are you?" the mage demanded, holding on to the girl with his slender hands that were, nevertheless, unbelievably strong.

"I—I am . . . ordinary," the girl faltered, staring at Raistlin with wide eyes.

"Ordinary!" Raistlin gripped her more tightly as she made a halfhearted attempt to break free. His eyes gazed in disbelief at the fine-boned, delicate face; the mass of hair that was the brilliance and color of silver starlight; the eyes that were as dark and soft and velvet-black as the night sky. "Ordinary! In my hands I hold the most beautiful woman I have seen in all my twenty-one years. What is more, I hold in my hands *a woman who does not age!*" He laughed mirthlessly. "And she calls herself 'ordinary!' "

"What about you?" Trembling, the girl's hand reached up to touch Raistlin's golden-skinned face. "And what do you mean—I do not age?"

The mage saw fear in the girl's eyes as she asked this question, and his own eyes narrowed, studying her intently. "My golden skin is my sacrifice for my magic, as is my shattered body. As for you not aging, I mean you do not age in my sight. You see, my eyes are different from the eyes of other men . . ." He paused, staring at the girl, who began to shiver beneath the unwavering scrutiny. "My eyes see time as it passes, they see the death of all living things. In my vision, human flesh wastes and withers, spring trees lose their leaves, rocks crumble to dust. Only the young among the long-lived elves would appear normal to me and even then I would see them as flowers about to lose their bloom. But you—"

"Raist!" Caramon boomed from below. There was a crash. Endeavoring to shake off the gully dwarf—who was holding his hands firmly over the big man's eyes, blinding him—Caramon landed headlong on a table, smashing it to splinters.

The mage did not move, nor did the girl. "You do not age at all! You are not elven," Raistlin said.

"No," the girl murmured. Her eyes still fixed on the mage, she tried unsuccessfully to free herself from his grasp. "You—you're hurting me . . ."

"What are you?" he demanded.

She shrugged, squirming and pushing at his hands. "Human, like yourself," she protested, looking up into the strange eyes. "And I thank you for saving me, but—"

Suddenly she froze, her efforts to free herself ceased. Her gaze was locked with Raistlin's, the mage's gaze fixed on hers. "No!" she moaned helplessly. "No!" Her moan became a shriek, echoing above the howling of the storm winds outside the inn.

Raistlin reeled backward, slamming into the wall as though she had driven a sword into his body. Yet she had not harmed him, she had done nothing but look at him. With a wild cry, the girl scrambled to her feet and ran up the stairs, leaving the mage slumped against the wall, staring with stunned, unseeing eyes at where she had crouched before him on the staircase.

"Well, I took care of the scum, small thanks to you," Caramon announced, coming up beside his brother. Wiping blood from a cut on the mouth, the big warrior looked over the railing in satisfaction. Four men lay on the floor, not counting the one his brother had stabbed, whose inert body huddled at the foot of the staircase. The gully dwarf was sticking out of a barrel, upside down, his feet waving pathetically in the air, his ear-splitting screams likely to cause serious breakage of the glassware.

"What about damages?" Slegart demanded, coming over to survey the ruin.

"Collect it from them," Caramon growled, gesturing to the groaning members of the "hunting" party. "Here's your dagger, Raist," the warrior said, holding out a small silver knife. "I cleaned it as best I could. Guess you didn't want to waste your magic on those wretches, huh? Anyway—hey, Raist—you all right?"

"I'm . . . not injured. . . ." Raistlin said softly, reaching out his hand to catch hold of his brother.

"Then what's the matter?" Caramon asked, puzzled. "You look like you've seen a spirit. Say, where's the girl?" He glanced around. "Didn't she even stay to thank us?"

"I—I sent her to her room," Raistlin said, blinking in confusion and looking at Caramon as though wondering who he was. After a moment, he seemed more himself. Taking the dagger from his brother's hand, the mage replaced it on the cunningly made thong he had attached around his wrist. "And we should be going to our rooms, my brother," he said firmly, seeing Caramon's gaze drift longingly to the pitcher of ale still on their table. "Lend me your arm," the mage added, taking hold of his staff. "My exertions have exhausted me."

"Oh, uh, sure, Raist," Caramon said, his thirst forgotten in his concern for his brother.

"Number thirteen," grunted Slegart, helping the ruffians drag their wounded comrade off into a corner.

"It figures," Caramon muttered, assisting his brother up the stairs. "Hey, you got a good look at that girl? Was she pretty?"

"Why ask me, my brother?" Raistlin replied softly. Pulling his hood down low over his face again, he evaded his brother's question. "You know what these eyes of mine see!"

"Yeah, sorry, Raist." Caramon flushed. "I keep forgetting. Damn! That one bastard broke a chair over my back end when I was bending over. I know I got splinters. . . ."

"Yes, my brother," Raistlin murmured, not listening. His gaze went to the door at the end of the hall, a door marked with the number sixteen.

Behind that door, Amberyl paced restlessly, clasping and unclasping her hands and occasionally making that low, moaning cry.

"How could this happen?" she asked feverishly, walking back and forth, back and forth, in the small chamber. The room was chill and dark. In her preoccupation, Amberyl had allowed the fire to go out. "Why did this happen? How could it happen? Why didn't any of the wise foresee this?" Over and over again she repeated these words, her feet tracing the circular path of her thoughts out upon the grime-encrusted wooden floor.

"I must see him," she said to herself suddenly. "He is magi, after all. He may know some way . . . some way to . . . help. . . . Yes! I'll see him."

Grabbing up her scarf, she wound it around her face again and cautiously opened the door. The hallway was empty and she started to creep out when she realized she had no idea which room was his.

"Perhaps he isn't even staying the night," she said, sagging against the door frame in despair. "What would I say to him anyway?" Turning, she started back into her room when she stopped. "No, I *must* see him!" she said, and closed the door firmly so that she might not be tempted back inside. "If he isn't up here yet, I'll go after him."

Moving down the hall, Amberyl crept near each door, listening. Behind some she heard groans and muttered oaths and hurriedly shied away from these, realizing that her attackers were inside, recovering from their fray with the mage and his brother. At another door there was the shrill giggle of a female and the deeper laughter of a man. Amberyl continued to number thirteen.

"But, Raist! What am I supposed to say to the girl? 'Come down to our room. My brother wants you'?"

Recognizing the voice, Amberyl pressed closer against the door, listening carefully.

"If that is all you can think of saying, then say that."

The whispering, sneering voice, barely heard above the howling of the storm wind, sent tiny prickles of pain through Amberyl's body. Shivering, she drew closer still.

"I don't care what you do, just bring her to me!"

Amberyl heard a shuffling sound and a deprecating cough. "Uh, Raist, I don't know how grateful you think she's gonna be, but from what I've seen of her—"

"Caramon," said the whispering voice, "I am weary and sick, and I have no more patience to cope with your stupidity. I told you to bring the girl to me. Now do so. . . ." The voice trailed off in coughing.

There came the sound of heavy footsteps nearing the door. Fearful of being caught listening, yet unable to leave, Amberyl wondered frantically what to do. She had just decided to run back to her room and hide when the door opened.

"Name of the gods!" Caramon said in astonishment, reaching out and catching hold of Amberyl as she shrank backward. "Here she is, Raist! Standing outside in the hall. Eavesdropping!"

"Is she?" The golden-eyed, golden-skinned mage looked up curiously from where he sat huddled by the fire as his brother half-dragged, half-led Amberyl into the room. "What were you doing out there?" he asked, his eyes narrowing.

For a moment, Amberyl could say nothing. She just stood staring at the mage, twisting the bottom of her scarf in her hands.

"Hold on, Raist," Caramon said gently. "Don't yell at her. The poor thing's freezing. Her hands are like a ghoul's. Here, my lady," the big man said awkwardly, leading her closer to the fire and drawing up a chair for her. "Sit down. You'll catch your death." He put his hand on her scarf. "This is wet from the snow. Let me take—"

"No!" Amberyl cried in a choked voice, her hands going to the scarf. "No," she repeated more softly, flushing to see Raistlin look at her with a grim smile. "I—I'm fine. I . . . never . . . catch cold. Please. . . ."

"Leave us, Caramon," Raistlin ordered.

"What?" The big man looked startled.

"I said leave us. Go back to your pitcher of ale and the barmaid. She appeared not insensible to your attractions."

"Uh, sure, Raist. If that's what you want. . . ." Caramon hesitated, looking at his brother with such a dumbfounded expression on his face that Amberyl started to laugh, only it came out in a sob. Hiding her face in her scarf, she tried to check her tears.

"Leave us!" Raistlin commanded.

"Sure!" Amberyl heard Caramon backing out the door. "Just . . . just remember, you're not strong, Raistlin. . . ."

The door closed gently.

"I—I'm sorry," Amberyl faltered, raising her face from the scarf and using the tip to dry her eyes. "I didn't mean to cry. I lost control. It—it won't happen again."

Raistlin did not answer her. Comfortably settled in a battered old chair, the mage sat calmly staring at Amberyl, his frail hands clutching a mug of tea that had long ago gone cold. Behind him, near at hand, his staff leaned against the wall. "Remove the scarf," he said finally, after a long silence.

Swallowing her tears, Amberyl slowly reached up and unwound the scarf from her face. The expression in the golden eyes did not change; it was as cold and smooth as glass. Amberyl discovered, looking into those eyes, that she could see herself reflected there. She wouldn't be able to enter again, not as she had on the stairs. The mage had put up barriers around his soul.

Too late! she thought in despair. Too late. . . .

"What have you done to me?" Raistlin asked, still not moving. "What spell have you cast upon me? Name it, that I may know how to break it."

Amberyl looked down, unable to stand the gaze of those strange eyes a moment longer. "No—no spell," she murmured, twisting the scarf round and round. "I—I am not . . . not magi . . . as surely as you can tell—"

"Damn you!" Raistlin slid out of the chair with the speed of a striking snake. Hurling the mug to the floor, he grabbed hold of Amberyl's wrists and dragged her to her feet. "You're lying! You have done something to me! You invaded my being! You *live* inside me! All I can think of is you. All I see in my mind is your face. I cannot concentrate! My magic eludes me! What have you done, woman?"

"You—you're hurting me!" Amberyl cried softly, twisting her arms in his grasp. His touch burned. She could feel an unnatural warmth radiate from his body, as though he were being consumed alive by some inner fire.

"I will hurt you much worse than this," Raistlin hissed, drawing her nearer, "if you do not tell me what I ask!"

"I—I can't explain!" Amberyl whispered brokenly, gasping as Raistlin tightened his grip. "Please! You must believe me. I didn't do this to you deliberately! I didn't mean for this to happen—"

"Then why did you come here . . . to my room?"

"You—you are magi. . . . I hoped there might be some way . . . You might know—"

"—how to break the enchantment," Raistlin finished softly, loosening his grip and staring at Amberyl. "So—you are telling the truth. It is happening to you. I see that now. That's the real reason you came here, isn't it? Somehow *I* have invaded your being as well."

Amberyl hung her head. "No. I mean yes. Well, partly." Raising her face, she looked at the mage. "I did truly come here to see if there wasn't some way . . ."

Laughing bitterly, Raistlin dropped her hands. "How can I remove a spell when you won't tell me what you have cast?"

"It isn't a spell!" Amberyl cried despairingly. She could see the marks his fingers had left on her flesh.

"Then what is it?" Raistlin shouted. His voice cracked, and, coughing, he fell backward, clutching his chest.

"Here," Amberyl said, reaching out her hands, "let me help—"

"Get out!" Raistlin panted through lips flecked with blood and froth. With his last strength, he shoved Amberyl away from him, then sank down into his chair. "Get out!" he said again. Though the words were inaudible, his eyes spoke them clearly, the hourglass pupils dilated with rage.

Frightened, Amberyl turned and fled. Opening the door, she plummeted out into the hallway, crashing headlong into Caramon and the barmaid who were heading for another room.

"Hey!" Caramon cried, catching Amberyl in his arms. "What is it? What's the matter?"

"Your—your brother," Amberyl said in confusion, hiding her face in her long hair. "He . . . he's ill."

"I warned him . . ." Caramon said softly, his face crumpling in worry as he heard his brother's rasping cough. Forgetting the barmaid, who was setting up a disappointed cry behind him, the big warrior went back into his room.

Amberyl ran blindly down the hall, yanked open her door, and stumbled inside her room to stand, shivering, against the wall in the darkness.

She may have slept. She wasn't certain. Her dreams were too near her waking thoughts. But she'd heard a sound. Yes, there it was again. A door slamming. Though it could have been any one of the rooms in the inn, Amberyl knew instinctively whose door it was.

Rising from the bed on which she'd been lying, fully dressed, the girl opened her door a crack as a voice echoed down the hall.

"Raist! It's a blizzard out there! We'll perish! You can't take this!"

"I am leaving this inn! Now!" came the mage's voice. No longer whispering, it was hoarse with anger and fear. "I am leaving, and I go with you or without you. It's up to you!"

The mage started walking down the hall, leaning upon his staff. Stopping, he cast a piercing glance at Amberyl's room. Panic-stricken, she ducked back into the shadows. He headed toward the stairs, his brother standing behind him, hands spread helplessly.

"This has to do with that girl, doesn't it?" Caramon shouted. "Name of the Abyss, answer me! I— He's gone." Left alone in the hall, the big warrior scratched his head. "Well, he won't get far without me. I'll go after him. Women!" he muttered, hurrying back into the room and reappearing, struggling to lift a pack to his back. "Just after we got out of that damn magic forest, too. Now, I suppose we'll end up right back in it."

Amberyl saw Caramon look down the hall toward her room and, once more, ducked back.

"I'd like to know what's going on, my lady," the big man said in her general direction. Then, shaking his head, Caramon shouldered the pack and clumped hastily down the stairs.

Amberyl stood for a moment in the darkness of her room, waiting until her breathing calmed and she could think clearly. Then, grabbing her scarf, she wound it tightly around her face. Pulling a fur cloak from her own pack, she crept cautiously down the hall after Caramon.

Amberyl could recall no worse storm in her life and she had lived many years in the world, though she was young yet by the standards of her kind. The snow was blinding. Blown by a fierce wind, it blotted out all traces of any object from her sight—even her own hands held out before her were swallowed up by the stinging, blinding white darkness. There was no possible way she could have tracked Raistlin and his brother—no way except the way she did it—by the bond that had been accidentally created between herself and the mage.

Accidental. Yes, it must have been accidental, she thought as she trudged through the drifts. Though the snow had been falling only a matter of hours, it was already knee-deep. Strong as she was, she was having some difficulty plowing her way through the steep drifts and she could imagine the magic-user . . . in his long robes. . . .

Shaking her head, Amberyl sighed. Well, the two humans would stop soon. That much was certain. Wrapping her scarf tighter about her face, covering her skin from the biting snow, she asked herself what she intended to do when they did stop. Would she tell the mage?

What choice do I have? she argued with herself bitterly and, even as she asked the question, she slipped and stumbled. There! she thought, a sickening wave of fear convulsing her. It's beginning already, the weakness that came from the bond. And if it was happening to her, it must be happening to him also! Would it be worse in a human? she wondered in sudden alarm. What if he died!

No, she would tell him tonight, she decided firmly. Then, stopping to lean against a tree and catch her breath, she closed her eyes.

And after you've told—then what?

"I don't know . . ." she murmured to herself brokenly. "The gods help me. I don't know!"

So lost in her fear and inner turmoil was Amberyl that, for a moment, she did not notice that the snow had suddenly ceased falling, the cutting, biting wind had lessened. When she became aware of the fact, she looked around. There were stars, she saw, and even moonlight! Solinari shone brightly, turning the snow silver and the white-covered woods into a wondrous realm of the most fantastic beauty.

The woods. . . . She had crossed the boundary. Amberyl laid her hand gently upon the trunk of the tree against which she leaned. She could feel the life pulsing in the bark, the magic pulsing within that life.

She was in the magical Forest of Wayreth. Though the blizzard might rage unabated not one foot away from her, here, within the shelter of these trees, it could be summer if the wizards commanded it. But it wasn't. The wind, though it had ceased its inhuman howl, still bit the flesh with teeth of ice. The snow was piled thigh-deep in places. But at least the storm was not permitted to vent its full fury inside the forest. Amberyl could see now quite clearly. Solinari's light against the snow was bright as the sun. No longer was she stumbling in the dark, led on only by the burning remembrance of the mage's golden eyes, his touch. . . .

Sighing, Amberyl walked on until she found tracks in the snow. It was the humans. Yes, her instincts had led her unerringly. Not that she had ever doubted her powers. But would they hold true in this forest? Ever since she had come to this land, she had been hearing tales about the strange and magical wood.

Pausing, Amberyl examined the tracks, and her fear grew. There were two sets—one pair of footprints that went through the deepest drifts without stopping. The other, however, was a wide swath cut through the snow, the swath left by a man floundering along in heavy, wet robes. In more than one place, she could see quite clearly the marks of hands, as though the mage had fallen. Her heart began to beat painfully when she saw that one set of tracks—the mage's—had come to an end. His brother must be carrying him! Perhaps he . . . perhaps he was . . .

No! Amberyl caught her breath, shaking her head. The mage might be frail-looking, but there was a strength in him greater than the finest steel blade ever forged. All this meant was that the two must stop and find shelter, and that would work to her advantage.

It wasn't long before she heard voices.

Dodging behind a tree, keeping within its moon-cast shadow, Amberyl saw a tiny bit of light streaming outside what must be a cave in the side of a cliff, a cliff that had apparently appeared out of nowhere, for she could have sworn she had not seen it ahead of her.

"Of course," she whispered to herself in thankfulness, "the wizards will take care of one of their own. Do they know *I* am here?" she wondered suddenly. "Would they recognize me? Perhaps not. It has been so long, after all. . . ." Well, it did not matter. There was little they could do. Hopefully, they would not interfere.

"I've got to get help, Raist!" she heard the big warrior saying as she drew near. Caramon's voice sounded tense and anguished. "You've never been this bad! Never!"

There was silence, then Caramon's voice rose again in answer to words Amberyl could not hear.

"I don't know! Back to the inn if I have to! All I know is that this firewood isn't going to last until morning. You yourself tell me not to cut the trees in this forest, and they're wet anyway. It's stopped snowing. I'll only be gone a few hours at most. You'll be safe here. Probably a lot safer in these accursed woods than I will." A pause, then. "No, Raist. This time I'm doing what *I* think best!"

In her mind, Amberyl could almost hear the mage's bitter curse, and she smiled to herself. The light from the cave was obliterated for an instant by a dark shadow—Caramon coming out. It hesitated. Could the man be having second thoughts? The shadow half-turned, going back into the cave.

Quickly murmuring words to herself in a language that none on the continent of Ansalon had heard for countless centuries, Amberyl gestured. Barely visible from where she stood, a glimmer of firelight burst into being far off in another part of the forest.

Catching a glimpse of it from the corner of his eye, Caramon shouted. "Raist! There's— A fire! Someone's close by! You stay wrapped up and . . . and warm. . . . I'll be back soon!"

The shadow merged with the darkness, then Amberyl saw the bright glint of armor in the moonlight and heard the heavy footsteps and labored breathing of the big man slogging through the snow.

Amberyl smiled. "No, you won't be back very soon, my friend," she told him silently as he passed right by the tree where she was hiding, "not very soon at all."

Waiting until she was certain Caramon was well off on his pursuit of the elusive blaze that would, she knew, keep always just beyond his reach, Amberyl drew a deep breath, said a silent prayer to her god, and crept swiftly through the sparkling silver snow toward the cave.

Pushing aside the blanket Caramon had strung up in a pathetic attempt to block out the elements, Amberyl entered. The cave was cold, damp, and dark, lit only by a fire that sputtered feebly near the doorway to allow for ventilation. Glancing at it, Amberyl shook her head. What firewood Caramon had been able to find was wet with snow and ice. It was a tribute to the big man's skill in woodlore that he had been able to coax a flame from it at all. But it wouldn't last long and there was no wood at all to replace it when it was gone.

Peering into the shadows, Amberyl couldn't find the mage at first, though she could hear his rattling breath and smell the spicy fragrance of his spell components. Then he coughed. A bundle of clothes and blankets near the fire moved, and Amberyl saw a thin hand snake out to clasp hold of a steaming mug that stood near the blaze. The fingers trembled, nearly dropping the mug. Hurriedly kneeling by his side, Amberyl caught hold of it.

"Let me help you," she said. Not waiting for an answer, she lifted the mug in her hand, then assisted Raistlin to sit. "Lean on me," she offered, seeing the mage endeavoring weakly to prop himself up.

"You're not surprised to see me, are you?" she asked.

Raistlin regarded her for a few moments with his flat, golden eyes, then—with a bitter smile—rested his frail body against Amberyl's as she settled down beside him. Chilled as he was, Amberyl could feel that strange warmth emanate from the thin body. He was tense and rigid, his breathing labored. Raistlin lifted the mug to his lips, but began to cough again, a cough that Amberyl could feel tear at him.

Taking the mug from him, she set it down, and held onto him as he choked and gasped for breath, wrapping her arms around him as though she would hold his body together. Her own heart was torn, both in pity for him and his suffering and with fear for herself. He was so weak! What if he died?

But, finally, the spasm eased. Raistlin was able to draw a shuddering breath and motioned for his drink. Amberyl held it to his lips, her nose wrinkling at the foul smell.

Slowly, Raistlin sipped it. "I wondered if you would find us here," he whispered. "I wondered if the wizards would allow you inside the forest."

"I wondered the same myself," Amberyl said softly. "As for me finding you"—she sighed—"if I hadn't, you would have found me. You would have come back to me. You couldn't help yourself."

"So that's the way it is," Raistlin said, his breathing coming easier.

"That's the way it is . . ." Amberyl murmured.

"Help me lie down," Raistlin ordered, sinking back among his blankets. Amberyl made him as comfortable as possible, her gaze going to the dying fire. A sudden gust of wind blew the blanket aside. A flurry of snow hissed and danced on the glowing embers.

"I feel myself growing strangely weak, as though my life were being drained off," the mage said, huddling into the wet blankets. "Is that a result of the spell?"

"Yes . . . I feel it, too. And it isn't a spell," Amberyl said, doing what she could to stir up the blaze. Coming to sit in front of the mage, she clasped her arms around her legs, looking at him as intently as he stared at her.

"Take off your scarf," he whispered.

Slowly, Amberyl unwound the scarf from her face, letting it fall about her shoulders. She shook out her snow-wet hair, feeling drops of water spatter on her hands.

"How beautiful you—" He broke off. "What will happen to me?" Raistlin asked abruptly. "Will I die?"

"I—I don't know," Amberyl answered reluctantly, her gaze going to the fire. She couldn't bear to look at him. The mage's eyes burned through her, touching something deep inside, filling her with sweet pain. "I have . . . never heard of this . . . happening to—to a . . . human before."

"So you are not human," Raistlin remarked.

"No, I am not," Amberyl replied, still unable to face him.

"You are not elven, nor any of the other races that I am familiar with who live upon Krynn—and I tell you— What is your name?"

"Amberyl."

"Amberyl," he said it lingeringly, as though tasting it. She shivered again.

"I tell you, Amberyl," he repeated, "I am familiar with all the races on Krynn."

"Wise you may be, mage," Amberyl murmured, "but the mysteries of this world that have yet to be discovered are as numberless as the snowflakes."

"You will not reveal your secret to me?"

Amberyl shook her glistening hair. "It is not my secret alone."

Raistlin was silent. Amberyl did not speak either. Both sat listening to the hissing and popping of the wood and the whistling of the wind among the trees.

"So . . . I am to die, then," Raistlin said, breaking the silence at last. He didn't sound angry, just weary and resigned.

"No, no, no!" Amberyl cried. Reaching out impulsively, she took his thin, wasted hand in her own, cradling her cheek against it. "No," she repeated. "Because then *I* would die."

Raistlin snatched his hand from hers. Propping himself up weakly on his elbow, his golden eyes glittering, he whispered hoarsely, "There *is* a cure? You can break this . . . this enchantment?"

"Yes," Amberyl answered without a voice, feeling the warm blood suffuse her face.

"How?" Raistlin demanded, his hand clenching.

"First," said Amberyl, swallowing, "I—I must tell you something about . . . about the *Valin*."

"The what?" Raistlin asked quickly. Amberyl could see his eyes flicker. Even facing death, his mind was working, catching hold eagerly of this new information, storing it away.

"The *Valin*. That is what it is called in our language. It means . . ." She paused, frowning, trying to think. "I suppose the closest meaning in your language is *life-mate*."

The startled expression on the mage's face was so funny that Amberyl laughed nervously. "Wait, let me explain," she said, feeling her own face growing more and more flushed. "For reasons of our own, in ages so far back that they are past reckoning, my people fled this land and retreated to one where we could live undisturbed. Our race is, as you were able to detect, long-lived. But we are not immortal. As all others, in order for our race to survive, we must produce children. But there were few of us and fewer still as time went by. The land we chose to live in is a harsh one. We tend to be loners, living by ourselves with little interaction even among our own kind. What you know as families are unknown among us. We saw our race begin to dwindle and the elders knew that soon it must die out completely. They were able to establish the *Valin* to ensure that our young people . . . that they . . ."

Raistlin's face had not changed expression; his eyes continued to stare at her. But Amberyl could not continue speaking beneath that strange, unblinking gaze.

"You chose to leave your land?" Raistlin asked. "Or were you sent away?"

"I was sent to this land . . . by the elders. There are others here as well. . . ."

"Why? What for?"

Amberyl shook her head. Picking up a stick, she poked at the fire, giving herself an excuse to avoid his eyes.

"But surely your elders knew that something like this must happen if you go out into other lands," Raistlin said bitterly. "Or have they been away *that* long?"

"You have no conception of how long we have been away," Amberyl said softly, staring at the fire that was flickering out despite her best efforts to keep it going. "And, no, it should *not* have happened. Not with one who is not of our race." Her gaze went back to Raistlin. "And now it is my turn to ask questions. What is there about *you* that is different from other humans? For there is something, something besides your golden skin and eyes that see death in the living. Looking at you, I perceive the shadow of another. You are young, yet there is a timelessness about you. Who are *you*, Raistlin, that this has happened between us?"

To her amazement, Raistlin blanched, his eyes widening in fear, then narrowing in suspicion. "It seems we both have our secrets." He shrugged. "And now, Amberyl, it appears that we will never know what caused this to happen. All that should really concern us is what must be done to rid ourselves of this . . . this *Valin*."

Shutting her eyes, Amberyl licked her lips. Her mouth was dry, and the cave was suddenly unbearably cold. Shivering, she tried more than once to speak.

"What?" Raistlin's voice grated.

"I . . . must bear . . . your child," Amberyl said weakly, her throat constricting.

For long moments there was silence. Amberyl did not dare open her eyes, she did not dare look at the mage. Ashamed and afraid, she buried her face in her arms. But an odd sound made her raise her gaze.

Raistlin was lying back on his blankets, laughing. It was almost inaudible laughter, more a wheeze and a choking but laughter nonetheless—taunting, cutting laughter. And Amberyl saw, with pity in her heart, that its sharp edge was directed against himself.

"Don't, please, don't," Amberyl said, crawling nearer.

"Look at me, lady!" Raistlin gasped, his laughter catching in his throat, setting him to coughing. Grinning at her mirthlessly, he gestured outside. "You had best wait for my brother. Caramon will be back soon. . . ."

"No, he won't," Amberyl said softly, creeping closer to Raistlin. "Your brother will not be back before morning."

Raistlin's lips parted. His eyes—filled with a sudden hunger—devoured

Amberyl's face. "Morning," he repeated.

"Morning," she said.

Reaching up a trembling hand, Raistlin brushed back the beautiful hair from her delicate face. "The fire will be out long before morning."

"Yes," said Amberyl softly, blushing, resting her cheek against the mage's hand. "It—it's already growing cold in here. We will have to do something to keep warm . . . or we will perish. . . ."

Raistlin drew his hand over her smooth skin, his finger touching her soft lips. Her eyes closed, she leaned toward him. His hand moved to touch her long eyelashes, as fine as elven lace. Her body pressed close to his. He could feel her shivering. Putting his arm around her, he drew her close. As he did so, the fire's last little flame flickered and died. Darkness warmer and softer than the blankets covered them. Outside they could hear the wind laughing, the trees whispering to themselves.

"Or we will perish . . ." Raistlin murmured.

Amberyl woke from a fitful sleep wondering, for a moment, where she was. Stirring slightly, she felt the mage's arm wrapped around her protectively, the warmth of his body lying next to hers. Sighing, she rested her head against his shoulder, listening to the shallow, too rapid breathing. She let herself lie there, surrounded by his warmth, putting off the inevitable for as long as possible.

Outside, she could no longer hear the wind and knew the storm must have ended. The darkness that covered them was giving way to dawn. She could barely make out the blackened remnants of the firewood in the gray half-light. Turning slightly, she could see Raistlin's face.

He was a light sleeper. He stirred and muttered at her movement, coughing, starting to wake. Amberyl touched his eyelids lightly with her fingertips, and he sighed deeply and relaxed back into sleep, the lines of pain smoothing from his face.

How young he looks, she thought to herself. How young and vulnerable. He has been deeply hurt. That is why he wears the armor of arrogance and unfeeling. It chafes him now. He is not used to it. But something tells me he will become all too accustomed to this armor before his brief life ends.

Moving carefully and quietly so as not to disturb him—more by instinct than because she feared she would wake him from his enchanted sleep— Amberyl slid out from his unconscious embrace. Gathering her things, she wrapped the scarf once more about her head. Then, kneeling down beside the sleeping mage, she looked upon Raistlin's face one last time.

"I could stay," she told him softly. "I could stay with you a little while. But then my solitary nature would get the better of me and I would leave you and you would be hurt." A sudden thought made her shudder. Closing her eyes, she shook her head. "Or you might find out the truth about our race. If you ever discovered it, then you would loathe me, despise me! Worse still"—her eyes filled with tears—"you would despise our child."

Gently, Amberyl stroked back the mage's prematurely white hair, and her hand caressed the golden skin. "There is something about you that frightens me," she said, her voice trembling. "I don't understand. Perhaps the wise will know. . . ." A tear crept down her face. "Farewell, mage. What I do now will keep pain from us both"—bending down, she kissed the sleeping face—"and from one who should come into this world free of all its burdens."

Amberyl placed her hand upon the mage's temples and, closing her eyes, began reciting words in the ancient language. Then, tracing the name *Caramon* upon the dirt floor, she spoke the same words over it as well. Rising hurriedly to her feet, she started to leave the cave. At the entrance she paused. The cave was damp and chill; she heard the mage cough. Pointing at the fire, she spoke again. A blazing flame leapt up from the cold stone, filling the cave with warmth and light. With a final backward glance, a last, small sigh, Amberyl stepped out of the cave and walked away beneath the watchful, puzzled trees of the magical Forest of Wayreth.

Dawn glistened brightly on the new-fallen snow when Caramon finally made his way back to the cave.

"Raist!" he called out in a frightened voice as he drew nearer. "Raist! I'm sorry! This cursed forest!" He swore, glancing nervously at the trees as he did so. "This . . . blasted place. I spent half the night chasing after some wretched firelight that vanished when the sun came up. Are—are you all right?" Frightened, wet, and exhausted, Caramon stumbled through the snow, listening for his brother's answer, cough . . . anything.

Hearing nothing from within the cave but ominous silence, Caramon hurried forward, tearing the blanket from the entrance in his desperate haste to get inside.

Once there, he stopped, staring about him in astonishment.

A comfortable, cheery fire burned brightly. The cave was as warm—warmer—than a room in the finest inn. His twin lay fast asleep, his face peaceful as though lost in some sweet dream. The air was filled with a springlike fragrance, as of lilacs and lavender.

"I'll be a gully dwarf," Caramon breathed in awe, suddenly noticing that the fire was burning solid rock. Shivering, the big man glanced around. "Mages!" he muttered, keeping a safe distance from the strange blaze. "The sooner we're out of this weird forest the better, to my mind. Not that I'm not grateful," he added hastily. "Looks like you wizards saved Raist's life. I just wonder why it was necessary to send me on that wild swimming-bird chase." Kneeling down, he shook his brother by the shoulder.

"Raist," Caramon whispered gently. "Raist. Wake up!"

Raistlin's eyes opened wide. Starting up, he looked around. "Where is—" he began.

"Where is who? What?" Caramon cried in alarm. Backing up, his hand on the hilt of his sword, he looked frantically around the small cave. "I knew—"

"Is . . . is—" Raistlin stopped, frowning.

"No one, I guess," the mage said softly, his hand going to his head. He felt dizzy. "Relax, my brother," he snapped irritably, glancing up at Caramon. "There is no one here but us."

"But . . . this fire . . ." Caramon said, eyeing the blaze suspiciously. "Who—"

"My own work," Raistlin replied. "After you ran off and left me, what else could I do? Help me to my feet." Stretching out his frail hand, the mage caught hold of his brother's strong one and slowly rose up out of the pile of blankets on the stone floor.

"I—I didn't know you could do anything like that!" Caramon said, staring at the fire whose fuel was rock.

"There is much about me you do not know, my brother," Raistlin returned. Wrapping himself up warmly in his cloak, he watched as Caramon hurriedly repacked the blankets.

"They're still a little damp," the big man muttered. "I suppose we ought to stay and dry them out. . . ."

"No," Raistlin said, shivering. He took hold of the Staff of Magius, which was leaning against the cavern wall. "I have no desire to spend any more time in the Forest of Wayreth."

"You've got my vote there," Caramon said fervently. "I wonder if there are any good inns around here. I heard that there was one, built near the forest. It's called the Wayward Inn or some such thing." The big man's eyes brightened. "Maybe tonight we'll eat hot food and drink good ale for a change. And sleep in a bed!"

"Perhaps." Raistlin shrugged, as if it didn't much matter.

Still talking of what he had heard about the rumored inn, Caramon picked up the blanket that had hung over the cave entrance, folded it, and added it to the ones in his pack. "I'll go ahead a little way," he said to his brother. "Break a trail through the snow for you."

Raistlin nodded, but said nothing. Walking to the entrance of the cave, he stood in the doorway, watching his strong twin wade through the snowdrifts, making a path the frail twin could follow. Raistlin's lip curled in bitterness, but the sneer slipped as, turning, he looked back inside the cave. The fire had died almost instantly, upon Caramon's leaving. Already, the chill was creeping back.

But there lingered on the air, still, the faint fragrance of lilac, of spring. . . .

Shrugging, Raistlin turned and walked out into the snow-blanketed forest.

The Wayward Inn looked its best in summer, a season that has this happy influence on just about anything and everyone. Great quantities of ivy had been persuaded to cradle the inn in its leafy green embrace, thus hiding some of the building's worst deficiencies. The roof still needed patching; this occurred to Slegart every time it rained, when it was impossible to go out and fix it. During dry weather, of course, it didn't leak and so didn't need fixing. The windows were still cracked, but in the heat of summer, the cool breeze that wafted through the panes was a welcome one.

There were more travelers at the inn during these journeying months.

Dwarven smiths, occasionally an elf, many humans, and more kender than anyone cared to think about, generally kept Slegart and his barmaids busy from morning until late, late at night.

But this evening was quiet. It was a soft, fragrant summer evening. The twilight lingered on in hues of purple and gold. The birds had sung their night songs and were now murmuring sleepily to their young. Even the old trees of Wayreth seemed to have been lulled into forgetting their guardian duties and slumbered drowsily at their posts. On this evening, the inn itself was quiet, too.

It was too quiet, so two strangers thought as they approached the inn. Dressed in rich clothing, their faces were covered with silken scarves—an unusual thing in such warm weather. Only their black eyes were visible and, exchanging grim glances, they quickened their steps, shoving open the wooden plank door and stepping inside.

Slegart sat behind the bar, wiping out a mug with a dirty rag. He had been wiping out that same mug for an hour now and would probably have gone on wiping it for the next hour had not two incidents occurring simultaneously interrupted him—the entry of the two muffled strangers through the front door and the arrival of the servant girl, running breathlessly down the stairs.

"Your pardon, gentlemen both," Slegart said, rising slowly to his feet and holding up his hand to check one of the strangers in his speech. Turning to the servant, he said gruffly, "Well?"

The girl shook her head.

Slegart's shoulders slumped. "Aye," he muttered. "Well, p'rhaps it's better so."

The two strangers glanced at each other.

"And the babe?" Slegart asked.

At this, the servant girl burst into tears.

"What?" Slegart asked, astonished. "Not the babe, too?"

"No!" the servant girl managed to gasp between sobs. "The baby's fine. Listen—" A faint cry came from overhead. "You can hear 'er now. But . . . but—oh!" The girl covered her face with her hands. "It's dreadful! I've never seen anything like it—"

At this, one of the strangers nodded, and the other stepped forward.

"Pardon me, innkeep," the stranger said in a cultivated voice with an unusual accent. "But some terrible tragedy appears to have happened here. Perhaps it would be better if we continued on—"

"No, no," Slegart said hastily, the thought of losing money bringing him to himself. "There, Lizzie, either dry your tears and help, or go have your cry out in the kitchen."

Burying her face in her apron, Lizzie ran off into the kitchen, setting the door swinging behind her.

Slegart led the two strangers to a table. "A sad thing," said the innkeeper, shaking his head.

"Might we inquire—" ventured the stranger casually, though an astute observer would have noticed he was unusually tense and nervous, as was his companion.

"Nothin' for you gentlemen to concern yourselves with," Slegart said. "Just one of the serving girls died in childbirth."

One of the strangers reached out involuntarily, grasping hold of his companion's arm with a tight grip. The companion gave him a warning glance.

"This is indeed sad news. We're very sorry to hear it," said the stranger in a voice he was obviously keeping under tight control. "Was she—was she kin of yours? Pardon me for asking, but you seem upset—"

"I am that, gentlemen," Slegart said bluntly. "And no, she warn't no kin of mine. Came to me in the dead 'o winter, half-starved, and begging for work. Somethin' familiar about her there was, but just as I start to think on it"— he put his hand to his head—"I get this queer feelin'. . . . 'Cause of that, I was of a mind to turn her away, but"—he glanced upstairs—"you know what women are. Cook took to her right off, fussin' over 'er and such like. I got to admit," Slegart added solemnly, "I'm not one fer gettin' attached to people. But she was as pretty a critter as I've seen in all my born days. A hard worker, too. Never complained. Quite a favorite she was with all of us."

At this, one of the strangers lowered his head. The other put his hand over his companion's.

"Well," said Slegart more briskly, "I can offer you gentlemen cold meat and ale, but you won't get no hot food this night. Cook's that upset. And now,"— the innkeeper glanced at the still-swinging kitchen door with a sigh—"from what Lizzie says, it seems like there's somethin' odd about the babe—"

The stranger made a sudden, swift movement with his hand, and old Slegart froze in place, his mouth open in the act of speaking, his body half-turned, one hand raised. The kitchen door stopped in midswing. The servant girl's muffled cries from the kitchen ceased. A drop of ale, falling from the spigot, hung suspended in the air between spigot and floor.

Rising to their feet, the two strangers moved swiftly up the stairs amid the enchanted silence. Hastily, they opened every door in the inn, peered inside every room, searching. Finally, coming to a small room at the very end of the hall, one of the strangers opened the door, looked inside, and beckoned to his companion.

A large, matronly woman—presumably Cook—was halted in the act of brushing out the beautiful hair of a pale, cold figure lying upon the bed. Tears glistened on the cook's kindly face. It had obviously been her work-worn hands that had composed the body for its final rest. The girl's eyes were shut, the cold, dead fingers folded across the breast, a small bunch of roses held in their unfeeling grasp. A candle shed its soft light upon the young face whose incredible beauty was enhanced by a sweet, wistful smile upon the ashen lips.

"Amberyl!" cried one of the strangers brokenly, sinking down upon the bed and taking the cold hands in his. Coming up behind him, the other stranger laid a hand upon his companion's shoulder.

"I'm truly sorry, Keryl."

"We should have come sooner!" Keryl stroked the girl's hand.

"We came as quickly as we could," his companion said gently. "As quickly as she wanted us."

"She sent us the message—"

"—only when she knew she was dying," said the companion.

"Why?" Keryl cried, his gaze going to Amberyl's peaceful face. "Why did she choose to die among . . . among humans?" He gestured toward the cook.

"I don't suppose we will ever know," said his companion softly. "Although I can guess," he added, but it was in an undertone, spoken only to himself and not to his distraught friend. Turning away, he walked over to a cradle that had been hastily constructed out of a wood box. He whispered a word and lifted the enchantment from the baby, who drew a breath and began whimpering.

"The child?" the stranger said, starting up from the bed. "Is her baby all right? What the servant girl said . . ." There was fear in his voice. "It isn't, it isn't dea-" He couldn't go on.

"No," said his friend in mystified tones. "It is not what you fear. The servant girl said she'd never seen anything 'like it.' But the baby seems fine—Ah!" The stranger gasped in awe. Holding the baby in his arms, he turned toward his friend. "Look, Keryl! Look at the child's eyes!"

The young man bent over the crying baby, gently stroking the tiny cheek with his finger. The baby turned its head, opening its large eyes as it searched instinctively for nourishment, love, and warmth.

"The eyes are . . . gold!" Keryl whispered. "Burning gold as the sun! Nothing like this has ever occurred in *our* people. . . . I wonder—"

"A gift from her human father, no doubt. Although I know of no humans with eyes like this. But that secret, too, Amberyl took with her." He sighed, shaking his head. Then he looked back down at the whimpering baby. "Her daughter is as lovely as her mother," the man said, wrapping the baby tightly in its blankets. "And now, my friend, we must go. We have been in this strange and terrible land long enough."

"Yes," Keryl said, but he made no move to leave. "What about Amberyl?" His gaze went back to the pale, unmoving figure upon the bed.

"We will leave her among those she chose to be with at the end," his companion said gravely. "Perhaps one of the gods will accept her now and will guide her wandering spirit home."

"Farewell, my sister," Keryl murmured. Reaching down, he took the roses from the dead hands and, kissing them, put the flowers carefully in the pocket of his tunic. His companion spoke words in an ancient language, lifting the enchantment from the inn. Then the two strangers, holding the baby, vanished from the room like a shower of silver, sparkling rain.

And the baby was beautiful, as beautiful as her mother. For it is said that, in the ancient of days before they grew self-centered and seduced by evil, the most beautiful of all races ever created by the gods was the ogre. . . .

V

A child deeply wanted,
a son of the midlife,
the only daughter
with the father's eyes,
for you, dear children,
we build these castles
that the walls may encircle
your borrowed lives.

Surrounded by stone,
by tower and crenel,
there is no courage
that is not stone,
and drawbridge and battlement,
merlon and parapet
assemble to keep you
redeemed and alone.

O child well-loved,
O son of the midlife,
who measured the tendon
in the span of your hand?
And glittering daughter,
image of memory,
is the heart of your blossoming
apportioned and planned?

Where is your country
and where are your people?
Where the unblessed
discontentment with walls?
Where is the siegecraft
of heart and autonomy,
encircling the castle
as the battlement falls?

The Sacrifice

Chapter One

The last ringing echoes of the chimes, hanging in the clock tower of the Temple of Paladine, were punctuated by the sounds of shutters closing, doors slamming shut, keys turning in locks, and the shrill protests of disappointed kender, who had been discovered poking about among the shelves and were now being tossed into the streets. Six strikes of the bell brought the day's business to an end. Shopkeepers set about closing for the night; last minute buyers were eyed with impatience and hustled out of the stores as soon as their cash was in hand.

"Close up, Markus," Jenna told her young assistant.

He promptly left his seat at the entrance and began to draw the heavy wooden shutters over the pane glass windows.

The shop darkened. Jenna smiled. She enjoyed her work, but she liked this time of day best. All the customers were gone, the din of their voices quieted, and she was alone. She paused to listen to the stillness, to breathe in the smells that would have told Jenna—had she been blind and deaf—that she was in a mageware shop: the perfume of rose petals; the spicy smells of cinnamon and clove; the faint, sickening odor of decay, of bats' wings, and turtle skulls. The smell was always strongest this time of day. The sunlight brought forth the various fragrances, and the darkness enhanced them.

Markus appeared in the doorway.

"Anything else I can do for you, Mistress Jenna?" he asked eagerly.

He was newly hired and already in love with her. Hopelessly in love, as only a nineteen-year-old can be in love with a woman five years his senior. All Jenna's assistants fell in love with her. She had come to expect it, would have been disappointed—and probably angered—if they had not. Yet she did nothing to encourage the young men, beyond simply being herself, which, since she was beautiful, powerful, and mysterious, was quite enough. Jenna loved another man, and all in Palanthas knew it.

"No, Markus, you may be off to the Boar's Head for your nightly carousing with your friends." Jenna grabbed a broom and began briskly sweeping the floor.

"They're just kids," Mark said scornfully, his eyes following her every move. "I'd much rather stay and help you clean up."

Jenna brushed dried mud and a few scattered mint leaves out the door, and brushed Markus playfully along with them. "There's nothing you can do for me in the shop, as I've told you. Best for both of us if you keep out of it. I don't want your blood on my hands."

"Mistress Jenna, I'm not frightened—" he began.

"Then you have no sense," she interrupted, with a smile to take away the sting of her words. "Locked in that case is a brooch that will steal away your soul and take you directly to the Abyss. Next to the brooch lies a ring that could turn you inside out. See those spellbooks on the far shelf? If you were to so much as glance at the inscriptions on the covers, you would find yourself descending into madness."

Markus was somewhat daunted, but didn't intend to show it. "Where does it all come from?" he asked, peering into the shadowy shop.

"Various places. That White Robe who just left brought me the brooch of soul-stealing. The brooch is evil, you see, and she would never consider using it. But she traded the brooch to me for several spellbooks that she has long wanted, but could not afford. You remember the dwarf who came this morning? He brought these knives." Jenna gestured to a display case in which innumerable small knives and daggers were arranged in a fan leaf design.

"Are they magic? I didn't think mages were permitted to carry weapons."

"We may not carry swords, but knives and daggers are permissible. And, no, these are not magic, but the dwarves make many items that can later be imbued with magic. A wizard might cast a spell on one of these knives, if he chose to do so."

The young man said stoutly, "You're not afraid, Mistress Jenna. Why should I be?"

"Because I know how to handle such arcane objects. I wear the Red Robes. I have taken and passed the Test in the Tower of High Sorcery. When you do the same, then you may come into my store. Until then," she added, with a charming smile that went to the young man's head like spiced wine, "you stand guard at my door."

"I will, Mistress Jenna," he promised rapturously, "and . . . and maybe I will study magic . . ."

She shrugged and nodded. All her assistants said the same thing when they first came to work for her; none of them ever followed through. Jenna made sure of that. She never hired anyone who had the slightest proclivity toward magic. Her wares would be too strong a temptation for a young mage to resist. Besides, she needed brawn, not brain, to guard her door.

Only those who wore the robes and the few tradesmen who dealt in arcane merchandise were permitted to enter Jenna's shop, its doorway marked by a sign with three moons painted on it: the silver moon, the red, and the black. Magic-users drew their powers from these moons, and the few stores in Ansalon that dealt in mageware always marked their shops with these symbols.

Most citizens of Palanthas avoided Jenna's shop; many, in fact, crossed the street to walk on the other side. But there were always a few—either curious or drunk or acting on a dare—who attempted to enter. And, of course, kender. Not a day passed but that Jenna's assistant had to strong-arm, throttle, or otherwise remove the light-fingered kender from the premises. Every mage in Ansalon knew the story of the Flotsam mageware shop. It had vanished under mysterious circumstances, never to reappear. Horrified eyewitnesses reported having seen a kender enter just seconds before the entire building winked out of existence.

Markus shuffled off disconsolately down the street, to drown his unrequited love in ale. The fabric merchant next door to Jenna locked his door, then bowed to her in respect as he passed by on his way home. He had not been pleased when she had first moved in next door, but when his sales—particularly of white, black, and red cloth—increased, his protests decreased proportionally.

Jenna wished him a good evening. Stepping inside her shop, she shut her door, locked it, and placed a spell of warding on it. She lived above the shop, keeping her own guard on her wares during the night. Casting a final glance around, she mounted the stairs that led to her quarters.

A knock on the door halted her.

"Go home, Markus!" she called out irritably.

Three nights ago, he had come back to sing love songs beneath her window. The incident had been most embarrassing.

The knock was repeated, this time with more urgency. Jenna sighed. She was tired and hungry; it was time for a cup of tea. She turned, however, and went back down the stairs. Owners of Three Moon Shops were expected to open their stores to any mage at need, no matter what time, day or night.

Jenna opened a small window set into the door and peered out, expecting to see a Red Robe, humbly apologizing for disturbing her, but could he possibly have some cobweb? Or a Black Robe, imperiously demanding bat guano. Jenna was startled and displeased to find two tall and heavily cloaked and hooded men standing on her stoop. The rays of the setting sun glinted on swords, which both wore on their hips.

"You have the wrong shop, gentlemen," Jenna said in excellent Elvish. By their slender legs, expensive, well-tooled leather boots, and fancifully designed leather armor, she guessed them to be elves, although their faces were hidden in the hoods of their cloaks.

She was about to slam shut the window when one of the men said, speaking halting Common, "If you are Jenna, daughter of Justarius, head of the Wizard's Conclave, we do not have the wrong shop."

"Suppose I am Jenna," Jenna replied haughtily, though she was now extremely curious. "What do you want of me? If you have a magic item to sell," she added, as an afterthought, "please return in the morning."

The two men glanced at each other. She could see the glitter of almond-shaped eyes in the shadows of their hoods.

"We want to talk to you," said one.

"Talk away," Jenna said.

"In private," said the other.

Jenna shrugged. "The street is deserted this time of day. I don't mean to be rude, but you must know that owners of Three Moon Shops are careful about who they let into their shops. It's for your safety more than mine."

"Our business is serious, not to be discussed on the street. Believe me, mistress," the elf added, in a low voice, "we like this no more than you do. You have our word that we will touch nothing!"

"Did my father send you?" Jenna asked, playing for time.

If Justarius had sent them, he would have told her first, and she'd had no word from him in months, ever since their last quarrel. He strongly disapproved of her lover.

"No, mistress," said the elf. "We come on our own."

Odd, Jenna thought. One of the elves is Qualinesti, the other Silvanesti. She could tell the difference by their accents, though probably no other human in Solamnia could have done so. But Jenna had spent a great deal of time around elves, one elf in particular.

Long, long ago, the elves had been one nation. Bitter wars, the Kinslayer War, had divided them into two, Qualinesti and Silvanesti. Neither nation had any love for the other. Even now, after the War of the Lance had united every other race on Ansalon, the two elven states—though ostensibly one— were, in reality, farther apart than ever.

Her curiosity aroused, Jenna opened her door and stepped back to permit the elves to enter. She wasn't the least bit fearful. They were elves, and that meant that they were upstanding, law-abiding, and good to the point of boredom. Plus, she had a spell on her lips that would blow them back out into the street if they tried anything.

The two elves stood together in the very center of the shop. They kept their elbows locked to their sides, fearful of even touching a display case. They stood near each other—on the defensive—but were studiously careful to avoid touching each other. Allies, but unwilling allies, Jenna guessed. Her curiosity was now almost overpowering her.

"I believe you two gentlemen will be much more at home in my chambers upstairs," she said, with an impish smile. "I was about to make tea. Won't you join me?"

The Silvanesti elf had covered his mouth and nose with a handkerchief. The Qualinesti elf had half-turned and come literally eye-to-eye with a jar filled with eyeballs, floating in their protective fluid. He blenched and backed up a step.

Jenna gestured up the stairs. "You will find my chambers quite comfortable. And ordinary. My laboratory is downstairs, in the cellar," she added, for reassurance.

The elves again exchanged glances, then both nodded stiffly and began to ascend the stairs behind their hostess. The elves appeared vastly relieved to see that Jenna's small living room looked like any other human's living room, replete with table and chairs and soft-cushioned couches. Jenna stirred up the fire and brewed tea, using a leaf mixture imported from Qualinesti.

The elves drank their tea and nibbled at a cookie, for politeness's sake, nothing more. Jenna made small talk; elves never discussed business while eating and drinking.

The elves made suitable comments but offered nothing of their own, and the conversation dwindled away altogether. As soon as they could, without insulting their hostess, both elves set down their teacups, indicating they were prepared to discuss serious matters. But, now that they were here, they didn't seem to know where to begin.

Jenna could either let them stew or offer to help. Since she was expecting far more pleasant company later this evening, she wanted these elves gone, and so she prodded them along.

"Well, gentlemen, you've come to me—a red-robed magic-user. What is it you need of me? I must tell you, in advance, that I do not travel out of the city. If you want me to work magic, it must be magic that can be done here, within the confines of my own laboratory. And I don't mix love potions, if that's what you're in the market for . . ."

Jenna knew very well that love wasn't what they sought—not two bitter enemies, coming to her shop in secret, in the twilight. But it never hurt to feign ignorance.

"Don't be ridiculous," said the Qualinesti elf abruptly. "I . . . I . . . " He snapped his mouth shut, collected his thoughts, and started over. "This is most difficult for me. For us. We have need to talk to . . . someone. A special someone. And we have been advised that you were the one person who might be able to help us."

Ah, thought Jenna. Well, well, well. Isn't this interesting. She gave them a sweet and limpid smile. "Indeed? Someone I know? I can't imagine who that might be. You gentlemen appear to be of high birth. Surely, all doors on Ansalon would be open to you."

"Not this particular door," said the Silvanesti elf harshly. "Not the door to . . . " His voice dropped. "The Tower of High Sorcery."

"The dark tower," added the Qualinesti. "The tower located here, in Palanthas. We want to speak . . . to the master."

Jenna studied them. Two high-born elves; that much was proclaimed by their expensive clothing, their ornate swords, the fine jewels adorning their fingers and dangling from around their necks. Both elders, too, for though it was sometimes difficult to tell the ages of elves, these two were obviously in their middle years.

High-birth, high-rank, longtime enemies, short-time allies.

And they wanted to talk to the worst enemy each could possibly have in this world—the Master of the Tower of High Sorcery in Palanthas.

"You want to talk to Dalamar," Jenna said calmly.

"Yes, mistress." The Qualinesti's voice cracked. He coughed, angry at himself.

The Silvanesti, it seemed, had no voice at all. His face was rigid and set, his lips pursed together, his hand tightly clenched over the hilt of his sword. They were both obviously hating this.

Jenna bit her lip to keep from laughing. No wonder these elves had been so intent on privacy. Dalamar was one of their own, an elf of Silvanesti, but he was one who had been exiled, banished from elven society in disgrace. He was what they termed a "dark elf"—one who has been cast out of the light. His crime was the study of evil magic, the donning of the Black Robes. Such a heinous deed could never be condoned in elven society. For these two to even look on Dalamar would be considered a shocking act. To actually speak to him! . . .

Jenna could hardly wait to hear Dalamar's reaction. She decided to make these two suffer a little first, however.

"What makes you think that I can gain you such an interview?" she asked, in all innocence.

The Qualinesti flushed. "We have been informed that you and . . . er . . . the tower's master (he would not say the name) are friends . . ."

"He was my *shalafi*.[1] And he is my lover," Jenna replied, and enjoyed watching the elves squirm.

They again exchanged glances, as much as to say, What can you expect of a human?

The Silvanesti had apparently had enough. He rose to his feet. "Let us end this as swiftly as possible. Can you . . . will you . . . put us in touch with the Master of the Dark Tower?"

"Perhaps." Jenna was noncommittal. "When?"

"As soon as possible. Time is pressing."

Jenna arched a shapely eyebrow. "A word of caution. If you are considering laying a trap for Dalamar—"

The Qualinesti eyed her. "I assure you, madam," he said grimly, "no harm will come to him."

"No harm come to him!" Jenna laughed. "Why, what possible danger could you be to Dalamar? He is the most powerful of all the black-robed mages. He is head of the Order of Black Robes, and he will, when my father retires, take over the leadership of the entire Wizards' Conclave.

"Please, I'm sorry. Forgive me," she added, trying to stifle her laughter. The two were obviously deeply offended. "I was thinking of *your* safety, gentlemen. A friendly warning. Don't try any tricks with Dalamar. You won't enjoy the consequences."

"Of all the insolence!" The Silvanesti was livid with rage. "We don't have to—"

"Yes, we do," said his companion in a low voice.

The Silvanesti choked, but kept silent.

---

[1]Elvish for "master." Red-robed mages, being neutral in all things, may apprentice themselves to a master of any alignment, good, neutral, or evil.

"When may we meet with the Master of the Tower?" the Qualinesti asked coldly.

"*If* Dalamar agrees to meet with you, you will find him here, tomorrow night, in my chambers. I trust this place will be satisfactory to you? Or perhaps you would rather meet in the Tower of High Sorcery itself? I could sell you a charm—"

"No, mistress." The elves knew she was mocking them. "This room will be quite suitable."

"Very well." Jenna rose to her feet. "I will see you tomorrow night, at about this same time. Pleasant dreams, gentlemen."

The Silvanesti's face flushed red. He seemed prepared to strike her, but the Qualinesti halted him.

"Pleasant dreams—what a tactless remark," Jenna murmured, lowering her eyes to hide her amusement, "considering the terrible tragedy that has befallen Silvanesti. Forgive me."

She escorted them down the stairs and out the door, kept watch until they had disappeared down the street. When they were gone, she replaced the spell of warding, and—laughing out loud—went upstairs to prepare for her lover's arrival.

Chapter Two

The two elves were prompt. Jenna admitted them into her shop. Serious, demure, she led them to the stairs. At the foot, however, the elves came to a halt. They both were wearing green silk masks that covered the top half of their faces.

They looked, Jenna thought, decidedly silly, like children dressed in costume for the Festival of the Eye.

"Is he here?" asked the Qualinesti, with dread solemnity.

His gaze went up the stairs. Evening's shadows had gathered at the top. Undoubtedly the elf saw a different form of darkness, one more solid, more substantial.

"He is," Jenna replied.

Both elves hesitated, prey to inner turmoil. By even speaking to a dark elf, they were committing a crime that could well bring upon them the same fate—disgrace, banishment, and exile.

"We have no choice," said the Silvanesti. "We discussed this."

The Qualinesti nodded. The green silk was sticking to his face. Beads of sweat gathered on his upper lip.

The two mounted the stairs. Jenna started to follow.

The Silvanesti turned. "This conversation is private, madam," he said harshly.

"You are in my house," Jenna reminded him.

The Qualinesti hastened to make amends. "Forgive us, mistress, but surely you can understand . . ."

Jenna shrugged. "Very well. If you need anything, you will find me in my laboratory."

Dalamar heard the elven voices, heard the light tread of booted feet ascending the staircase. He smiled.

"This is my moment of triumph," he said softly to the darkness. "I always knew this would happen. Sooner or later, you self-righteous hypocrites, who cast me out in shame and disgrace, would be forced to come crawling back to me, begging for my help. I will grant it, but I will make you pay." Dalamar's slender fist clenched. "Oh, how I will make you pay!"

The two elves appeared in the doorway. Both were wearing masks—a sensible precaution, to prevent him from recognizing them—which meant, of course, that he knew them, or at least knew the Silvanesti.

"How long has it been since I was cast out of my homeland?" Dalamar muttered. "Twenty years, at least. A long time to humans, a short time for elves."

And the memory was burned into his mind. Two hundred years might pass, and he would not forget.

"Please, gentlemen," Dalamar said, speaking Silvanesti, his native tongue, "enter and be seated."

"Thank you, no," said the Qualinesti. "This is not a social call, master. It is strictly business. Let us understand this from the very beginning."

"I have a name," Dalamar said softly, his eyes intent on the elves, much to their discomfiture.

They found it difficult to look at him—to look on the black robes, decorated with arcane symbols of power and protection; on the bags of spell components hanging from his belt; on his face—youthful, handsome, proud, cruel. He was powerful, in control. Both men knew it, but neither man liked it.

"You had a name," said the Silvanesti. "It is no longer spoken among us."

"What a pity." Dalamar folded his hands in the sleeves of his robes. He bowed, prior to making his departure. "Gentlemen, you appear to have wasted your time . . ."

"Wait!" The Qualinesti gulped. "Wait, D-Dalamar." He mopped sweat from his lip. "This is not easy for us!"

"Nor for me," Dalamar returned coldly. "How do you think it makes me feel to hear, for the first time in all these years, the language of my homeland?" His throat constricted. He was forced to turn away, to stare into the fire, let the heat burn away his sudden, unexpected tears.

Neither answered. He heard them shift uncomfortably.

His unwelcome emotions tamped down, Dalamar turned to face them.

"And so, General, and you, Senator, what do you want of Dalamar the Dark?" he demanded brusquely.

The two stared at him in glowering astonishment, dismayed at his recognition.

"I . . . I don't know to whom you are . . . referring . . ." The Silvanesti general attempted to bluster his way out.

Dalamar gave the two a sardonic smile.

"Next time you want to travel incognito, I suggest that you, General, remove your ceremonial sword, and that you, Senator, take off your ring of office."

"I think . . . I will sit down," said the senator, the Qualinesti. He sank into a chair.

The general, the Silvanesti, remained standing, hand on the hilt of the sword that had betrayed him.

"You begin," the senator said to his companion.

The general crossed his arms over his chest, stood with feet apart. "I must tell you first what I think will be welcome news, even to you, Dalamar." He spoke the name with the tip of his tongue against his teeth, as if fearful that taking the name into his mouth might poison him. "Silvanesti has at last been reclaimed. Lorac's evil dream, which held our land in thrall, has been defeated. The few pockets of draconians and goblins holding parts of our land have been routed. Twenty years it took us, but now Silvanesti is ours again. Its beauty has returned."

"Congratulations," Dalamar said, his lip curling in a sneer. "So Porthios led you to victory. Yes, you see, I keep up with the politics of my homeland. Porthios, a Qualinesti, married Alhana, Lorac's daughter, Silvanesti queen. A united elven kingdom—I believe was what the two had in mind. And for the last twenty years, the Qualinesti Speaker of the Sun, Porthios, has risked his life to save the Silvanesti homeland. And he has succeeded. How have you repaid him for his services?"

"He has been imprisoned," said the general gravely.

Dalamar began to laugh. "How very elven! Imprison the man who saves your miserable lives. What was his crime? No, let me guess. I know Porthios, you see. He never let you Silvanesti elves forget that it was the Qualinesti who had come to your rescue. He spoke often of how the Qualinesti and the Silvanesti would unite, but implied that it would be the Qualinesti who would rule over their weaker brethren. Am I right?"

"Near enough." The general was not pleased. He could hear plainly the sarcasm in the dark elf's voice.

Dalamar turned to the senator. "And how do you Qualinesti feel about this? Your Speaker of the Sun imprisoned?"

The senator gasped, tugged on his mask. "This thing is stifling me." He drew a deep breath, then spoke carefully, "We have no quarrel with the Silvanesti. Their queen, the wife of Porthios, Alhana Starbreeze, is my guest in Qualinost."

Dalamar sucked in a deep breath, then let it out slowly. "The things I've missed, locked away in my dull tower. A 'guest,' you say. A guest who is undoubtedly weary of your hospitality but finds it difficult to leave. What is *her* crime?"

"This is not generally known, but Alhana Starbreeze is pregnant." The senator was nervously twisting his ring of office around and around on his finger.

Dalamar was intrigued. "So, after twenty years, the marriage of convenience has heated up, has it? I'm surprised Porthios found the time. Or the inclination."

"If the child is born in elven lands," the senator went on, pretending he hadn't heard, "while the parents rule, the child will be heir to the thrones of both kingdoms. The unification will be complete."

"This must not be allowed to happen." The general's hand clenched over the sword's hilt.

"And what do you propose to do to stop it?" Dalamar asked. "Assuming murder is not a consideration."

The senator stiffened in outraged dignity. His silk mask was wet around the forehead and clung to his face. "Exile. Both of them."

"I see," said Dalamar. "Like myself." His voice was soft, bitter. "Death would be kinder."

The senator frowned. "Are you implying—"

"I imply nothing." Dalamar shrugged. "Merely making a comment. But I don't quite see how I fit into this neat little treasonous plot of yours. Unless you are offering me the rulership of the elves?"

The two regarded him in horror, eyes wide and staring.

"Please, gentlemen, you take yourselves too seriously!" Dalamar laughed, reassuring. "I spoke in jest, nothing more."

Both appeared relieved, but still somewhat suspicious.

"House Protector will rule Silvanesti, until such time as a member of House Royal is deemed prepared to take over," said the general. "House Protector has ruled Silvanesti for these past twenty years, while we fought the dream. My people are accustomed to martial law. And they don't like Porthios."

"As for the Qualinesti . . . " The senator hesitated. He glanced uneasily down the staircase.

"Don't worry," said Dalamar. "Jenna isn't the sort to eavesdrop. And, believe me, she has little interest in the politics of the elven kingdoms."

"This is far too delicate a matter to take the chance of word leaking out," the senator said, and he beckoned Dalamar near.

The dark elf, looking amused, shrugged and walked over.

Coming as close to Dalamar as the senator could without actually touching him, the Qualinesti elf spoke in a low and urgent voice.

Dalamar listened, smiled, and shook his head. "You know, of course, that there will be a problem with the parents."

"That is where you can be of inestimable help to us," the senator said.

"You being his father's friend," the general added.

Dalamar considered the matter. His gaze shifted from one elf to the other, measuring their determination, their resolve. Both bore his gaze stolidly.

"Very well." Dalamar agreed. "I will deal with my friend, see to it that neither he nor his wife interfere. But my help will cost you."

The senator waved a deprecating hand. "Our coffers are well filled. Name your price—"

Dalamar scoffed. "What do I need with more wealth than I already possess? I could probably buy and sell Qualinesti itself! No, this is my price."

He paused, let them sweat, then said softly, "A month in my homeland."

The senator was startled at first; then, thinking about it, he was relieved. Dalamar was Silvanesti, after all. He would be spending a month in Silvanost.

The general had the same thought. His jaw worked. He was almost gibbering with fury.

"Out of the question!" he managed to snarl. "Impossible! You are mad to ask such a thing!"

Dalamar turned away. "Then, gentlemen, our business is at an end."

The senator rose swiftly, took hold of the other elf's shoulder. The two began a heated discussion.

Dalamar, smiling, walked back to the fire. He was seeing, in his memory, the beautiful trees of his homeland. He heard the birds singing, walked among the wondrous flowers. He lay in the fragrant grass, felt the sun warm on his face. He breathed fresh air, ran through lush meadows. He was young, innocent, without stain or shadow. . . .

"A month only," the senator said. "No longer."

"I swear by Nuitari," Dalamar vowed, and enjoyed watching the two wince at his naming of the god of dark magic.

"You will come and go in secret," the senator continued. "No one must know. No one must see you. You will speak to no one."

"I agree."

The senator looked at the general.

"I suppose there's no help for it," the general muttered ungraciously.

"Excellent," Dalamar said briskly. "Our business is concluded satisfactorily. Let us seal it, as custom demands."

Walking over, he took hold of each elf and kissed each of them on the cheek. The general could barely contain himself. He went rigid at the touch of the cool, dry lips. The senator flinched as though a snake had bitten him. But neither drew back. They had asked for this alliance. They didn't dare offend.

"Now, my brothers," said Dalamar pleasantly, "tell me the plan."

Chapter Three

Tanis Half-Elven had been searching throughout his house for his wife. He finally discovered her in the library on the second floor. She was seated near the window, in order to catch the last rays of the afternoon sun. He heard the scratching of her pen across parchment before he saw her, and he smiled to himself.

He had caught her this time.

Soft-footed, he padded up to the door and peered inside. She sat in a pool of sunlight, her head bowed, working with such concentration that he knew he could have stomped up the stairs and she would not have heard him. He paused a moment to admire her, to realize—awed and wondering—that she loved him as he loved her, a love their years of marriage had strengthened, not diminished.

Her long, golden hair was brushed loose and tumbled over her shoulders, down her back. Usually, these days, she wore her hair pulled back, the shining strands twisted in a chignon at the base of her neck. The severe style suited her; gave her an air of dignity and stature quite useful in negotiations with the humans, who (those who did not know her) sometimes tended to treat the youthful-looking elven woman like a child—well-meaning but interfering in adult affairs.

That generally lasted for only about fifteen minutes, by which time Laurana had them sitting up and taking notice. How could they have forgotten she'd been a general during the War of the Lance? That she had led men to war? Well, twenty-some years had passed, and humans had short memories. When they left her presence, they had remembered.

She was the diplomat of the family; her husband was the planner. They worked well together as a team, for Laurana was quick to glide in smoothly where Tanis would have trampled roughshod. And he could offer her insight into the human mind and heart—two areas she sometimes found baffling.

She was beautiful, so beautiful that Tanis's heart ached to look at her. And they were together. Not for long. The human blood in his veins was burning up the elven. He had already lived far more years than any human, but he would not enjoy the long life span of the elves. Some already mistook Laurana for his daughter. The day would come when they would mistake her for his granddaughter. He would age and die while she remained a relatively young woman. Such a shadow might have darkened their relationship. For them, it deepened it.

And, then, there was Gil. Their son—new life, created from love.

"Got you!" Tanis shouted triumphantly and bounded into the room.

Laurana gasped, jumped. A guilty flush spread over her face. Hastily, in considerable confusion, she attempted to hide the writing by covering the paper with another blank sheet.

"What is that?" Tanis demanded, glaring at her in mock severity.

"Only a list," Laurana ventured, shuffling more papers on the desk. "A list . . . of things I have to do while we're home— No! Tanis, stop it!"

He made a deft grab and snatched the paper out from beneath her hand. Laughing, she tried to recapture it by capturing him, but he backed out of her reach.

" 'My dear Sir Thomas,' " he read, " 'I would once again urge you to reconsider your stance against the Unified Nations of the Three Races treaty—' " Tanis shook the paper accusingly at his wife. "You were working!"

"Just a letter to Sir Thomas," Laurana protested, her flush deepening. "He's wavering. He's nearly ready to come over to our side. I thought perhaps a nudge—"

"No nudging," Tanis intoned. He hid the letter behind his back. "You promised. You made me promise! No work. We're home at last, after a month on the road. This is to be our time—yours and mine and Gil's."

"I know." As Laurana hung her head, her hair drifted about her in a radiant cloud. "I'm sorry." She sidled near him, put her hands on his chest, and playfully smoothed his shirt collar. "I promise. I won't do it again."

She kissed his bearded cheek. He started to kiss her, but at that moment she reached around him, caught hold of the letter, and snatched it from his grasp. Of course, he couldn't refuse such a challenge. He caught hold of her and the letter.

The letter eventually fluttered to the floor, forgotten.

The two stood by the window, warm and comfortable in each other's arms.

"Damn and blast it all!" Tanis swore, nuzzling his chin in his wife's golden hair. "Look—there's a stranger riding up the road."

"Oh, not a guest!" Laurana sighed.

"A knight, by the horse's trappings. We'll have to entertain him. I should go down—"

"No, don't!" Laurana clasped her husband tighter. "If you go, you'll be courtesy-bound to invite him in and this knight will consider himself courtesy-bound to stay. There goes Gil up to meet him. Gil can handle him."

"Are you sure?" Tanis was doubtful. "Will he know how to act, what to say? The boy's only sixteen—"

"Give him a chance," Laurana said, smiling.

"We can't afford to insult the knights now, of all times . . ." Tanis gently put aside his wife's arms. "I think I'd better go—"

"Too late. He's riding away," Laurana reported.

"There, what did I tell you?" Tanis was grim.

"He doesn't look insulted. Gil's coming into the house. Oh, Tanis, we can't let him think we've been spying on him. You know how touchy he is these days. Quick! Do something!"

Laurana hastily sat back down in her chair. Grabbing up a sheet of paper, she began writing furiously. Tanis, feeling foolish, walked across the room and stared at a map of Ansalon, spread out on the table.

He was startled and discomfited to see the word Qualinesti leap out at him.

Only logical, he supposed. Whenever he looked at his son these days, Tanis was drawn back to his own childhood. And that brought memories of Qualinesti, the land of his birth—his ignominious birth.

All these years, hundreds of years, and the memories still had the power to hurt him. Once again he was sixteen and living in his mother's brother's house, an orphan, a bastard orphan.

"Touchy" Laurana had described their son.

Tanis had been "touchy" himself at that age. Or, rather, he'd been more like some infernal gnomish mechanical device, the human blood boiling in him, building up steam that either had to find an outlet or explode.

Tanis didn't see himself in his son physically. Tanis hadn't been frail, like his son. Tanis had been strong, robust, far too strong and robust to suit elven tastes and style. Tanis's broad shoulders and strong arms were an insult to most elves, a constant reminder of human parentage. He flaunted his human side; he could admit that much now. He'd goaded them into driving him away, then he was hurt when they did so.

It was in more subtle ways that Tanis saw himself in his boy. Inner turmoil, not knowing who he was, where he belonged. Although Gil had said nothing to him—the two rarely talked—Tanis guessed that was how Gil was feeling these days. Tanis had prayed for his son to be spared such doubt and self-questioning. Apparently, his prayers had not been answered.

Gilthas of the House of Solostaran[2], was Tanis's son, but he was Laurana's child—a child of the elves. Gilthas was named for Gilthanas, Laurana's brother (whose strange and tragic fate was never spoken of aloud). Gil was tall, slender, with delicate bone structure, fine-spun, fair hair, and almond-shaped eyes. He was only one-quarter human—his father being half-human—and even that alien blood had been further diluted, it seemed, by the unbroken line of royal elven ancestors bequeathed to him from both sides.

Tanis had hoped—for his son's own peace of mind—that the boy would grow up elven, that the human blood in him would be too weak to trouble him. He saw that hope dwindle. At sixteen, Gil was not the typical docile, respectful elven child. He was moody, irritable, rebellious.

And Tanis—remembering how he himself had bolted—was keeping an extra tight grip on the reins that held his son in check.

Staring hard at the map, Tanis pretended not to notice when Gil came into the room. He didn't look up, because he knew what he would see. He would see himself standing there. And because he knew himself, knew what he had been, he feared seeing that likeness in his son.

And because he feared it, he couldn't speak of it, couldn't admit it.

And so he kept silent. He kept his head down, stared at the map, at a place marked Qualinesti.

Gilthas knew the moment he entered the room that his parents had been watching him from the window. He knew it by the faint flush of self-consciousness on his mother's face, by the fact that his father was intensely interested in a map Tanis himself had termed outdated—by the fact that neither looked up at him.

Gil said nothing, waited to let his parents give themselves away. At length, his mother looked up and smiled at him.

"Who were you talking to outside, *mapete*?" Laurana asked.

The aching, familiar knot of irritation tightened Gil's stomach. *Mapete!* An elven term of endearment, used for a child!

On not receiving an answer, Laurana looked even more self-conscious and realized she had made an error. "Um . . . were you talking to someone outside? I heard the dogs barking . . ."

"It was a knight, Sir Something-or-other," Gil replied. "I can't remember his name. He said—"

Laurana laid down her pen. Her manner was calm, and so was her voice. "Did you invite him inside?"

[2]Customarily, among elves, a son takes the name of his father's house. But since Tanis Half-Elven is of illegitimate birth and questionable bloodline, his son Gilthas was given the name of his mother's father's house, which is Solostaran

"Of course, he did," Tanis said sharply. "Gil knows better than to treat a Knight of Solamnia with discourtesy. Where is he, Son?"

Admit it. You watched the knight ride off, Gil told them silently. Do you take me for a complete fool?

"Father, please!" Gil was losing control. "Let me finish what I was saying. Of course, I invited the knight in. I'm not a dolt. I know the proper forms of etiquette. He said he couldn't stay. He was on his way to his home. He stopped by to give you and Mother this."

Gil held out a scroll case. "It's from Caramon Majere. The knight was a guest at the Inn of the Last Home. When Caramon found that Sir William was riding this direction, he asked him to bring this message."

Coldly, Gil handed the scroll case to his father.

Tanis gave his son a troubled look, then glanced at Laurana, who shrugged and smiled patiently, as much as to say, We've hurt his feelings. Again.

Gil was being "touchy," as his mother would say. Well, he had a right to be "touchy."

A frail and sickly child, whose birth was much wanted and long in coming, Gil had been in ill health most of his life. When he was six, he had very nearly died. After that, his anxious, adoring parents kept him "wrapped in silk," as the saying went. Cocooned.

He had outgrown his illnesses, but now suffered from painful, debilitating headaches. These would begin with flashes of light before his eyes and end in terrible agony, often causing him to lapse into a state of near unconsciousness. Nothing could be done for the malady; the clerics of Mishakal had tried and failed.

Tanis and Laurana were both away from home a great deal of the time, both working hard to preserve the slender threads of alliances which held the various races and nations together after the War of the Lance.

Too weak to travel, Gil was left in the care of a doting housekeeper, who adored him only slightly more than did his parents. To them all, Gil was still that frail little boy who had nearly burned up with fever.

Due to his illness, Gil was not permitted to play with other children, supposing there had been any other children living near them, which there weren't. Tanis Half-Elven liked his privacy, had deliberately built his house far from those of his neighbors. Often alone, left to his own thoughts, Gil had developed many strange fancies. One of these was that his headaches were caused by the human blood in his veins. He had the nightmarish impression, brought on by the horrible pain, that if he could cut his veins open and drain out this alien blood, the pain would end. He never spoke of such fancies to anyone.

Laurana was not ashamed of having married a half-human. She often teased Tanis about the beard he wore, a beard no elf male could grow. Tanis wasn't ashamed of being half-human.

His son was.

Gil dreamt of the elven homeland he had never seen, probably would never see. The trees of Qualinesti were more real to him than the trees in his father's garden. Gil couldn't understand why his parents rarely visited Qualinesti, why they never took him with them when they did. But he knew (or believed he knew) that this alienation was his father's fault. And so the young man came to resent Tanis with a passion that sometimes frightened him.

"There is nothing of my father in me!" Gil would say to himself reassuringly every day, as he peered anxiously into the mirror, fearful that unsightly human hair might start sprouting on his chin.

"Nothing!" he would repeat in satisfaction, surveying his clear, smooth skin.

Nothing except blood. Human blood.

And because Gil feared it, he couldn't speak of it, couldn't admit it.

And so he kept silent.

The silence between father and son had been built brick by brick over the years. It was now a wall not easily scaled.

"Well, aren't you going to read the letter, Father?" Gil demanded.

Tanis frowned, not liking his son's insolent tone.

Gil waited for his father to reprimand him. The young man wasn't sure why, but he wanted to goad his father into losing his temper. Things would be said . . . things that needed to be said . . .

But Tanis put on the patient smile he had taken to wearing around his son and removed the scroll from its case.

Gil turned his back. Stalking over to the window, he stared unseeing down on the lush and elaborately laid out garden below. He had half a mind to walk out of the room, but he wanted to hear what Caramon Majere had to say.

Gil had no use for most of the humans he'd met, those who came to visit his parents. He considered them loud, clumsy, and oafish. But Gil liked the big, jovial Caramon, liked his wide, generous smile, his boisterous laugh. Gil enjoyed hearing about Caramon's sons, particularly the exploits of the two elder boys, Sturm and Tanin, who had traveled all over most of Ansalon in search of adventure. They were now attempting to become the first men born outside of Solamnia to enter the knighthood.

Gil had never met Caramon's sons. A few years ago, after returning from some secret mission with Tanis, Caramon had offered to take Gil to visit the inn. Tanis and Laurana had refused to even consider it. Gil had been so furious that he had moped about his room for a week.

Tanis unrolled the scroll and was rapidly scanning through it.

"I hope all is well with Caramon," Laurana said. She sounded anxious. She had not returned to her writing, but was watching Tanis's face as he read the message.

Gil turned. Tanis did look worried, but when he reached the end, he smiled. Then he shook his head and sighed.

"Caramon's youngest boy, Palin, has just taken and passed the Test in the Tower of High Sorcery. He is a white-robed mage now."

"Paladine save us!" Laurana exclaimed in astonishment. "I knew the young man was studying magic, but I never thought he was serious. Caramon always said it was a passing fancy."

"He always hoped it was a passing fancy," Tanis amended.

"I'm surprised Caramon permitted it."

"He didn't." Tanis handed her the scroll. "As you will read, Dalamar took the matter out of Caramon's hands."

"Why wouldn't he let Palin take the Test?" Gil asked.

"Because the Test can be fatal, for one thing," Tanis said dryly.

"But Caramon plans to let his other sons test for the knighthood," Gil argued. "That can be pretty fatal, too."

"The knighthood's different, Son. Caramon understands battle with sword and shield. He doesn't understand battle with rose petals and cobwebs."

"And then, of course, there was Raistlin," Laurana added, as if that concluded the matter.

"What has his uncle got to do with it?" Gil demanded, though he knew perfectly well what his mother meant. He was in a mood to argue these days.

"It's natural for Caramon to fear Palin would walk the same dark path as Raistlin took. Though now that seems hardly likely."

And what path do you fear I'll walk, Mother, Father? Gil wanted to shout at them. Any path? Dark or light? Any path that leads me away from this place? Someday, Mother . . . Someday, Father . . .

"May I read it?" Gil asked petulantly.

Wordlessly, his mother handed the scroll over. Gil read it slowly. He could read human script as easily as elven, but he had some trouble deciphering Caramon's gigantic, round-handed, and excited scrawl.

"Caramon says here he made a mistake. He says he should have respected Palin's decision to study magic instead of trying to force him to be something he isn't. Caramon says he's proud of Palin for passing the Test."

"Caramon says that now," Tanis returned. "He would have said something far different if his boy had died in the tower."

"At least he gave him a chance, which is more than you will me," Gil retorted. "You keep me locked up like some sort of prize bird—"

Tanis's face darkened.

Laurana intervened hastily. "Now, Gil, please don't start. It's nearly dinnertime. If you and your father will get washed up, I'll tell Cook that we're—"

"No, Mother, don't change the subject! It won't work this time!" Gil held the scroll tightly, drawing reassurance from it. "Palin's not much older than I am. And now he's off traveling with his brothers. He's seeing things, doing things! I've never been farther from home than the fencerow!"

"It's not the same, Gil, and you know it," Tanis said quietly. "Palin's human—"

"I'm *part* human," Gil returned with bitter accusation.

Laurana paled, lowered her eyes. Tanis was silent a moment, his lips, beneath the beard, compressed. When he spoke, it was in the infuriatingly calm tone that drove Gil to distraction.

"Yes, you and Palin are near the same age, but human children mature faster than elven children—"

"I'm not a child!"

The knot inside Gil twisted until he feared it would turn him inside out.

"And you know, *mapete*, that with your headaches, travel would be—" Laurana began.

The knot snapped.

"Stop calling me that!" Gil shouted at her.

Laurana's eyes widened in hurt and surprise. Gil was remorseful. He hadn't meant to wound her, but he also felt a certain amount of satisfaction.

"You've called me that name since I was a baby," he continued in a low voice.

"Yes, she has." Tanis's face, beneath the beard, was dark with anger. "Because she loves you. Apologize to your mother!"

"No, Tanis," Laurana intervened. "I owe Gil the apology. He is right." She smiled faintly. "It is a silly name for a young man who is taller than I am. I am sorry, my son. I won't do it again."

Gil hadn't expected this victory. He didn't quite know how to handle it. He decided to ride on, press home the advantage against a weakened opponent. "And I haven't had a headache for months now. Perhaps I'm rid of them."

"But you don't know that, Son." Tanis was trying hard to control himself. "What would happen if you fell ill while you were on the road, far from home?"

"Then I'd deal with it," Gil retorted. "I've heard you tell about times when Raistlin Majere was so sick his brother had to carry him. But that never stopped Raistlin. He was a great hero!"

Tanis started to say something. Laurana gave him a warning glance, and he kept quiet.

"Where is it you want to go, Son?" she asked.

Gil hesitated. The moment had arrived. He hadn't expected the subject to come up quite this way, but it had and he knew he should take advantage of it.

"My homeland. Qualinesti."

"Out of the question."

"Why, Father? Give me one good reason!"

"I could give you a dozen, but I doubt you'd understand them. For starters, Qualinesti isn't your home—"

"Tanis, please!" Laurana turned to Gil. "What put this idea into your head, *mapet*—Son?"

"I received an invitation, a very handsome invitation, very proper and fitting to my station as an *elven prince*." Gil emphasized the words.

His mother and father exchanged alarmed glances.

Gil ignored them and continued on. "The invitation is from one of the senators of the Thalas-Enthia. The people are having some type of celebration to welcome Uncle Porthios back from Silvanesti, and this senator thinks I should be in attendance. He says my absence from formal occasions like this has been noticed. People are starting to say that I am ashamed of my elven heritage."

"How dare they do this?" Tanis spoke with barely concealed fury. "How dare they interfere? Who is this senator? The meddling ass. I'll—"

"Tanthalas, listen to me." Laurana called him by his full elven name only when the matter was serious. "There's more to it than that, I fear."

She drew near him; they spoke together in an undertone.

Whispering. Always the whispers. Gil tried to look as if he hadn't the slightest interest in what they were saying, though he listened closely. He caught the words "political" and "move cautiously" but nothing more.

"This does concern me, you know, Father," Gil stated abruptly. "*You* weren't invited."

"Don't speak to me in that tone, young man!"

"Gil, dear, this is a very serious matter," Laurana said, using a soothing note to her son, laying a soothing hand on her husband's arm. "When did you receive this invitation?"

"A day or two ago, when you were both in Palanthas. If you'd been home, you would have known about it."

Again, the two looked at each other.

"I wish you'd told us earlier. What reply did you send?"

His mother was clearly nervous, her hands twisted together. His father was furious, but Tanis kept silent. He was being forced to keep silent.

Gil knew himself suddenly, for the first time in his life, in control. It was a good feeling that eased the tight knot in his stomach.

"I haven't sent my answer," he said coolly. "I know this is political. I know this is serious. I waited to talk the matter over with you both."

He had the satisfaction of seeing his parents look ashamed. Again, they had underestimated him.

"You did right, Son. I'm sorry we misjudged you." Tanis sighed and scratched his bearded chin in frustration. "More than that, I'm sorry you had to be dragged into this. But I guess I should have expected it."

"We both should have," Laurana added. "We should have prepared you, Gil."

Her voice dropped. She was talking to Tanis again. "It's just that I never thought . . . He's part human, after all. I didn't suppose they would . . . "

"Of course, they would. It's obvious to me what they're after . . . "

"What?" Gil demanded loudly. "What are they after?"

Tanis didn't seem to hear him, for he continued to talk to Laurana. "I had hoped he would be spared this, that he wouldn't have to go through what you and I did. And if I have anything to say about it, he won't."

He turned to Gil. "Bring us the invitation, Son. Your mother will frame the proper refusal."

"And that's it," Gil said, glaring from one to the other. "You won't let me go."

"Son, you don't understand—" Tanis began, his temper starting to flare.

"You're damn right I don't understand! I—" Gil paused.

Of course. It was all so simple, really. But he had to be careful. He mustn't give himself away.

He'd stopped talking in midsentence—a stupid move. They might suspect. How to cover it?

Diplomacy, learned from his mother.

"I'm sorry for yelling, Father," Gil said contritely. "I know you have only my best interests at heart. It was foolish of me to want to go—to visit my mother's homeland."

"Someday, Son," Tanis said, scratching his beard. "When you're older . . ."

"Certainly, Father. Now, if you two will excuse me, I have my studies to attend to." Turning, Gil walked out of the room with dignity. He shut the door behind him.

Pausing outside the door, he listened.

"We've known this was coming," his mother was saying. "It's only right he should want to go."

"Yes, and how will he feel when he sees the hate-filled glances, the curled lips, the subtle insults . . ."

"Maybe that won't happen, Tanis. The elves have changed."

"Have they, dearest?" Tanis asked her sadly. "Have they really?"

Laurana made no response, at least not one that Gil could hear.

He wavered in his decision. They were only trying to protect him, after all.

Protect him! Yes, just as Caramon had tried to protect Palin. He had taken the Test and passed. He'd proven his worth—both to his father and to himself.

Resolve hardened, Gil ran down the hall, took the stairs to his room two at a time. Once inside, he closed and locked the door. He had kept the invitation hidden in a golden filigree box. Reading the invitation again, Gil scanned the lines until he found what he was searching for.

> *I will be staying at the Back Swan, an inn that is about a day's ride from your parents' house. If you would care to meet me there, we could journey to Qualinesti together. Let me assure you, Prince Gilthas, I would be honored by your company and most pleased to introduce you into the very highest levels of elven society.*
>
> Your servant, Rashas of the House of Aronthulas.

The man's name meant nothing to Gil, wasn't important anyway. He dropped the invitation and gazed out his window, down the road that led south. To the Black Swan.

Chapter Four

Wrapped in his cloak, Tanis Half-Elven was lying on the hard, cold ground. He was sleeping deeply, peacefully. But Caramon's hand was on his shoulder, shaking him. Tanis, we need you! Tanis, wake up!

Go away, Tanis told him, rolling over, hunching himself into a ball. I don't want to wake up. I'm tired of it all, so very tired. Why can't you leave me alone? Let me sleep. . . .

"Tanis!"

He woke with a start. He'd slept longer than usual, longer than he'd intended. But his sleep had not been restful, had left him feeling heavy-limbed, fuzzy-brained. He blinked. Looking up, he half expected to see Caramon.

He saw Laurana.

"Gil's gone," she said.

Tanis struggled to shake off the dream, the heaviness. "Gone?" he repeated stupidly. "Where?"

"I don't know for certain, but I think—" Her voice broke. Wordlessly, she held out to Tanis a sheet of gold leaf paper.

Rubbing his eyes, Tanis leveraged himself to a sitting position. Laurana slid onto the bed beside him and put her arm around his shoulder. He read the invitation.

"Where did you find this?"

"In . . . in his room. I didn't mean to snoop. It was just . . . He didn't come down to breakfast. I thought he might be ill. I went to check." Her head drooped, and tears slid down her cheeks. "His bed wasn't slept in. His clothes are gone. And this . . . this . . . was on the floor . . . by the window . . ."

She broke down. After a moment's silent struggle, she regained control of herself. "I went to the stable. His horse is gone, too. The groom didn't hear or see anything—"

"Old Hastings is deaf as a post. He wouldn't have heard the Cataclysm. Caramon tried to warn me this would happen. I didn't listen." Tanis sighed. Subconsciously, he'd listened. That was what the dream meant.

Let me sleep . . .

"Everything's going to be fine, dearest," Tanis said cheerfully. Kissing his wife, he held her close. "Gil left this behind, knowing we'd find it. He wants us to come after him. He wants to be stopped. This is his rooster crow of independence, that's all. I'll find him at the Black Swan—exhausted, but too proud to admit it, pretending he's going to ride on, secretly hoping I'll argue him out of it."

"You won't scold him . . ." Laurana asked anxiously.

"No, of course, not. We'll have a man-to-man talk. It's long coming. Maybe he and I will even spend the night away from home, ride back together in the morning."

Tanis warmed to the idea. Now that he thought of it, he had never spent the day alone with his son. They would talk, really talk. Tanis would let Gil know that his father understood.

"This might actually prove to be good for the boy, my dear." Tanis was up, out of bed, and dressing for travel.

"Perhaps I should go, too. . . ."

"No, Laurana," Tanis said firmly. "This is between Gil and me." He paused in his preparations. "You don't really understand why he's done this, do you?"

"No elven youth would do such a thing," Laurana said softly, the tears shining in her eyes.

Tanis bent down, kissed her lustrous hair. He remembered a half-elven youth who had run away from his people, his home; a half-elven youth who had run away from her. He guessed that she must be remembering the same.

The hunger for change—the human curse.

Or blessing.

"Don't worry," he said. "I'll bring him back safely."

"If only he understood! We would sacrifice anything for him . . . "

Laurana talked on, but Tanis wasn't listening, not to her. He was listening to the voice of another woman, another mother.

What would you sacrifice for your own son—your wealth? Your honor? Your very life? These were Sara's words—Sara, surrogate mother of Steel Brightblade.

Chilled, fearful, Tanis remembered the vision. He had not thought about it for years, had put it out of his mind. Once again he stood in the evil fortress of Lord Ariakan, Knight of Takhisis. Dark clouds parted; Solinari's silver light shone through, giving Tanis a swift glimpse of danger and peril, swirling about his frail son like the driving rain. And then Solinari was swallowed by dark clouds. The vision was gone. And he had forgotten it.

Until now.

"What's wrong?" Laurana was staring at him, frightened.

How well she knew him! Too well . . .

"Nothing," he said, forcing a reassuring smile. "I had a bad dream last night, that's all. I guess it's still affecting me. About the war. You know."

Laurana knew. She had those dreams, too. And she knew he wasn't telling her the truth, not because he didn't love her or trust her or respect her, but simply because he couldn't. He had learned at an early age to keep his inner torments and hurts and fears well-hidden. To betray any weakness would give someone the advantage over him. She couldn't blame him. She'd seen how he'd been raised. A half-human in elven society, he was permitted to live in Qualinesti out of charity and pity. But he had never been accepted. The elves had always let him know he was—and would ever be—an outsider.

"What about Rashas?" she asked, tactfully changing the subject.

"I'll deal with Rashas," Tanis said grimly. "I might have known he'd be behind this. Always plotting. I wonder why Porthios puts up with him."

"Porthios has other worries, my dear. But now that Silvanesti is free of Lorac's dream, Porthios can finally return home and deal with matters in his own land."

Lorac's dream. Lorac had been an elven king, ruler of Silvanesti before the War of the Lance. Afraid that his land was about to fall victim to the invading armies of the Dark Queen, Lorac had tried to use one of the powerful, magical dragon orbs to save his people, his land. Instead, tragically, Lorac had fallen victim to the orb. The evil dragon, Cyan Bloodbane, had taken over Silvanesti, whispered dark dreams into Lorac's ears.

The dreams had become reality. Silvanesti was a haunted and devastated land, crawling with evil creatures that were both real and, at the same time, a product of Lorac's fear-twisted vision.

Even after Lorac's death and the Dark Queen's defeat, Silvanesti had not been completely freed of the darkness. For long years, the elves had fought the remnants of the dream, fought the dark and evil creatures that still roamed the land. Only now, had they finally defeated them.

Tanis thought of Lorac's story, thought grimly that it had relevance in this day. Once again, some of the elves were acting irrationally, out of fear. Some of the old, set-in-their-ways elves like Senator Rashas . . .

"At least now Porthios has something to take his mind off his troubles— now that Alhana is pregnant," Tanis said, trying to present a cheerful front, even as he began lacing on his leather armor.

Laurana looked at the armor, which he never wore unless he expected trouble. She bit her lip, but said nothing about it. She continued the conversation, followed his lead.

"I know Alhana is pleased. She has wanted a child for so long. And I think Porthios is pleased, as well, though he tries to act as if fatherhood were nothing special. Just doing his duty by the people. I see a warmth between them that has been missing all these years. I really believe that they are beginning to care for each other."

"About time," Tanis muttered. He had never much liked his brother-in-law. Tying his traveling cloak around his shoulders, he picked up a knapsack, then leaned over to kiss his wife's cheek. "Good-bye, love. Don't fret if we're not back right away."

"Oh, Tanis!" Laurana gazed at him searchingly.

"Don't be afraid. The boy and I need to talk. I see that now. I should have done it a long time ago, but I had hoped . . ." He stopped, then said, "I'll send you word."

Buckling on his sword, he kissed her again, and was gone.

His son's trail was easy to pick up. Spring rains had deluged Solanthus for a month; the ground was muddy, the horse's hoofprints deep and clear. The only other person who had ridden this road lately was Sir William, delivering Caramon's message, and the knight had ridden in the opposite direction, toward Solamnia, whereas the Black Swan was located on the road that led south to Qualinesti.

Tanis rode at a relaxed pace. The morning sun was a slit of fire in the sky, and the dew glittered in the grass. The night had been clear, cool enough to make a cloak feel good, but not chill.

"Gil must have enjoyed his ride," Tanis said to himself. He remembered, with guilty pleasure, another young man and another midnight journey. "I had no horse when I left. I walked from Qualinesti to Solace in search of Flint. I had no money, no care, no sense. It's a wonder I made it alive."

Tanis laughed ruefully, shook his head. "But I was shabby enough that no robber looked twice at me. I couldn't afford to sleep in an inn, and so I stayed out of fights. I spent the nights walking beneath the stars, feeling that at last I was able to breathe deeply.

"Ah, Gil." Tanis sighed. "I did the very thing I promised myself a hundred times I would never do. I bound you and fettered you. The chains were made of silk, forged by love, but they were still chains. Yet how could I do otherwise? You are so precious to me, my son! I love you so much. If anything were to happen . . .

"Stop it, Tanis!" he sternly reprimanded himself. "You're only borrowing trouble, and you know what the interest on that debt can cost you. It's a lovely day. Gil will have a fine ride. And we'll talk tonight, really talk. That is, you'll talk, Son. I'll listen. I promise."

Tanis continued to follow the horse's tracks. He saw where Gil had allowed the animal its head, saw signs of a mad gallop, both horse and rider giddy with freedom. But then the young man had calmed the horse, proceeded forward at a sensible pace, not to tire the animal.

"Good for you, boy," Tanis said proudly.

To take his mind off his worry, he began considering what he would say to Rashas of the Thalas-Enthia. Tanis knew the elf well. Near the same age as Porthios, Rashas was enamored of power, enjoyed nothing more than political intrigue. He had been the youngest elf ever to sit on the senate. Rumor had it that he hounded his father until the elder elf finally collapsed under the pressure and relinquished his seat to his son. During the War of the Lance, Rashas had been a burr beneath the saddle of Solostaran, Speaker of the Sun. Solostaran's successor, Porthios, was now having to cope with this irritant.

Rashas persistently advocated elven isolation from the rest of the world. He made no secret of the fact that, in his opinion, the Kingpriest of Istar had been right in offering bounties on dwarves and kender. Rashas would have made one change, however: He would have added humans to the list.

Which made all this completely inexplicable. Why was this cagey old spider trying to lure Gilthas, of all people—a quarter-human—into his web?

"At any rate," Tanis muttered into his beard, "this will give me a chance to settle my own score with you, Rashas, old childhood friend. I remember every one of your snide comments, the whispered insults, the cruel little practical jokes. The beatings I took from you and your gang of bullies. I wasn't allowed to hit you then, but, by Paladine, there's nobody going to stop me now!"

The delightful anticipation of smashing his fist into Rashas's pointed chin kept Tanis entertained throughout the better part of the morning. He had no idea what Rashas wanted with his son, but he guessed it couldn't be anything good.

"It's too bad I didn't tell Gil about Rashas," Tanis mused. "Too bad I never told him much of anything about my early life in Qualinesti. Maybe it was a mistake to keep him away from there. If we hadn't, he would have known about Rashas and his type. He wouldn't have fallen for whatever clever scheme the senator's plotting. But, I wanted to protect you, Gil. I didn't want you to suffer what I suffered. I . . . ."

Tanis stopped his horse, turned the animal around. "Damn it to the Abyss." He stared down at the dirt road, cold dread constricting his heart.

He slid off his horse for a better look. The mud, now slowly hardening in the bright sun, told the tale all too clearly. There was only one creature in all of Krynn that left tracks like this: three front claws that dug deep in the ground, a back claw, and the sinuous twisting mark of a reptilian tail.

"Draconians . . . four of them."

Tanis examined the prints. His horse, snuffling at them, shied away in disgust.

Catching the animal, Tanis held its head near the tracks until it became accustomed to the smell. Remounting, he followed the trail. It could be coincidence, he told himself. The draconians could merely be traveling the same direction as Gil.

But Tanis became convinced, after another mile, that the creatures were stalking his son.

At one point, Gil had turned his horse off the trail, led the animal down an embankment to a small stream. At this juncture, the draconians also left the trail. Tenaciously tracking the horse's hoofprints down to the creek, the draconians trailed the horse along the water's edge, followed the hoof marks back up to the road.

In addition, Tanis saw signs that the draconians were taking care to keep out of sight. At various points, the clawed footprints would leave the trail and seek the safety of the brush.

This road was not particularly well traveled, but farmers used it, as did the occasional venturing knight. If these draconians were ordinary raiders, living off the land, they would not hesitate to attack a lone farmer, steal his wagon and horses. These draconians were hiding from those who passed along the road; they obviously were on a mission.

But what connection could draconians have with Rashas? The elf had his faults, certainly, but conspiring with creatures of darkness wasn't one of them.

Fearful, alarmed, Tanis spurred his horse. The tracks were hours old, but he wasn't far from the Black Swan. The inn was located in the fairly substantial town of Fair Field. Four draconians would never dare venture into a populated area. Whatever their intention, they would have to strike before Gil reached the inn.

Which meant Tanis might well be too late.

He rode along the trail, traveling at a moderate pace, keeping his eyes on the prints—both the clawed prints and those made by Gil's horse. The young man obviously had no idea he was being followed. He was riding along at an easy walk, enjoying the scenery, reveling in his newfound freedom. The draconians never deviated from their course.

And then, Tanis knew where they would strike.

A few miles outside of Fair Field, the road entered a heavily wooded area. Oak and walnut trees grew thick, their tangled limbs branching across the trail, blocking out the sunlight, keeping the road in deep shadow. In the days after the Cataclysm, the forest was reputed to have been a refuge for robbers and, to this day, was known unofficially as Thieves Acres. Caves honeycombed the hillsides, providing hiding places where men could hide and gloat over their loot. It was the perfect spot for an ambush.

Sick with fear, Tanis left off tracking, urged his horse forward at a gallop. He almost rode down a startled farmer, who shouted at him, wondering what was the matter. Tanis didn't waste time bothering to answer. The forest was in sight, a long length of dark green banding the road ahead of him.

The shadows of the trees closed over him; day turned to dusk in the blink of an eye. The temperature dropped noticeably. Here and there, patches of sunlight filtered through the overhanging tree limbs. Compared to the darkness around him, the light was almost blinding in its intensity. But soon even these few glimpses of the sun were lost. The trees closed in.

Tanis slowed his horse. Though he grudged the wasted time, he dared not miss whatever tale the ground had to tell him.

All too soon, he read the story's end.

He couldn't have missed it, no matter how fast he was riding. The dirt road was churned and cut up to such an extent that Tanis found it impossible to decipher what exactly had occurred. Horse's hooves were obliterated by draconian claws; here and there he thought he saw the impression of a slender elven foot. Add to this a strange set of claw prints. These looked vaguely familiar, but he couldn't immediately identify them.

He dismounted, searched the area, and forced himself to be patient, not to overlook the slightest detail. What he discovered brought him no comfort, only increased dread. From the point beyond the churned up mud, no tracks proceeded onward down the road.

Gil had made it this far, and no farther.

But what in the name of all that was holy had happened to him?

Tanis went back over the ground, expanded his search into the trees. His patience was rewarded.

Horse's hooves had been led off the main road and into the woods. The hooves were flanked by the draconian claw marks.

Tanis swore bitterly. Returning to his own horse, he tethered the animal on the roadside, then removed his longbow and quiver of arrows from his saddle. He slid the bow over his shoulder and slung the quiver on his back. Loosening his sword in its sheath, he entered the woods.

All his old skills in hunting and stalking came back to him. He blessed the foresight—or had it been that vision at Storm's Keep?—that had prompted him to wear his soft leather boots, bring along the bow and arrow that he rarely carried in these days of peace. His gaze swept the ground. He moved through the trees and brush without a sound, treading lightly, careful not to snap a stick, cause a branch to rustle with his passing.

The woods grew deeper, denser. He was a long way from the road, tracking four draconians, and he was alone. Not a particularly wise move.

He kept going. They had his son.

The sound of guttural voices, speaking a language that made flesh crawl and brought back unpleasant memories, caused Tanis to slow his pace. Holding his breath, he crept forward, moving from tree trunk to tree trunk, nearing his prey.

And there they were, or most of them, at least. Three draconians stood in front of a cave, conversing in their hideous tongue. And there was the horse, Gil's horse, with its fine leather trappings and silken ribbons tied in its mane. The animal was shivering in fear, bore marks of having been beaten. It wasn't a trained war-horse, but it had apparently fought its captors. One of the draconians was cursing the animal and pointing to a bleeding slash on a scaled arm.

But there was no sign of Gil. He was probably in the cave with the fourth draconian. But why? What terrible things were they doing to him?

What had they done?

At least Tanis could take cold comfort from the fact that the only blood visible on the ground was green.

He chose his target, the draconian standing nearest to him. Moving more silently than the wind, Tanis lifted his bow, fitted an arrow to it, raised the bow to his cheek, and pulled. The arrow struck the draconian in the back, between the wings. The creature gave a gurgle of pain and astonishment, then toppled over dead. The body turned to stone, held the arrow fast. Never attack a Baaz with a sword if you can help it.

Swiftly, Tanis had another arrow nocked and ready. The second draconian, its sword drawn, was turning his direction. Tanis fired. The arrow hit the draconian in the chest. It dropped the sword, clutched at the arrow with its clawed hands, then it, too, fell to the ground.

"Don't move!" Tanis ordered harshly, speaking the Common language he knew the creatures understood.

The third draconian froze, its sword halfway drawn, its beady eyes darting this way and that.

"I have an arrow with your foul name on it," Tanis continued. "It's pointed straight at what you slime call your heart. Where is the boy you took captive back there? What have you done to him? You have ten seconds to tell me, or you meet the same fate as your comrades."

The draconian said something in its own language.

"Don't give me that," Tanis growled. "You speak Common better than I do, probably. Where is the boy? Ten seconds is almost up. If you—"

"Tanis, my friend! How good to see you again," came a voice. "It's been a long time."

An elf, tall, handsome, with brown hair, brown eyes, wearing black robes, emerged from the cave.

Tanis fought to keep the bow raised and aimed, though his hands trembled, his fingers were wet with sweat, and the fear tore him up inside.

"Where is my son, Dalamar?" Tanis cried hoarsely. "What have you done with him?"

"Put the bow down, my friend," Dalamar said gently. "Don't make them kill you. Don't make me."

Blinded by tears of rage and fear and helpless frustration, Tanis kept the bow raised, was ready to loose the arrow, not caring what he hit.

Clawed fingers dug into his back, dragged him to the ground. A heavy object struck him. Pain burst in Tanis's head and, though he fought against it, darkness closed around him.

Chapter Five

Gil was riding through a particularly dark and gloomy portion of forest, thinking, uncomfortably, that this would be a perfect place for an ambush, when a griffin sailed down through an opening in the trees and landed on the road directly in front of the young man.

Gil had never before seen one of the wondrous beasts, who were friends to the elves and no other race on Krynn. He was alarmed and startled at the sight. The beast had the head and wings of an eagle, but its rear portion was that of a lion. Its eyes were fierce; its wickedly sharp beak could—according to legend—rip through a dragon's scales.

His horse was terrified; horseflesh is one of a griffin's favorite meals. The animal neighed and reared in panic, nearly throwing its rider. Gil was a skilled horseman; such exercise having been advocated as good for his health, and he immediately reined in the horse and calmed it down with soothing pats on the neck, gentle words of reassurance.

The griffin's rider—an elder elf clad in rich clothing—watched with approval. When Gil's horse was under control once again, the elf dismounted and walked over. Another elf—one of the oddest-looking elves Gilthas had ever seen—waited behind. This strange elf was clothed in practically nothing, leaving bare a well-muscled body decorated with fantastic, colorfully painted designs.

The elder elf introduced himself.

"I am Rashas of the Thalas-Enthia. And you, I believe, must be Prince Gilthas. Well met, grandson of Solostaran. Well met."

Gil dismounted, said the polite words as he'd been taught. The two exchanged the formal kiss of greeting and continued through the ritual of introduction. During this proceeding, the griffin glared around, its fierce-eyed gaze penetrating the forest shadows. At one point, it gnashed its beak, its claws churned the ground, and its lion tail lashed about in disgust.

The elf accompanying Rashas spoke a few words to the griffin, which twisted its head and flexed its wings and seemed to—somewhat sullenly—settle down.

Gil was watching the griffin, trying to keep his horse calm, casting oblique glances at the painted elf servant, and attempting, at the same time, to make the correct, polite responses to the senator. Small wonder he became confused.

Rashas noticed the young man's difficulty. "Permit me to apologize for frightening your horse. It was thoughtless of me. I should have realized that your animal would not be accustomed to our griffins. The horses of Qualinesti are trained to be around them, you see. It never occurred to me that the horses of Tanthalas Half-Elven were not."

Gil was shamed. The griffins had long been friends of the elves. To be unacquainted with these magnificent beasts seemed to him tantamount to being unacquainted with one's own kind. He was intending to stammer an apology for his father, but to his astonishment found himself saying something quite different.

"Griffins come to visit us," Gil said proudly. "My parents exchange gifts with them yearly. My father's horse is well-trained. My own horse is young—"

Rashas politely cut him off.

"Believe me, Prince Gilthas, I do understand," he said earnestly, with a glance of cool pity that brought hot blood to the young man's face.

"Believe me, sir," Gil began, "I think you mistake—"

Rashas continued on, as if he hadn't heard, "I thought it might be enjoyable, as well as enlightening, for you to take your first glimpse of Qualinesti from the air, Prince Gilthas. Therefore, on impulse, I flew to meet you. I would be greatly honored if you were to ride back with me. Don't worry, the griffin can easily carry us both."

Gil forgot his anger at the insult. He gazed at the wondrous beast with awe and longing. To fly! It seemed all his dreams were coming true at once! But his elation quickly evaporated. His first concern must be for his horse.

"I thank you for your kind offer, Senator—"

"Call me Rashas, my prince," the elf interrupted.

Gil bowed, acknowledging the compliment. "I could not leave my horse alone, unattended." He patted his horse's neck. "I hope you are not offended."

On the contrary, Rashas appeared pleased. "Far from it, my prince. I am glad to see you take such responsibilities seriously. So many young people do not, these days. But you won't have to miss out on the trip. My Kagonesti servant here"—Rashas waved a hand in the general direction of the strange-looking elf—"will return the horse to your father's stables."

Kagonesti! Now Gil understood. This was one of the famed Wilder elves, fabled in legend and song. He had never seen one before.

The Kagonesti bowed, indicating silently that nothing would give him greater pleasure. Gil nodded awkwardly, all the while wondering what he should do.

"I see you hesitate. Are you not feeling well? I have heard it said that your health is precarious. Perhaps you should return home," Rashas said solicitously. "The rigors of the flight might not be good for you."

That remark, of course, decided the matter.

His face burning, Gil said that he would be pleased to accompany Senator Rashas and the griffin.

Gil gave over the care of his horse to the Kagonesti servant without another thought. Only when he was securely mounted on the griffin did it occur to the young man to wonder how the senator had known Gil had decided to travel to Qualinesti. And how had Rashas known where to meet him?

It was on the tip of Gil's tongue to ask, but he was in awe of the elder elf, in awe of Rashas's elegant and dignified air. Laurana had trained her son well, taught him to be diplomatic. Such a question would be impolite, would imply that Gil didn't trust the elf. Undoubtedly there was a logical explanation.

Gil settled back to enjoy the ride.

Chapter Six

As long as he lived, Gil would never forget his first glimpse of the fabled elven city of Qualinost. A first glimpse, yet a familiar sight to the young elf.

Rashas turned to witness the young man's reaction. He saw the tears sliding down Gil's cheeks. The senator nodded approval. He even prevented Gil from wiping the tears away.

"The beauty fills the heart to bursting. The emotion must find an outlet. Let it fall from your eyes. Your tears do you no shame, my prince, but rather great credit. It is only natural that you should weep at the first sight of your *true* homeland."

Gil did not miss the senator's emphasis on the word true, and could only agree with him. Yes, this is where I belong! I know it now. I've known it all my life. For this is not my first sight of Qualinost. I've seen it often in my dreams.

Four slender spires made of white stone, marbled with shining silver, rose above the tops of the aspen trees, which grew thick within the city. A taller tower, made of gold that gleamed in the sunlight, stood in the city's center, surrounded by other buildings formed of glittering rose quartz. Quiet streets wound like ribbons of silk among the aspen groves and gardens of wildflowers. A sense of peace settled over Gilthas's soul—peace and belonging.

Truly, he had come home.

The griffin landed in the center courtyard of a house made of rose quartz, decorated with green jade. The house itself seemed delicate, fragile, yet it had, so Rashas boasted proudly, withstood the tremors and fiery winds of the Cataclysm. Gil gazed at the spires, the latticework, the fluted columns and slender arches, and mentally compared this with his parent's manor house. That house, which Laurana had named "Journey's End," was rectangular, with sharp angles, gabled windows, and a high-pitched roof. Compared to the graceful, beautiful elven homes, Gil recalled his house as bulky and solid and ugly. It seemed . . . human.

Rashas thanked the griffin politely for its services, gave it several fine gifts, and bid it farewell. Then he led Gilthas into the house. It was more lovely inside than out, if that were possible. Elves love fresh air; their houses are more window than wall, as the saying goes. Sunlight, streaming through the latticework, danced among the shadows to form patterns on the floor, patterns that seemed alive, for they were constantly shifting with the movement of the sun and clouds. Flowers grew inside the house, and living trees sprang up from the floor. Birds soared in and out freely, filling the house with music. Lullabies whispered by gently splashing water from indoor fountains formed a soft counterpoint to the birdsong.

Several Kagonesti elves—tall and heavily muscled, with strange markings on their skin—greeted Rashas with bows and every appearance of deference.

"These are my Wilder elves," Rashas said to Gil in explanation. "Once they were slaves. Now—in accordance with modern decrees—I am required to pay them for their services."

Gil wasn't certain, but he thought uneasily that Rashas sounded rather put out. The elder elf glanced at him and smiled, and Gil concluded the senator had been jesting. No one in this day and age could possibly approve of slavery.

"Only myself and my servants live here now," Rashas continued. "I am a widower. My wife died during the war. My son was killed fighting with the armies of Whitestone, armies led by your mother, Gilthas." Rashas gave the young man a strange look. "My daughter is married and has a house and family of her own. Most of the time, I am alone.

"But today I have company, an honored guest staying with me. I hope you, too, my prince, will consider my house your own. I trust you will grace my dwelling with your presence?" The senator appeared eager, anxious for Gilthas to say yes.

"I am the one who would be honored, Senator," Gil said, flushing with pleasure. "You do me too much kindness."

"I will show you your room in a moment. The servants are making it up now. The lady who is my guest is most anxious to meet you. It would be impolite of us to keep her waiting. She has heard a great deal about you. She is, I believe, a close friend of your mother's."

Gil was mystified. Following her marriage, his mother had retained few friends among the elves. Perhaps this person had been one of his mother's childhood companions.

Rashas led the way up three flights of gracefully winding stairs. A door at the top opened onto a spacious hallway. Three doors opened off the hall, one at the far end and two on each side. Two of the Kagonesti servants stood outside the far door. They bowed to Rashas. At a signal from him, one of the Wilder elves knocked respectfully on the door.

"Enter," said a woman's voice, low and musical, quiet and imperious.

Gil stood back to permit Rashas to enter, but the senator bowed, gestured. "My prince."

Embarrassed, yet pleased, Gilthas walked into the room. Rashas followed behind him. The servants shut the door.

The woman had her back to them; she was standing by a window. The room was octagon-shaped, a small arboretum. Trees grew in the center, their branches carefully coaxed and trained to form a living ceiling of green. Tall, narrow windows were set into the walls. These windows were not opened, Gil noticed, but were all closed and draped in silk. He supposed the room's occupant did not like fresh air.

Two doors—one on each side of the room—led to private chambers off this main one. The furniture, a sofa, table, and several chairs, was comfortable and elegant.

"My lady," said Rashas respectfully, "you have a visitor."

The woman remained standing with her back to them a moment longer. Her shoulders seemed to stiffen, as if bracing herself. Then she turned slowly around.

Gil let out a soft breath. He had never in his life seen or imagined such beauty existed, could be embodied in a living being. The woman's hair was the black of the sky at midnight, her eyes the deep purple of amethyst. She was graceful, lovely, ethereal, ephemeral, and there was a sorrow about her that was like the sorrow of the gods.

If Rashas had introduced the woman as Mishakal, gentle goddess of healing, Gil would not have been the least surprised. He felt strongly compelled to fall on his knees in worship and reverence.

But this woman was not a goddess.

"My prince, may I present Alhana Starbreeze—" Rashas began.

"Queen Alhana Starbreeze," she corrected, softly, haughtily. She stood tall and—oddly—defiant.

"Queen Alhana Starbreeze," Rashas amended with a smile, as if he were indulging the whim of a child. "Please permit me to present Gilthas, son of Lauralanthalasa of the House of Solostaran . . . and her husband, Tanthalas Half-Elven." Rashas added the last almost as an afterthought.

Gil heard the distinct pause in Rashas's words, a pause that effectively separated his father from his mother. Gil felt his skin flame in embarrassment and shame. He could not look at this proud and haughty woman, who must be pitying and despising him. She was talking, not to him, but to Rashas. Such was Gil's confusion that he couldn't understand what she was saying at first. When he did, he raised his head and stared at her in pleased astonishment.

" . . . Tanis Half-Elven is one of the great men of our time. He is known and revered throughout Ansalon. He has been awarded the highest honors each nation has to offer, including the elven nations, Senator. The proud Knights of Solamnia bow before him with respect. Revered Daughter Crysania of the Temple of Paladine in Palanthas considers him a friend. The dwarven king of Thorbardin calls Tanis Half-Elven brother—"

Rashas coughed. "Yes, Your Majesty," he said dryly. "I understand the half-elf has friends among the kender, too."

"Yes, he does," Alhana returned coolly. "And considers himself fortunate to have won their innocent regard."

"No accounting for taste," Rashas said, his lip curling.

Alhana made no response. She was looking at Gil, and now she was frowning, as if a new and unpleasant thought had suddenly occurred to her.

Gil had no idea what was going on. He was too dazed, too rattled. To hear such glowing praise of his father, praise given by the queen of Qualinesti and Silvanesti. His father—one of the great men of our time . . . proud knights bow to him . . . dwarven king calls him brother . . . highest honors of each nation. . . ."

Gil had never known that. Never known any of that.

He realized suddenly that a deafening silence had descended on the room. He was extremely uncomfortable, wished someone would say something. And then he was alarmed.

"Maybe it's me!" he said to himself, panicked, trying to recall his mother's lessons in entertaining royalty. "Maybe I'm supposed to be the one making conversation."

Alhana was studying him intently. Her lovely eyes, turned upon him, effectively robbed him of coherent speech. Gil tried to say something, but discovered he had no voice. He looked from the senator to the queen and knew then that something was wrong.

The sunlight was not permitted to enter this room. Curtains had been drawn across the windows. The shadows had at first seemed cool and restful. Now they were ominous, unnerving, like the pall that falls over the world before the unleashing of a violent storm. The very air was dangerous, charged with lightning.

Alhana broke the silence. Her purple eyes darkened, deepened almost to black.

"So this is your plan," she said to Rashas, speaking Qualinesti with a slight accent that Gilthas recognized as belonging to her people, the Silvanesti.

"Quite a good one, don't you think?" Rashas answered her. He was calm, unmoved by her anger.

"He is only a boy!" Alhana cried in a low voice.

"He will have guidance, a wise counselor at his side," Rashas replied.

"You, of course," she said scathingly.

"The Thalas-Enthia elects the regent. I will, of course, be happy to offer my services."

"The Thalas-Enthia! You have that band of old men and women in your pocket!"

Gil felt the knot tighten his stomach, the blood start to pound painfully in his head. Once again, adults were talking over, around, below, and above him. He might as well be one of those trees sprouting up out of the floor.

"He doesn't know, does he?" Alhana said. Her look on Gil now was one of pity.

"I think perhaps he knows more than he lets on," Rashas said with a sly smile. "He came of his own free will. He wouldn't be here if he didn't want this. And now, Your Majesty"—he said the title with fine sarcasm—"if you and Prince Gilthas will both excuse me, I have pressing business elsewhere. There is much to do in preparation for tomorrow's ceremony."

The senator bowed, turned on his heel, and left the room. The servants shut the door immediately on his leaving.

"Want what?" Gil was bewildered and angry himself. "What's he talking about? I don't understand. . . ."

"Don't you?" she said to him.

Before he could reply, Alhana turned away. Her body was rigid, both fists clenched, nails digging into flesh.

Feeling like a child who has been shut up in the nursery when the adults are having a party in the living room below, Gil stalked over to the door and flung it open.

Two of the tall, strong Kagonesti elves planted their bodies before the door. Each held a spear in his hand.

Gil started to shove between them.

The elves did not move.

"Excuse me, perhaps you don't understand. I'm leaving now," Gil said politely, but in a stern tone to show them he meant what he said.

He stepped forward. The two said nothing. Their spears crossed in front of the door, in front of him.

Rashas was just disappearing down the staircase.

"Senator!" Gilthas called, trying to keep calm. The flame of his anger was starting to waver in fear's chill wind. "There's some sort of misunderstanding. These servants of yours won't let me out!"

Rashas paused, glanced back. "Those are their orders, my prince. You'll find the suite of rooms you will be sharing with Her Majesty quite comfortable, the best in my household, in fact. The Wilder elves will provide you with whatever you want. You have only to ask."

"I want to leave," Gilthas said quietly.

"So soon?" Rashas was pleasant, smiling. "I couldn't permit it. You've only just arrived. Rest, relax. Look out the windows, enjoy the view.

"And by the way," the senator added, proceeding down the stairs, his words floating upward. "I'm truly glad you find Qualinesti so beautiful, Prince Gilthas. You're going to be living here a long, long time."

Chapter Seven

"Dalamar!" Tanis beat on the bolted door. "Dalamar, damn you, I know you're out there! I know you can hear me! I want to talk to you! I—"

"Ah, my friend," came a voice, practically in his ear. "I'm glad you've finally regained consciousness."

At the unexpected sound, Tanis nearly jumped through a stone wall. Once his heart had quit racing, he turned to face the dark elf, who stood in the center of the room, a slight smile on the thin lips.

"Do stop this shouting. You're disrupting my class. My students cannot concentrate on their spells."

"Damn your students! Where is my boy?" Tanis shouted.

"He is safe," Dalamar replied. "First—"

Tanis lost control. Heedless of the consequences, he leapt at Dalamar, hands going for the dark elf's throat.

Blue lightning flared, crackled. Tanis was thrown backward. He crashed painfully into the wooden door. The shock of the magic was paralyzing. His limbs twitched; his head buzzed. He took a moment to recover, then, frustrated with his own helplessness, he started toward Dalamar again.

"Stop it, Tanis," the dark elf said sternly. "You're acting like a fool. Face the facts. You are a prisoner in the Tower of High Sorcery—my tower. You are weaponless and even if you did have a weapon, you could do nothing to harm me."

"Give me my sword," Tanis said, breathing heavily. "We'll see about that."

Dalamar almost, but not quite, laughed. "Come now, my friend. I told you, your son is safe. How long he remains so is up to you."

"Is that a threat?" Tanis demanded grimly.

"Threats are for the fearful. I merely state facts. Come, come, my friend! What has happened to your renowned logic, your legendary common sense? All flown out the window when the stork flew in?"[3]

"He's my son. Those draconians— I was afraid—" Tanis gave up. "How could you understand? You've never been a parent."

"If degenerating into a mindless idiot is what it means to be a parent, I shall certainly take care that I never achieve such a dubious distinction. Please, sit down. Let us discuss this like rational men."

Glowering, Tanis stalked over to a comfortable armchair, placed near a welcome fire. Even on a warm spring day, the Tower of High Sorcery was dark and chill. The room in which he was imprisoned was furnished with every luxury; he'd been provided with food and drink. His few minor wounds—scratches, mostly, from the draconian's claws and a bump on the head—had been carefully tended.

Dalamar seated himself in a chair opposite. "If you will listen with patience, I will tell you what is transpiring."

"I'll listen. You talk." Tanis's voice softened, almost broke. "My son is all right? He is well?"

"Of course. Gilthas would be of little use to his captors if he were not. You may take comfort in that fact, my friend. And I am your friend," the dark elf added, seeing the angry flash in Tanis's eyes. "Though I admit appearances are against me.

"As for your son," Dalamar continued, "he is where he has longed to be—his homeland, Qualinesti. It is his homeland, Tanis, though you don't like to hear that, do you? The boy is lodged quite comfortably, probably being afforded every courtesy. Only natural for the elves to treat him with deference, respect—since he is to be their king."

Tanis couldn't believe he'd heard right. He was on his feet again. "This is some sort of bad joke. What is it you want, Dalamar? What is it you're really after?"

The dark elf stood up. Gliding forward, he laid his hand gently on Tanis's arm.

"No joke, my friend. Or, if it is, no one is laughing. Gilthas is in no danger now. But he could be."

Once again, Tanis saw the vision he'd seen on Storm's Keep—dark clouds, swirling around his son. Tanis lowered his head, to hide his burning tears. Dalamar's grip on him tightened.

"Get hold of yourself, my friend. We don't have much time. Every minute is critical. There is a great deal to explain. And," Dalamar added softly, "plans to make."

---

[3]It is a kender belief that the stork delivers babies to fortunate households by dropping the babies down the chimney. Certainly, this might almost be true, for kender women have a wonderfully easy time during pregnancy and delivery. Babies really do seem to appear by magic. Thus kender families tend to be quite large; a good thing, since the attrition rate among kender is high. Relatively few kender ever live to a ripe old age.

Chapter Eight

"King?" Gil repeated in astonishment. He stared at Alhana in disbelief. "Speaker of the Sun and Stars! Me? No, you can't be serious. I . . . I don't want to be king!"

The woman smiled, a smile that was like winter sunshine on thick ice. The smile lit her face, but did not warm her. Or him.

"I am afraid that what you want, Prince Gilthas, does not matter."

"But you're queen."

"Queen!" Her voice was bitter.

"My uncle Porthios is the Speaker." Gil went on, baffled and—though he didn't admit it—frightened. "I . . . This doesn't make sense!"

Alhana gave him a cool glance, then she turned away, walked back to the window. Parting the curtain, she stared outside, and in the light he could see her face. She had seemed cold and imperious in the shadows. In reality, in the sunlight, she was careworn, anxious, and afraid. She, too, was afraid, though he had the impression that her fear was not for herself.

I don't want to be king, Gil heard himself whine, like a child complaining about being sent to bed. He blushed deeply.

"I'm sorry, Lady Alhana. So much has happened . . . and I don't understand any of it. You are saying that Rashas brought me here to crown me Speaker of the Sun and Stars, to make me king of Qualinesti. I don't see how that's possible—"

"Don't you?" she asked, shifting her gaze. The purple eyes were hard and dark with suspicion.

Gilthas was shocked. "My lady, I swear! I don't know . . . Please, believe me . . ."

"Where are your parents?" Alhana asked abruptly. She was looking back outside now.

"Home, I suppose," said Gil, a choking sensation in his throat. "Unless my father rode after me."

Hope rose in Gil's heart. Certainly his father would come after him. Tanis would find the invitation, right where Gil had left it (his declaration of his right to do as he pleased). Tanis would ride to the Black Swan and . . . and discover that Gil had never been there.

"I let Rashas's servant have my horse! He . . . he could have told my parents anything!" Gil sank despondently into a chair. "What a fool I've been!"

Alhana let fall the curtain. She studied the young man intently a moment. Then, coming over, she laid the fingertips of her hand on his shoulder. Her touch was chill, even through the fabric of his shirt.

"You say that your parents knew nothing of this?"

"They didn't, my lady," Gil admitted shamefacedly. "They told me not to come. I . . . didn't listen. I ran away. I left . . . in the night."

"I think you had better tell me the whole story." Alhana seated herself— erect and regal—in a chair across from him.

Gilthas did so. He was astonished, at the end of his recital, to see her face relax. She brushed her hand across her eyelashes.

"You were afraid my parents were behind this!" Gil said in sudden realization.

"Not behind it, perhaps," Alhana said, sighing, "but that they approved. Forgive me, Prince. If your father and mother were here, I would beg their forgiveness, too."

Reaching out her hand, she clasped his. "I've been alone for so long. I began to think everyone I had ever trusted had betrayed me. But we are in this together, it seems." She squeezed his hand gently, then released it. Sinking back into her chair, she stared unseeing at the curtained window, then sighed again.

"My father and mother both know I planned to come to Qualinesti. They must know I'm here, no matter what the servant told them. They'll come after me, my lady," Gil said stoutly, hoping to comfort her. "They'll rescue both of us."

But Alhana only shook her head. "No, Rashas is far too clever to permit that to happen. He has concocted some means to keep your parents from reaching you."

"You make it sound as if we could be in danger! From Senator Rashas? From our own people?"

She raised her gaze to meet his. "Not your own, Gilthas. You are different. That's why they chose you."

You are part human. The unsaid words hung in the air. Gil stared at her. He knew she had not meant it as an insult, especially not after the praise she had given Tanis. It was a habit of thought, bred into her by thousands of years of self-imposed isolation and the belief—however mistaken—that the elves are the chosen, the beloved, of the gods.

Gil knew this, yet he felt hot words rise up into his throat. He knew if he said them, it would make matters only worse. Yet . . .

Grace under pressure, my dear!

Gil heard his mother's voice, saw her rest her hand on Tanis's arm. Gil remembered meetings held at their house, remembered watching his mother move with dignity and calm through the storms of political intrigue. He remembered her words to his father, reminding him to remain cool, under control. Gil remembered seeing his father turn red in the face, swallow hard.

Gil swallowed hard.

"I think you should tell me what's going on, my lady," he said in a low voice.

"It is really very simple," Alhana replied. "My husband, Porthios, is being held a prisoner in Silvanesti. He was betrayed by my people. I am being held a prisoner here, betrayed by his people. . . ."

"But why?" Gil was perplexed.

"We elves don't like change. We fear it, mistrust it. But the world is changing very rapidly. We must change with it—or we will wither away and perish. The War of the Lance taught us that. At least I thought it did. The younger elves agree with us; the elder do not. And it is the elder—like Senator Rashas—who wield the power. I never supposed he would dare go this far, however."

"What will happen to you and Uncle Porthios?"

"We will be exiled," she said softly. "Neither kingdom will accept us."

Gil knew enough of his people to realize that exile for an elf is far worse punishment than execution. Alhana and Porthios would be known as "dark elves"—elves who have been "cast out of the light." They would be exiled from their homelands, prohibited any communication with their people. They would have no rights anywhere on Ansalon and, as such, would be in constant peril. Rightly or wrongly, dark elves are considered evil. They are hounded, persecuted, driven out of every city and town. They are fair targets for bounty hunters, thieves, and other scum. Not surprising that, in order to survive, most dark elves did seek refuge in the shadow of Takhisis.

Gil could think of nothing to say that would be of any help or comfort. He looked up at Alhana.

"Why me, my lady? Why now?"

"I am with child," she said simply. "If our baby is born, he or she will be heir to the throne. As it is, should anything happen to Porthios, your mother is rightful heir. But your mother's marriage to a half-human bastard—"

Gil sucked in his breath.

Alhana glanced at him, sympathetic, but not apologetic. "That is how most of the Qualinesti think of your father, Gilthas. It is one reason Tanis Half-Elven has never been eager to return to his homeland. Life here was not very pleasant for him when he was young. It would be worse now. What's the matter? Didn't you ever stop to consider this?"

Gil shook his head slowly. No, he'd never considered his father's feelings, never thought about Tanis at all.

I only thought about myself.

Alhana was continuing, "Your mother's marriage precludes her from ruling . . ."

"But, I'm part human," Gil reminded her.

"So you are," Alhana replied coolly. "Rashas and the Thalas-Enthia do not see that as a problem. In fact, they probably view your bloodline as an asset—to them. Rashas considers all humans weak, tractable. He thinks that, because you are part human, he can lead you around by the nose."

Gilthas flushed in anger. He lost control. Fists clenched, he bounced up out of the chair.

"By all the gods! I'll show Rashas," Gil proclaimed loudly. "I'll show them all. I'll . . . I'll . . ."

The door opened. One of the Kagonesti guards, his spear in his hand, glared suspiciously into the room.

"Calm down, young man," advised Alhana in a soft voice, speaking Silvanesti. "Don't start trouble you cannot finish."

Gil's anger flared, sputtered, then burned out like a gutted candle.

The Kagonesti eyed him, then began to laugh. He said something to his fellow guard in Kagonesti and shut the door. Gil didn't speak the Wilder elf language, but the Kagonesti words were mixed with enough Qualinesti to bring a blush of shame to Gil's cheek. Something about the pup trying to bark like an old dog.

"So you are saying that even if I am king, I'll really be their prisoner. Are you suggesting I get used to that, too, my lady?" He spoke bitterly.

Alhana was silent a moment, then she shook her head. "No, Gilthas. Never get used to being their pawn. Fight them! You are the son of Tanthalas and Lauralanthalasa. You are strong—stronger than Rashas thinks. With such noble blood in your veins, how can you be otherwise?"

Even if it is mixed blood, he thought, but did not say. He was pleased at her confidence. He resolved to be worthy of it, no matter what happened.

Alhana smiled at him reassuringly, then walked again to the window. Parting the curtain, she looked outside.

It occurred to him, at this moment, that she must be doing something other than admiring the view.

"What is it, my lady? Who's out there?"

"Hush! Keep your voice down."

She closed the curtain, then opened it, then closed it. "A friend. I have given him the signal. He saw them bring you in. I have just told him we can trust you."

"Who? Porthios?" Gil was suddenly, buoyantly hopeful. Nothing seemed impossible.

Alhana shook her head. "One of my own people, a young guardsman named Samar. He fought with my husband against the dream in Silvanesti. When Porthios was captured, Samar remained loyal to his commander. Porthios sent Samar to warn me. He came too late; I was already Rashas's prisoner. But now Samar has completed his arrangements. The Thalas-Enthia meets this evening to plan for tomorrow's coronation."

"Tomorrow!" Gil echoed the word in disbelief.

"Do not be afraid, Gilthas," Alhana said. "Paladine willing, all will be well. Tonight, while Rashas is attending the meeting, you and I will escape."

Chapter Nine

"Rashas planned this all very carefully. Of course, Tanis, you were meant to think that draconians had abducted the boy," Dalamar told him. "You fell into the trap quite neatly. The Wilder elf led the horse into the forest, left it as a tempting bit of bait out in front of the cave. The rest, you know."

Tanis was barely listening. Laurana, he thought. She'll worry when she doesn't hear from me. She'll realize something's wrong. She'll go to Qualinesti. She'll put a stop to this . . . .

"Ah, you are wondering about your wife," Dalamar said.

Discomfited at having his thoughts laid bare, Tanis shrugged, lied. "I was only thinking of sending her a message, telling her I was all right. So she won't worry . . ."

"Yes, of course," said Dalamar, his half-smile indicating he wasn't fooled. "The thoughtful husband. You'll be pleased, then, to know that I've already taken care of the matter. I sent one of the servants from the Black Swan with a note for your wife saying that all was well, that you and your son needed time alone together. You should thank me . . ."

Tanis replied with a few words in human that were not, in any way, shape, or form, an expression of gratitude.

Dalamar's smile darkened. "I repeat, you should thank me. I may have saved Laurana's life. If she had gone to Qualinost and tried to interfere . . ." He paused, then shrugged his slender shoulders.

Tanis had been pacing the room. He stopped in front of Dalamar. "You're implying she might be in peril? From Rashas and the Thalas-Enthia? I don't believe you. By the gods, these are elves we're talking about—"

"I am an elf, Tanis," Dalamar said quietly. "And I am the most dangerous man you know."

Tanis started to say something, but his tongue froze to the roof of his mouth. His throat constricted, shutting off his breathing. He swallowed, then managed to whisper huskily, "What are you saying? And how do I know I can trust you?"

Dalamar did not immediately answer. He spoke a word, and a wine decanter appeared in his hand. Rising, he walked over to a table on which stood a silver tray and two thin-stemmed crystal glasses. "Will you have some? The wine is elven, very fine, very old, part of the stock of my late *shalafi*."

Tanis was on the verge of refusing. It is generally a wise idea never to eat or drink anything while incarcerated in a Tower of High Sorcery with a dark elf wizard.

But Tanis's "renowned logic" reminded him that he would get nowhere behaving like a thick-headed lout. If Dalamar wanted to dispose of him, the mage would have done so by now. And, then, too, Dalamar had made a subtle inference to Raistlin, his *shalafi*. Once, Raistlin and Tanis had fought on the same side. Once, Dalamar and Tanis had fought on the same side as well. The dark elf had said something earlier about making plans.

Silently, Tanis accepted the glass.

"To old alliances," Dalamar said, echoing Tanis's thoughts. He tilted the wine to his lips and took a sip.

Tanis did the same, then set the glass down. He didn't need a fuzzy head, a fevered brain. Silently, he waited.

Dalamar held his glass to the firelight, studied the wine's crimson color. "Like blood, isn't it?"

His gaze shifted to Tanis. "You want to know what is going on? I'll tell you. The Dark Queen is back in the game. She is arranging her pieces on the board, putting them into position. She has stretched forth her arm, sent out her seductive call. Many feel her touch, many hear her voice. Many are moved to do her bidding—without ever realizing that they are acting for her.

"But then," Dalamar added wryly, "I'm not telling you anything you don't already know, am I, my friend?"

Tanis took care to look blank.

"Storm's Keep?" the dark elf pursued. "Surely you haven't forgotten your visit to Ariakan's fortress?"

"Why are you telling me these things?" Tanis demanded. "You're not thinking of changing robes, are you?"

Dalamar laughed. "White is not my color. Don't worry, my friend. I'm not betraying any of my queen's secrets. Takhisis understands the mistakes she made in the past. She has learned from them. She won't repeat them. She is moving slowly, subtly, in ways completely unexpected."

Tanis snorted. "You're claiming this business with my son is all a plot of Her Dark Majesty's?"

"Think about it, my friend," Dalamar advised. "As perhaps you know, I have little love for Porthios. He cast me, in shame and humiliation, from my homeland. On his orders, I was blindfolded, bound hand and foot, and hauled in a cart, like one of your human slaughter animals, to the borders of Silvanesti. There, with his own hands, he threw me into the mud. I would not weep to see the same happen to him.

"But even I admit that Porthios is an effective leader. He is courageous, swift to action. He is also rigid and inflexible and proud. But these flaws have, over the years, been tempered by the virtues of his wife."

Dalamar's voice softened. "Alhana Starbreeze. I saw her often in Silvanesti. I was of low caste, she—a princess. I could view her only from a distance, but that didn't matter. I was a little bit in love with her."

"What man isn't?" Tanis growled. He made an impatient gesture. "Get on with whatever point it is you're making."

"My point is this—the treaty of the Unified Nations of the Three Races."

Tanis shook his head, apparently mystified. "I don't know what you're talking about."

"Then let me enlighten you. An alliance of the elven kingdoms of Qualinesti and Silvanesti with the human kingdoms of Solamnia, Southern and Northern Ergoth, and the dwarven kingdom of Thorbardin. For nearly five years you and Laurana have worked to bring this about—ever since your clandestine visit to Storm's Keep. Porthios, urged on by Alhana, has finally agreed to sign. It would have been a powerful alliance."

Dalamar lifted his delicate hand, snapped his fingers. A spark of blue flame flared around the white skin; a puff of smoke wafted in the air, wavered a moment, then drifted away.

"Gone."

Tanis regarded him grimly. "How did you find out?"

"Ask, rather, my friend, how did Senator Rashas find out?"

Tanis was silent, then he began to swear softly beneath his breath. "Rashas told you he knew? He betrayed his own people? I can't believe that, not even of Rashas."

"No, the senator still has some smattering of honor left in him. He is not a traitor—not yet. He gave me some lame excuse, but I think the truth is fairly obvious. When were the final papers to have been signed?"

"Next week," Tanis said bitterly, staring into the flickering flames.

"Ah, there." Dalamar shrugged again. "You see?"

Tanis did see. He saw the Dark Queen, whispering her words of seduction into elven ears. Senator Rashas would be shocked to the core of his being at the suggestion that he was being seduced by evil. In his mind, he was acting only for good—the good of the elves, keeping them safe, isolated, insulated.

All the hard work, all the endless hours of traveling back and forth, all the hard-fought negotiations: convincing the knights to trust the elves, convincing the dwarves to trust the Ergothians, convincing the elves to trust anybody. All gone in a puff of smoke.

And Lord Ariakan and his dread Knights of Takhisis growing stronger by the hour.

This was a terrible blow to their hopes for peace, yet, at the moment, all Tanis could think of was his boy. Is Gilthas safe? Is he well? Does he know what Rashas plots? What will he do if he finds out?

Hopefully, nothing. Nothing rash, nothing foolish. Nothing to put himself—or others—into danger. Gil had never been in any sort of danger or difficulty before now. His father and mother had seen to that. He wouldn't know how to react.

"We always protected him," Tanis said, not realizing he was talking aloud. "Maybe we were wrong. But he was so sick, so fragile. . . . How could we do otherwise?"

"We raise our children to leave us, Tanis," Dalamar said quietly.

Startled, Tanis looked at the dark elf. "Caramon said that."

"Yes, he said it to me, after Palin had taken his test. 'Our children are given to us for only a short time. During that time, we must teach them to live on their own, because we won't always be around.' "

"Wise words." Recalling his friend, Tanis smiled fondly, sadly. "But Caramon wasn't able to follow his dictum, not when it came to his own son."

He was silent a moment, then said quietly, "Why are you telling me all this, Dalamar? What's in it for you?"

"Her Dark Majesty has a very high regard for you, Tanis Half-Elven. Neither she nor I consider it conducive to our cause to have your son on the elven throne. I think we would do far better with Porthios," Dalamar added dryly.

"What about the treaty?"

"That victory is already ours, my friend. No matter what happens among the elves, the treaty is so much scrap paper. Porthios will never forgive the Silvanesti for betraying him. He won't sign now. You know it. And if the two elven nations refuse to sign, the dwarves of Thorbardin will refuse to sign. And if the dwarves—"

"Hang the dwarves!" Tanis said impatiently. "Does this mean you'll help me bring Gilthas home?"

"Your son's coronation is planned for tomorrow," Dalamar said, raising his wineglass to Tanis in a mocking salute. "It is a solemn occasion, one no father should miss."

Chapter Ten

Twilight enhanced the beauty of the elven land. The soft, glowing colors of the setting sun shone through the silken curtains, burnished every object in the room with gold. Its beauty was wasted on Gil. Nervously, he paced away the hours.

The house was still. The Kagonesti guards hardly ever spoke, and when they did, it was only briefly and in their own language—a language that sounded like the calls of wild birds. The guards brought in dinner: bowls of fruit and bread, wine and water. Then, after a swift searching glance around the room, they left, shutting the door behind them. Alhana could eat nothing.

"This food tastes like ashes," she said.

Despite his trouble, Gilthas was hungry. He ate not only his meal, but— when he saw she wasn't going to eat—hers as well.

Alhana smiled faintly. "The resiliency of youth. It is good to see. You are the future of our race." She pressed her hand against her abdomen. "You give me hope."

Night was forbidden to truly settle over Qualinesti. The darkness was lit by thousands of tiny sparkling lights, shining in the trees. Alhana lay down, closed her eyes, and tried to find some rest before the evening's long and possibly dangerous journey.

Gil continued pacing in the darkness, attempting to sort through the confused jumble of his thoughts.

Home! How he had longed to leave it. Now, perversely, he longed to be back.

"Father came after me. I know he did. And maybe I've put him in danger." Gil sighed. "I've made a mess of things. Whatever happens to Father will be my fault. He warned me not to go. Why didn't I listen? What's wrong with me? Why do I have these horrible feelings inside me? I—"

He stopped. Voices, loud voices, speaking Qualinesti, came floating up from far below. Alarmed, thinking perhaps that Alhana's plot had been discovered, Gil wondered if he should wake her.

She was already awake, sitting up, her eyes open wide. She listened several moments, then sighed in relief.

"It is only a few members of the Thalas-Enthia—Rashas's cohorts. They're planning on entering the senate chambers together, to present a solid front."

"Then all the senators aren't behind Rashas?"

"The younger members are opposed to him, though there are too few of them to matter. But many of the elder are wavering. If Porthios were here, there would be no contest, and Rashas knows it."

"What will happen tomorrow when you're gone and I'm not here to be crowned?"

Alhana was scornful. "The people will wake to discover that they have no ruler. Rashas will be forced to send for Porthios. The Thalas-Enthia will be chastened and we can get on with our lives—such as they are."

Gil had heard his parents talk about the marriage of Alhana and Porthios. It wasn't a happy one. Husband and wife rarely saw each other. Porthios was fighting Lorac's dream in Silvanesti. Alhana spent her time shuttling between the two kingdoms, trying desperately to hold them together. But she spoke of her husband with respect and pride, if not affection.

Gil gazed at her with adoring eyes. I could live off her beauty alone. If she were mine, I wouldn't need anything else. I could do without water, food. How could any man not love her? Porthios must be a great fool.

A brief burst of cheering erupted from down below. The sound of voices began to diminish.

"They're leaving," said Alhana. "Now the guards will relax."

The house was silent. Then, once certain Rashas was gone, the Kagonesti guards outside their door began to talk and laugh. Spears clattered to the floor. More laughter, and strange clicking sounds.

Puzzled, Gil looked at Alhana.

"Those are sticks you hear, being tossed onto the floor. The Kagonesti are playing a game of their people. They do this whenever Rashas leaves, but don't imagine they are letting down their guard," she warned. "They would trade their betting sticks for spears the moment you tried to open that door."

"Then how are we going to escape?"

It was a long drop to the garden below; Gil had already looked.

"Samar has everything planned," Alhana said, and would say no more.

Time passed. Gil was edgy, nervous.

"How long will the meeting of the Thalas-Enthia last?"

"Far into the night," said Alhana quietly. "After all, they are plotting sedition."

The Wilder elves' game was becoming increasingly entertaining, judging by the bursts of laughter and the occasional excited, friendly argument. Gil walked over to the door and put his ear to it to hear better. He would like to join in such a game sometime, and wondered how it was played. Sticks clattered; then there would be moments of breath-held silence, followed by a gasp of relief or howls of dismay. At the end, cries of success came from the winners, good-natured swearing from the losers.

Then, suddenly, there was the sound of a strange voice. "Good evening, gentlemen. Who is winning?"

Alhana—deathly pale—rose to her feet. "It is Samar," she whispered. "Get away from the door! Quickly!"

Gil jumped back. He heard shouts, confused scrambling outside the door—men reaching for their spears. Swift, strange words, spoken in a language that he didn't understand, halted those sounds, changed them to muffled groans, followed by several thuds, as of heavy bodies tumbling to the floor. And then no more sounds for the space of ten heartbeats—rapid, frightened heartbeats.

The door opened. A young elven warrior strode into the room.

"Samar! My trusted friend." Alhana smiled at him. Gracious and calm as if she were in her own audience chamber, she extended her hand.

"My queen!" Samar fell to one knee before her. His head bowed in homage.

Gil peered curiously out the door. The Wilder elves were stretched out, comatose, on the floor. Some had their spears still clutched in their hands. What appeared to be a rolled-up piece of parchment was ablaze in the center of the room. As Gil watched, the parchment vanished, consumed by the fire. Thin tendrils of green smoke drifted on the still air.

Gil was about to step out to take a closer look.

"Take care, young man," Samar warned. Rising swiftly to his feet, he pulled Gil back. "Don't go anywhere near that smoke, or you'll be slumbering as peacefully as they."

"Prince Gilthas, son of Laurana Solostaran and Tanis Half-Elven," Alhana performed the introductions. "This is Samar of House Protector."

Samar's gaze—cool and appraising—raked over Gil, who felt suddenly weak and frail in the presence of this seasoned warrior. Samar gave the young man a cold nod, then turned immediately back to his queen.

"All is prepared, Your Majesty. The griffins are waiting to meet us in the wilderness. They were furious when they heard that Rashas had taken you prisoner." Samar smiled grimly. "I don't believe he will be riding by griffin back anymore. If you are ready, we should leave at once. Where are your possessions? I will carry them for you."

"I travel lightly, my friend," Alhana said. She spread her hands, showed them empty.

"But your jewels, my queen—"

"I have what is important to me." She placed her hand over a ring she wore upon her finger. "My husband's token of faith and trust. All else means nothing."

Samar frowned. "They took your jewels from you, didn't they, my queen? How dare they?"

Alhana's voice was gentle, but stern. "The jewels belong to the Qualinesti people. The matter is trivial, Samar. You are right. We should leave at once."

The warrior bowed in silent acquiescence. "The downstairs guards, too, are silenced. We will go that way. Cover your nose and mouth, my queen. You, too, Prince," he ordered Gil curtly. "Don't inhale the magical smoke."

Alhana pressed an embroidered silken handkerchief over her face. Gil held the hem of his cloak over his mouth. Samar led the way, his hand on the hilt of his sword. They stepped over the slumbering bodies of the Wilder elves and detoured cautiously around the smoldering ashes of the spell scroll. When they reached the top of the stairs, Samar brought them to a halt.

"Stay here," he whispered.

Descending the steps, he looked around, then—satisfied that all was safe—he motioned for Alhana and Gil to follow.

Halfway down the last flight of stairs, Samar suddenly grabbed hold of Alhana, dragged her into the shadows. A fierce look from the warrior and an urgent "Get back!" warned Gil to do the same.

Not daring to breathe, he flattened himself against the wall.

A Wilder elf, this one a female, emerged from a doorway directly below them. She was carrying a silver bowl filled with fruit. Humming a song to herself, she crossed the entryway, heading for a courtyard, bright with the tiny, sparkling lights. Another Kagonesti servant met the woman at the door. They conferred a few moments. Gil caught the Qualinesti word for "party." The two disappeared into the courtyard.

Gil was impressed. How in the name of Paladine had Samar heard the woman coming? She moved as silently as the wind on her bare feet, except for that soft song. Gil regarded the warrior with undisguised admiration. Samar was apologizing in an undertone to his queen.

"Forgive me, Your Majesty, for my roughness."

"There is nothing to forgive, Samar. Let us hurry, before she comes back."

Swiftly, silently, the three ran down the stairs.

Samar put his hand on the door handle.

The door opened, but it was not the warrior who opened it.

Senator Rashas stood in the doorway.

"What is this?" he demanded in an amazed tone, staring from the warrior to Alhana. The senator's face went livid with anger. "Guards! Seize them!"

Qualinesti elves, wearing the swords and uniform of the city guard, surged past Rashas. Samar drew his sword, threw himself in front of his queen. The guards drew their swords.

Gil had no weapon, wouldn't have known what to do with one anyway. The blood pounded in his ears. He had been almost paralyzed with fear when Rashas first appeared. That fear had evaporated. Gil's blood burned. He felt light-headed and calm, ready to fight. Tensing, he was about to leap . . .

"Stop this madness!"

Alhana flung herself in the midst of the combatants. Her hands, soft and white, grabbed the blade of Samar's sword and thrust aside the blade of the guard threatening him.

"Samar, put your weapon away," she ordered, speaking Silvanesti, her voice shaking with emotion and anger.

"But my queen!" he began, pleading.

"Samar! That is my command!" she returned.

Slowly, reluctantly, Samar lowered his sword. But he did not sheathe it.

Alhana turned to face Rashas.

"So this is what it has come to," she said. "Elf killing elf. Is this what you want, Rashas?"

Alhana held out her hands. Her flesh was cut, bleeding.

Rashas was unmoved, his face hard and cold. The Qualinesti guards, however, looked uncomfortable, lowered their weapons, and backed up a pace. Gil stared at the blood on the queen's hands and was deeply ashamed of his own bloodlust.

"It is not I who brought us to this pass, my lady," Rashas said coolly, "but you. By attempting this escape, you have flaunted the lawful decree of the Thalas-Enthia."

"Lawful!" Alhana regarded him with disdain. "I am your queen. You have no right to hold me against my will!"

"Not even a queen is above elven law. We know about the secret treaty, Your Majesty. We know that you and the traitor Porthios have plotted to sell us out to our enemies."

Alhana stared at him, not understanding. "Treaty . . ."

"The treaty known as the Unified Nations." Rashas sneered. "A treaty that would make us slaves!"

"No, Senator. You don't understand! You have it all wrong!"

"Do you deny that you conducted talks in secret with the humans and the dwarves?"

"I don't deny it," Alhana answered with dignity. "The talks had to be kept secret. The matter is too delicate; it is too dangerous. There are things happening in the world you don't know about. You can't possibly understand—"

"You are right, my lady," Rashas interrupted. "I do not understand. I do not understand how you could sell us into bondage, give away our lands."

Alhana was imperious, calm. "You are a blind fool, but that is beside the point. Our negotiations were legal. We broke no law."

"On the contrary, my lady!" Rashas was losing patience. "Elven law demands that all treaties be voted on by the Thalas-Enthia!"

"We were going to present it to the senate. I swear this to you—"

"A Silvanesti oath?" Rashas laughed in disdain.

"Forgive me, my queen, for my disobedience," Samar said in a low voice. Taking hold of Alhana, the warrior shoved his queen protectively into Gil's arms.

Sword raised, the Silvanesti warrior sprang at Rashas.

The Qualinesti guard closed with him. Steel rang as swords clashed. Rashas stumbled backward into a safe corner. Gil placed his own body in front of Alhana. She watched in horror, powerless to intervene.

The Qualinesti guards outnumbered Samar four to one. He fought valiantly, but they managed to overwhelm and disarm him. Even then, he fought on. The guards struck him with their fists and the flat of their blades until he fell, senseless, to the floor.

It was the first time Gil had seen blood drawn in violence. He was sickened by the sight and by his own impotent rage.

Alhana knelt beside the fallen Samar.

"This man is badly injured." She looked up at the Qualinesti. "Take him to the healers."

The guard turned to Rashas. "Is that your will, Senator?"

Alhana paled, bit her lip.

Rashas was once more in control of the situation. "Take him to the healers. When they are finished with him, throw him into prison. He may well pay for this act of treason with his life. One of you guards, return with me to the senate. I must inform them of what has occurred. The rest of you escort Alhana Starbreeze back to her chambers. No, not you, Prince Gilthas. I want to have a word with you."

Defiant, Gil shook his head.

Alhana rose, came to him, rested her hand on his arm. "You are a Qualinesti prince," she said to him earnestly, intently. "And the son of Tanis Half-Elven. You have courage enough for this."

Gil didn't quite understand, but it occurred to him that he might bring more trouble down on her if he refused to listen to Rashas.

"Will you be all right, *Queen* Alhana?" he asked, emphasizing the word.

She smiled at him. Then, walking with dignity, accompanied by her guards, Alhana left the room.

When she was gone, the senator turned to Gil.

"I am deeply sorry for this unfortunate incident, my prince. I take the responsibility completely upon myself. I should never have quartered you with that cunning woman. I should have foreseen that she would coerce you into going along with her treacherous scheme. But you are safe now, my prince." Rashas was soothing, reassuring. "I will find other quarters for you this night."

Gil knew what his father would do in this situation. Tanis would have swallowed hard and then he would have slugged Rashas.

Grace under pressure.

Hitting Rashas would solve nothing, however, only make matters worse. Gil knew what his mother would do.

Sighing regretfully, Gil assumed a calm and placid expression that gave away nothing of his thoughts, an expression he'd seen more than once on his mother's face.

"I thank you for your concern, Senator."

Rashas nodded, then continued smoothly on. "The members of the Thalas-Enthia want very much to meet you, Prince Gilthas. They asked me to bring you to tonight's meeting. That is why I returned early. I was sent to bring you to the senate chamber. Fortunate, don't you think? It shows the gods are with me."

One god, at least, Gil thought grimly. Or should I say goddess?

"But you don't look well." Rashas was all sympathetic concern. "Not surprising. You were in grave danger from that conniving female." He lowered his voice. "There are some who say she is a witch. No, no. Don't try to talk, my prince. I will convey your apologies to the senate."

"Please, do that, Senator," Gil said. He could play this game, too. He only wished he had a clearer understanding of the rules.

Rashas bowed. "Sleep well, tonight, Prince Gilthas. You have a busy schedule ahead of you tomorrow. It is not every day that a man is crowned king."

With a gesture, the senator summoned one of his Kagonesti servants. "Take His Highness to new quarters—away from the witch. And see to it that he is not disturbed."

Chapter Eleven

All that night, Gil lay in his bed and made plans for morning. It had occurred to him, shortly after he had been escorted to his room, that he and Alhana were worrying over nothing. He knew what to do, how to handle the situation. It was all very simple. He was only sorry he couldn't tell Alhana that she had nothing to fear.

Gil rehearsed in his mind several times what he would say to Rashas. Anxiety eased, the young man fell asleep.

The sound of knocking woke him. He sat up, glanced out the window. It was still dark.

A Kagonesti guard opened the door, permitting three serving women to enter Gil's room. One of the women carried a large basin of fragrant rose water; orange blossoms floated on the surface. Another brought in a lamp and food on a tray. The third held—carefully—soft yellow robes, draped over her arms.

The Kagonesti woman carrying his breakfast was very young, not more than Gil's age. She was very lovely, too. Her body was not painted, as were the older elves', either as a matter of taste or perhaps the custom was dying out among the young.[4] She had the darkly tanned skin of her people, however, and her hair was burnished gold. Her eyes—by the soft light of the lamp—were large and brown. She smiled shyly at him as she placed the tray of food on the table by his bedside.

Gil smiled back, not thinking of what he was doing. He was then deeply embarrassed when the two older women laughed, said something in their lilting language. The young girl blushed and moved hastily away from Gil's bed.

"Eat. Wash. Dress," said one of the older women, embroidering her crude Qualinesti speech with darting motions of her hands. "The master will be shortly with you. Before sun rises."

[4]The Qualinesti consider the custom of body-painting barbaric and have been working to halt the practice among the Wilder elves, especially those who come to live and work in Qualinesti. The elder Kagonesti adhere rigidly to the old ways, but the younger elves—particularly those who want to remain in Qualinesti—have given up the custom. This has not pleased many of the Kagonesti, who have accused their cousins of attempting to lure their young away from them, perhaps even eradicate the Kagonesti race.

"I want to see Queen Alhana," Gil said firmly, trying to sound as dignified as possible, considering that he was more or less trapped in his bed by these women.

The Kagonesti woman slid her eyes toward the guard, who was standing watchfully in the door. He frowned, barked a sharp command, and the women hastened out.

"I want—" Gil began again loudly, but the guard only grunted and slammed the door shut.

Gil drew a deep breath. Soon, apparently, he must confront Rashas. He went over the words again and again as he performed his morning ablutions. With barely a glance at the yellow robes—the ceremonial robes of the Speaker of the Sun and Stars—Gil put on his traveling clothes, the clothes he had worn to Qualinesti, the clothes he intended to wear home.

Home! The reminder brought tears to his eyes. He would be so glad to return; he doubted if he'd ever leave again. His gaze went to the tray of food. He remembered the lovely girl who had carried it, remembered her eyes, her smile.

Well, maybe he wouldn't leave home for a short while. He would come back here, when all this was over, when Alhana and Porthios were once more rightful rulers. And next time, he would come back with his parents.

He tried eating breakfast, but gave it up. He sat on the bed, in the lamplit darkness, waiting with impatience for Rashas.

A tinge of rose-colored light glistened on the windowpane. It was nearly dawn. Gil heard footsteps and then Senator Rashas entered the room. He strode in abruptly, hurriedly, without knocking. The senator's gaze went first to the robes of the Speaker, lying untouched on Gil's bed, then to Gil himself.

He had risen to his feet, was standing respectfully, but certainly not humbly, before the senator.

"What is this?" Rashas demanded in surprise. "Didn't the women tell you? . . . Damn their ears! Those barbarians never get anything right. You are to dress yourself in the robes of the Speaker, Prince Gilthas. Obviously, you misunderstood—"

"I didn't misunderstand, Senator," Gil said, using the formal appellation.

His hands were cold. His mouth was so dry he feared his voice would crack, which would ruin the effectiveness of his carefully prepared speech. But there was no help for that now. He had to go on as best he could. He had to do what was right, do what he could to make amends for all the trouble he'd caused.

"I'm not going to be your Speaker, Senator. I refuse to take the vow."

Gil paused, expecting Rashas to argue, ridicule him, or even remonstrate and plead.

Rashas said nothing. His face was unreadable. He crossed his arms over his chest, waited for Gil to continue.

Gil licked dry lips. "Perhaps, Senator, you assumed that because my parents didn't choose to raise me in Qualinesti I have been kept ignorant of my heritage. That is not true. I know all about the ceremony to crown the Speaker of the Sun and Stars. My mother explained it to me. I know that one thing is required. The Speaker must take the vow of his *own free will*."

Gil emphasized the words. The speech was coming easier. He was too absorbed in it to realize that Rashas's reaction—or nonreaction—might bode trouble.

"I won't take the vow," Gil concluded, drawing in another deep breath. "I can't be your Speaker. I don't deserve such an honor."

"You're damn right you don't," Rashas said suddenly, softly, with suppressed fury. "You arrogant little half-breed. Your father was a bastard. He never knew the name of the man who rutted with the whore that was his mother. She should have been cast out in her shame. I said as much, but Solostaran was a soft-hearted, doddering old idiot.

"As for your own mother! What decent elven woman dons armor and rides to battle like a man? I have no doubt she found it most entertaining— surrounded day and night by so many soldiers! Your mother was nothing more than a glorified camp follower. The half-elf was the only man to have her after the others were done with her! With such a heritage, to even let you sniff the air of Qualinesti is a greater honor than you deserve, Prince Gilthas!" Rashas sneered when he spoke the name.

"And now, by the gods, you have the temerity to refuse—to refuse—to be Speaker! By all rights you should be down on your knees before me, weeping in your thankfulness, that I should pick you up out of the muck and make something of you!"

Shocked to the core of his being, Gil stared at the senator in appalled horror. He began to shake. His stomach wrenched; he was physically sickened by what he had heard. How could this man be so twisted? How could he think such things, let alone say them? Gil struggled to reply, but anger— choking and hot—caught him by the throat.

Rashas eyed him grimly. "You are more thick-headed than I had supposed you could be, though I might have expected it. You are most definitely your father's son!"

Gil stopped shaking. He stood rigid, his hands clenched tightly behind his back. But he managed a smile. "I thank you for the compliment, sir."

Rashas paused, frowning, considering. "I see I am going to have to resort to extreme measures. Remember, young man. Whatever happens, you brought this on yourself. Guard!"

Grabbing up the robes of the Speaker with one hand, Rashas dug his bony fingers into Gil's arm and shoved him, stumbling, toward the door. The Kagonesti guard took a firm grip on Gil.

He struggled to free himself. Rashas said something in Kagonesti. The guard tightened his grip.

"He'll break your arm, if I order him to," Rashas said coldly. "Come, come, Prince." Again, the sneer. "Stop wasting my time."

Rashas led the way out of Gil's room, up the stairs, back to the part of the house where Alhana Starbreeze was being held prisoner. Before now, Gil had been too furious to think clearly. His anger was starting to be replaced by fear.

Senator Rashas was obviously insane.

No, he's not, Gil realized with a sense of dread. If he were insane, no one would listen to him, no one would follow him. But he truly believes those terrible things he said about my parents. He truly believes that Alhana is a witch. He believes what he said last night about the treaty, about the elves becoming slaves of the humans. He's got everything twisted around so that, in his mind, what is good is evil and what is evil is good!

How is this possible? I don't understand . . . And what can I do to stop him?

They reached Alhana's chambers. The Kagonesti guards flung the door open at Rashas's snarling command. He stalked into the room. The Kagonesti guard dragged Gil in after.

Pulling away from the Wilder elf, Gil made an attempt to recover his dignity. He glared defiantly at Rashas.

Alhana was on her feet, regarded him with calm disdain. "Well, why have you come here, Senator? Shouldn't you be proceeding with the coronation?"

"The young man has proven obstinate, Lady Alhana." Rashas was smooth, cool. "He refuses to take the vow. I thought perhaps you could persuade him that what he is doing is not in his best interests—or in yours."

Alhana rewarded Gil with a warm and approving smile; a smile that eased his fear and filled him with renewed strength, renewed hope. "Quite the contrary. I think the young man has shown remarkable wisdom and courage for one of his years. Obviously, you misjudged him, Rashas. I would not dream of attempting to talk him out of this decision."

"I believe you will change your mind, Lady Alhana," Rashas said smoothly. "As will the young man."

Rashas said a few words in Kagonesti. One of the Wilder elf guards put down his spear and removed a bow he wore slung over his shoulder. Rashas gestured at Alhana. The Wilder elf nodded. He drew an arrow from his quiver and began to fit it to the bow.

Alhana was extremely pale, but not, apparently, from fear. She regarded the senator with a look that might almost have been pitying. "You are being seduced by darkness, Rashas. Stop this course of action before it destroys you!"

Rashas was amused. "I am not the one in league with the Dark Queen—as you, her servant, should know. I do all in my power to keep the shadows of her wickedness away from my people. Paladine's holy light shines upon me!"

"No, Rashas," Alhana said softly. "Paladine's light illuminates. It does not blind."

His face hard, expression scornful, Rashas turned from Alhana. The senator faced Gil, who was only now beginning to comprehend what was happening.

"You can't do . . . such a thing!" Gil gasped. He stared at Rashas in disbelief. "You can't . . ."

The senator flung the yellow robes of the Speaker at him. "It is time you dressed for the ceremony, Prince."

Chapter Twelve

The last time Tanis had been in the Tower of the Sun had been during the dark days just prior to the War of the Lance. Evil dragons had returned to Krynn. A new and terrible foe—the draconians—were joining with other servants of the Dark Queen to form immense armies under the captaincy of powerful Dragon Highlords. Victory against such mighty forces seemed impossible. In this tower, the elves of Qualinesti had come together for possibly the last time, to plan the exodus of their people from their beloved homeland.

Tiny flickering flames of hope had burned steadily through that dark night: Hope in the form of a blue crystal staff and a woman wise and strong enough to wield it; hope in the unlikely form of a merry kender who decided to help in "small ways"; hope in the form of a knight whose courage was a blazing beacon to those who cowered in fear beneath the Dark Queen's dread wings.

Goldmoon, Tasslehoff, Sturm—they and the rest of the companions had been with Tanis in this room, in this tower. He sensed their presence with him now. Looking around the chamber of the Speaker of the Sun, he was cheered. All would be well. He glanced up into the dome, at the glittering tile mosaic, which portrayed the blue sky and the sun on one half; the silver moon, the red moon, and the stars on the other.

"Please the gods," Tanis prayed softly. "I'll take you home, my son, and we'll start over. And this time things will be better. I promise."

Dalamar, standing beside Tanis, was also gazing upward. The dark elf gave an amused chuckle. "I wonder if they know that the black moon is now visible on their ceiling?"

Shocked, Tanis stared. Then he shook his head. "It's only a hole. A few tiles have fallen out. That's all."

Dalamar gave him a sidelong glance. The dark elf smiled.

Tanis, uncomfortable, ceased to look at the mosaic.

The tower's white marble walls glistened red in the dawn. The huge, round room in which they stood was currently empty, except for a rostrum, placed directly beneath the domed ceiling. People had not yet gathered; they would wait until the sun was completely over the horizon. Tanis and Dalamar had arrived early, traveling the corridors of magic—a brief, but nerve-jolting journey that left Tanis confused and disoriented.

Before they left the Tower of High Sorcery, Dalamar had given Tanis a ring carved from crystal-clear quartz.

"Wear this, my friend, and no one will be able to see you."

"You mean I'll be invisible?" Tanis asked, regarding the ring dubiously, not touching it.

Dalamar slid the ring on Tanis's index finger.

"I mean no one will be able to see you," the dark elf replied. "Except myself."

Tanis didn't understand, then decided that he didn't particularly want to understand. Holding his hand awkwardly, not daring to touch the ring for fear of disrupting the spell, he wished impatiently for the ceremony to begin. The sooner started, the sooner over, and he and Gil would be safely home.

The bright sunlight shone through small windows cut into the tower, reflected off mirrors placed in the shining marble walls. The Heads of Household began to file into the chamber. Several walked over to stand directly in front of Tanis. He stiffened, waiting to be spotted. Elves walked very near him, but none paid any attention to him. Relaxing, Tanis glanced over at Dalamar. He could see the dark elf, and the dark elf could see him, but no one else could. The magic was working.

Tanis searched the crowd.

Dalamar leaned near, spoke softly, "Is your son here?"

Tanis shook his head. He tried to tell himself all was well. It was early. Gil would probably enter with the Thalas-Enthia.

"Remember the plan," Dalamar added unnecessarily. Tanis had thought of nothing but the plan all during a long and sleepless night. "I must make physical contact with him in order to magically transport him. Which means we must reveal ourselves. He will be alarmed, may try to break away. It will be up to you to calm him. We must act quickly. If any elven White Robes should see us—"

"Stop worrying," Tanis said impatiently. "I know what to do."

The chamber filled rapidly. The elves were excited, tense. Rumors sprouted faster than weeds. Tanis heard the name Porthios pronounced several times, more in sorrow than in anger. Whenever Alhana's name was spoken, however, it was generally accompanied with a curse. Porthios obviously was a victim of the seductive Silvanesti woman. The word "witch" was used by several elder elves standing near Tanis.

He stirred restlessly, found it difficult to contain himself. He would have given all his wealth to be able to bang their heads together, knock some sense into these hidebound old fools.

"Easy, my friend," Dalamar warned softly, resting his hand on Tanis's arm. "Do not give us away."

Tanis set his jaw, tried to calm down. An argument erupted on the opposite side of the chamber. Several young elves—who had become Heads of Household on the untimely death of a parent—were in loud disagreement with their elders.

"The winds of change are blowing in the world, bringing new ideas, fresh thoughts. We elves should open our windows, air out our houses, rid ourselves of stale and stagnant ways," one young woman was proclaiming.

Tanis silently applauded these young men and women, but was sorry to note that their numbers were few, their youthful voices easily shouted down.

A silver bell rang once. Silence fell over the assembly. The members of the Thalas-Enthia were arriving. The other elves made way respectfully for the senators. Clad in their robes of state, they formed a circle around the rostrum.

Tanis searched the group for Gil, but could not find him.

A white-robed mage, a member of the Thalas-Enthia, lifted her head. She glanced sharply and with lowered brows around the chamber.

"Damn it to the Abyss," Dalamar muttered, and he plucked Tanis's sleeve. "Watch out for that wizardess, my friend. She senses something's wrong."

Tanis looked alarmed. "Does she see you? Us?"

"No, not yet. I'm like a bad smell to her," Dalamar said. "Just as she is to me."

The White Robe continued to search the crowd, then the silver bell rang out four times. All the elves began to crane their necks, the shorter standing on tiptoe to see over the heads and shoulders of the taller. Their eyes focused on a small alcove adjacent to the central chamber, an alcove Tanis suddenly remembered. In that room, he and his friends had waited until called to the come before old Solostaran, Speaker of the Sun and Stars, Laurana's father, a man who had been foster father to Tanis.

In that alcove, Tanis knew, with a painful constricting of his heart, was his son.

Gilthas entered the chamber.

Tanis forgot their danger, forgot everything in his concern, his astonishment, and—it must be admitted—his pride.

The little boy who had run away from home was gone. In his place walked a young man, with grave and solemn countenance, a young man who stood upright, tall and dignified in the yellow, shimmering robes of the Speaker.

The elves murmured among themselves. They were obviously impressed.

Tanis was impressed. From this distance, his son looked every inch a king.

And then Gilthas stepped into a shaft of brilliant sunlight. The father's loving eye caught the tremor in the young man's clenched jaw, the pallor of the face, his expression, which was carefully and deliberately blank. Rashas and the white-robed elven wizardess both moved to stand beside him.

"That's Gilthas. Let's go."

Hand on his sword, Tanis started forward. Dalamar caught hold of him, dragged him back.

"What now?" Tanis demanded angrily, and then he saw the look on the dark elf's face. "What's wrong?"

"He's wearing the sun medallion," Dalamar said.

"What? Where? I don't see it."

"It's hidden beneath his robes."

"So?" Tanis didn't understand the problem.

"The medallion is a holy artifact, blessed by Paladine. The medallion's power protects him from the likes of me. I dare not touch him."

The dark elf drew near, whispered in Tanis's ear. "I don't like this, my friend. What's Gilthas doing with the sun medallion? Only the Speaker of the Sun and Stars may wear it. Porthios would never give it up voluntarily and, because of its holy properties, the medallion can't be taken from him by force. Something sinister is at work here."

"All the more reason to get Gil out! What do we do now?"

"Your son has to take off the medallion, Tanis. And he must do it of his own free will."

"I'll see to that!" Tanis said, and again started forward.

"No, wait!" Dalamar cautioned. "Patience, my friend. Now is not the time—not with the cursed White Robe standing near him. Let us see what transpires. The proper moment will come. When it does, you must be ready."

The half-elf slowly released his grip on his sword hilt. It was his instinct to act, to do, not to wait around. But Dalamar was right. Now was not the time. Restlessly, Tanis shifted from one foot to the other, forced himself to be patient.

Gilthas had come to stand near the side of the rostrum. He was shorter than the elves around him. He would never be the normal height of an elf—a result of his human bloodline. For a moment, he looked undersized, not very kingly.

Rashas prodded him forward, had his hand on Gil's shoulder.

Gil turned and stared at Rashas coldly.

Smiling, lips tight, Rashas removed his hand.

Turning his back on Rashas, Gilthas walked slowly up to the rostrum. Once he was there, he raised his head and cast one swift, searching, hopeful glance around the room.

"He's looking for me," Tanis said. He had his hand on the ring. "He knows I'll come for him. If he could only see me . . ."

Dalamar shook his head. "He might accidentally give us away."

Tanis watched helplessly and saw his son's hope die.

Gil's head bowed. His shoulders slumped. Then, drawing a deep breath, he raised his head and stared unseeing, with stoic calm, out into the crowd.

Rashas was getting along with business, moving through it hastily, dispensing with all the ritual and ceremonial trappings elves love.

"The situation is grave. Last night, the Qualinesti guards caught an intruder, a Silvanesti spy!"

The elder elves looked suitably shocked and irate. The young ones exchanged glances, shook their heads.

"The spy was captured and will stand trial. But who knows if he is the only one? Who knows but that he might not be the forerunner of an invasion army! Therefore," Rashas was talking loudly, practically shouting, "in the interests of this nation's security, the senate has decided to pursue the only course of action left open to us.

"It is the decision of the Thalas-Enthia that, for crimes against his people, the current Speaker of the Sun and Stars, Porthios of the House of Solostaran, should be stripped of his title. That, further, he shall be exiled, cast out from this land, and from all lands where good men walk."

"We challenge that ruling!" called a loud voice.

The elder elves were horrified, demanded to know who dared to do such a thing. The group of young elves stood together, defiance hardening their faces.

"The Heads of Household had no say in this," continued the young elf, his voice rising over the outraged calls for silence. "And therefore we challenge the ruling."

"This is not a matter for the Heads of Household," said Rashas in icy tones. "By law, the Speaker determines if an elf is to be cast out. In the case where it is the Speaker himself who has committed a serious crime, the Thalas-Enthia is granted power to stand in judgment."

"And who decided Porthios committed a crime?" the young man pursued.

"The Thalas-Enthia," Rashas answered.

"How convenient!" The young man sneered.

His cohorts backed him up. "Put it to a vote of the Heads of Household," several shouted.

"We want to hear from Porthios," a young woman called out. "He should have a right to defend himself."

"He was offered that right," said Rashas smoothly. "We sent word to Silvanesti. Our messenger told the Speaker that he had been brought up on charges of treason and that he should return immediately to answer them. As you see, Porthios is not present. He remains in Silvanesti. He disdains not only these proceedings, but his own people."

"Clever, very clever," Dalamar murmured. "Of course, Rashas fails to mention the fact that Porthios is locked in a prison cell in Silvanesti."

Tanis stood watching the proceedings in grim silence. His fear for his son was growing. Rashas, it seemed, would stop at nothing. Dalamar had been right. The senator was now in the clutches of the Dark Queen.

Rashas was forging ahead, "And here is the supreme mark of the disdain of Porthios for his people. Show them, Prince Gilthas."

Gilthas lifted his head. He appeared to hesitate. Rashas said something to him. Gilthas glanced at the man, loathing and hatred in that glance. Then, slowly, he reached his hand into his yellow robes and drew forth the glittering, golden medallion formed in the image of the sun.

Anger, like a gust of wind, swept through the chamber.

The sun medallion was an ancient, holy artifact, handed down through the centuries from one Speaker to his successor. Tanis had no very clear idea what its powers were. These had long been a well-kept secret among the descendants of Silvanos.

How much did Dalamar know about it? Tanis wondered uneasily. And how he had found out? Not that it mattered. The dark elf was right. Porthios would have never voluntarily relinquished the holy medallion.

The White Robe was whispering in Rashas's ear. Dalamar tensed, but the White Robe was apparently offering advice, not issuing a warning.

"All has been done in accordance with the law," Rashas said, "but, if some of our younger and more inexperienced members request a vote, then we will allow it."

The vote took place. Porthios lost, by a considerable majority. The sun medallion had clinched the matter. In the eyes of the elves, Porthios had renounced his own people. The young elves were the only ones to loyally support the absent Speaker.

Rashas proceeded relentlessly. "Leaderless, we turn to another member of the illustrious lineage of Silvanos. It is my pleasure and honor to present Gilthas, son of Lauralanthalasa, daughter of Solostaran, and the next Speaker of the Sun and Stars."

At a nudge from Rashas, Gilthas bowed to the crowd politely. He was exceedingly pale.

"The Thalas-Enthia has carefully examined the lineage of Prince Gilthas. We find it completely satisfactory."

"What about the fact that his father's a half-human?" One of the younger elves was making a final try.

Rashas smiled benignly. "Surely, in these enlightened times, such a factor should not count against the prince. Don't you agree?"

The young man scowled, unable to answer. He and his cohorts had been neatly caught in their own trap. If they protested against Gilthas further, they would appear as bigoted and rigid as their elders. The young Heads of Household exchanged glances. Then, of one accord, they turned and walked out of the proceedings.

A troubled murmur, like the rumble of thunder, rolled around the chamber. The elves didn't like this. Some appeared to be having second thoughts. Rashas gave instructions to the White Robe and made a gesture. Apparently, she was being ordered to go after the rebellious members. She seemed to remonstrate, but Rashas frowned. His gesture was repeated, this time more forcibly.

The White Robe, with a shake of her head, left the rostrum and hurried out of the chamber.

"Thank you, Takhisis!" Dalamar breathed.

Tanis offered a similar prayer to Paladine.

The two slipped forward, began moving cautiously through the crowd. "Don't bump into anyone!" Dalamar warned. "We may be invisible, but we're not wraiths!"

The elves in the chamber were restless, muttering among themselves.

Rashas saw the situation rapidly deteriorating. Obviously, he had to wrap this up swiftly. He called for silence. The elves gradually settled down, gave him their full attention.

"We will proceed with the Taking of the Vow," he said, casting a sweeping glance around the chamber.

No one said a word in challenge now. Tanis and Dalamar had very nearly reached the rostrum. Gilthas was gripping the rostrum with white-knuckled hands, as if he needed its support to hold him up. He seemed oblivious to what was going on around him. Tanis glided near. He kept fast hold of the magic ring.

Rashas had turned to face Gilthas. "Do you, Gilthas of the House of Solostaran, hereby agree, of your own free will, to take the Vow of the Sun and Stars? To serve your people for the rest of your days as their

Speaker?"

Gil's face was without expression, his eyes lifeless. Moistening parched lips, he opened his mouth.

"No, Son! Stop!" Tanis yanked the ring off.

Gil stared in amazement at his father, who had apparently leapt straight out of nothing.

Tanis grasped hold of his son's arm. "Take off the sun medallion!" he commanded. "Quickly!"

Dalamar appeared on Gil's left. The young man looked dazedly from his father to the dark elf. A babble of confused sound broke out, shouts and cries. Gil's hand closed spasmodically over the medallion.

Rashas, standing next to the young man, said something to him in a low voice.

Tanis ignored the senator. He would deal with him later.

"Gil, take the medallion off," Tanis repeated quietly, patiently. "Don't worry! You'll be safe. I've come to bring you home."

Tanis's words jolted the young man to action, though not the action Tanis wanted.

Gil pulled himself away from his father's grasp. The young man was deathly pale, but his voice was strong.

"You are wrong, Father." Gil glanced at Rashas. "I am already home."

Rashas began calling out loudly for the guards. At the sound of the commotion, the White Robe wizardess ran into the room.

"Quickly, my friend!" Dalamar urged in a low voice. "Unless you want to see a magical battle that will bring this tower down around our ears!"

"Gil, listen to me," Tanis began angrily.

"No, Father, you listen to me." Gilthas was calm. "I know what I'm doing."

"You're a child!" Tanis raged. "You have no idea what you're doing—"

A crimson streak stained Gil's face, as though Tanis had struck him. Wordlessly, he gazed at his father, silently asking for his trust, for his understanding. The medallion—holy artifact of the elves—gleamed on his breast, its bright light reflected in blue eyes.

How many times, when Tanis was a child, had he looked up to see that medallion gleaming above him, like the sun itself, far out of reach?

"Take that damn thing off!" He stretched out his hand.

White light flashed like the sun itself exploding. Pain burned through Tanis's arm, pain terrible enough to burst his heart. He was falling. Strong hands caught him, supported him, and a strong voice was chanting strange words.

He heard, as from a far distance, Gilthas say, "I will take the vow. I will be the Speaker of the Sun and Stars."

Tanis fought to free himself, but the room grew darker, the darkness began to swirl around him, and he realized, in frustrated despair, that he was trapped inside Dalamar's magic.

Chapter Thirteen

The next instant, Tanis was on his hands and knees, kneeling on a grassy lawn, blinking in the bright sunlight. He was dizzy and half sick, his arm ached, and his hand felt useless and numb. Sitting back on his heels, he stared around. Dalamar stood over him.

"Where in the Abyss are we?" Tanis demanded.

"Hush! Keep quiet!" Dalamar ordered in a low voice. "We are outside Rashas's house. Put the ring on! Swiftly. Before someone sees us."

"His house?" Tanis found the ring in a pocket. With his left hand, he struggled to replace the ring on a finger that had no feeling in it. His right arm could move, but it didn't seem to be his arm. "Why did you bring us here?"

"My reasons will soon become apparent. Keep silent and come with me."

Dalamar strode rapidly across the lawn. Tanis hurried to catch up.

"Send me back to that chamber. I'll go alone!"

Dalamar shook his head. "As I told you, my friend, there's something sinister going on here."

When they were in sight of the house, Dalamar halted.

A Wilder elf stood guard, blocking the door.

Putting his hand to the side of his mouth, Dalamar called out, speaking the Kagonesti tongue, "Come quickly! I need you!"

The guard jumped, turned around, and peered into a grove of aspen trees growing in back of the large house.

Cloaked in magic, Dalamar was standing practically in front of the porch, but his voice had come from the grove.

"Hurry, you slug!" Dalamar called again, adding a favorite Kagonesti insult.

The guard left his post, ran toward the aspen grove.

"One of Raistlin's old illusionist tricks. I learned much from my *shalafi*," Dalamar said, and he glided silently inside the house.

Mystified, unable to imagine what the dark elf was after, Tanis followed.

In the entryway, a Kagonesti woman was busily scrubbing at a large stain on one of the elegant carpets. Dalamar pointed to the stain, drawing Tanis's attention to it.

The stain was fresh; the water in the servant's bucket, the rag in her hand, were crimson.

Blood. Tanis's lips formed the word, he did not speak it aloud.

Dalamar did not reply. He was standing at the foot of a flight of stairs, peering upward. He began to climb, motioned to Tanis to accompany him. The servant, unaware of their presence, continued at her task.

Tanis kept his hand on his sword. He was not particularly good at fighting left-handed, but he would at least have the advantage of surprise. No enemy would see him coming.

They crept up the stairs, walking cautiously, testing each board before setting foot upon it. The house was deathly silent; a single creaking board would give them away. The steps proved sturdy and solid, however.

"Only the finest for Senator Rashas," Tanis muttered, and he began to climb more rapidly. He was now beginning to have an idea of why they had come.

Reaching the top of the stairs, Dalamar held up a warding hand. Tanis halted. A door stood open, revealing a spacious hallway. Three doors opened off the hall, one door at the far end and two on each side. Only a single door—the one at the far end—was guarded. Two Kagonesti, holding spears, stood in front of it. Tanis glanced at Dalamar.

"You take the man on the left," said the dark elf. "I'll take the right. Make your attack swift and silent. There are probably more guards inside the room."

Tanis considered using his sword, then decided against it. Positioning himself directly in front of the oblivious Kagonesti, Tanis clenched his fist, aimed a swift, sharp jab to the jaw. The Wilder elf never knew what hit him. Tanis caught the stunned guard as he fell and lowered him silently to the floor. Glancing over, he saw the other Kagonesti asleep on the floor, a scattering of sand over his inert body.

Tanis put his hand on the door handle. Dalamar's thin fingers closed over the half-elf's wrist.

"If what I think is true," Dalamar whispered into Tanis's ear, "any move to open that door could be fatal. Not to us," he added, noting Tanis's look of astonishment. "To the person inside. We will return to the corridors of magic."

Tanis scowled and shook his head. Walking those "corridors" left him feeling disoriented and slightly nauseous. Dalamar smiled in understanding.

"Close your eyes," the dark elf advised. "It helps."

Keeping fast hold of Tanis's wrist, Dalamar spoke quick words. Almost before Tanis had his eyes shut, he felt those same fingers dig into his arm, warning him to look around. Opening his eyes, he blinked in the bright light.

He was in a large sunlit arboretum. Seated on a couch near a window was a woman. Her wrists and ankles were bound together with silken cord. She sat rigidly straight, regal and imperious, her cheeks flushed—not with fear, but with anger. Tanis recognized, with shock, Alhana Starbreeze.

Directly opposite Alhana stood a Kagonesti guard, armed with bow and arrow. The bow was raised, one arrow nocked and ready to fire. The arrow was aimed at Alhana's breast.

"And they exiled *me!*" Dalamar said quietly.

Tanis could say nothing. He could barely think coherently, much less speak. He guessed now what threat had been used to induce Porthios to give up the sun medallion—the same threat that had forced Gilthas to accept it. Horror and outrage, shock and fury, and the dreadful memory of the terrible things he'd said to his son combined to overpower Tanis. He was as numb and useless as his arm. He could do nothing except stand staring in sick and unwilling disbelief.

Dalamar tugged on Tanis's sleeve, gestured at the Kagonesti guard, who stood with his back to them. The dark elf made a motion with a clenched fist.

Tanis nodded to show he understood, though he wondered what Dalamar had in mind. At the first sound they made, the Kagonesti would fire. Even if they managed to kill him, his fingers might spasmodically unleash the arrow.

Alhana sat unmoving on the couch, staring at death with a disdain that seemed to invite it.

Dalamar, invisible to everyone in the room except Tanis, walked over, came to stand directly in front of the Kagonesti. The arrow was now pointed at the dark elf's breast. With a sudden movement, Dalamar grabbed hold of the bow, yanked it away from the guard. Tanis—both fists clenched—clouted the guard on the back of the head. The Kagonesti went down without a sound.

Alhana didn't move, didn't speak. She gazed at the fallen guard in bewilderment. Unable to see either Tanis or Dalamar, it must have looked to her as if the guard had just fought with himself and lost.

Tanis took off his ring. Dalamar threw off his magical cloak.

Alhana shifted her disbelieving gaze to them both.

"Your Majesty," Tanis said, hastening to her side. "Are you all right?"

"Tanis Half-Elven?" Alhana stared dazedly at him.

"Yes, Your Majesty." He touched her hand, let her know he was flesh and blood, and began to untie her bindings. "Did they hurt you?"

"No, I am fine," Alhana said. She rose hurriedly. "Come with me. We have no time to lose. We must stop Rashas . . ."

Her voice died. She had seen the expression on Tanis's face.

"Too late, Your Majesty," he said quietly. "When I left, Gilthas was taking the vow. Before that, the Thalas-Enthia decreed that you and Porthios are to be exiled."

"Exiled," Alhana repeated.

The blood drained from her cheeks, left her as pale as if it had taken her life with it. Her gaze went involuntarily to Dalamar, a dark elf—the personification of her doom. Shuddering, she averted her gaze, put her hand over her eyes.

Dalamar's lip curled. "You have no right to turn your face from me, my lady. Not now."

Alhana flinched. Shivering, she pressed her hand over her mouth and leaned unsteadily on the back of a chair.

"Dalamar—" Tanis began harshly.

"No, Half-Elven," Alhana said softly. "He is right."

Lifting her head, the mass of dark hair falling disheveled around her beautiful face, she held out her hand to him. "Please forgive me, Dalamar. You speak the truth. I am now what you are. You saved my life. Accept my apology and my gratitude."

Dalamar's hands remained folded in the sleeves of his black robes. His face was ice hard with disdain, frozen by bitter memory.

Alhana said nothing. Slowly, her hand lowered.

Dalamar gave a sigh that was like the wind in the leaves of the aspen trees. His black robes rustled. He touched Alhana's fingertips, barely brushing them, as if fearing he might inadvertently do her some harm.

"You are wrong, Alhana Starbreeze," he said quietly. "They may send you from your homeland, term you 'dark elf,' but you will never be what I am. I broke the law. I did it knowingly. I would do it again. They had every right to cast me out."

Pausing, keeping hold of her hand in his, he looked at her intently, spoke earnestly. "I foresee dark days ahead for you, my lady. If you or your child are ever in need of aid or comfort, and you are not afraid to turn to me, I will do whatever is in my power to assist you."

Alhana stared at him wordlessly. Then she smiled, pale, wan. "Thank you for your offer. I am grateful. And, I do not believe that I would be afraid."

"Davat! Where are you?" An angry voice sounded from below. "Why aren't you at your post? You men, over here!"

"It's Rashas," said Tanis, listening. "Probably with more of his Kagonesti slaves."

Dalamar nodded. "I was expecting him. He must have guessed we'd come here. We could make our stand." The dark elf looked at Tanis grimly, expectantly. "Fight them . . ."

"No! There will be no fighting!" Alhana caught hold of Tanis's sword arm, held him back as he would have drawn his blade. "If blood is shed here, all chance for peace is lost!"

Tanis stood irresolute, his sword half in and half out of its sheath. In the rooms below, Rashas could be heard, dispersing his guards, sending them throughout the house.

Alhana's grip tightened. "I am no longer queen. I have no right to command. Therefore, I beg of you . . ."

Tanis was angry, frustrated. He wanted to fight, would have enjoyed nothing more. "After what they did to you, Alhana? You'll meekly let them exile you?"

"If the alternative is killing my own people, yes!" Alhana said calmly.

"Make your decision, Tanis!" Dalamar warned. The footsteps were very near.

"You're too late," Tanis said, thrusting his sword back into its scabbard. "You know that, Alhana. Too late."

She tried to speak, but her words came out as a sigh. Her hand slid nervelessly off Tanis's arm.

"In that case," said Dalamar, "I will take my leave. Do you travel with me, Half-Elven?"

Tanis shook his head.

The dark elf folded his hands in his sleeves. "Farewell, Queen Alhana. Walk with the gods. And do not forget my offer."

He bowed to her respectfully, spoke words of magic, and was gone.

Alhana stared at where he had been standing. "What is happening in this world?" she murmured. "I am betrayed by my friends . . . befriended by my foes . . ."

"Evil times," Tanis replied, voice bitter. "The night returns."

In his vision, the silver moon shone through the storm clouds, its light lasting long enough to illuminate the path, and then was gone, swept away by darkness.

The door burst open. Kagonesti guards ran inside. Two grabbed hold of Tanis by both arms. One guard divested him of his sword; another put a knife to Tanis's throat. Two more started to take hold of Alhana.

"Traitors! Do you dare lay rough hands on me?" she demanded. "Until I cross that border, I am your queen."

The Kagonesti appeared daunted, and they looked at each other uncertainly.

"Leave her be. She will give you no trouble," Rashas ordered. The senator stood in the doorway. "Escort the witch to the Abanasinian border crossing. By order of the Thalas-Enthia, cast her out."

Alhana walked disdainfully past Rashas. She did not look at him, as if he were beneath her notice. The Kagonesti accompanied her.

"You can't send her out into Abanasinia alone, defenseless," Tanis protested angrily.

"I don't intend to," Rashas replied, with a smile. "You, half-human, will accompany her." He glanced around the room, his brow darkening. "Was this man by himself?"

"Yes, Senator," the Kagonesti replied. "The evil mage must have escaped."

Rashas turned his gaze on Tanis. "You conspired with the outlaw wizard known as Dalamar the Dark in an attempt to disrupt the ceremony crowning the rightful Speaker of the Sun and Stars. Therefore, you, known as Tanis Half-Elven, are hereby banished from Qualinesti for life. Such is the law. Do you dispute it?"

"I could dispute it," Tanis said, speaking Common, a language the guards would not understand. "I could mention the fact that I'm not the only person standing in this room who conspired with Dalamar the Dark. I could tell the Thalas-Enthia that Gilthas did not take that vow of his own free will. I could tell them that you are holding Porthios prisoner, his wife hostage. I could tell them all that. But I won't, will I, Senator?"

"No, half-human, you won't," Rashas replied, also in the human tongue, but spitting the words, as if they left a bad taste in his mouth. "You'll keep quiet because I have your son. And it would be a pity for the new Speaker to meet an untimely and tragic end."

"I want to see Gilthas," Tanis said in Elvish. "Damn it, he's my son!"

"If by that name, you mean our new Speaker of the Sun and Stars, may I remind you, half-human, that under elven law the Speaker has no father, no mother, no family ties of any kind. All elves are considered his family. All *true* elves."

Tanis took a step toward Rashas. A tall Wilder elf stepped protectively in front of the senator.

"At this moment, our new Speaker is receiving the accolades of his people," Rashas continued coolly. "This is a great day in his life. Surely, you would not want to ruin it by embarrassing him with your presence?"

Tanis struggled inwardly. The thought of leaving without seeing Gil, without having a chance to tell him he understood, that he was proud of him, was intolerable, heartbreaking. Yet, Tanis knew well enough that Rashas was right. The appearance of his half-breed bastard father would cause only trouble, make things far more difficult for Gil than they were already.

And they would be difficult enough.

Tanis let his shoulders sag. He shrugged bitterly, appeared whipped, beaten.

"Take him to the border," Rashas said.

Tanis started to walk meekly past the senator. Pausing in front of Rashas, Tanis pivoted, rocked forward, and swung his fist. It connected—satisfyingly—with bone.

The senator toppled over backward, crashed into an ornamental tree.

The Kagonesti raised his sword.

"Leave him be," Rashas mumbled, rubbing his jaw. A trickle of blood dribbled from the corner of his mouth. "This is how the servants of evil fight against righteousness. I would not give him the satisfaction of striking back."

The senator spit out a tooth.

Tanis, nursing bruised knuckles, strode out the door.

He'd been wanting to do that for over two hundred years.

Chapter Fourteen

The griffins refused to answer any form of summons from the Qualinesti elves—another fact that gave Tanis grim satisfaction, though it forced him to make the journey to the border on foot. The distance was not far, however, and Tanis had a legion of bitter, unhappy reflections to keep him company.

His thoughts crowded in around him so thick and deep that he took no notice of where he was. He realized they had reached the border only when the Qualinesti captain brought his men to a halt.

"Your sword, sir." The captain handed over the weapon in a courteous manner. "The path leads to Haven one way, to Solace another. If you take the fork to the left—"

"I know the damn path," Tanis told him. Long ago, during the war, he and his companions had taken that path into Qualinesti.

He thrust the sword into its scabbard.

"I was about to advise you, sir, to avoid Darken Wood," the captain added politely.

Tanis, struck by the elf's manner, looked at the captain intently. Was he in agreement with all this? Or was he one of the malcontents? He was young, but then most members of the elven army were young. What did they think about this? Would they back the Thalas-Enthia? . . . On and on, the questions spun their spiderwebs in Tanis's brain.

He would have liked to ask, but could think of no way to frame the question. Besides, other soldiers were listening. He might well get the captain in trouble. Tanis mumbled an ungracious thanks.

The captain saluted gravely, then stood waiting to watch Tanis cross the invisible line which divided the elves from the rest of the world.

Tanis took six steps down the path, six steps that were the longest and most difficult he'd ever taken in his life. Six steps, and he was out of Qualinesti. Though the sun shone brightly, his eyes were blinded by tears and a lowering darkness. He heard the captain give a command and heard the soldiers march off.

Tanis wiped his eyes and nose, looked around, and suddenly recalled he was supposed to meet Alhana Starbreeze at this location.

She was nowhere in sight.

"Hey!" Tanis yelled angrily, taking two long, swift strides back toward the border. "Where is Lady Alhana—"

An arrow zipped out the trees, landed at Tanis's feet. A hairbreadth to the right, and it would have gone through the toe of his boot. He looked up into the trees, but could not see the elven archers. The next arrow, he knew, was aimed at his chest.

"Captain!" he bellowed. "Is this how elves keep their word? I was promised—"

"My friend," came a gentle voice at his shoulder.

Tanis's heart lurched. He whipped around and found Dalamar standing at his side.

"I suppose . . . I should be used to your dramatic appearances by now," Tanis said.

The dark elf smiled. "Actually, I used no magic. I've been waiting for you beside the path for the past hour. You were so intent on your shouting that you did not hear me." He glanced into the leafy branches of the aspen trees. "Let us remove ourselves from this location. I offer a rather tempting target. Not that their puny weapons could hurt me, of course, but I do hate wasting my energy.

"I will answer your questions," he added, seeing Tanis's frown. "We have much to discuss."

Tanis cast the elves a final, baleful glance, then accompanied Dalamar in among giant oak trees that stood on the fringes of Darken Wood, now haunted more in legend than in fact. The shadows were cooling. In a clearing, Dalamar had spread a white cloth. There was wine and bread and cheese. Tanis sat down, drank some wine, but couldn't stomach the food. He kept constant watch on the path.

"I offered Lady Alhana some refreshment before her journey," Dalamar said, with his irritating habit of answering Tanis's thoughts. The dark elf settled himself comfortably on a cushion on the grass.

"She's left then?" Tanis was back on his feet. "Alone?"

"No, my friend. Please, do sit down. I have to strain my neck to look up at you. The lady has a champion, who will accompany her to her destination. Samar is somewhat battered and bloodied, but stalwart and strong for all that."

Tanis stared, mystified.

"The blood we found on the floor belonged to a Silvanesti warrior-mage," Dalamar explained. "Samar tried to help Alhana and your son escape. The warrior was being held in a Qualinesti prison as a spy, facing execution. I snatched him right out from under the nose of that White Robe, who'd been sent to guard him." Dalamar took a sip at his wine. "A most enjoyable experience."

"Where are they going?" Tanis asked, staring into the trees in the direction of the path that could, for Alhana, lead only to darkness.

"Silvanesti," said Dalamar.

Tanis protested. "That's crazy! Doesn't she realize—"

"She realizes, my friend. And I believe we should accompany her. That is why I waited for you. Think a moment, before you refuse. Rashas has looked on the face of rebellion. He knows now that some of his own people may rise up against him. He's afraid. My dread queen loves those who are afraid, Tanis. Her nails are dug into him deeply, and she will continue to drag him down."

"What are you saying?" Tanis demanded.

"Only this—it's bound to occur to Rashas that Porthios is a threat, that exile won't stop him."

"That Porthios mustn't be allowed to live."

"Precisely. We may already be too late," Dalamar added offhandedly, with a shrug.

"You keep saying 'we.' You can't go into Silvanesti. Even with your powers, you'd be hard pressed to fight all the elven magic-users. They'd kill you without hesitation."

"My people won't welcome me home with open arms," Dalamar replied, smiling slyly. "But they can't stop me from entering. You see, my friend, I've been granted permission to visit Silvanesti. For services rendered."

"You don't give a damn about Porthios." Tanis was suddenly angered by the dark elf's coolness. "What's your stake in this?"

Dalamar answered with a sidelong glance. "A high one, you may be certain. But don't expect me to reveal my hand to you. For now, we are partners in this game." He shrugged again. "What will it be, Tanis Half-Elven? In a snap of my fingers, we could be in your home. You will, of course, want to talk to your wife. Tell Laurana what has happened. She will need to accompany us. She will be most valuable in talking sense to that stiff-necked brother of hers."

Home. Tanis sighed. He wanted very much to go home, to shut himself up in his fine house and . . . do what? What was the point now? What was the use?

"When Alhana reaches Silvanesti," Tanis said slowly, thinking this through to its bitter conclusion, "the Silvanesti elves will hear of the insult the Qualinesti offered their queen. That will mean bloodshed. Alhana won't be able to stop it this time. Once, long ago, we elves fought among ourselves. You're talking about starting another Kinslayer War."

Dalamar shrugged, unconcerned. "You are behind the time, Tanis. The war has already started."

Tanis saw the truth of this, saw it with the same vivid clarity he'd seen the vision of Gilthas. Only now, instead of Solinari illuminating the young man's future, Tanis saw it lit by flame and lightning, saw it stained with blood.

The war would come . . . and he would be pitted against his own son.

Tanis closed his eyes. He could see Gil's face, so young, trying so desperately to be brave, wise. . . .

"Father? Is that you?"

For a moment, Tanis thought the voice was in his mind, that the image of his son had conjured it into being. But the word was repeated, stronger, with a ragged edge of joy and longing.

"Father!"

Gilthas stood on the path, just inside the border of Qualinesti. The white-robed wizardess lurked jealously near him. She did not look pleased to see Tanis. She had obviously not expected to find him here. She laid a firm hand on Gilthas's arm, appeared ready to whisk him away.

A rustle in the treetops was a warning, all the warning Tanis was likely to receive.

"Tanis!" Dalamar called. "Be careful!"

Tanis ignored him, ignored the White Robe, ignored the elves in the trees with their bows and arrows. He strode toward his son.

Gilthas jerked away from the wizardess's grasp. She clasped hold of him again, more firmly this time.

An angry flush stained Gilthas's face, but he swallowed hard. Tanis could see his son choke down his anger, could see—in Gilthas—himself. Gilthas said something in a low, conciliatory voice.

The White Robe, still looking displeased, removed her hand and backed off. Tanis stepped across the border. Reaching out, he caught hold of his son in his arms.

"Father!" Gilthas said brokenly. "I thought you'd gone. I wanted to talk to you. They wouldn't let me . . ."

"I know, Son. I know," Tanis said, clasping his boy close. "I understand. Believe me, I understand it all now." Hands on Gil's shoulders, Tanis looked intently into his son's face. "I do understand."

Gil's face darkened. "Is Queen Alhana safe? Rashas assured me that she was, but I made them bring me here to see for myself . . ."

"She is safe," Tanis said quietly. His gaze shifted to the White Robe, who stood to one side, her baleful gaze divided between her charge and the black-robed wizard hovering in the shadows. "Samar is with the queen. He will guard her well, as you have reason to know, I believe."

"Samar!" Gil's face brightened. "You rescued him? I'm so glad! They were going to make me sign the order for his execution. I wouldn't have done it, Father. I don't know how"—the youthful face hardened—"but I wouldn't have."

Tanis glanced at the White Robe. Dalamar could stop her from taking any action. But could he, at the same time, prevent the archers from shooting? They would, however, be reluctant to endanger the life of their new Speaker . . .

"Gil," Tanis spoke in Common, "you didn't take that vow of your own free will. You were coerced into making it. You could leave, now. Dalamar will help us . . ."

Gilthas bowed his head. There was no doubt what answer he wanted to give. He looked up with a wistful smile. "I gave the wizardess my word, Father. When I found you here, I promised her I would return with her, if she would grant me permission to . . . to . . . tell you good-bye."

His voice broke. He paused a moment, struggling, then continued quietly, "Father, I heard you once tell Lord Gunthar that, if it had been up to you, you would have never, of your own free will, fought in the War of the Lance. You were drawn into it by force of circumstance. And that was why it made you uneasy to hear people call you a hero. You did what you had to do—what any right-thinking person would do."

Tanis sighed. Memories—mostly dark—came back to him. His grip on Gilthas tightened. Tanis knew that, in a moment, he would have to let his son go.

"Father," Gil said earnestly, "I'm not fooling myself. I know I won't be able to do much to change things. I know Rashas intends to use me for his own evil ends and, right now, I don't see any way of stopping him. But, do you remember what Uncle Tas said when he told the story about saving the gully dwarf from the red dragon? 'It's the small things that make the difference.' If I can manage, in small ways, to work against Rashas, Father . . ."

We raise our children to leave us.

Without even knowing it, Tanis had done so. He could see that now, could see it in the face of the boy—no, the man—standing in front of him. He supposed he should feel proud . . . and he did. But pride was a very small fire to warm his heart-numbing chill of loss.

The White Robe was clearly growing impatient. She removed from her belt a jeweled silver wand.

Dalamar, seeing this, called out quietly, "Tanis, my friend, I am here, if you have need of my services."

Tanis embraced his son one last time. He took advantage of their closeness to whisper. "You are the Speaker now, Gilthas. Don't forget that. Don't let Rashas and his kind forget it. Keep fighting him. You won't fight alone. You saw the young elves who walked out of the meeting today? Win them to your side. They won't trust you at first. They'll think your Rashas's pawn. You'll have to convince them otherwise. It won't be easy. But I know you can succeed. I'm proud of you, my son. Proud of what you did this day."

"Thank you, Father."

A last embrace, a last look, a last brave smile.

"Tell Mother . . . I love her," Gil said softly.

He swallowed hard. Then, turning, he left his father and went back to stand beside the White Robe. She spoke a word.

The two were gone.

Without a backward glance—Tanis couldn't have seen anything anyway, blinking away the tears that blinded him—he walked back across the border. But he held his head high, as would any proud father whose son has just been made ruler of a nation.

He'd keep his head high until night, until darkness. Until he was home. Until he had to tell Laurana that she might never see her beloved son again. . . .

"So," said Dalamar, keeping in the shadows beneath the oak trees, "you couldn't talk Gilthas into coming back with you."

"I didn't try," Tanis returned, his voice harsh and grating. "He gave them his word of honor he'd go back."

Dalamar regarded his friend intently a moment. "He gave them his word. . . ."

The dark elf shook his head and sighed. "As I said before, the son of Tanis Half-Elven is the last person Takhisis wanted to see sitting on the elven throne. If it is any comfort, my friend, Her Dark Majesty did not mean things to turn out exactly as they did. She is extremely sorry that we failed."

Tanis supposed that news should bring him some consolation.

Dalamar removed the cloth, the cushion, the wine, the bread, and the cheese with a wave and a word. He slid his hands into the sleeves of his black robes.

"Well, my friend, have you made a decision? What will you do?"

"What I have to do, I suppose," Tanis said bitterly. "I can't let Rashas murder Porthios. And, once Porthios is free, I've got to stop him from murdering Rashas and the rest of the Qualinesti—none of which looks very promising."

He walked out from beneath the oak trees and came to stand on the path that led back to Qualinesti. He looked into the sunlit, quivering leaves of the aspen trees of his childhood home.

"There are so many things I meant to teach you, Gilthas," Tanis said softly, "so much I meant to tell you. So many things I meant to say. . . ."

Dalamar rested his hand on Tanis's shoulder. "You may not have said the words aloud, my friend. But I think your son heard you."

Tanis turned away from Qualinesti, turned toward the path that led to darkness. He turned back to a house that, no matter how many people it held, would always be empty.

"Let's go," he said.

Epilogue

A prospect of birds
in the cancelling winter,
first fables of prophets
and roses and swords,
Margaret believed in us all,
believed in our stories:
a patient astronomer
drawn by a gap in the sky
who knows from a thousand years' calculation
that the next star is coming
that all that remains
is the waiting and prayer
and the long tiring business
of notebook and telescope,
until the brightness
consumes the dark,
a brightness conceived
and cradled for centuries,
she can say *this is something*
I have always expected
this is the harvest of years

And then when she speaks
the heavens remember
that she was the one
bearing money and flowers
and trips to the city,
incandescence of fireworks
when we gathered in dozens
on the summer nights
by the vanishing lake,
and most of all words
she brought us
arrayed like galaxies
into the forms of belief.

At home by the lake
she began the story,
building word after difficult word
until in the telling the world appeared,
until in the waters the stars came down,
and all of the planets
the heavens encircle—

Chislev and Zivilyn,
Raistlin and Caramon,
Palin and Tanin,
Raoul and the little one,
the trining moons
that herald the tides of her magic,
all in the choir of her memory,
where the voice of love
moved on the water
and sang in attendance
as the story rose out
of the lake and the midnight,
the attar of roses
on the farthest shore,
and the winter reverted
to incredible spring
as it always reverts,
and the snow and the spirits
went where they wish
in the lands of belief
as the story begins again.

Appendix

Song of Huma

Tales of Huma, the ancient and almost mythical heroic Knight of Solamnia, have inspired many performance pieces over the centuries. No two pieces agree on the details of his history, and many were written in support of various personal causes.

This song is one of the oldest known on Krynn, and was written only a few years after the disappearance of Huma at the conclusion of the Dragon War. Despite the fact that it undoubtedly was created by those who knew Huma, the text of the song—more appropriately called a hymn—is completely lacking in any helpful details about Huma's life.

The spelling of the name with an "h" appended is intended to honor the sound of his name when sung.

Song of Huma

♩= 95 *Maestoso Deciso*

Words & Music by
Tracy Hickman

Dra — co Hum — mah co ni par ai fam Sa at mas So — lam — nis
13
molt. rit.
ff
a tempo
veg — ri nogh Co - ni Est Lor Tar — i — kan!
Hu — mah Su — lar — us Hum —
ff
p
16
Kar ram Hu mah!
Sol — am nis hu ma dur vey!
mah!
So lam nis Hu mah dur — vey!
mp
19
mf
f
Kar — am nes Hu ma dur — vey!
Karam nes Hu ma dur — vey!
Mi thas!
mf
f
23

poco accel.
ff
Hu- mah dix kar— ai Ex dix! O — par — ru est dix!
ff
27
Hu — mah — kar — am Su — lar — us! —
So — lam — nis Lor A — lan Pa — la — dine!
30
Allegro
ff
mp
Hu ma mi thas Hu – mah mi - thas Est mi - thas — ah!
mp
ff
33
molto rit.
fff
Dra — co Hu — mah dur — vey!
fff
37

Knights of Takhisis
Dark Warriors

Many readers who love the novels of the DRAGONLANCE® saga go on to live the adventure by playing Ansalonian characters in the ADVANCED DUNGEONS & DRAGONS® role-playing game. The following expansion of existing campaign rules provides players yet another option for their gaming.

The Knights of Takhisis are a new nonplayer character (NPC) class in the DRAGONLANCE world of Ansalon. Nonexistent during the War of the Lance, these lawful evil knights were formed some twenty years after the downfall of Neraka, when the Queen of Darkness was banished back to the Abyss. The knights are an emerging and cohesive force of order and darkness in a world still reeling from years of war. What does their emergence mean for the forces of freedom in a shattered world?

Game Statistics

Characters must meet the basic warrior ability requirements in order to qualify for any of the orders of the Knights of Takhisis. (See the AD&D® 2nd Edition Players Handbook.) All characters start in the Order of the Lily and may progress to other orders later if they so choose.

All beginning characters of this class start with a patron (Lily), sponsor (Skull), or mentor (Thorn). This is an elder NPC who has brought the new character into the order. Knights of Takhisis never just "sign up" or enlist. They must always be sponsored by an older knight (7th level or higher) of any of the three orders.

This NPC becomes guarantor and advocate for the character. The advocate's commands and judgments are the final law and always unquestionably obeyed. It is the responsibility of the advocate to forward the advancement of the character in the knighthood—or to kill the character who is disobedient.

The advocate assumes the role of parent, judge, executioner, and, depending on the relationship, occasionally lover. Regardless of the relationship, the NPC will hunt down and destroy the character without compassion if he or she shows the least sign of disobedience to the order. To do otherwise would bring death on the advocate from his or her own sponsor.

As with the Knights of Solamnia, women may enter the ranks of the Knights of Takhisis. One of the most renowned leaders during the War of the Lance was Dragon Highlord Kitiara Uth Matar, and despite the fact that she was, in large part, responsible for the death of Lord Ariakan's father, Kitiara is celebrated as one of the heroes of the knights, for her courage and daring in battle. Women may enter any order without restriction and may rise as high as their own abilities take them.

Class Ability Requirements

Class	Str	Dex	Con	Int	Wis	Cha
Knight of Takhisis	14	12	10	–	13	–

Racial Class Limitations

Race	Subrace	Level Limitation
Human		Unlimited
Kender		NA
Gnomes		NA
Elves	Dark	Unlimited
	Qualinesti	NA
	Silvanesti	NA
	Kagonesti	NA
	Dimernesti/Dargonesti	NA
	Half Elves	14th Level
Dwarves	Fatherless	Unlimited*
	Hill Dwarves	NA
	Mountain Dwarves	NA
	Gully Dwarves	NA
Irda		NA
Minotaurs		Unlimited

*Cannot become Knights of the Thorn

History

The capture and subsequent imprisonment of Ariakan, son of the powerful Dragon Highlord Ariakas and—so it is rumored—the sea goddess Zeboim, was one of the best-kept secrets of the War of the Lance. His very existence was not even suspected by the forces of the west until the fall of the Temple of Neraka.

Solamnic Knights discovered the young man during the occupation of the evil temple. He had been hiding in one of the lower levels of the temple, his father having left his son under the protection of a large draconian force led by nine of Lord Ariakan's most trusted lieutenants. In the fierce battle that ensued, the young man did not accept the mercy that was offered him, but refused to surrender. He fought bravely and skillfully, killing five of the Solamnic Knights in combat before being forcibly subdued.

On his capture, Ariakan made no secret of his lineage, revealing his parentage proudly. Although the knights did not believe the bold youth, they were impressed by his obvious skill, courage, and intelligence. The fact that he was being guarded by such a strong force indicated he was someone in whom the late Dragon Highlord took an interest. The knights removed Ariakan to the High Clerist's Tower for holding and questioning. At length, they credited his story and realized what a valuable prisoner had fallen into their hands. Ariakan was to remain their prisoner for more than six years.

During this time, Ariakan learned all that he could about the structure, organization, and mentality of the Solamnic Knights. A personable youth, handsome and charming, he soon won both the favor and admiration of his captors. The knights were, of course, eager to indoctrinate him in the Oath and the Measure, believing that such a course of study would benefit the young man and teach him the error of his ways. The error, however, was on the part of the knights.

Ariakan studied the knighthood as any warrior would study his enemy—in detail. It was only a matter of time before he knew all the right things to say that would convince the knights of his total rehabilitation and conversion. Indeed, after two years, he was given an early release from the High Clerist's Tower, but he asked to stay and finish his studies. His request was happily granted.

It has been rumored that the knights actually considered offering Ariakan knighthood. Everyone now denies it, of course, but the lord knights all fall noticeably silent when the subject is broached. If knighthood was offered to Ariakan, he most politely and graciously refused. At the end of six years, having learned all he could from the knights, he offered his farewells.

Many among the knighthood were sorry to see him go, for Ariakan was a charming companion, a knowledgeable scholar, and an excellent fighter. Only after he had left the knights did it occur to them that—during all the time he was with them—he had been careful never to actually proclaim any true allegiance, swear any vow, take any oath.

Ariakan was in his mid-twenties when he rode out onto the Solamnic Plain. He had an escort—knights bound for other parts of the realm—but he soon managed to divest himself of his unwanted companions. Immersed in their own affairs, attempting to put back together a country shattered by war, the Solamnic Knights made only a halfhearted attempt to locate Ariakan, but to no avail. He had led them to believe he was going to enter the mercenary line of work and, though they considered this a lowly occupation, they agreed that he must be off in some realm, selling his sword to earn his living.

Ariakan had no thought of selling his sword. He had learned much more from the knights than just their culture, tradition, and history. Using the skills the knights had taught him, he eluded their watch and slipped back across the plains. Amidst a raging blizzard, he climbed the forbidding mountains of Neraka.

He soon lost his way. Frozen and starving, he would undoubtedly perish without help. He collapsed in a snowdrift and, with his last breath, prayed to his mother, Zeboim, for aid.

He had no more than ended his prayer when he saw, in the snow before him, a seashell. Accepting this as a sign from his goddess mother, Ariakan struggled to his feet. A trail of seashells led him to a cavern. Here he found shelter against the storm, a cache of food, and dry wood for a fire. He ate and, exhausted, soon fell fast asleep.

He woke from a sound sleep to find a warrior, clad all in shining black armor, seated near the fire. Ariakan did not fear the warrior; the man seemed familiar to him, and he thought deep in his heart that this might be some manifestation of his dead father. The warrior spoke with Ariakan, encouraged him to relate his experiences.

Ariakan spoke in admiration of the discipline and training of the Solamnic knighthood. He explained how they had achieved victory over the forces of darkness through their willingness to sacrifice themselves for the good of the cause.

"We are our own worst enemy," he told the dark warrior. "Each commander in our armies was out for his or her own personal gain. Our troops lacked discipline because their leaders lacked discipline. Our soldiers had no respect for their commanders. Our commanders had no respect for each other. The Knights of Solamnia refer to this as 'evil feeding upon itself' and have proclaimed that this is an inherent trait of all evil beings. Such disorder, lack of discipline and loyalty, would always bring us to defeat."

"And what do you propose to do about this?" the dark warrior demanded.

Ariakan was somewhat daunted, but he went on to tell of his dream—a holy mission that would be his life's work. He wanted to form an order of knights that would rival and eventually supplant the Solamnic Knights as the dominant force for order in the world.

It was then that the dark warrior revealed herself—a vision of Takhisis from the Abyss. Though she was not pleased by such a blunt description of her own failings, she was wise enough to listen to Ariakan's proposal and give serious thought to it.

Takhisis ordered him to continue.

Awed, Ariakan poured out his heart and soul to his queen. He had witnessed the strengths of the Solamnic Knights—and also their failings.

"We must not be like the giant oak trees, which do not bend and are often toppled at the roots. We must not be stone, which never yields but can be broken and is worn away by the elements. We must not be water, which yields too easily and follows every path.

"My knights," Ariakan said, "will be like the ironwood trees. The strong trunks are impervious to blows, yet the branches sway with the wind. Such trees live forever—they maintain their strength while yielding sufficiently to the ways of the world in order to survive.

"The keys to victory," Ariakan maintained, "are order, discipline, and vision. Bring order to our followers, and they will accomplish. Discipline them, and they will achieve. Give them the vision, and they will move forward toward a common goal."

Takhisis was pleased with Ariakan and granted him her blessing.

So began the recruiting. Cautiously, carefully, Ariakan began building the knighthood.

He proclaimed as the foundations of the Knights of Takhisis the Vision, the Blood Oath, and the Code.

The Vision, the Blood Oath, and the Code

The Vision is—in simple terms—a statement of the ultimate goal of the knighthood. For knights of the warrior rank or less (5th level or below), the Vision is embodied in the phrase: "One World Order." The goal is no less than the total and unquestioned domination of the entire world of Krynn. The Blood Oath and the Code are established to work toward that end.

When knights moving beyond warrior rank have passed the Test of Takhisis (see *Tests of Takhisis*), part of the ceremony for investment is the Deep Vision—a magical impression on the knight's mind of the will of Takhisis and the goals of the knighthood. Experienced after four days of fasting and prayer to the Dark Queen, the Vision gives the knight a clear understanding of the goals of the knighthood and the knight's own place in the grand plan.

The Blood Oath is simple: "Submit or die." When joining the knighthood, each knight dedicates body and soul utterly to the cause. All thoughts of self are submerged, sublimated. Yet this does not mean that knights may not think for themselves, which brought about the creation of the Code.

The Code is complex in the extreme, yet elegant in its detail. The strict, unyielding exactitude of the Solamnic Knights' "Oath and Measure" had caused their long fall from the Age of Might, ending in their continuing weakness. Despite the fact that the knights and other forces for good had emerged victorious, they were a long way from bringing peace and order to Ansalon.

Knowing the weaknesses of all mortal creatures, Ariakan crafted a detailed set of laws that relate principally to military situations, but that also can be extended into the lives of each member of the knighthood. Strict adherence to the Code is required, but each case is considered on its own merits, and exceptions can be made.

The Knights of Solamnia hold knightly councils to consider changes or alterations in their Measure. Having sat through many of these council meetings, Ariakan determined them to be a waste of time, spent in endless arguing and bickering over trivial points of law and honor. Ariakan established his Code so that there would be no need to argue fine points. The law was as written. Violations were obvious and dealt with summarily.

However, he did recognize the need to be flexible, as occasion demanded, and so established a means by which an exception to the Code might be considered and either accepted or rejected on its own merits.

Exceptions to the Code are adjudicated by a single knight selected from a chosen few in command positions. The role of adjudicator is generally reserved for knights of 12th level or higher. (Occasionally those of less than 12th level are granted the right, but that would be up to Lord Ariakan. Many of higher rank are not, including most of the Knights of Thorns.) The outward, visible sign of an adjudicator is a scepter, presented to the knight by Lord Ariakan himself.

If the adjudicator decides that the Code has been broken and that no exception to the Code may be permitted, punishment is meted out to the offender. Since a knight who violates the Code is seen to have also violated the Vision and broken the Blood Oath. The punishment is generally death.

Unlike the Solamnic Knights, the Knights of Takhisis are permitted to lie, steal, or commit murder, but *only* if such acts can be proven to advance the Vision and are not committed for personal gain or through loss of self-control. Thus, Knights of Takhisis do not "rape, pillage, and plunder." Such acts are seen as adverse to the advancement of the Vision, which is to establish an ordered world, free of chaos.

Execution is carried out by the advocate, if that knight is present, or by the knight's commander if the advocate is not. The knights do not view death as the ultimate end, but rather as advancement to a higher rank. Takhisis is the final judge of a knight's life, and the knight is rewarded by Her Dark Majesty or punished eternally as she decides. The knight does not fear death, therefore, but could have reason to fear the wrath of the queen in the afterlife. A knight who wishes to appeal the ruling of the adjudicator may do so. Once his soul is dispatched to Takhisis, she will hear the plea.

The Dark Queen has been known to send knights wrongfully judged back to "correct the error." Such undead knights are known as revenants. (Refer to *Monstrous Manual*, page 302.) Because of this, all adjudicators will want to be extremely sure of the facts and will order a knight's execution only after serious prayer and consideration.

Part of the Code deals specifically with the establishment and maintenance of lines of communication and authority. Thus, when an order is given from above, it is quickly dispatched and acted on. But Ariakan knew that the knights probably would find themselves in situations where they would be on their own, cut off from the chain of command. Therefore, major sections of the Code are devoted to acting on the Vision. When communication with the knighthood is severed, individuals who have a clear concept of the Vision will act independently to carry out the will of the knighthood until such time as communication can be reestablished. In this way, order is maintained in times of chaos.

Even within the bounds of orders as given, the knights have broad discretion as to how these orders are carried out. As long as a knight's actions do not violate the Vision, the standing orders of their knighthood, or the specific orders that they have been given, a knight is free to act.

The Code is divided into several basic precepts, which guide the three major orders of knighthood:

The Lily: Independence breeds chaos. Submit and be strong.
The Skull: Death is patient. It flows both from without and from within. Be vigilant in all and skeptical of all.
The Thorn: One who follows the heart finds it will bleed. Feel nothing but victory.

These divisions of the Code lead to the natural specialization of the knights and help to define the duties of the knights in the new world that they propose to create.

Organization of the Knights

The Order of Battle for the Knights of Takhisis is as follows:

Division	Complement	Officers, Numbers (Level)
Talon	9 Knights of various types	1 (6th), 1 (3rd)
Wing	5 Talons (45 knights)	1 (7th), 3 (6th)
Compgroup	7 Wings (350 knights)	1 (8th), 3 (7th)
Shield	5 Companies (1,575)+support	1 (10th), 3 (9th)
Quadron	4 Battalions (6,300)+support	1 (12th), 3 (11th)
Army	7 Regiments (44,100)+support	1 (14th)

Knights are primarily organized at the Compgroup level, each Compgroup consisting of approximately 350 persons. While individual Compgroups may have different organizations, the following chart is typical.

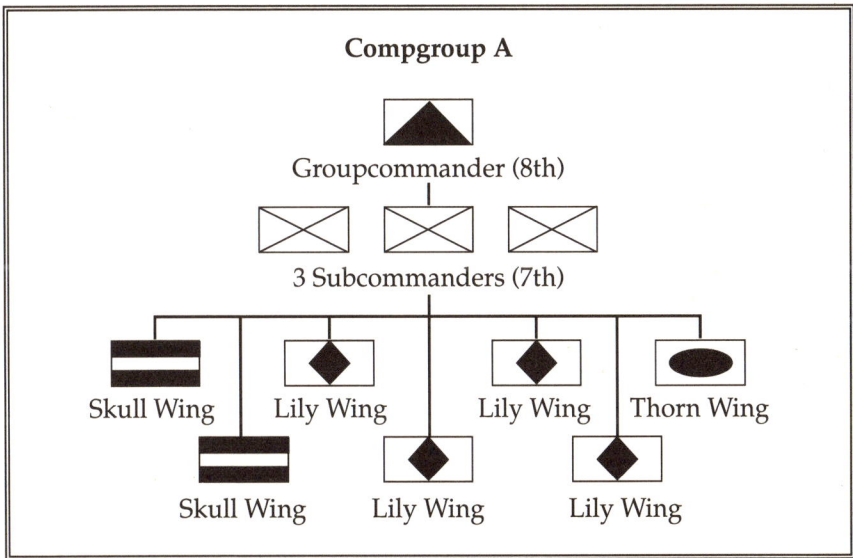

Compgroup A

Groupcommander (8th)

3 Subcommanders (7th)

Skull Wing   Lily Wing   Lily Wing   Thorn Wing

Skull Wing   Lily Wing   Lily Wing

Note that Wings composed primarily of Knights of the Skull work side-by-side with ranks of Lily Knights and Thorn Knight sorcerers. It is this organizational cooperation that makes the knighthood such a deadly and efficient fighting force.

Knights of the Lily

As with the Knights of Solamnia, any who would enter into the Knights of Takhisis must begin as a Petitioner (1st level) in the Order of the Lily. All Knights of Takhisis remain under the Order of the Lily until they attain the rank of Warrior and are ready to advance to Novice (from 5th level to 6th level). At this level, knights may choose entry into either Skull or Thorn, or remain with the Lilies.

The Knights of the Lily are the military might of the knighthood and the center of political power as well. The Order of the Skull and the Order of the Thorn are separate, with their own particular skills and areas of responsibility. While it may look to an outsider as if the Knights of the Lily are the dominant force in the knighthood, all three orders provide necessary functions and are considered equal in power and authority, differing only in jurisdiction and function.

Knights of the Lily Levels

Level	Experience Points	Hit Dice (d10)	Title (Lily/Fighters)
1	2,500	2	Petitioner
2	5,000	3	Supplicant
3	10,000	4	Follower
4	18,500	5	Believer
5	37,000	6	Warrior
6	85,000	7	Novice of Night
7	140,000	8	Night Acolyte
8	220,000	9	Night Warrior
9	300,000	10	Black Bard
10	600,000	11	Dark Wanderer
11	900,000	12	Dark Warrior
12	1,200,000	12+1	Warrior of the Lily
13	1,500,000	12+2	Master of the Lily
14	1,800,000	12+3	Champion of the Lily
15	2,100,000	12+4	Master of the Lily (147 only)
16	2,400,000	12+5	Protector of the Lily (21 only)
17	2,700,000	12+6	Lord of the Lily (7 only)
18	3,000,000	12+7	Lord of Night (1 only)

Tests of Takhisis

For all orders, continuation past the rank of Warrior (5th level) requires that the knight pass of a test of loyalty. Just as the wizards on Krynn must pass the dread Test of the Towers of High Sorcery, so, too, must all the Knights of the Lily pass a similar test in order to advance. Failure in this test results in death. There has never been a case where a failed knight has survived. Even if a knight manages to escape, the members of all three orders use their powers to track the knight down.

The test for the Knights of the Lily generally centers around the three themes of Vision, Order, and Obedience. The test is every bit as difficult as the Test in the Tower of High Sorcery. Typical problems posed are: Will the knight sacrifice whatever is necessary—power, fortune, a loved companion, life itself—in order to fulfill the Vision? Will order and obedience win out over sentiment and the heart? Will the knight obey an order at the sacrifice of the knight's own life or the lives of kin or loved ones?

As in the tower, the test may be an illusion, though the tested knights truly believe that what they are undergoing is real. Or, in some instances, the knights may be sent on missions or quests designed to prove their worthiness. The test is dangerous and often cruel in the extreme, but those who pass are as strong as steel forged in the fires of Neraka.

The nature of the test is determined by the knight's advocate—the one person who knows the knight best. The advocate understands and appreciates the fact that a knight must be strong in order to fulfill the Vision. There can be no weak links in the chain. Therefore, the test is never made easy for the supplicant. Quite the contrary, no advocate wants to be known as the sponsor of a weak and ineffective knight, and, therefore, the test is designed to be as difficult as possible.

Knights who pass the test are free to choose the order they wish to enter. Often this is the order of their advocate, but this need not strictly be the case. The ascension of the knight into the next order takes place in a solemn ceremony at the knighthood's headquarters, in the hidden northern fortress known as Storm's Keep.

The knight is kept in seclusion in the Temple of Takhisis, fasting and praying, for four days prior to the ceremony. At the end of this period, during which the knight receives the Deep Vision, the knight is blessed by dark clerics and sent forth. The knight comes before the rank and file of knights (all those currently in residence), including Lord Ariakan himself. The Procession of Knights is enacted. The knight is formally presented by his advocate. The advancement in rank is bestowed upon the knight by Lord Ariakan, and the knight is officially accepted into the order of choice.

The knight then undergoes a period of training of about six months. This grueling instruction generally takes place in Storm's Keep, but occasionally extends into other regions if the training specifically requires. Only after this training is the knight considered a full member of the order.

Knights of the Skull

These Knights form the clerical order of the knighthood. They practice the healing arts and are also in charge of both external intelligence and internal security.

Skull Knights work their art by stealth and subtlety rather than by force, leaving that to the other two orders.

Knights of the Skull are dedicated solely to Takhisis, to the exclusion of all other gods and goddesses (including other dark deities). Her Dark Majesty rewards such loyalty by renewing their spells on a daily basis, in a manner similar to other clerics. This is unlike the Knights of Solamnia, who must fast and pray to attain their spells.

Although it is well known that the sea goddess Zeboim favors the knighthood (in honor of her son, Ariakan), the Skull Knights do not pray to her. Ariakan sets aside one day a year in honor to his mother. It is considered a matter of courtesy for all knights to ask the goddess Zeboim's blessing during a sea voyage.

Knights of the Skull may advance through the ranks as high as 14th level before they must vie for a position among the lord knights. (See *Order of Lords*).

Knights of the Skull Levels

Level	Experience Points	Hit Dice* (d8)	Title (Skull/Priests)
6	85,000	1	Bone Novice
7	140,000	2+1	Bone Acolyte
8	220,000	3+1	Bone Warrior
9	300,000	4+2	Skull Abbot
10	600,000	5+2	Skull Bishop
11	900,000	6+3	Skull Cardinal
12	1,200,000	7+3	Skull Knight
13	1,500,000	7+4	Skull Paladin
14	1,800,000	7+5	Skull Champion
15	2,100,000	7+6	Master of the Skull (147 only)
16	2,400,000	7+7	Protector of the Skull (21 only)
17	2,700,000	7+8	Lord of the Skull (7 only)
18	3,000,000	7+9	Lord of Night (1 only)

*These dice rolls are *in addition* to the hit points already accumulated from the 6d10 rolled so far. Thus, if a Knight of the Skull had previous total hit points of 32 (from 6d10), the new Skull Knight would now roll an additional d8 for further hit points. If the result is 6, the new Blood Novice would now have 38 hit points.

Knights of the Skull Priest Spells per Level

Cleric Level	Title	1	2	3	4	5	6	7
6	Bone Novice	1						
7	Bone Acolyte	2						
8	Bone Warrior	2	1					
9	Skull Abbot	3	2					
10	Skull Bishop	4	2					
11	Skull Cardinal	4	2	1				
12	Skull Knight	5	3	1	1			
13	Skull Paladin	6	4	1	1	1		
14	Skull Champion	7	5	2	1	1	1	
15	Master of the Skull (147 only)	8	6	3	2	1	1	1
16	Protector of the Skull (21 only)	9	7	3	2	1	1	1
17	Lord of the Skull (7 only)	9	8	4	3	3	2	1
18	Lord of Night (1 only)	9	9	5	4	3	2	1

The "Spells per Level" columns (1 2 3 4 5 6 7) are headed by **Spells per Level**.

Knights of the Thorn

Knights of the Thorn are an order of wizards. They operate completely outside the Towers of High Sorcery on Ansalon, refuse to swear any allegiance to any of the three robes, including black, and are therefore considered renegade wizards by all members of the conclave.

Unlike the wizards of the conclave, the Gray Robe Knights, as they are known, work with dark priests—Knights of the Skull—in maintaining order both in conquered lands and their own home territories. The Thorn Knights are of a special type. They may not wear armor while casting spells, and reduce their weapon proficiencies to those available to wizards (they may still use weapons they have been proficient in earlier, such as swords). Their THAC0 is either as a wizard or 5th-level fighter, whichever is better.

Knights of the Thorn Levels

Level	Experience Points	Hit Dice (d4)*	Title (Thorn/Mages)
6	85,000	1	Blood Novice
7	140,000	2+1	Blood Acolyte
8	220,000	3+1	Blood Apprentice
9	300,000	4+2	Thorn Apprentice
10	600,000	5+2	Sorcerer
11	900,000	6+3	Wizard
12	1,200,000	7+3	Seer
13	1,500,000	7+4	Master
14	1,800,000	7+5	Nightlord
15	2,100,000	7+6	Master of the Thorn (147 only)
16	2,400,000	7+7	Protector of the Thorn (21 only)
17	2,700,000	7+8	Lord of Thorns (7 only)
18	3,000,000	7+9	Lord of Night (1 only)

*These dice rolls are *in addition* to the hit points already accumulated from the 6d10 rolled so far. Thus, if a new Knight of the Thorn had previous total hit points of 32 (from 6d10), the new Thorn Knight would now roll an additional d4 for further hit points. If the result is 3, then the new Blood Novice would now have 35 hit points.

Knights of the Thorn Wizard Spells per Level

Level	Title	Spells per Level								
		1	2	3	4	5	6	7	8	9
6	Blood Novice	3	2	1						
7	Blood Acolyte	4	3	1						
8	Blood Apprentice	3	3	2	1					
9	Thorn Apprentice	4	3	2	1	1				
10	Sorcerer	4	4	3	2	1	1			
11	Wizard	4	4	3	2	2	2	1		
12	Seer	5	4	4	3	3	2	1		
13	Master	5	4	4	3	3	3	1	1	
14	Nightlord	5	5	4	4	4	3	2	1	
15	Master of the Thorn (147 only)	5	5	5	4	4	3	2	2	
16	Protector of the Thorn (21 only)	5	5	5	5	4	3	2	2	1
17	Lord of Thorns (7 only)	5	5	5	5	5	4	3	2	2
18	Lord of Night (1 only)	5	5	5	5	5	4	3	3	3

Thorn Knights and the Moons of Krynn

The sorcerer Knights of the Thorn have their own schools of magic. They wear gray or black robes and have no relationship to the Black Robes of the Towers of High Sorcery.

Unlike the orders of the towers, the knights draw on the power of all three of Krynn's moons as the source of their magic, rather than from one moon. This grants a far more powerful magical edge to Thorn Knights. Just how they have accomplished this feat remains unknown to the conclave. It is not surprising that the robed wizards of Ansalon are extremely disturbed by the appearance of this new and powerful order of sorcery in the world. They view it as a distinct threat to themselves, and wizards of all robes are exerting all their efforts to both study it and eradicate it.

Moon Phase Effects

Moon Phase	Saving Throw	Additional Spells	Effective Level
Low Sanction	−1	0	Even
Waning	Normal	+1	Even
Waxing	+1	+2	+1
High Sanction	+2	+3	+2
Any two moons aligned	+2	+3	+2
All three moons aligned	+3	+4	+2

Saving throw adjustments apply to all required saving throws.

Additional spells may be of any level that the wizard is capable of casting.

Effective level refers to the level of the sorcerer for purposes of determining spell ranges and powers. *Only a knight of at least 8th level who has an intelligence of 15 or greater gains this benefit from the moons.*

Utilize the system detailed in the Wizard Group section of the *Tales of the Lance* boxed set for determining the location of the moons and tracking their movement.

Order of Lords

In all classes of the knighthood, once characters have reached 14th level they have the opportunity to enter into the Order of Lords. There are a limited number of lord positions, and in order for a character to rise a level, a vacancy must already exist within the order the candidate wishes to enter. Such a vacancy may be created. Advancement through formal challenge and knightly combat is not only permissible but encouraged.

While each of the Orders of Lords are equivalent in rank, there is considerable variation in the power and nature of the ranks depending upon the order to which the knight belongs. Thorn Knights, for example, continue to advance as wizards, using the Thorn Knights tables for experience points and hit dice. All prohibitions for the order still apply.

The assignment and mission of a lord knight need not be constrained to those of his own order, however. Indeed, it is common for a lord knight sorcerer to be placed in command of a legion of Knights of the Lily, or to find a clerical lord knight in command of a unit comprising the Order of the Thorn.

Lord Ariakan realized that, since most large military units of the Knights of Takhisis comprise elements of all three orders of knighthood, it was conceivable that lord knights might well favor their own order over the others. Ariakan took care to see that this did not happen. Those who have risen to such high levels in the ranks have been indoctrinated in the concept of "Power through Diversity," that a wise leader uses *all* of the assets available to ensure victory. Indeed, it is a point of honor among the Knights of Takhisis that no favoritism is shown, and the accusation of such impropriety is a challenge to one's honor that never goes unanswered.

When a vacancy in the upper ranks of the knighthood comes about as the result of attrition (such as a lord knight dying of natural causes or being killed in battle, outside single combat), all applicants must present themselves before a lord knight tribunal. The tribunal is made up of a majority of knights in that particular order. It is entirely up to the discretion of the reviewing tribunal to determine the criteria under which the position shall be won. Typically such criteria will consist of elimination tournaments or particularly hazardous ventures.

Those who wish to force a vacancy in the knighthood may challenge a lord knight in that position to single combat. In this latter case, victory assures the assumption of the defeated knight's rank by the victorious knight. A tribunal is not called into session in such an instance.

Assassination is not an option, this being viewed as an act of cowardice.

It is only after assuming a place in the next level of knighthood that characters may advance in hit points and any other abilities. When characters do advance, they use the tables as listed for the order of knighthood through which they rose to their position. In other words, once a character is a Knight of the Thorn, that character remains a Thorn Knight up through 18th level, even though the rank places the character in common with knights of all orders.

Storm's Keep

The main stronghold and current headquarters of the Knights of Takhisis is located far north and west of the continent of Ansalon, on a vast rock peak somewhere in the Sirrion Sea. The fortress is difficult to discover, for the elements themselves guard it. Storm clouds, dark and churning, conceal the fortress from the air. The goddess Zeboim and those creatures of the deep loyal to her make certain that no unwanted visitors arrive by sea.

Storm's Keep is immense and impregnable. Some say the fortress was dragged up from the bottom of the ocean floor by Zeboim, as a gift to her son Ariakan. The less romantic maintain that since the structure is similar in design to those favored by the minotaurs on their isle of Mithas, the knights probably hired minotaurs to build it.

The fortress is not marked on any map. Lord Ariakan has forbidden the making of such maps, knowing that they could conceivably fall into the hands of enemies. The only two outsiders—Tanis Half-Elven and Caramon Majere—purported to have slipped inside the fortress, traveled there on dragon back during a storm-ridden night and are unable to give any indication of the fortress's location.

The layout of the fortress itself is also unknown. Arriving in the confusion of a mock battle, fearful for their lives, Tanis and Caramon were able to furnish few details, beyond the estimation (given to Lord Gunthar) that a direct assault launched by the combined armies of the peoples of Ansalon, including the good dragons, would likely have no more effect on the fortress than the raindrops that constantly pelt it. (Lord Gunthar, naturally, believes Tanis Half-Elven to be exaggerating.)

It was hoped that Sara Dunstan, the only person ever known to have escaped Storm's Keep, would be able to furnish detailed drawings of the fortress. But—fearful for the life of Steel Brightblade, the young Knight of the Lily whom she loves as a son—Sara has thus far refused to reveal any of the keep's secrets. She is, of course, in hiding for her very life.

It is either known or assumed that the fortress has barracks for the housing of the knights; outbuildings where live servants, slaves, and workers; storehouses; a stronghold for the wealth of the knighthood; stables for horses; a large courtyard; an infirmary; several turreted main buildings with watchtowers; and, at the heart, the Temple of Takhisis. An enormous wall, which appears to have been built of the same rock as the peak on which the fortress stands, surrounds and protects it.

In addition, the Conclave of Wizards speculates that the Knights of the Thorn have their own magical Tower of High Sorcery located on this isle. Here are stored all books and scrolls and other magical artifacts, many of them undoubtedly newly created by the Knights of the Thorn. The conclave estimates that the knights have spent much time and research on the development of magical weapons of tremendous destructive power.

The Knights of Takhisis are not confined to this one fortress. Groups of them are currently abroad in Ansalon. Secret, hidden—even from other forces of darkness in Krynn—the knights and their Dread Queen are quietly preparing to conquer the world.

What is Currently Known on Ansalon About the Knights

Twenty years after the War of the Lance, very few people in Ansalon have any knowledge of the existence of the Knights of Takhisis. Among those who do know, most either refuse to believe what they have been told (the Knights of Solamnia) or are simply too involved in their own political turmoil to care (the elves).

Surprisingly enough, this lack of knowledge extends even among those who might be considered to be the Dark Queen's loyal subjects (dark priests, draconians, and minotaurs). Only someone who might be considered a suitable candidate for recruitment is ever approached by the knights, and then only after a long period of secret surveillance and evaluation. Such a recruit who decides to join would simply drop out of sight, vanish forever to the knowledge of friends and family. Either no recruit has ever turned down such an honor, or they have not survived to speak of it.

The only people truly concerned and aware of the terrible threat posed by this newly emerging force are the robed wizards of Krynn. Even this knowledge is primarily confined to the members of the conclave. All three robes, Black, Red, and White, view these renegade wizards with alarm.

It is speculated that the conclave actually attempted to magically penetrate the secret confines of the Thorn Knights' Tower of High Sorcery. Rumor has it that this attempt was not only easily repelled, but that it had nearly disastrous consequences for the members of the conclave.

All members of the conclave, and in particular Dalamar the Dark, head of the Tower of High Sorcery in Palanthas, are avidly seeking information about the Knights of Takhisis in general, the Gray Robe Knights of the Thorn in particular.

The rest of the people of Ansalon are too busy quarreling and fighting with each other to pay any heed to the deadly lilies that have been planted and are now being cultivated right in their own gardens.